Also by Killarney Traynor:

Summer Shadows

Necessary Evil

Killarney Traynor

This is a work of fiction.

Names, characters, businesses, organizations, places, events, and incidents are either products of the author's imagination, or are used fictiously. Any resemblance to actual events, locales, organizations, or persons (living or dead) is entirely coincidental.

ISBN: 1517390338
ISBN 13: 9781517390334

Cover Design by Adriana Hanganu, adipixdesign.com

Author photograph provided by Monica Bushor of Bushor Photography

For Ernest and Reuben

I have read, in the marvelous heart of man,
That strange and mystic scroll,
That an army of phantoms vast and wan
Beleaguer the human soul.

- Longfellow

Fear of the Lord is the beginning of knowledge.
Proverbs 1:7

CONTENTS

CAST OF CHARACTERS

Present Day:
Madeleine Warwick
Susanna Chase, *her aunt*
Michael Chase, *her uncle, deceased*
Prof. Gregory Randall, *of Hadley University, MA*
Prof. Joseph Tremonti, *of Breaburn College, CA*
Prof. Anthony Maddox, *of Breaburn College, CA, deceased*
Darlene Winters, *author and neighbor*
Allison Winters, *her daughter, missing*
Lindsay Khoury, *farm hand*
Jacob Adamski, *farm hand*
Che Che Randazzo, *co-worker*
Melanie Randazzo, *her daughter*
Mark Dulles, *TV personality*
Charlene Schaeffer, *Charleston Historian*
Charlie White, *local newsman*

From the Past:
Alexander Chase, *the accused thief*
Mary Welles Chase, *his mother*
Obadiah Chase, *his step-father*
Avery Chase, *his step-brother*
Jeremiah Beaumont, *Alexander's friend*
Jaspar McInnis, *Alexander's South Carolinian employer*
Mary Anna McInnis, *his daughter*

PROLOGUE

Life can change in the blink of an eye. What was once running along safely, smoothly, predictably, can be derailed in an instant as forcibly and as irretrievably as a train running into a granite mountain.

For the want of a nail, they say, the kingdom was lost. My life is proof of that. Not so much for the want of a nail, but for something far more inconsequential. Or so it felt at the time.

My name is Madeleine Warwick. On a bright, beautiful June morning, on a back trail I've been riding since I was four years old, my life changed forever.

I've been picking up the pieces ever since.

TWO YEARS AGO

From an article in ***The Triple Town Sentry***

Chase Letter Authenticated

Professor Anthony Maddox announced today that he has authenticated the much disputed Chase/Beaumont letter.

In a public speech at Braeburn College, in Sundale, California, the distinguished Professor of American History announced his findings on the controversial letter, citing lab tests and other evidence that brought about his conclusion.

"Using the finest scientific techniques and after consultations with my knowledgeable colleagues, coupled with my own research, I'm happy to announce that this letter, written by Jeremiah Beaumont to Mary Chase in 1862, is authentic. It is a valuable find, one that will influence historical studies of the time period. I am proud to have been among the first to comprehensively study it."

Beaumont, born in Georgia, was a non-combatant during the Civil War and worked with Alexander Chase when both were in the employ of a Charleston merchant, Jasper McInnis. The letter was addressed to Alexander's mother, Mary Chase of New Hampshire, and was written while Beaumont was in prison in Baltimore during the summer of 1863. Ostensibly a letter of consolation, it explained the circumstances surrounding the death of her son, who had been serving as a private in the Union in the 3rd New Hampshire Voluntary Infantry, as well as explaining the disappearance of a large collection of household goods that Chase was accused of stealing back in 1861.

"I regret, thinking on your new widowhood, that there is nothing of Alex's that I can send back to you," Beaumont

wrote. "Some 'goods' which we had the good fortune to come into were lost on the gaming tables in this very city shortly after their acquisition. I have since repented of my actions, but the goods, now lost, cannot be recovered."

The letter was discovered in the bottom of a trunk three months ago in the still active Chase farm in Chester, New Hampshire. Susanna Chase, the discoverer, and descendant of Alexander Chase by marriage, immediately recognized the significance of the find and submitted it to Maddox for examination.

Professor Maddox admitted that he was initially skeptical as the contents of the letter "seemed, at first glance, to fly in the face of what we knew about both Alexander Chase and his friendship with Jeremiah Beaumont, especially in regards to the amount reportedly lost on the 'gaming tables.' However, this does set to rest some questions about the activities of Alexander Chase, particularly in regards to the McInnis affair."

While the letter references two obscure historical Civil War persons, the local repercussions of the authentication are momentous. Alexander Chase was a controversial figure, son of a prominent local family well-known for their political activism and public spirit. Their reputation was tarnished when the McInnis family charged the deceased Alexander with theft of their large family fortune and brought suit against the Chase family when the Civil War ended. While the family disclaimed all knowledge of such treasure, public opinion said that it was buried somewhere on the Chase farm. The lawsuit stretched on for years, ending only with the death of Jamison McInnis, grandson of Jasper. Rumors of treasure persisted, however, and many treasure hunters and historians have searched the farm, to no avail.

The Chase treasure was largely forgotten until a year ago, when the Chase family farm was featured in the popular documentary series, Lost American Treasures. Even though

Michael Chase, the farm's owner, assured the viewers that there was nothing hidden in his fields, the episode generated new interest in the treasure. Amateur and professional treasure hunters flocked to the farm, now a respected stable and riding school, searching with metal detectors and shovels and ignoring posted "No Trespassing" signs. Then tragedy struck: Michael Chase was killed when his horse stumbled in a hole left by a treasure hunter.

His death had a stunning effect on the community.

"We were devastated," said Darlene Winters, a resident, and author of the bestselling novels, ***To Pluck a Butterfly's Wing*** *and* ***Too Close to the Sun****. "Michael was a rock in this community, a true gentleman and a generous man. His death was just tragic. He was far too young."*

The Chase Farm is still in operation, now under the management of his wife, Susanna, and niece Madeleine Warwick, who divides her time between the farm and her full-time job at a veterinary office. Both were relieved by Maddox's announcement.

"This letter absolutely disproves the buried treasure theory," Ms. Warwick said in a telephone interview. "We're hoping that this will discourage treasure hunters once and for all."

Scholars agree with Warwick's assessment of the letter. Beaumont doesn't specifically refer to the McInnis treasure, but his letter does mention an item that was included in the lawsuit's list of stolen items: a set of silver Kirk spoons. While Beaumont mourns the effect the 'rumors' had on Alexander's reputation, he neither confirms nor denies the theft itself, something that Professor Maddox believes is tantamount to a confession.

"Beaumont and Chase were friends, working for a man who was acknowledged to be a harsh taskmaster, even by the standards of the time," he stated in his address to the press. "Beaumont wrote this letter while serving time for disturbing

the peace. He knows that the jailers are going to be reading it before they mail it, so he can't come right out and say, 'Yes, we stole the goods. Then we got drunk and lost them gambling.' He'd never get out of prison. So he skirts the issue, but makes sure to mention the spoons specifically. I think Beaumont was telling Mary Chase, 'Look, you know and I know what kind of man your son was. I'm only telling you what you already know. And there's nothing left.'"

The Professor also announced his intention to step down from his position in the history department, retiring to focus on personal projects. His successor has yet to be determined, but popular historian and author Joseph Tremonti is rumored to be in the running.

Back east, the authentication is a mixed blessing. This paper was unable to reach the McInnis family for comment; but the Chase family, speaking through Ms. Warwick, reported that they were relieved by the discovery of the letter: "It only proves what people have thought for years. Every family has their share of rogues and colorful characters."

When asked, Warwick admitted that they were still troubled by trespassers. She hopes to add the Chase Farm, founded in the 1680s, to the New Hampshire roster of Historical Places. In the meantime, she continues her uncle's work, boarding, raising, and breeding horses as well as offering lessons and summer riding camps.

"Chase Farm is fortunate in both our stock and our riders," Warwick said. "We count many prize-winning riders and horses among our stable family. We're looking forward to our annual horse show and competition this coming August."

She acknowledges that life without her uncle is hard, especially on her aunt, Michael's widow. But, "We're forging ahead and every day gets easier. We're looking at a bright future."

1

Early September

Oppressive humidity weighed heavily on my chest as I pounded along the riding trail, the last hurrah of a long hot miserable summer. My running shoes hit the hard-packed dirt, and I winced as I felt pebbles and variations in the ground through my now-thin soles. Only two months old and already I needed a new pair, my fourth this year alone.

Tree frogs and early morning birds sang as I jogged through the wooded trail. The sun lit the eastern sky on my right, glowing faded gold through the tall pines and scrubby bushes. Two squirrels chased each other around the base of a grand old oak, pausing briefly as I passed. My iPod played on, but my earphones dangled over my shoulders, so all I heard of the music was rhythmic squeaking and tapping. I had been listening earlier, but even my favorite rock songs couldn't chase the anxious thoughts that whirled around my head. The cheerful sound grated on my soul, and I had to pull them out just to get a grip on myself.

Anxiety is a good exercise partner. It runs alongside of you, a relentless drill sergeant who shouts in your ear the whole time, "Can't you go faster? I'm running circles around you. I'm getting bored here, soldier. Next time you want a stroll, take your grandmother."

I'm not much of a runner, really. I can sprint, but even after loads of training, my long distance running skills are still decidedly sub-par. My legs are sturdy, but thick, better suited for riding. I'm short, too, which I like to think has something to do with it, but my biggest handicap is that I don't like running at all. While clear days aren't too bad, most mornings I feel like I'm running through soup, fighting a losing battle against gravity. Some runners talk of "runners high" and extoll the relief they feel after a run. All I feel is tired and sore.

Nevertheless, I rose every morning before six, tied on my sneakers, and hit one of the several riding trails we have on the farm. I varied my route - decades of constant use has left a network of trails snaking all throughout the farm and the wooded areas.

We still have decent acreage for a New England farm. Back in the 1800s, the Chase family owned about a third more, as well as having family members on the Chester town council, the state legislature, and Congress in DC, all before the outbreak of the Civil War. Our fortunes have ebbed considerably since then, both in land and in influence.

The trail I had chosen wove in and out of woods and fields. Through the breaks in the trees, the paddocks lay quiet and shrouded in morning mist, a lovely view of old New England countryside. I've had photographer friends stage shoots here, and gotten inquiries from local reenacting groups to use the land. It's beautiful, but I hardly noticed. It's one thing to visit the property – it's another to be responsible for it.

As I ran, I automatically noted where the grass was thinning, scanned the fences for breakages, and gave the simple summer stables a glance to determine their upkeep. We have some paddocks devoted to training, equipped with defined tracks and jumping tools, but these so-called summer paddocks are out of sight of the main house and used only for pasturing. The stables are clean and I keep them in good condition, but they're only used in the summer months, unless really pressed for space. Since Uncle Michael died, space hasn't been a problem.

As I passed one of the paddocks, I saw that two horses had been let out. Lindsay Khoury waved to me as she secured the gate. Her dark hair, pulled up high on her head, swung jauntily as she walked along. Only seventeen years old and a devoted equestrian, Lindsay was my right hand on the farm. She arrived before school every morning to prep the horses for the day and came back most afternoons for lessons and chores. During summer vacation, she helped run the summer camps, becoming the mother hen and adored riding instructor for over a dozen well-to-do middle school girls.

Next fall she'd be off to college and as I ran, I worried about what I'd do without her. Even with two years of experience under my belt and business as slow as it was, running such a large farm by myself was a daunting prospect.

On paper, the farm was run by both my Aunt Susanna and myself, but in reality, Lindsay and I did the work. When Uncle Michael died, Aunt Susanna quickly became overwhelmed, so I stepped away from school to help out. I'd thought it'd be simple. After all, I'd spent most of my childhood here, being raised by my aunt and uncle and learning the business. Now, two years later, I was deeper in debt than ever before and I was running out of ideas.

I worried about Aunt Susanna, too. My aunt used to be the type to make up ridiculous songs on the spot or take cha-cha lessons just for the fun of it. She was interested in everything to do with the farm, adored the horses, and rode like a pro, winning prizes all over New England.

All that changed with Uncle Michael's death. She'd aged decades in a day and sunk into a deep depression that lasted more than a year. Where once she never let a day pass without riding, usually bareback, now she shuddered at the very idea.

"I'm too old," she'd say. "Riding is a sport for young girls, like you and Lindsay."

I'd learned better than to argue with her.

Now she spent hours alone, chain-watching sad movies and going for long solitary walks, often coming back in a dither when she found some evidence of trespassing.

We used to be troubled with that a lot, until the article about the Beaumont letter was published. Then as interest in the farm died down, Aunt Susanna began to recover - so slowly at first that I hardly noticed, but it was steady. I was still too jaded to believe in the progress when she shocked me in August by saying, "I think I'll go for a ride. Does Sunshine need exercise?"

I don't remember answering. I ran to the paddock to bring the pretty mare in for her. I was outside when Aunt Susanna slipped and fell down the narrow back staircase. She was still lying there when I came in to look for her.

Her face was gray and she was breathing heavily. I stood over her, fighting back panic - my mind automatically flashing back to the morning of my uncle's accident - when she spoke.

"Maddie," she said, and every syllable was an effort. "Maddie, I can't get up."

The doctor at the hospital said she'd broken her hip, bad enough that she would need replacement surgery. Thus began a month of seemingly never-ending appointments, check-ups, and tests, from which they concluded that not only would she need the surgery, but that one of her knees was ready for replacement.

"But that can wait until she recovers from her hip," her doctor assured me.

Despite the doctor's reassurances that she'd make a full recovery, my aunt slipped silently back into depression. Although we never spoke of it, partially because I wouldn't allow us to, I knew she felt guilty. Even with insurance, caring for an invalid is time-consuming and expensive and my workload didn't allow me a lot of time to take care of her myself. I found myself relying heavily on our neighbor and good friend, Darlene Winters, who appointed herself as Susanna's part-time caregiver.

Farm work is never ending: there are horses to groom, exercise, feed, and care for, lessons to give, stables to muck out and supplies to haul, lawns to mow, and crops to take in, as well as all the paperwork, social media, and phone negotiations that a business requires. With the bills piling up and lessons dwindling with summer's end, I'd starting asking my boss for extra work at the office just to keep us afloat. I work behind the receptionist desk at the veterinary office - a rather ironic twist of fate, considering I was in veterinary school until my uncle's accident.

The path took a turn, leading me away from the bright fields and deeper into the woods.

I slowed to a jog and kept going. My legs were feeling better, the morning stiffness loosening with the exertion. The trail unwound before me, arcing out to the east until it touched the bank of the Pocatague River, a tiny offshoot of the Exeter.

I paused, bending over to catch my breath and taking stock of myself. I wasn't a supermodel, but I was in good shape and I prided myself that I could more than pull my weight on the farm. Work and worry had taken its toll on me, though: my face was weathered, my hands unusually strong for their size. I was capable, but I didn't often feel pretty or attractive – not that it really mattered. There was little time for that sort of thing anyway.

I didn't stand still for long. I'd forgotten, as I usually did, that insects like the moisture around the boggy river's edge. They swarmed, I swatted, and then I started to run again.

I've been running since last summer, and even I have noticed a marked improvement in my endurance. I run for my health, my figure, to relieve stress, and to give me time in the morning before I have to face the day. It's not the only reason I run every day, but I didn't like to think of that other reason, so I would put that aside, too, and run on.

Sometimes I wondered if I wasn't trying to outrun my past, if the punishment I took on the hard-packed trails wasn't some form of penance for crimes committed but unwritten, a forgotten neglect of duty, or a violation of a social custom. Perhaps it was a form of bargain, a sacrifice on the altar to the God of the Old Testament – I will flagellate myself in this way every morning and You keep the tenuous balance of my life from shifting back into chaos.

That was blasphemy and I knew better. I'm a Roman Catholic and we don't believe in bargaining with God. He knows best and we, as good and willing servants, do our duty with hope and joy and expectation. I told myself that's what Aunt Susanna and I were doing: our duty, looking with expectation towards a bright future.

Yet every morning, I tied my sneakers and worked out my penance on the unforgiving trails.

2

I first learned that Maddox was dead when I came into the kitchen from my run that morning. I was beet-red, drenched in sweat and early morning fog, and ravenous.

The kitchen was large, silent, and clean. Decorated in shades of gray and cream, it looked almost institutional in the mornings, but there were so many warm memories here that I felt both at home and alien at the same time.

Aunt Susanna was sitting on one of the stools at the counter, so quiet and still that she was nearly lost in the palette. Her blonde and white hair was pinned in the usual milkmaid braids around the crown of her head, only a little mussed by a night's sleep. Her gray silk robe with the pink and black Asian print had aged well, but it was too big for her now. Folds of fabric spilled on the counter as she crouched over her laptop, emphasizing her recent, involuntary weight loss. Engrossed in her reading, she didn't look up to acknowledge me, but there was an extra mug of steaming coffee on the counter beside hers.

Her walker was parked within easy reach, but under the lip of the counter, out of her line of sight. She hated it almost as much as I did, and I felt a twinge of sympathy as I skirted around it. The walker was used. Our doctor had procured from a woman who, he assured us, recovered just fine from the same surgery. He thought it would help, but it didn't. The walker offended my aunt's sense of autonomy, and the cheerful bunny stickers that the previous owner decorated it with only made things worse.

I tossed my iPod on the counter, and took the mug of coffee gratefully. You're supposed to have something healthy after an intense workout, like water, juice, or something with electrolytes. I always rebelliously opted for caffeine, as though striking back against a strict coach: You can force me to run, but you cannot control what I drink.

I took a sip and recognized the bitter brew of Dark French Roast, too strong for my tastes. I added milk, then reached past my aunt for the sugar shaker. She noticed and shifted a little to make room.

"Sorry, I forgot," she said.

"No worries."

I glanced at her breakfast plate as I shook crystal granules into my cup. Toast, unbuttered, and burnt again. There was a time when she would have turned up her nose at such fare, calling it a poor excuse for a meal. Had she come upon Uncle Michael or myself eating that, she would have rolled up her sleeves and whipped up one of her famous omelets, or - if she was feeling particularly continental - French Toast dipped in rum-based batter and dripping with butter and real Vermont maple syrup. You could protest about your waistline all you wanted, but she would have her way. She had been lively, youthful, and unstoppable in those days. But she was a different woman now. She was a woman who had quite simply stopped.

I was too accustomed to this new way of life to feel more than slight regret. As I put the shaker back on the shelf and checked my watch, Aunt Susanna turned to me with wide, blue eyes. She looked so alert and so *alive* all of a sudden that I was startled.

"What is it?" I demanded.

"Did you hear about Professor Maddox?" she asked.

My heart jumped and I started, hot coffee sloshing over my hand and onto the spotlessly clean tiles. I shook the hot liquid from my hand, then reached for the paper towels, wishing I had better control of myself. As it was, I was barely able to keep my expression placid under my aunt's keen gaze.

"Something happen?" I asked, as I dabbed at the floor. I was praying, *Please, please, let it be something normal. Please, please...*

She turned back to her laptop and waved at the screen.

"He's dead," she said.

"*Dead?*" I leaped up to stare at the screen. Relief washed over me, followed quickly by guilt.

It wasn't an obituary my aunt had found, but an article about the funeral. It briefly informed the reader of Professor Maddox's accomplishments as an eminent scholar, author, lecturer, father, husband, and long-time professor of American History at Braeburn College in California. He died at home, surrounded by his loving family. The eulogy was read by his colleague, the respected Professor Joseph Tremonti, on loan to a Massachusetts university for the year.

My heart beat faster at that line. Joe was back on the East Coast?

Not now, Maddie...

"Such a nice man," Aunt Susanna said, as I followed a link to Maddox's college, where his list of accomplishments was more thoroughly outlined. "We should send a donation and a card to his wife, don't you think?"

"Mmm hmm..."

I found what I was looking for in the second to last paragraph: "Among his significant finds were the 1862 Beaumont letter and the Carignan diaries, both of which shed light on little-known aspects of the American Civil War."

It was inaccurate – Maddox hadn't found the letter, only authenticated it– but the mention was mercifully brief and unlikely to cause harm. I breathed a sigh of relief as I turned the computer over to Aunt Susanna. I didn't know what I was worried about, really. The matter, so important to us, was unlikely to interest the college or the media very much, not when compared to Maddox's other, considerable contributions to historical knowledge.

Aunt Susanna was looking at me curiously and I realized that I hadn't responded to her question.

"What did you say, Aunt Susanna?"

"I was saying, we ought to do something for Mrs. Maddox. They were both so kind to us about the letter. What do you think?"

I picked up my mug again and took a sip as I tossed the paper towel wad into the trash can. "Yes, we really should. You're thinking of a donation to the scholarship fund?"

Mentally, I brought up the checkbook and estimated how much we could spare. Even with my income from the veterinary office and the lessons split between Lindsay and me, we ran the farm on a frayed shoestring, and the number I was comfortable with contributing was embarrassing compared with what Maddox's university colleagues were likely to give.

There's no shame in being poor, I reminded myself, but the twinge remained.

The Chase family hadn't been wealthy since the 1800s; but still, Uncle Michael had been well able to keep both himself and his wife comfortable while contributing to my college fund. That I was barely keeping the place open spoke volumes, I thought, of my inability to husband the farm he'd so carefully built up.

There was some consolation in the idea that the financial trouble had started before Uncle Michael's accident. Ever since the debut of the *Lost American Treasures* episode featuring the mythical (in my opinion) Alexander Chase treasure, our respectable family farm had been inundated with treasure hunters and curious tourists who frightened off our clientele and, worse still, left the marks of their search behind them, with devastating effects.

The Chase Treasure story itself is a fairly typical buried treasure myth: Alexander Chase, the black sheep of the respectable Mayflower family, stole money and goods from his employer, merchant Jasper McInnis of Charleston. It was just before the Battle of Fort Sumter, and it included a box of prized silver Kirk spoons, intended as the wedding dowry of McInnis' daughter, Mary Anna. Local lore has it that he buried booty somewhere on the Chase property when he came home for a brief visit in April of 1861, just before he joined the 3rd New Hampshire Voluntary Infantry. The location of the treasure was lost when Chase died after the Battle of Sucessionville in 1862. "Treasurists" - a term invented by my Uncle Michael - believe that the McInnis treasure is still on the property somewhere, proof that Chase family counted thieves among their members.

Family members and some historians disagreed.

Anti-Treasurists bring up the fact that Alexander Chase's reputation was fairly clean, aside from occasional bouts of drinking and gambling, and insist that he was as ardent an abolitionist as was his father. They maintain that the thievery charges brought against him by the McInnis family after the war's end were just another case of so-called 'lost causers' trying to recoup their wartime losses.

A third theory, one that I subscribed to, is that Alexander Chase did steal from the McInnis money, and then lost it gambling in one of the seaports that he frequented. These people believe that he was a thief and probably indifferent to slavery, a position that my Uncle Michael found repugnant in the extreme. A mild-mannered man, he was known to actually argue with people about Alexander, holding until his dying day that the private died a slandered but essentially good man.

Those who believe in the treasure have two pieces of evidence to support their theory. One is that Avery Chase, Alexander's half-brother, spent his entire lifetime searching for the treasure, even while refuting the McInnis' claims. The second piece of evidence comes from one of Alexander's own letters, which was discovered by my uncle in an old box in the barn several years ago. Written to his mother just weeks before his death, Alexander commended his "earthly" treasures to her care, and reminded her of his favorite hymn, 'no. 29'. Chase's step-father, Obadiah, was a deacon, and Alexander and Avery were practically raised in the pew. On page twenty-nine of *Psalms and Hymns*, an 1853 hymnal that Alexander would have been very familiar with, are two songs: *Come, Ye Thankful People, Come*, and *Gather the*

Golden Grains. Treasurists are adamant that this rather benign sentiment is actually a clue to the treasure's location.

As Mark Dulles, the handsome Ivy League host of *Lost American Treasures,* pointed out, both are songs of thanksgiving that speak of the fields. *Come, Ye Thankful People, Come,* even specifically mentions corn and wheat fields. Since Obadiah Chase was a conscientious log-book keeper, who recorded every ear of corn that ever grew on his farm, this clue led generations of hapless treasure seekers to search particular fields on our land, some of which we still use for haying now.

While filming, Mark Dulles and his crew worked in the fields, demonstrating with the latest equipment that there was nothing buried there. They were forced, reluctantly, to conclude that there was nothing to find, something that should have ended all further attempts.

However, in the closing scene of the episode, Mark Dulles looked out over the fields of tender green shoots, and in a voice-over, said, "Whatever our conclusions today, one thing remains: the mystery of Alexander Chase and the McInnis treasure remains unsolved, an intriguing footnote in the tragic history of America's Civil War."

I can still remember Uncle Michael's satisfied tone when he called me at my dorm that night after watching the special.

"This will get people talking," he said. "Only now, they won't be so focused on the treasure - now they'll be talking about Alexander and what really happened during the Civil War."

Even before finding the letter, my uncle had been Alexander's fiercest defenders. A quiet, peaceable man by nature, he surprised Aunt Susanna and me by allowing Dulles to film on his property. When we asked, he'd explained, "I'm getting nowhere with my own research. I want to bring this Chase treasure business into the public eye, then maybe someone else will take on the project."

The night of broadcast, he was sure that someone would.

"They cut out most of my interview, but I think there was enough left in there to intrigue people," he said.

I was in veterinary school at the time, a straight-A student who thought a little too much of her own intelligence. I felt obliged to point out that people didn't often react in the ways we wished them to.

"It's more likely we're going to get a few more treasure hunters trespassing," I said – prophetically, as it turned out.

He snorted. "After Dulles and his team failed? No one will be looking for that nonsensical treasure anymore."

"I hope you're right," I said, sincerely.

But he wasn't.

Not long after the episode aired, we started finding people wandering about our fields with metal detectors, shovels, and copies of *Come, Ye Grateful People, Come,* or *Gather the Golden Grains.* They were a nuisance, leaving test holes when we didn't catch them in time. Uncle Michael felt sorry for them, while I was only annoyed. While he spoke sadly of their disappointment, I would rail about destruction of property.

At first, the incursions were few; but as time passed, the story began to permeate. All over the web, Treasure Hunter websites spread word about the special, and the siege began in earnest. Hunters from across all fifty states, and even beyond, flooded our small town and congregated on our front stoop.

These visitors ranged from passersby who wanted their picture taken in front of the house, to Civil War enthusiasts looking for more information, to invasive hunters with metal detectors who often forgot to ask for permission before they started digging up likely sites, leaving pockmarks in the fields, paddocks, and trails.

It was like being under siege. The police did their best, but they were unable to handle the problem. These invaders disrupted the lessons, disturbed the horses, wearied my aunt with phone calls and visits, and drove my sweet uncle to such a nervous state that the normally hawk-eyed sage never saw the gouge in the trail before his horse, a fine spirited stallion, tripped in it. The stallion broke his leg. My uncle broke his neck. The finest man I'd ever known was killed over an empty promise of treasure.

The incident broke my aunt's heart, and she withdrew into herself to grieve. My uncle was a popular man, and his funeral was a big affair; but even with all of the news coverage, and the increased police protection, the incursions on our land didn't stop. The morning of my uncle's funeral, I found a fresh excavation in the north pasture.

Even death doesn't stop the gold hungry.

I don't know what we would have done without the Beaumont letter. While cementing the charge of theft, it conclusively proved that the treasure had never been buried on the farm. Its discovery and public authentication by Professor Maddox was covered by the press, and picked up by the treasure hunter blogosphere. It took long enough for things to calm down, but now it'd been months since I'd found any evidence of trespassers. For that, my family owed a debt of gratitude to Professor Maddox.

I agreed with Aunt Susanna that the farm should send something, but with the mortgage due on top of the usual bills, and this year's disappointingly small sign-up for summer classes, there wasn't much capital to spread on lavish gifts.

"What were you thinking of sending?" I asked and braced myself. Aunt Susanna sometimes forgot that we had no money and I hated whenever I had to remind her that we couldn't afford something.

She was looking at the on-screen picture of Professor Maddox, a kindly looking man in the obligatory tweed jacket. We'd met him in person only once, but it was enough to impress upon us that he was as kind as he looked.

The thought of that kindness and that reputation made my stomach churn and I turned away from the picture, pretending to look out the back window.

"Would it be foolish to send flowers?" Aunt Susanna asked.

I looked at her, surprised.

She gestured to the screen. "It says to send a donation in lieu of flowers, but I dunno, a donation seems – seems so impersonal."

"Sure, why not?" I said.

She nodded and turned back to her computer. "I wish they lived closer. I'd send them some in one of my baskets."

Basket weaving was the only hobby that my aunt kept up in the past few years. I suspected that was largely due to Darlene, who wove with her, but the nature of the activity - the simplicity of the supplies, the tidy, methodical weave, the satisfaction of the final product – has a soothing effect on the practitioner. Before Aunt Susanna's fall, the hobby required her to spend hours outside collecting supplies, or pouring over guides and handbooks, looking for trickier weaves or new techniques. Aunt Susanna and Darlene would collect willows, and then spend afternoons weaving them into the most fantastically shaped baskets, some of which won prizes at local fairs. She had three to enter this year and I was determined to see to it that she went to the fair, her protestations of weakness notwithstanding.

"You can't really mail a basket of flowers from here to California," she was saying wistfully. "Which is too bad, because the one I'm making now would be perfect for her." She checked her watch and started to rise. "I've got to rush. Darlene will be here any minute."

I handed her the walker, then turned to the cabinets, rummaging for my breakfast. "You have an appointment today?" I asked.

"No, Mass."

Despite myself, I felt my spine stiffen. Of course. It was Sunday, and if there was one thing that Aunt Susanna never forgot to do, no matter how deep her depression, it was to go to Mass. I used to be as faithful, but lately, I've been overbooked. I knew she wasn't going to be happy about my absence.

"Oh, right," I said, keeping my back to her.

"We're going to the eight a.m. Mass today," she informed my back. "We like the music there better. They've got that new keyboardist, the one who went to Berkeley. He's very good – you should come and hear him."

"I can't today, but thanks."

Silence for a moment. I found some stale corn flakes and made a mental note to go to the grocery store, wondering when on earth I'd find time to do that, too. Suddenly, I felt overwhelmed and fought the urge to bury my face in my hands and scream.

Aunt Susanna asked, "Are you going later?"

I shook my head. "I've got lessons all morning, then Lindsay and I have to do the stall cleaning."

We thoroughly clean out the stalls at least once a month while the horses are out in the paddocks, and always try to do it on a dry day, so the horses don't immediately track mud in. It's a long, hard afternoon's work, but necessary and overdue. I prayed that my aunt would know to let this go.

She didn't.

"Maddie," she said, with that note of quiet concern in her tone that was meant to comfort me, but instead set my teeth further on edge. "You can't do this anymore. You have to take time out, to rest, to pray, to spend time with God. You can't let work be your life. Come on, Maddie. Cancel the classes and come with me instead."

"*Cancel* the classes!" I barked, turning on her. "Cancel the classes? Susanna, I already had to reschedule the Bailey girl twice this week and Mrs. Taylor is already upset because it's me and not Lindsay teaching her kids. These people will *leave* us if we don't pay attention to them. The Baileys will take Greybeard with them, and if there's one thing we can't afford to do, it's lose a paying customer. We're *barely* keeping afloat and you want me to take the day off? No. I can't go. You go. And say 'hi' to God for me while you're at it."

I turned again and yanked a bowl out of the cupboard, annoyed at myself as much as at her. I heard Aunt Susanna shuffle slowly out of the kitchen and down the hall, to where we'd set up a temporary bedroom for her in what had been the TV room. Immediately, a wave of regret washed over me. I shouldn't have lost my temper, not at her. But sometimes her simple faith drove me crazy. She believed in miracles – I believed in that old maxim: the Lord helps them that help themselves. At that moment, neither of us had much to show for our beliefs.

By the time she finished dressing, I'd calmed down enough to apologize and she accepted, but I could tell she was not happy.

That made two of us.

3

That night, Aunt Susanna found me sitting dreamy-eyed in the office, with Joe Tremonti's professional page pulled up on my computer screen. She was in a good mood, having spent the better part of the day with Darlene and a few church friends.

"What are you looking at?" she asked. The desk was near the door and despite her handicap, she was able to see the screen before I could switch it. "Joe Tremonti! Goodness, he hasn't changed, has he?"

I disagreed. The years had touched him, but gently, aging him to perfection - hardening the always admirable jaw line and dusting his thick, dark hair with the right amount of gray. His smile was just as I remembered it: mischievous and even dangerous - and in this professional photo, even after all these years, it was enough to set my heart pattering.

"Did you know that he was back in the area?" I asked, as casually as I could manage, which was quite the trick.

Aunt Susanna glanced at the photo and the long list of accomplishments, and shook her head. "I didn't. I was surprised when I read the article." She leaned over, took my mouse, and began scrolling down, slowly. "Has he been in touch with you?"

"No."

My face was flaming, both at being caught and from the knowledge that a crush from my teenage years could still be so powerful.

I got up abruptly, offered her the chair, then grabbed an armload of files and hurried over to the cabinet to put them away. I said, casually, "When I saw his name in the article today, I became curious and searched for him. He's guest lecturing at that university while writing a book." I pulled open a drawer and began to sort files.

Aunt Susanna scanned the write-up with interest. "I read his book, you know," she said softly.

"Which one?" I asked. He'd written several bestsellers, two historical and one historical fiction. I'd read them all, several times.

"The one that mentioned the dig," she said, clicking in a distracted way. "The one here on the farm. You remember."

I remembered. Ten years ago, when I was seventeen, Joseph Tremonti was an assistant at the local college who'd just gotten a grant from the state to do a historical dig. A popular teacher for obvious reasons, he had the volunteer manpower to do it but was at a loss for a site. When Strawberry Banke in Portsmouth turned him down, a student oh his - one of our riders- remembered that my uncle, while digging out a section of the yard for a cement pad, discovered an old knife that dated back to 1820. Joe went to see it on display at the library, then offered my uncle a deal: if he allowed his team to conduct a dig, Joe would pay to install the cement pad himself. Uncle Michael, excited by more by the idea of the dig than the cement pad, was easily persuaded.

It was the most exciting thing that had ever happened to me. I was a rough and tumble kid who hadn't much interest in either history or boys. The dig changed that. For six weeks, our yard was covered with college kids and the teacher with the Hollywood good looks who insisted that I join in on the fun. With his flashing smile, intelligent humor, and graceful yet rugged mannerisms, I was a goner before I even knew I had a heart. That summer was momentous: I grew up, and Uncle Michael discovered his passion for the past - a passion that would lead to his untimely accident.

I looked at the wall over the filing cabinet. In a dusty old frame was the group photo we'd taken at the Dig's End Party, the last night we'd all been together. Joe Tremonti was in the middle, his confidence radiating even through the passage of time.

It amused Aunt Susanna then that the team was mostly comprised of girls. I remember mixed feelings of jealousy, admiration, and kinship with those older, seemingly sophisticated young women. In the group photo, I'd somehow managed to stand next to Joe. A messy-haired, sun-browned kid, I was beaming like a lottery winner - standing next to my crush, who'd condescended to put his arm around my shoulder. I'd felt like a woman then.

Now, looking at the photo, I saw me as I was: a child who was about to experience her first heartbreak over a boy, a girl who didn't see the impossibility of a seventeen-year-old's love for a twenty-four-year-old.

That was ten years ago and I'd aged considerably. A lot had happened since then.

But that night wasn't the last time I'd seen Joe. That had been at Uncle Michael's funeral.

We buried Uncle Michael on a miserably hot and humid day. The church had no air conditioning, so we sweltered during the Mass and the lengthily eulogies. Then the priest, with a stately elegance no humidity could touch, incensed the coffin, and we formed a line to follow him to the cars.

Aunt Susanna's brother and his wife, both from North Carolina, escorted her, staying close as she silently wept, leading the long train of neighbors and friends outside, where it was only slightly cooler. They were too absorbed in their own grief to notice when I slipped away to the side, hiding in the shadow of the choir loft staircase. When the doors closed and I was alone, I sat down and cried for the first time.

I hadn't time to cry before. There were too many arrangements to make, too many decisions that Aunt Susanna was too prostrate to handle, and I was afraid that my tears would only add to her grief.

So I sat in the silent staircase, and sobbed. When the door wrenched open unexpectedly, I barely contained a scream.

Joe Tremonti was framed in the doorway. "Maddie?"

No one had expected the rising academic star to show up at the funeral, least of all me. Aside from that summer, our family had no connection with the man; but there he was, late, his impeccably tailored suit adorably untucked, rushing only to find that the grieving party had already left for the cemetery and me, a shivering, miserable wreck, crying on the choir loft stairs.

Seeing him was like discovering a freshwater lake in the middle of the desert: tall, handsome, and kind, pulling me into his arms and letting me sob on his shoulder. I wasn't too upset to notice that he still wore the same cologne that he'd used when we were at the dig together.

"Maddie," he whispered in my hair. "I'm so sorry, Maddie."

I'd dreamed about Joe coming back into my life. I'd scripted dozens of witty conversations, imagined me throwing my head back, laughing, looking like Audrey Hepburn in *Sabrina*, only with reddish curly hair. But that day, tears overflowing my swollen eyes, my scripted lines left me. My wits as well.

"They killed him, Joe," was the first thing I said. "They killed him."

We sat hidden together on the choir loft stairs for a long time. He listened while I cried. I told him about the treasure hunters, and the holes, and the accident, reliving the scene as I spoke. I must have sounded like a mad woman – all I could see were trespassers, flooding our land, leaving holes and destruction, gold-blind to the death they caused, and I began to shiver uncontrollably, despite the heat.

"They killed him and they're still there, Joe," I whispered, trying to swallow the lump in my throat. "They just. Keep. *Digging*. I found another hole this morning. Another bloody *hole*!"

If I hadn't just cried myself tearless, I would have crumbled again. But I had nothing left to give, just a hollow emptiness and a dreadful fear: that we'd never be free of this cursed treasure story, nor of the ever-present intruders.

"Oh, Maddie," Joe said again.

The others had returned by then. We heard them entering the church basement, the faint sounds of laughter and chatter signifying warmth, security, and kinship. I felt alone, as though I were a million miles away, kept away by a force far more insurmountable than distance. And even though Joe was there, his profile in sharp relief against the light of the doorway, his shoulder brushing mine, his handkerchief crumbled in my hands – even he was there only temporarily. I, and I alone, would have to face the future.

To keep myself from sliding into despair, I turned to anger.

"*They* won't believe that there is *nothing to find*," I snapped in a whisper. "They will keep looking for it – why would they stop now when even Mark Dulles' failure wouldn't stop them?"

"They'll stop," Joe said softly, "once definitive proof is found."

I laughed, bitterly. "Definitive proof! How can you prove something *isn't* there?"

He looked at me, with just the slightest hint of a smile.

"That," he said, "is the right question."

I don't know how long I'd been staring at the photo, but I was in a deep enough reverie to be startled when Aunt Susanna said, "He's writing another book!"

Shaking my head clear, I put the files on top of the cabinet and went back to the desk to take a look. "He is? What about?"

She pointed at the screen. She had followed a link to the Braeburn College Journal, where the headline announced, *Popular lecturer on loan to Mass.*

Still reading, Susanna said, "According to this, he's writing a book on the Carignan Diaries while he's guest lecturing. That had some connection to the Civil War, too, which I remember was a favorite subject of his. He was forever talking to Michael about it." She frowned, seeming confused. "Now, I wonder why he's doing that, and not something about the Beaumont letter. He was so interested when you sent it to him, and now that he's in the area, he'd be able to see it whenever he wants..."

Before she could think too much about it, I pointed out the second to last paragraph of the article. "It says right there. Apparently, this was the project that Professor Maddox was working on when he died and the family asked him to finish it."

"For joint credit, I'll bet," she said, and before I could question her remark, she read aloud, "Professor Tremonti is looking forward to his return to New England, where he received his Masters and first worked as a student-teacher. 'I'm looking forward to connecting with old friends,' he stated. 'And as much as I love sunny California, it'll be great experiencing a real New England winter again.' Professor Tremonti confirmed that he will be bringing his skis and snowshoes." She sat back in her chair. "I didn't know he was an outdoorsman."

"Oh, sure you did," I said. "Don't you remember all those afternoons he stayed late to ride with Uncle Michael and me, and that time we took him waterskiing on Winnipesauke? He took a group up Mount Washington, the *hard* way. I remember because you wouldn't let me go." I stroked the keyboard and went back to the original page, musing, "I still have his phone number. I should send him a text sometime."

I must have looked even dreamier than I thought, because there was a sharp note in Aunt Susanna's voice when she said, "He's still married, Maddie."

Like a bucket of ice water, that jolted me out of my half-formed daydream, and before I could stop myself, my eyes went to his hands. Yes – there was that gold band. I hadn't noticed before. Something like an iron band snapped around my heart and I experienced a sharp, embarrassing jolt of disappointment.

He was married. I hadn't been the only heartbroken girl when he announced it that night at the Dig's End party, but I was probably the hardest hit. I remember him standing in the glow of the bonfire, his cheeks flushed, his hands trembling as he lifted his soda can high and shouted, "Congratulate me, my friends. She said 'yes'!"

Most of the other girls had brought boyfriends or friends with them to the party, so they had support when they cheered in celebration. But I had no one except Uncle Michael and Aunt Susanna, and I was too embarrassed to confide in them. I remember holding it together until the congratulations calmed down, then I made an excuse and hid in the stables to cry until Aunt Susanna found me.

"Men like him are always breaking young girls' hearts," she'd told me that night. "His kind aren't worth it, Maddie."

Back then, I'd wondered why she'd taken such a dislike to Joe. When Aunt Susanna, now gathering her walker to leave the room, said, "Although I doubt a little thing like *that* would really discourage a man like him," I learned that time had done little to change her mind.

I wasn't seventeen anymore and had no business mooning over a married man. All the same, I felt the need to defend Joe. Aunt Susanna didn't know the debt of gratitude she owed him. How could she, when I never told her how that Beaumont letter got into the trunk in the attic?

"Geez!" I said lightly. "I was thinking about getting a coffee together, not starting a passionate romance! I's a *good* girl, I am," I added, and she laughed as she began her slow march into the kitchen.

"I'm making tea. Want some?" she called over her shoulder.

"Sure, after I bed the tenants," I said.

I made a habit of checking all the occupied stables every evening before turning in. I pulled on my boots, called for our dog Trusty, and went out.

It was a beautiful night. Above my head, the trees were rustling as a September breeze brushed by with its touch of frost. There was already a hint of red and gold about the green, although they wouldn't fully turn until the beginning of October, when busloads of 'Leaf Peepers' would make their annual foliage pilgrimage. I took a deep breath as Trusty ran ahead of me, her ears flying behind her.

Fall is my favorite time of year. Clean, cool air replaces summer's humidity, we exchange salads for thick, warm soups, and the fiery leaves set the stage for the holiday season. There is something refreshing and reviving about the autumn, something as promising as the new books we used to start the school year with. As I checked the horses and found all peaceful and undisturbed, a wave of contentment swept over me.

Despite it all, I thought, *we'll be okay. It'll be tight, but Aunt Susanna will get better. The bills will come and only two thirds of our stalls are used right now, but we will get more tenants, more clients, and more students. My desk job will keep groceries on the table and the bank from repossessing the farm, at least for a little while.*

I marveled at my own optimism and it wasn't until I walked back to the house that I realized one reason: Joe was back in town. Further, I hadn't seen one trespasser or abandoned hole in weeks.

We've done it, I thought, my spirits rising. *We've beaten the curse!*

Thanks to Professor Maddox and the Beaumont letter, we'd finally convinced the gold-seeking public that there was nothing to find on Chase Farm. The siege was over – recovery could begin.

I felt so good, I wanted to call Joe right then and there and tell him, but I remembered and I restrained myself.

No matter, I thought. *It's going to be tough for a little while, but we're going to make it after all.*

I looked up at the sky and grinned. "Thanks," I said and went into the house with Trusty, feeling confident for the first time in years.

The next day was Monday and I was late for work. It had taken me the better part of an hour to fill in and disguise the prospector's hole I'd discovered on my morning run.

My celebration had been premature.

THE BEAUMONT LETTER

Authenticated by Professor Anthony Maddox

Dear Mrs. Chase – ma'am:

I have recently received your kind letter of April 19th, it having followed me from my former apartments to where I am currently living. I am in good health and am in want of nothing, unless it is a restoration of my liberties. I am, however, content to serve my sentence.

You asked for particulars regarding Alex's death – I am sorry to say that I was not present at his passing. We did meet when his regiment passed through where I was working, and he was in good health and spirits, despite missing home and family as any man would. He encouraged me to follow his example and take up arms against the rebels, but pressing personal obligations kept me from following his honorable example and I learned of his passing from mutual friends.

No doubt you have heard disturbing rumors regarding the circumstances of our departure from Mr. McInnis' employment in Charleston, just before the Declaration of War. That Mr. McInnis was robbed is not in doubt – whether the goods are still intact is a matter of some dispute, even while the wisest and most knowledgable of men know that it is likely the items would have been lost on the gaming tables, as thieves and brigands are not adept in husbandry. Even the sad passing of your son is not enough to lay to rest the vicious rumors about his noble character.

Thinking on your widowhood, I regret that there is nothing of Alex's that I can send to you. While noble in character, we nevertheless indulged in an occasional gaming. Even what little we had was lost and is irretrievable, including the Kirk spoons, which you mentioned in your letter.

I hope to join the army upon my release, though I am torn in loyalties – my heart belongs to Georgia, while my wit believes in the Union. I trust I shall be guided in the right. Should I learn anything more regarding my friend, Alexander, I will be sure to contact you. I am grateful for your concern and care, and remain,

Yours faithfully,

J. Beaumont

4

Early May

The months slipped by. I said nothing to Aunt Susanna about the hole I'd discovered in September, nor about the ones I continued to find, but there was no keeping the secret from Lindsay. In the course of her workweek, she covered almost as much of the farm as I did, and it was she who discovered the third hole back in October.

I was out in one of the near paddocks, working one of the new mares, an old thoroughbred I'd bought as a favor off an old friend, hoping that I could train her as a teaching horse. We'd been working for a short time, Lucy going through her paces with the eagerness of a former show horse, and I was feeling pretty good about the purchase when Lindsay came to the gate.

"I have to show you something," she said.

I reined up so sharply that Lucy complained, tossing her head and dancing to one side. I barely paid attention, just slipped off her back and tugged her along with us.

Lindsay led us to one of the back paddocks, which - if Obadiah Chase's careful record-keeping is to be believed – was used for wheat and later for corn. Level and neglected-looking, it suffers from occasional flooding when the Exeter runs high. It was here that the treasure hunters left their mark.

The hole was shallow and wide, with the rocky soil thrown up in a tidy pile beside it. It was at the far side of the paddock, partially concealed by a barrel that we used for turning training. Lucy munched on the remaining grass while Lindsay and I filled the hole, patted it down, stomped on it, and rolled the barrel over it until the ground was safe enough to ride on.

"Are you going to call the police?" Lindsay asked when we were finished.

Calling the police meant publicity and I couldn't afford that. I shook my head grimly. "It won't do any good. We'll just have to keep watch, see if we can catch whoever is doing this. Hopefully, they'll get tired of looking and move on. Don't tell Susanna."

"Right, boss." She wiped her hands on her jeans, surveying our work. Then she shook her head.

"What?" I asked.

"I was just thinking – I'd never look here for the treasure. That Alexander Chase guy would have known about the flooding and, if I were him, I'd assume the soil would be washed away."

"You wouldn't be looking for the treasure anyway," I said, as we shouldered our shovels and led Lucy back to the barn. "You are smart enough to accept that there isn't any."

We came across two more holes before the ground froze for good at the end of November.

"This is such a pain," Lindsay complained, as we filled the last one. "I hope we find this guy."

"You and me both," I muttered, although I didn't really share the sentiment. Experience had taught me that others would come to replace him.

With the onset of snow, life went on in its dull, rhythmic routine. My job was going well enough, but even I was surprised at how quickly the weekly paycheck was eaten up by bills. We had a simple Christmas celebration, squeezed enough out of the checkbook to give Lindsay a decent Christmas bonus, then began making plans for the upcoming spring and summer season, our busiest of the year.

Aunt Susanna recovered enough from her hip surgery to have her knee operation. Physically recovered, I should say. Hobbling around like an elderly cripple for weeks on end left invisible scars, and she seemed to age even as she healed. The temporary downstairs bedroom slowly took on permanence, a sign of her surrender - and if it weren't for Darlene's caustic wit and sisterly bullying, I think she would have spent most of her winter inside.

It was a rough winter. Several of the mares became sick. In February, an ice storm damaged some of the detached stalls, and the barn roof showed signs of weakening. In March, I started negotiations with the bank to take out a second mortgage. In April, I was refused.

"What will we do?" Aunt Susanna asked, when she found out.

I shrugged. "We'll think of something else," I said. But I was fresh out of ideas. The best I could offer at that moment was the pathetic reassurance, "Summer's coming. We'll have plenty of work then."

Summer is easily our busiest and most profitable season. Aside from the usual lessons, arranging to have the fields planted and harvested, and the gardens, we always offer four riding camps: two in July, and two in August. The farm sees an increase in visitors as well. Riders prefer the trails to using the indoor ring, of course, and longer days encourage longer rides. They train more often, too - summer is prep-season for the fall shows.

This year, besides the lessons and the camps, we had two other major events. One was the annual August Chase Farm Horse Show, a tradition since the early 1960s, when it was open to only the farm riders and boarders. When Uncle Michael took over, he opened it up to everyone and turned it into one of the most popular and profitable events of the year.

Since his passing, attendance had dropped considerably, so I agreed to allow a wedding to take place on the grounds. It's a risk and an inconvenience, but the bride was an old friend of mine and the fee she offered for the privilege was an amount I couldn't, in good conscience, turn away.

"Maybe weddings will end up being a regular thing," I mused to Lindsay, as we discussed the schedule.

To my surprise, she was less than enthused.

"They are nothing but a huge pain," she pointed out. "My sister got married last year and the whole thing was a headache, start to finish. You'll make some money, sure, but you'll be lucky if it's worth the work."

She wasn't the only one who thought so. Joe Tremonti was of the same mind.

"Have you ever had to deal with a woman on her wedding day?" he asked me later that week, over a cup of coffee at our usual place in Salem. "Do you know what it's like?"

"What?" I asked reluctantly. I didn't like to be reminded that he had firsthand knowledge. "What's it like?"

He took a sip of his coffee, watching me over the rim of his mug, his eyebrows raised, his hazel eyes shifting colors. I thought again, *What did I do to deserve this?*

It was a happy thought, one that engendered others, and I had nearly forgotten the question when he answered it:

"You've read *Carrie,* right?"

I threw my napkin at him and he ducked, laughing - a rich, deep sound that made me shiver. *I could get used to this,* I thought; but as I looked at Joe, I couldn't help repeating the thought, this time with genuine confusion:

What did I do to deserve this?

For Joe had come back into my life, and it had been he who'd done the outreach, contacting me through social media. For a month or so, that's where it stayed – a message here and there, a joke picture passed back and forth. Then he invited me to a guest lecture.

"I remember how much you like local history," he'd explained in his message. "This woman really knows her stuff – I think you'll like her."

I went and I liked both the woman and the lecture, but it was the coffee afterwards, in a little Boston coffee shop, that I enjoyed most of all. Joe Tremonti was as handsome as ever, and he hadn't lost the knack of making you feel like you were the only person on the planet. But even as I reveled in the attention, I had to remind myself, *Married, married, married.*

It wasn't until he was walking me back to my car that he'd dropped the bomb. I asked him what made him accept the guest lecturing position. He was going through the usual reasons: prestige, time to write, new opportunities - when he broke off suddenly and stopped walking, his shoulders slumping.

The parking garage was nearly deserted, not a place I'd normally feel comfortable hanging around at night. The light from exit sign partially lit his face. His eyes, lost in the shadows, looked like hollow caverns and, for the first time since I'd known him, Joe Tremonti looked tired and beaten.

"Oh, what's the use?" he said. "There's no point in hiding it, not from you. Amber asked me to go. She wanted a divorce, but I… I convinced her to try separation. Give her time to think, to work things out."

He turned, leaving me with a curious, awkward feeling. I wanted to take his hand to make him feel better, but I knew better than to offer comfort.

"Has it helped?" I asked. It was all I could think to say.

"It did," he said. "She filed for divorce on Monday."

"I'm sorry," I whispered.

He turned and his weak grin was heartbreaking. "All I could think when she told me was, 'I'm so glad I'm here, near my friends.' You don't know how much you rely on them… Until something like this happens." He took my hand and squeezed it. "Thanks, Maddie."

I squeezed it back, feeling like a small child who'd just unwrapped the very present she'd asked for.

Aunt Susanna was sympathetic for his plight; but after Christmas, when we started meeting on a semi-regular basis, she was not happy.

"You need to be careful," she scolded. "The man is barely out of one relationship. He shouldn't be moving on this fast."

"Nothing like that is going on," I said, even while I blushed. "He's in need of a friend, that's all. He doesn't really know anyone at the college."

"He hardly knows you, either," she said. "If he's looking for a rebound relationship, let it be with one of his colleagues, not my niece."

I turned on her with a fury that surprised both of us. "We are *not* in a relationship!" I snapped. "We are *friends* and that's it! And I'm not going to stop – if it weren't for Joe, I wouldn't even *have* a social life right now."

As soon as I said it, I wished I could take it back. Aunt Susanna didn't need to be reminded that I was working two full time jobs essentially, just trying to keep the place running. I didn't need her slipping into guilt-induced depression.

Aunt Susanna never brought her concerns up again, even after I apologized. I was glad, because she was not exactly wrong about the situation – she just had it backwards. Joe never acted like anything more than a friend to me, but the more time I spent with him, the harder I fell. I hadn't realized how lonely I was, how much I'd longed for some attention, until I started spending time with him.

Joe knew how to treat a woman. He was the type who could hold the door open for you without looking like he was trying too hard, who knew just the right way to tease, when to compliment you on your hair, and when to ask, "How are *you* doing today?" And he worried about me, which made me feel special.

He was worried about me the day I mentioned the wedding plans.

"All those people running around, trampling on the grass," he said. His tone was doubtful.

"They can't be worse on it than we already are," I said, more cheerfully than I was feeling. I didn't really like the idea of turning our place into a wedding venue, but it was better than selling the farm, as my co-workers suggested. "It's not that big a deal. It'll be over in a week."

"If you're lucky," he said, and I had to laugh at his dire tone.

The days were stretching out longer, bringing with them the usual increased workload. Lindsay and I spent hours preparing lessons for the riding camps, organizing schedules, and planning the usual vet appointments and summer maintenance.

Lindsay loved the summer. Besides her passion for horses and the outdoors, she really connected with the children we work for. Which was a good thing, because between my aunt's slow recovery and my work schedule, the bulk of the training was going to fall on her slim shoulders.

"You feeling up to being Headmaster?" I had asked, as we ended a meeting.

"Oh, yeah." She grinned. "This is going to be a blast. I'll put them through their paces – they'll be equestrians *par excellence* by the end of August, you'll see."

Lindsay's enthusiasm was infectious, and I couldn't help but think how lucky I was to have her. I still didn't know what I was going to do when she went to college.

Even with Lindsay taking over most of the lessons, there was plenty for me to do: the advertising, the paperwork, the task of providing lunches and snacks every day for anywhere from five to fifteen finicky little girls, and scheduling the ever-increasing number of lessons. I couldn't afford to turn people away. By the end of May, I was putting in fourteen hour days and seriously considering hiring two more part-time helpers.

Added to this were the usual daily irritations. Despite the letter's authentication, we were still getting requests from people to use the farm for everything ranging from filming horror movies to excavating on the off chance that there actually was treasure. By this point, I was immune to their passionate pleas and annoyed by their persistence. I had ordered Aunt Susanna to deny any requests that came by phone, and I deleted the email requests without replying. When Professor Randall's email came in, I must have followed the usual procedure and trashed it right away. I don't remember ever seeing it.

I have a particularly sharp memory of the early morning run on that Wednesday in May. It was a clear, unseasonably cool day, and my breath came out in gusts of condensation as I pushed along the riding trail. As I rounded the corner and headed back to the farmhouse, it loomed before me in clear relief against the foggy early morning, a solid, squat Colonial salt-house with additions marring its otherwise pure look.

I remember pausing at the gate that separates the horse farmyard from the main yard, chilled with sweat and hungry. The house was quiet, dark windows accenting the dark blue paint that, yet again, needed new coat.

It's an antiquarian's dream, our house. Built in the 1600s, it had stood through the revolutions, wars, and climate changes of America's rambunctious history, housing generation after generation of stalwart Chases. They were the archetype - in my opinion at least - of the original settlers: hardworking, quiet, civic-minded, and stubborn.

I loved the house. I loved it for more than just the sentimental memories of a happy childhood spent within its secure four walls. I loved the ideas it represented, its history, up to Alexander Chase. Of course, I loved the people who lived in it when I was child: my aunt and uncle had done the bulk of raising me, and I thought of them as more my parents than my real ones.

My biggest regret has always been that my name is Warwick. As a child, I'd write "Chase" on my kindergarten school papers, and argue with my teacher about the legality of it. When she sent me home with a note to my guardians, I begged Uncle Michael to change my name.

I'll never forget the look on his face as he answered, "Would if I could, Maddie. I would if I could."

He probably would have. My aunt and uncle loved children, yet were never able to have any of their own. If it wasn't for me, they probably would have adopted one, but they never did and now they had no one to carry on their own legacy.

No one, that is, but me. I suppose that's why I was so bound and determined to keep the farm open and working. I wasn't a Chase, so even if I did have children, they wouldn't have the name. The farm was my uncle's one legacy, and I had appointed myself guardian of it.

Vowing to preserve something is one thing. Bringing it about is quite another. I'd always known that Susanna and Michael Chase were not very interested in money, but I'd never known how close they played everything. Every month was a long, knock-down drag-out fight between me, the checkbook, and the bank, and the struggle was starting to tell on me. Even I could see that. My hobbies and interests had dwindled to almost nothing, my back was constantly stiff from both the burden and the broken mattress I couldn't afford to replace. A line had etched itself on my face, my romantic prospects (excepting, perhaps, the long-shot Joe Tremonti) were practically null, and my hands had grown calloused with time and work. Despite my best efforts, my manners had grown more brusque, almost rude.

Relinquishing the fight was not an option. Aunt Susanna deserved to keep her home and the Chase family legacy, tarnished though it was. Besides, I hadn't run out of ideas yet.

That morning in particular, I remember standing in its shadow, looking up at the familiar lines, thinking, *It's not over yet. I promise, Uncle Michael, I won't give up.*

Even as I said it, dread crept around the edges of my heart. I don't really believe in premonitions; but if I did, I would say that I knew, even then, that the fight was about to take a turn for the worse.

5

That Wednesday was one of the longest days of my life.

It started off normally enough. Aunt Susanna was in her room preparing for an exercise class with Darlene, and I, home from work, had my usual routine of stable mucking, bill paying, lessons, and teaching.

The bad news started right after she left. I was checking my emails and discovered one from the New Hampshire Board of Historical Properties, once again turning down my application for Historical Property status. It was a serious blow. Having them assume the financial responsibility for the buildings would have eased our struggle considerably, and perhaps even have given Aunt Susanna the freedom to do something else with her time and income, like get a winter place in Florida, maybe, or visit her sisters in the Carolinas.

The board's refusal changed nothing, aside from dashing my hopes again. I would have handled the disappointment much better if I hadn't also spotted the mortgage statement on the stack of yesterday's bills. I'd only just finished paying the minimum on our credit cards, and our checking account didn't have enough to cover this as well.

Thankfully, I had lessons to give, getting me out of that office. But watching little girls in pink helmets going in endless circles on the back of a shuffling pony only depressed me. They seemed oddly emblematic of my life. The concentration on their faces, the almost panicked way the new riders gripped the reins with their hands rather than the saddle with their knees struck a chord in me. I spend too much time in my head anyway; but sometimes, I wondered if I wasn't doing the same in my own life: riding in tethered circles with bad form.

Mrs. Fontaine's daughter, Alice, had a lesson that day, which didn't help my state of mind.

While Alice was a nice little girl with a smile so sweet it could give you cavities, her mother was a nervous, pushy sort who liked to speak her mind. She was unhappy with me because, after a year of lessons, her daughter still wasn't jumping. I had tried to explain to her that jumping was only for the more experienced, that it was perfectly normal for it to take two years or so before a rider was ready. Mrs. Fontaine was not unlike other parents when she insisted that Alice was especially talented, and could be trained at a faster pace than the others.

I knew better. Alice was a gentle girl with a level head, but she was not a natural equestrian. If anything, she needed more time, not less.

I never said that, of course, but my watered-down explanations were enough to upset Mrs. Fontaine. Unable to override me, she would instead try to undermine me with veiled threats.

"The Shoepflin Farm a few towns over offers more competitive training for girls Alice's age," she'd say. Or, "It's a long drive to here from Andover. I keep thinking we should go someplace closer."

I'd become used to over-anxious mothers and their badgering techniques, and I was determined that I would not let her upset me. The farm had a vested financial interest in keeping the Fontaine's business: not only did Alice take her lessons here, but Mrs. Fontaine's sister boarded two horses with us. If Mrs. Fontaine left, no doubt she'd take her sister with her.

Alice had her lessons at six p.m., after her piano lessons. They always arrived dressed in full gear, on time, expecting Alice's favorite pony - Red Rider - to be ready. Normally, we insisted that the rider prepare the pony, but as Mrs. Fontaine was nervous around horses and Alice was still so little, we waived this in their case.

At 5:45, I was heading to the barn to prepare Red Rider when I met Lindsay coming in the opposite direction. She was looking very cheerful.

"I've got the Hendersons at six," she said. "Do you mind if I take Missy out for a run before I go home?"

"Be my guest," I answered. "She could use the exercise. I've got one more lesson, then a long, leisurely night of balancing budgets to look forward to."

"You've got the Fontaine's tonight, right? Gosh, am I glad tonight is your turn in rotation."

"Why?"

"Red Rider threw his shoe. You'll have to use Greybeard, and you know how he loves little Alice's crop."

"Oh, terrific!" I exclaimed. "I'm going to have to keep them on the lunge line. Mrs. Fontaine will love that. I'll get the lecture about holding her daughter back. You wouldn't want to trade, would you?"

"Not on your life. I'll take the Henderson girl any day of the week."

She hurried off, and I glumly went into the barn to check on Red Rider and saddle up Greybeard.

As predicted, Mrs. Fontaine was not at all pleased. She was even more upset when she learned that we weren't going to be using the indoor ring.

"Why not?" she asked, practically pouting as I opened the door to let Alice lead her dark charge out into the yard.

"It's in use at the moment," I lied. It actually needed to be cleaned and the sand re-spread to make a smooth riding surface. It should have been done a week ago, but both Lindsay and I had been too busy to tend to it.

I wasn't about to admit as much to Mrs. Fontaine. The truth would have only made her more upset.

"We've used it before with other people in it," she pointed out. "Why is today different?"

"We're using Greybeard today and he isn't as comfortable around other horses," I said hastily, and instantly wished I'd said anything else.

Mrs. Fontaine's eyes grew wide with shock. I skipped ahead to help Alice lead her horse.

It was a lovely night. The sun was low in the sky, blinding us as we headed for the west fields, where the training paddocks were. I hadn't given much thought to which paddock we would use, but as the first two had jumping equipment set up in them, I decided that we'd use the far ring, instead of the usual outdoor training ring.

Alice was in her usual good mood, as unflappable as her mother was anxious. Dressed in immaculate riding garb, complete with shiny boots and a short crop, she crooned and rubbed Greybeard's nose as we walked along. I watched her, wishing that current child safety policies didn't make it absolutely imperative that a parent be present at these lessons.

Mrs. Fontaine would be much happier at home, I reasoned. *As it is, she's going to be catching up in a second to pester me. I should have stayed in veterinary school.*

Sure enough, Mrs. Fontaine soon caught up with us, her fashion boots clumping unsteadily on the trail, her eyes flashing behind long lashes.

"Do you mean to say that my daughter is on an *unsafe* horse?" she sputtered.

"Absolutely not. Greybeard is as gentle and nice as Red Rider. But we're, uh, training horses in the ring tonight and they're unsteady. Red Rider is older and wouldn't be bothered, but Greybeard is a young guy. He's absolutely lovely, really."

I went ahead to open the paddock gate. Alice, unmoved by her mother's unhappiness, led the pony in and up to the mounting stool. I stepped inside and was about to latch the gate behind me when Mrs. Fontaine caught my hand in a steel grip.

Prepared as I was for her temper, I was caught off guard by the unmasked anger in her eyes.

"Have you checked it first?" she hissed.

"Checked what?" Admittedly, my tone was snappy.

"The ground – have you checked it for holes?"

I stared at her. Lindsay and I had been finding evidence of treasure hunters with increasing regularity, but we'd been careful to keep it from the parents and students. The only rider who might have known would be Karen Guinta, who'd come across a hole a week ago, but I convinced her that it was there as part of a surveying project. So how did Mrs. Fontaine know? Had she found one? How could I ask without admitting to the danger?

Then Mrs. Fontaine went on. "I don't want an accident to happen to my daughter like it happened to Michael. I insist that you inspect the grounds before she rides."

I could hardly see for the anger. It took every ounce of restraint for me not to tell her off properly.

As I took a breath, I thought, *All this time and no progress. I still lose it whenever someone mentions his name.*

"It was inspected, Mrs. Fontaine," I said, carefully, politely, but she would have to be blind not to have seen the smoke pouring out of my ears. "Lindsay, used this paddock only this morning. And we haven't been bothered by trespassers in quite some time, just so you know."

"That's not what I've heard. Karen Guinta saw one of those prospecting holes only the other day."

Darn it. So Karen hadn't bought my story.

"Karen Guinta said that?" I asked sharply. "What else did she say?"

She shrugged. "I don't know. Charlie White told me about it. He called to ask me if I'd seen anything suspicious on your farm. *He* thinks that you're still being bothered by treasure hunters."

I sighed. Of course, Charlie White was behind this. A wannabe journalist who edited an online rag by the name of *New Hampshire News Now,* he was always looking for something sensational, a trick to pull off in the relatively tame Granite State. He'd been all over my uncle's death, writing opinion pieces and conducting interviews until finally even Aunt Susanna told him off. When the Beaumont letter was published, his coverage was brief and uninterested, partially because there was another, bigger story in Franklin. I'd thought we were finished with Charlie White, but it seemed that the story was not as dead as I'd thought.

I was still mulling this over when Mrs. Fontaine said, "I won't have my daughter riding on dangerous ground."

"We check all the paddocks every morning," I said automatically. "There aren't any treasure hunters on the property. Professor Maddox's discovery put an end to that."

"That's not what I heard..."

"I can't help the rumors, Mrs. Fontaine," I cut her off. "I can only tell you the truth."

I might have added, *Or a part of the truth.*

Mrs. Fontaine's green eyes flashed at me. "Well," she hissed. "The truth of the matter is, I've been uneasy bringing Alice here. My sister likes you, but I've seen nothing to convince me that you're any better than any other instructor, even though you charge like you've trained a triple-crown winner. I can't see that it's worth it, frankly. You may love horses, but you don't seem to have any discernable talent. You certainly aren't anywhere close to the reputation that your uncle had, and I'm not even sure that his reputation wasn't grossly overrated..."

That did it. I broke her monologue by smashing my hand against the rough, wooden rail. She jumped as though I'd hit her - which, frankly, had been my first instinct.

"Mrs. Fon*taine*," I snapped. "If you've got nothing better to do than insult me and my family, you can take your contract and your daughter and walk out right now."

She stared at me, and I stared back.

"Mom? Miss Warwick?"

Alice sounded frightened, and it takes a lot to snap that little girl out of herself.

The silence stretched long enough for regret to start infringing on my self-assurance. Mrs. Fontaine looked at me with disbelief mingled with caution. Then she stepped back, still smoldering, but nodding for me to go on. I took in her stance, her set jaw, the way she angrily fingered her phone, and I thought, *I've lost it. I've lost their account. We'll go under. I've lost.*

Yet, even then, I knew that if she'd said one more word about Uncle Michael, I would have verbally leveled her.

Just when all seemed lost, a cheery voice sounded from down the path.

"Hey, Alice! Mind if we join you?"

Lindsay approached with the Henderson girl jauntily astride the roan thoroughbred, her grandmother following at a distance. Beaming with confidence, my assistant looked like she had come to save the day.

Then, she did.

"Good grief, Mrs. Fontaine! Where *did* you get those boots? Please tell me that they make a cheap knock-off, because I totally need a pair."

To my shock, Mrs. Fontaine flushed with pleasure and said something about a sale. Lindsay continued to gush, then admired Alice's outfit - and in short order, she had Mrs. Fontaine laughing with Henderson's grandmother. She introduced the two girls to each other and had the pair of them working companionably in the ring, Alice on the lunge line while Henderson rode in circles around her.

I stood in the middle of the ring, holding the line, aware that the sudden peace was as fragile as the first ice over Walden Pond. Mrs. Fontaine's glances in my direction were enough to tell me that I was not in her good graces yet. For the sake of her daughter, and probably Lindsay, she stayed civil up until the party broke up in the barn. The Hendersons walked the roan back to his stall, Lindsay went into the tack room to clean the saddle, and we were alone.

Mrs. Fontaine sent Alice on ahead to the car, then she turned to me.

"I suppose you expect an apology," she said. She was in the doorway, the falling sun outlining her thin profile. She looked both impressive and brittle.

I was honest. I told her I wasn't, but I offered her one. She brushed it off and looked at me with scorn.

"I don't allow people I hire to speak to me the way you did," she said. "I would withdraw my daughter from this place and insist on a full refund, except for the fact that she really loves that girl, Lindsay. So we'll keep our account with you. For now. But I expect better service in the future, Miss Warwick, or I promise you, both Alice and my sister will find other stables and tell others why. Do you understand me?"

It was impossible to misunderstand her. Oh, how I wanted to fling the offer back in her face, to tell her to take her little girl and the two overindulged horses and find some other stable stupid enough to put up with her. I wanted to tell her that she could tell the world what she pleased, that it would take more than her insignificant voice to worry us. I wanted to hold my head up high and put her highness back into her place.

The problem was I knew exactly what her position was. Mrs. Fontaine might be more trouble than eight of my other clients put together, but I needed her business. Alice was one of a tight group of girls, all of whom had signed up for summer camps. If Alice left, that was bad enough, but I knew that she'd take others with her, and the farm couldn't handle it.

Mrs. Fontaine was implying that I couldn't do without her business, and she was right.

So I drew a deep breath, and I threw up a prayer, and I looked her in the eye.

"Thank you, Mrs. Fontaine," I said.

It was the hardest thing I'd ever had to say, but that was nothing compared with watching her draw herself up and stride off, the warrior triumphant. The proud Chase girl had joined her in battle and lost on her own ground. There would be no dealing with Mrs. Fontaine in the future. She knew her place and mine, and I was done.

But there was nothing I could do about it, so I cleaned her daughter's fancy tack and put it on her specially marked peg.

It was the least a peasant could do.

6

I entered the house, dirty, defeated, and so tired that I almost forgot to leave my boots by the back door, as Aunt Susanna had requested so many times. I called out to her as I untied them, but there was no answer. I went into the kitchen and flipped on the lights.

It was neat, with only a few dishes in the sink, and nothing prepared on the counter. I was famished, so I quickly washed my hands in the sink and pulled open the fridge. It was a discouraging sight: sparsely populated with eggs, a quart of milk, and a few limp vegetables. There weren't even any left-overs.

I sighed and slammed it shut, then went over to the bread box. Two stale crusts of wheat bread lay dejectedly on their sides. I'd meant to go to the grocery store, but the workload had put the need out of my mind. I wondered why Aunt Susanna hadn't gone, but realized that this was my week to do the shopping. So this was my fault.

I let the cover to the bread box fall shut and rubbed my eyes as my stomach growled. With a grunt, I pulled the cover open again and shoved one of the pieces of bread in my mouth. It was like eating sawdust.

Hopefully, Aunt Susanna had some ideas for dinner, because I was fresh out.

"Aunt Susanna!" I called again, through my mouthful.

Odd. She was usually in the kitchen at this time of night, preparing something, even if it wasn't her turn to cook.

I went to the hall and called again, but as I did so, the wall calendar caught my attention. Today's date was circled in red, with the words, *Class, 7pm,* written in my aunt's hand.

She wasn't even here. I was on my own for dinner.

I might have sworn aloud then. I probably did. I don't swear under normal circumstances, but I was tired and the incident with Mrs. Fontaine was still fresh on my mind. I had been hoping to discuss it with Aunt Susanna, but now it would have to wait until she returned and I was not happy about that.

I turned to go back into the kitchen to see if there were any frozen dinners left in the fridge, when something else caught my eye. The light to the living room was on.

Since becoming the one responsible for them, I was somewhat obsessive about the electric bills. If a room wasn't in active use, I insisted that the lights be turned off. My aunt had objected a little, saying that it made the house seem even emptier than it was, but even she had to concede that it was better to be in a dark house than have none at all. She was usually pretty good about turning things off, but if she was in hurry, like she'd probably been tonight in trying to get to class on time, she'd forget.

I sighed again. It seemed, in my childish piquancy, that everything was conspiring against me. I lumbered down the hall, taking another bite of the bread that remained in my hand.

The light switch is far enough in the room that you have to step into it in order to reach it, which I did. I was so focused on the bread that I didn't see anything else as I flipped the light switch.

"Hey!"

The protest erupted from somewhere in the darkness in front of me. It was a male voice, one I didn't recognize in a room that was supposed to be empty. I choked, but my hand was still on the switch and I had the presence of mind to flip it again as I coughed.

The warm yellow light infused the old living room with its battered furniture and out-of-style wallpaper with an almost neighborly sense of welcome. It was more welcoming, I'm sure, than the startled look I was giving the person at the couch.

A man sprang up from it, one hand still grasping the book he'd been reading, while the other was pulling off his large glasses. He was dressed in a well-fitting, but somewhat worn brown jacket over pressed pants that looked as though they were of good quality. A briefcase, also well-used, was on the floor by his leather-clad feet, and his hair, dark and thick, was neatly brushed and groomed.

"I *beg* your pardon," he said, haughtily. "I was reading in here. Next time you might want to look in a room before you turn the lights off."

He spoke in a clipped tone, clearly annunciating every word, like a seasoned Shakespearean actor. I was too startled to answer, and we looked each other up and down in silence for a moment.

His appearance matched his tone, I decided. He looked like a fussy sort of a man, one accustomed to a certain high manner of living without the income to maintain it.

The most striking thing about him was the color of his shirt - a dark, almost jewel-toned orange that set off his hair and dark eyes. While the rest of his outfit was the typical stuffy-professor look you'd expect in a movie or play, the shirt played against type. I wonder what it said about the stranger's character.

He held the coffee table copy of Uncle Michael's self-published book, *A Short History of the Chase Family,* and if his finger positioning was anything to go by, he was halfway through it. His face was young, probably younger than he actually was. The result, I thought, of a life of relative ease.

Oh, Lord, just what I need. A male version of Louisa Fontaine in my life.

The thought relaxed me a little. Whatever this man was doing here, it was not to cause me physical harm.

What he thought of me, I couldn't really say. I hadn't changed out of my work clothes, except for taking off my boots, so I must have presented a bedraggled appearance: dirty jeans and a sweat-stained plaid shirt thrown over a tank top. My mismatched stockings (I'd been putting off laundry, too) were hardly sophisticated, my hair was pulling loose out of my pony tail, and I still clutched a piece of wadded up week-old bread in my hand.

I looked a sight and I knew it, but when his expression changed ever so slightly to one that I took as distaste, my temper flared.

"*What* are you doing in here?" I demanded.

He didn't answer right away. He looked me up and down again, and then in the face.

"Madeleine Warwick?" he inquired, and I got the distinct impression that he was hoping I'd say no.

It pleased me to disappoint him. I folded my arms across my chest. "That's me," I said. "And who are you?"

He eyed me with more interest then, but he didn't answer. Instead, he reached into his pocket and pulled out a card. He took a step over to hand it to me, and I noted that he was a few inches taller than me. The scent of cologne, earthy and light, clung about him.

"You don't answer your emails," he said lightly.

I snatched the card from his grasp. "I answer the important ones."

I didn't wait for his response. I studied the card, frowning to focus. I was so upset that my hands were shaking, and my annoyance at my overreaction only made it worse. It took me a little time before I made out what I was supposed to be reading.

"Professor Gregory Randall?" I asked, and looked up.

He'd put his over-sized glasses back on and was pouring over the pages of Uncle Michael's book, but he glanced at me.

"Pleased to meet you," he said, before looking back down again.

Irritated, I looked at the card again and said, "Hadley University? Where's that? I've never heard of a *Hadley* University."

That got him to look up from the book.

"It's in Holbein," he said, with a wounded look - as though I ought to have recognized it right off the bat. "In the heart of beautiful western Massachusetts."

"Sorry." I handed the card back. "Doesn't ring a bell. Is it one of those new, online universities?"

"Certainly not!" he said, accepting the card and looking at the face of it, as though to make sure I hadn't changed anything. "Hadley University was established in 1914, and boasts an illustrious alumni and a sterling academic reputation." Then he shrugged as he put the card back in his pocket. "Don't feel too badly, though. We are a small, but growing community."

"How lovely," I said dryly, and one of his eyebrows raised in acknowledgement. "And may I be so bold as to inquire what brought one of the faculty from such an... an *august* establishment to trespass on my property?"

Even as I said the word, "trespass", I experienced a clutch in my heart. Trespassers on the Chase Property usually only had one object in mind. If this bookworm was expecting permission to hunt for buried treasure, he was going to be in for a shock.

Professor Randall looked wounded again. "I am not *trespassing*," he emphasized, pulling his glasses off as he spoke. "Your aunt let me in. She was in a hurry to get out the door to class or something, but she invited me to wait here to talk to you. If you don't believe me, why don't you call her and ask her. Trespass, indeed!"

He looked very put out and, without knowing why, I believed him. It was definitely something that Aunt Susanna would do: let a complete stranger sit alone in the house while I was unaware in the barn.

I sighed and decided that I probably was coming on a little too strong. After all, he hadn't meant to frighten me – Aunt Susanna should have sent me a text or something before she left.

"Poor choice of words on my part, I guess," I said. "What do you want, Professor?"

He gestured to my recliner. "Have a seat?"

"In these clothes?"

Professor Randall looked me over again, and nodded. "Perhaps you're right. I can wait if you'd like to..."

"What I'd like to do," I interrupted, trying to keep my tone light while still getting my point across, "is shower, eat, and go to bed as soon as possible. I don't want to be rude, Professor, but I'd appreciate it if you'd get right to the point."

I might have added, *So I can throw you out on your ear and get on with my life,* but I wanted to be sure of his intentions first. Besides, something told me that he had prepared himself for a hostile reception, a thought that made me feel even more frustrated.

I'm not a tyrant – I'm just tired of people trying to get rich off of my family's history.

But maybe I had this guy wrong. Maybe he didn't care about the treasure at all. Maybe he was a historian who was looking to do a proper history on the family, someone that I could trust with the family documents, someone who could set the record straight, who'd treat us with the dignity and respect that is the right of every decent, upright family…

Then he said, "Very well. Briefly, I want permission to search your family estate for the remains of the McInnis treasure."

With that pin-prick, my balloon deflated with a violent pop. I sagged against the wall in disappointment, a gesture he took no notice of. He had dropped back to the couch, pulled up his briefcase, and was working the old-fashioned combination lock as he spoke.

"I'm a historian, a researcher by trade," he said conversationally. "My preferred concentration is early United States Colonial and Republican history, but at the moment, I am involved in writing a biography on a lesser known Civil War participant, whose name I'm sure you wouldn't be familiar with. In conducting my research, I crossed paths with Professor Maddox…"

"Professor Maddox!" I exclaimed, in spite of myself.

He nodded, pulling a sheaf of papers from out of his case. "Yes. We'd worked together before, back when I was an undergraduate student at Braeburn. My research has lead me to some work that he'd been doing before his death. His widow was kind enough to let me go through his papers. Imagine my surprise when I discovered a connection to the Chase family and the McInnis affair."

As he spoke, his tone slipped into an authoritative cadence, like that of a professional lecturer going over an often-used lesson. My pulse quickened, but I kept calm. He was shuffling through the papers, so if my face was flushed, he didn't notice it. Randall didn't see my eye roll, either. He looked at me a second too late.

"You don't say," I sighed.

The professor frowned, and turned back to his papers. "Yes – remarkable, I thought. It seems my subject had a strong connection to one of the characters in the case. Naturally, when I began to look into the theft, it piqued my curiosity. As you probably know, unsolved cases are something of a hobby of mine."

"They are?"

He didn't hear. "My book is nearly finished. The final piece is this McInnis case, which I can only solve here, where the treasure disappeared."

"I think you mean Baltimore," I said.

Again he looked at me and again he grinned - a sly, unsettling expression.

"Yes…" he said and gestured to the pages in front of him. "I've been working on this only for a few weeks now and most of the material available is… Dubious to say the least, but some aspects are clear. There was, among other things, a silver spoon set that disappeared from the McInnis household at the same time Alexander Chase and Beaumont left his employ. Beaumont was a ruffian, but there's no indication that Alexander Chase was ever in trouble with the law beyond a drunken-disorderly. The idea that he would steal from his employer seems to be out of character. Are you sure you don't want to sit, Miss Warwick? You look tired."

He gestured to one of our chairs, but I waved him off.

"Just get to the point, all right?" I asked.

Randall blinked at me, then nodded.

"All right. It's simple enough. Alexander Chase's involvement in the theft is still very much in question, but what is *not* is the fact that there was a fortune that disappeared from the McInnis household, and evidence to suggest that it wound up here, on your property. I'm going to find it and hopefully, in doing so, bring to conclusion this whole matter and wrap up my biography at the same time." He paused, then went on. "I have cleared my summer schedule and have collected up all the evidence I can get my hands on. I expect to find more between now and when we begin the search, but what I need from you is, first of all, permission to..."

"No," I said.

Randall looked up at me, surprised. "No?"

"No."

He paused, then, "That's all you have to say? 'No'? You won't hear me out?"

"No, I won't." I sighed, rubbing my eyes. "You're looking for fool's gold, Professor. Every historian worth his salt has declared the treasure nothing more than a rumor, a local ghost story, one that has caused more pain and death than I'm willing to go through again. Now, I'm going to ask you politely to leave."

"I've done my legwork, Miss Warwick. I have evidence..."

"Don't bother showing it to me. If you're anything like the others, all you have are photocopies of some letters and diary entries from local citizens. I've heard every version and every theory and I'm getting tired of people trying to get rich off of my family's history."

Randall sputtered. "Rich off your... My dear Miss Warwick, you misunderstand me. I'm not here to take the treasure from your family. You can keep it, for all I care, once we've catalogued it."

"Oh, very generous of you, I'm sure," I scoffed.

"I'm not here for gold, I'm here to solve a mystery, a mystery which a member of your own family lays at the heart of. Aren't you even the slightest bit curious?"

"No, I'm not. Use whatever excuse you have, mister, I know a fortune hunter when I see one."

For a long moment we just stared at each other. I think it was then that I first noticed how dark his eyes were. The brown looked nearly black, the darkest eyes I'd ever seen, and I found myself wondering what lay within their depths.

At the moment, all I could detect was annoyance.

"A fortune hunter!" he said, and his enunciation was even clearer than before. He was the very picture of scandalized innocence as he shook his head and laughed. "You know, I'd been warned that you were less than hospitable, but no one said anything about outright slander. Aren't you even slightly interested in my evidence, in my theories?"

"I'm not," I said, in conscious imitation of his tone. "There's nothing that you can show me that I haven't already seen before."

"But think of what this might do for your family..."

"I am."

"Are you though? Or are you just skirting a painful, unresolved issue?" He waved away my open-mouthed objection and continued. "Look, imagine - just imagine, for a moment - that I'm right, that there is a treasure, just as everyone thought. Think of what that would do for your struggling farm, Miss Warwick. Instead of amateur treasure hunters leaving pot holes everywhere, you could hire the fields out to re-enactors. You could use the reputation of the find to build your business. Instead of trying to make ends meet at the end of every month, begging credit card companies to extend your credit, you'd be hiring help and building more stables to handle the overflow. With your family's reputation saved from the dumpheap of history, you'd finally be able to convince the state of New Hampshire that this monument to early American pride is worth the seal of 'Historical Significance'. You'd be able to focus on what you want to do, instead of worrying about where the next mortgage payment is coming from."

I stared at him, shocked and outraged. How did *he*, a stranger, know about the trouble the farm was in?

Randall wasn't finished. He went on, in an almost dreamy tone. "With the treasure found, you'd know, once and for all, the true story about your family. So, imagine that I find the treasure, which I will, make no mistake. I'm very good at this kind of thing. You've heard about the Dunstable Cache, I'm sure. Those papers and diaries of one of Washington's spies that was found in an old lady's attic in New York several years ago?"

He looked so proud of himself that I couldn't resist adding a bit of emphasis to my answer. "No, I hadn't heard. Was it important?"

I was getting used to his wounded look – it was almost cute.

"Yes, it was," he sniffed. "For years, the academic community denied the Dunstable connection and I nearly lost my position over it. I built my academic reputation as the man who can find things, and the Dunstable Cache... Honestly, Miss Warwick, don't you ever interest yourself in archeological and historical findings? I would have thought that someone with your family background would stay up to date on all such things."

"I've been busy, so sue me," I said. I remembered the piece of bread in my hand and slipped it into my pocket, to the obvious distaste of the professor. "But you can't find what isn't there, Professor. Trust me, if wishing could make something so, that treasure would have been found a century ago."

"By the parsimonious Avery Chase?" he asked.

"So you know Avery Chase's name and his obsession," I said stiffly. "You probably also know that he ruined his life looking for that stupid, non-existent treasure, and if anyone could have found it, it would have been him. After all, they were brothers."

Now Randall's smile was indulgent. "That," he said gently, like he was speaking to a child, "is a common mistake. People assume that because they were brothers, Avery would have known him better than most. But they were only half-brothers, and I know you don't have any siblings, Miss Warwick, but I do. Let me assure you that some of them are as strangers to me as if we had been born worlds apart, rather than mere years."

I bristled. "You researched *me*?" I sputtered.

"I told you, I'm…"

"Thorough, yes, I got that. I suppose you never considered that it might lead to a suit for breach of my privacy."

"For using what you posted online? I'm afraid you waived that right when you pushed 'post'."

Oh, Lord, how I wanted to slap his smug face.

"I'm not interested in you, your family affairs, or your *research*," I snapped. "I want you to leave."

"But about my project…"

"Your *treasure* hunt," I corrected. "Be honest about it and listen to me. There. Is. No. *Treasure.* There never was."

As soon as I said it, I recognized the slip of the tongue and, sure enough, he caught it.

"That's not what Beaumont said in his letter," Randall pointed out.

"So you've read the Beaumont letter?"

"Yes."

"Then what *else* do you want?" I exploded. "The man came out and said that the 'treasure' was lost in gambling dens all up and down the coast. There is no treasure."

"I don't believe it."

"Don't *believe* it? Don't *believe* the Beaumont letter?"

Randall looked at me inquisitively. Softly, almost in a whisper, he said, "No. I don't believe it."

There was something menacing in his tone. I threw up my hands again, desperate to look only exasperated and not frightened. "Look, it doesn't even matter – save yourself some heartache and backache, Mr. Randall, and listen to me: there is no treasure on Chase Farm. There never has been. You're on a fool's errand that's ruined better men than you."

"You mean," he said, in the same soft tone, "that it ruined Michael Chase."

For the second time today, my uncle's end had been thrown in my face for effect. Now fury replaced fear. If he wanted a fireworks display, I could oblige.

I grabbed the door knob and threw the door wide open. It bounced against the wall and nearly rebounded on me. I whirled on him and pointed at the doorway, but Randall hadn't moved. My display of temper didn't do anything more than make the set expression on his face even more firm.

"That," I hissed, "is *enough.* You get out of my house, Randall. Get out *now,* or I swear, I'll call the police."

There was another moment of quiet, so deep, so still, that it was frightening. Randall - for all his peculiarities, his snobbish, particular exterior - looked so calm, so still, that I thought, *I've lost.*

Just as I completed the thought, he leaned in. His dark eyes bored into mine, and I repressed a shiver.

"Tell me, Warwick," he asked, ever so softly. "Did that letter achieve its purpose? Has it stopped *anybody* from digging on your land?"

My mouth went dry and I leaned back against the wall, struggling to ask, "What are you talking about?"

Again, the look of feigned innocence. "The Beaumont letter. You published it in the local and national papers to ward off further trespassers. After all, the death of your uncle wouldn't have been enough to stop them, not when they're caught in the throes of gold fever." His head tilted, almost sympathetically. "His death – it nearly destroyed you, didn't it?"

The memory hit me like a tidal wave. I staggered, the images threatening to overwhelm me.

They come in solid moments, images like flashcards, moving too fast for me to stop. My uncle on the stallion. I could see clearly the solid set of his shoulders, the loose, practiced way he held his seat, the careless way he rejected his helmet. "Haven't been tossed in twenty years and there aren't any students around to see."

It was like being there again. The morning sun making the new leaves sparkle like jewels. The feeling of the saddle between my legs. The bite of the early morning chill.

He's ahead, standing in the stirrups.

"Let's see what you can do, boy!"

The stallion is magnificent. He's my first purchase for the farm, a stud that I'm sure we can breed racers from. Uncle Michael had teased me: "You take this horse thing seriously, don't you?"

I'm laughing breathlessly, trailing behind. The trail is smooth, empty. We're racing, flying, free and fast. A splendid day for a ride. My roan eats the ground, as enthused as I am.

The first crack is like a rifle shot. It's the sound of the stallion's front leg snapping. He falls, my uncle keeps going. The second crack, a sickening, wet sound, is when he hits the tree. The stallion is thrashing, but my uncle is still. He's dead before I can get to him. I pull up his head and call his name, but he's loose in my hands.

The shriek of the stallion, rolling over the abandoned fortune hunter's hole, echoes in the empty morning air.

Shattering doesn't begin to describe it. Earth shaking is closer. Everything changed that day.

Sharp tears sprung to my eyes, but I bit them back as I glared at Professor Randall. For a moment, I wondered if he knew that I run every morning, keeping guard against more holes.

Ridiculous, I thought, angry at myself for a moment. *He doesn't know anything.*

But my hands were shaking.

Randall said, "The letter hasn't stopped them, has it? There aren't legitimate hunters any more, but the amateurs are worse. People who are willing to trespass don't tend to enclose their sites or post warning signs. I bet you're still finding exploratory holes scattered about the place. I bet you've threatened a few with the police, but they've caught the scent and they won't stop until something is found. The Beaumont letter hasn't solved the problem, has it?"

I swallowed hard. He was right, absolutely right. The Beaumont letter had cut back on the incursions, but not nearly enough.

"You must have been so disappointed," he said.

"All right!" I snapped, my voice shaking. "I'll admit it – we published it to stop the intruders. I thought it would help, but it didn't and they still come. Not as bad as before, but they come. People will insist on believing in Santa Claus as long as they think they can get something out of it. The letter didn't work and I'll admit it. Now will you go?"

I gestured towards the door, but Professor Randall didn't move. He studied me for a long moment, his dark, fathomless eyes roaming my face, searching for I knew not what.

I didn't care what he saw. He had managed to touch that which should be left alone, and I was through with being his emotional puppet. I was ready for whatever weapon he cared to throw at me.

I *thought* I was prepared.

"If I were you, I'd get your money back."

His voice was soft, even gentle, but the words struck me as forcibly as arrows from a crossbow. My mouth went dry, my heart slowed to almost a stop. The dreadful calm I felt as I faced him, wide-eyed and an easy target, was almost as frightening as the look of certainty in his eyes.

I stammered. "What are you talking about?"

He sighed and lowered himself back down onto the couch, draping his clasped hands over the armrest. Then he fixed me with that dark-eyed stare again.

"I'm talking about the letter you forged," he said.

7

After what seemed like an eternity, I found my voice.

"You are *insane*," I gasped. "Absolutely *insane*."

My breath was shallow. A thousand moths beat their wings against my stomach lining and I instinctively wrapped my arms around myself before realizing what I looked like. I let go and drew myself up to glare at him.

"Insane," I repeated, but he only shook his head.

"Now, now, Miss Warwick, let's stop wasting each other's time. The letter's a fake. You know it. I know it. Let's move on."

"Professor Maddox, Professor *Anthony* Maddox, authenticated it. He was the finest in his field. Are you trying to say," I demanded, gaining confidence slowly, "that he made a mistake? He was too good to be mistaken. The letter is real, Randall. Maddox said so."

Professor Randall regarded me with amusement.

"My dear Miss Warwick," he said. It was a mild and mocking reproof.

Damn him. He was so implacable!

"Professor Maddox had the respect of the community," I said. "He was known as an ethical man who wouldn't put his name behind anything that wasn't absolutely true. You may not have known him, Professor Randall, but everyone said..."

"Actually, I knew him quite well," he interrupted. He turned to his papers and searched through them as he spoke. "I said before, I worked and studied under him for two years. He was, as you say, a man of principle. If he gave his word, it meant something. Which leads me to believe that he must have thought an awful lot of you and your family to do what he did."

I flinched. "I don't know what you mean. I barely knew the man."

"Then you must have had some impressive hold over him to make him commit perjury." He plucked out a folded piece of paper and sat back in the couch.

My face was hot. "You think I *blackmailed* Professor Maddox to authenticate the letter?"

"It wasn't my first theory, but it does fit."

"Where on earth would I get anything on a man like that? And why would I? I didn't gain anything. We couldn't even sell the letter. Except for local interest, it's worth nothing."

"No, that isn't strictly true," Randall said calmly. "A friend at Harvard University told me that he contacted you, hoping to add it to his collection. He offered you the usual, generous amount, but you turned him down flat. Surprised him greatly and made him curious. Neither he nor I could figure it out."

"So, you're basing this whole crazy forgery theory on the fact that I disappointed a collector friend of yours?"

"No. As I said, I can prove the forgery to you right here and now. Want me to show you?"

"No!" I said sharply. "You're crazy and I want you to leave. What's that?"

Professor Randall had opened the folded paper while I was ordering him out, insufferable amusement plain on his face.

"This?" he asked, innocently. "It's a copy of the letter. Surely you recognize the writing."

I did and felt the blood drain from my face. He had a copy – but what could he tell from that?

We'd been so careful, so very, very careful. Finding the proper nib and the right ink had been easy compared to finding paper that was the right age and from the right location. The search went on for weeks, and in the end, I had to settle for English stationary - reasoning that in a port town like Baltimore, Beaumont might have had access to English print supplies.

The letter was perfect enough that it accomplished the seemingly impossible: convinced Maddox that it was the real deal. It was a risk that cost me many nights sleep while he studied the letter; but in the end, it paid off, and with Maddox declaring the authenticity, no one questioned it. To be sure that no one ever did, I'd convinced Aunt Susanna to store the letter in the safety deposit box – for future generations, I'd said.

I thought I'd covered it all. It was such a small event in the academic world that I convinced myself that no one would pursue it. The Chases were locally interesting, but not enough to draw national attention - except, of course, for the treasure angle. With that out of the picture, I thought I'd ended it.

It appeared, in the form of Professor Randall, that I'd failed to kill all interest.

Where this was going seemed obvious, but how much money could he really expect to get out of us, knowing the pitiful state of the farm?

I decided to keep playing the game for as long as he was willing. I pointed to the letter he held and demanded, "Where did you get that? Did Maddox give it to you?"

"Copies are available to all interested parties," Randall said. "I thought you might be reluctant to show me the real thing, so I brought this to prove my claim to you."

"To prove that Professor Maddox was a liar."

"Or that his affection for you and your family was strong enough to override his natural honesty," he said calmly. "I have to confess, I haven't been able to discover the connection yet."

"If you think this will make me give you permission to run around my property, then you've got a big disappointment coming. I'll run you out of town, Professor. Don't think I won't file a harassment suit against you and your precious Hadley University for ruining my family name. "

Again, the grin, accompanied by a glitter in his eyes. "Oh, that won't be necessary. I'm sure that you and I can work things out so that no one's reputation is damaged."

There it was. The first demand. I felt deflated.

I folded my arms. "So it's blackmail," I stated, and noted that he flinched at the word. "I don't deal with blackmailers, but even if I did, if you've been as thorough as you claim, you'd know that we don't make enough to keep a mouse, let alone a greedy, self-serving..."

He cut in with a dismissive wave. "We'll get into the particulars later. First things first – while your aunt is out, suppose I show you what is wrong with your letter?"

Without waiting for my response, Professor Randall placed the letter on the coffee table, then reached into his suitcase to pull out a magnifying glass and a file folder. Reluctantly, I left the wall and went to look over his shoulder. I kept telling myself there was nothing he could prove from a mere copy – that his entire case had to be based on a hunch and that it would, if made public, turn into a case of my word against his. If that happened, I'd be in the better position of having the deceased, respected Professor Maddox on my side. Joe Tremonti would back me, too - but I preferred to leave him out of it, until absolutely necessary.

Logic notwithstanding, I was nervous as I peered over Randall's shoulder.

Randall smoothed the letter out and my eyes ran over the artistic strokes. It was a good letter, artfully done, with just the right blend of training in the pen-strokes and gruffness in the tone to be convincing as a letter from a carelessly educated man. It fooled Maddox. It should have fooled Randall, too.

"Show me," I demanded.

"Just a minute."

He pulled out a slim, paperback book, garishly yellow and red. I thought, *Typical – technology adverse.*

Randall placed the book face down and rubbed his hands together, satisfied that everything was in place.

"Now," he said, "I did say that I was working on a biography, but I didn't say who it was about. To save you the trouble of asking, it's about Ernst Raine, a Baltimore prison guard during the Civil War, and an interesting subject."

"I've never heard of him."

"Very few have. He played no significant part in the war and I'm the first historian to take any real interest in him. Raine's contribution was made in a lengthy, detailed diary he kept, in which he described his daily life and wrote brief sketches of his inmates. Raine was an amateur psychologist, although he wouldn't have known of the science at the time. He had a great deal of sympathy for those in his care, especially those who were injured, sickly, or crippled. Life in the 1860s was a rough sport, Miss Warwick, and it left scars. Do you see where I'm going with this?"

"No, and I wish you'd get to the point."

"I'm practically on top of it. You knew, of course, that Beaumont was arrested and tried for causing unrest in Baltimore shortly after Alexander Chase's death?"

"Of course," I said.

He grinned again, and flipped over the book so that I could see the title: *Handwriting Analysis – the science and psychology.*

He said, "And I'm sure you knew that he was right handed."

I felt such a rush of relief that I had to fight against showing it.

"I hate to disappoint you, professor, but I think if you analyze this letter, you'll find - as Maddox did - that the letter was written by a right-handed man," I said. "Maddox was, as I'm sure you'll remember, a thorough man."

And so were we, but I didn't say it.

Randall's smirk threatened to undermine my confidence.

"Oh, I remember," he said, and pulled a piece of paper out of the book. "You're right – this is the letter of a right-handed man. But that's the problem. At the time this letter was written, according to both Ernst Raine and the surviving Baltimore Prison Records, Jeremiah Beaumont was in the hospital, recovering from a severe beating he received in a prison riot. Among the injuries sustained were head injuries, the usual bruising, cuts to the legs, the torso – and breaking four out of the five fingers on his right hand. It took him two months to recover."

"Where?" I demanded and without a word, he handed the paper to me. There, copied from the original records, was the notation from the prison records. And lest I claim this was a forgery, the copy bore the stamp of the school library it came from. A precaution that was particularly sagacious on Professor Randall's part – it left me without recourse.

Not that I didn't try. Desperately I scrounged about for an explanation, any explanation. "Then, then someone else must have written it for him," I stammered. "Someone else – someone who – who..."

"Someone who took such care to imitate his handwriting? I had an analysis done on this letter, comparing this letter to the logs that Beaumont kept for McInnis back in Charleston. Even though this was a copy, the expert I hired told me that it was a near-perfect imitation. 'A very impressive piece of work,' was the phrase she used, actually."

I didn't say anything. I was thinking, *Stupid, stupid! Why didn't I check for hospital records?*

But there had been no indication that Beaumont had done anything other than complain about prison food and catch the lingering disease that killed him six months after his release. Why would I have looked further?

I felt my world crumbling about me. I could fight Randall, claim innocence, throw him out and deny access to the letter or make sure that it was lost or destroyed, leaving nothing for the authorities when they came looking to verify his claim. What would Aunt Susanna think? What would this do to her?

I can't let this touch her. I can't let this happen, I thought over and over again; but try as I might, I could think of no way to avoid this. Randall had me over a barrel, me and all those I held dear.

After a moment, Professor Randall said, "If you still have doubts, let me reassure you that I do have documentation to back my claims. The Baltimore Historical Society will verify the hospital records. I told them they could expect a call from you."

I glared at him.

He went on, folding the letter as he spoke. "Initially, I thought that you'd been had, Miss Warwick. I thought, as anyone would, that you lacked the motive, the means, and the cunning to carry out such a deception. But when I learned that it was your aunt who'd found the letter in your attic, I realized that there was no way a third party could have put it there. You had to be in on the fraud. I wondered if you were trying to keep others away. I thought, *She's found the treasure and now she's looking to dispose of it through underground channels,* but that didn't wash. None of it was turning up, and it's obvious you don't have an independent source of income. You're running yourself into the ground trying to keep this place open. That gave you opportunity without means or motive. I wrestled with this for a while. Then it came to me. The reason why you did what you did, and why you kept it from your aunt."

"How do you know I kept it from my aunt?" My voice was hoarse, foreign.

"I talked with her. She knows nothing."

I flared. "What did you tell her?"

"Nothing. She still thinks the letter is all right. You wouldn't tell her, and I didn't see any reason why she should know. After all, the deceit was to protect her, wasn't it? Both she and the family business were - are - being besieged by opportunists. You didn't believe in the treasure yourself, so you fabricated the letter to convince others that it didn't exist. You falsified history in order to protect your family's privacy. Isn't that right, Miss Warwick?"

He was studying me, those fathomless eyes wide with inquiry and something else that I couldn't decipher.

I opened my mouth, but what could I say? That he'd hit the target almost dead center? Admitting that would lead to other confessions, open lines of inquiry that I couldn't allow. Other people would be damaged – and, anyway, I wasn't about to expose myself, my farm, or my aunt to his control. Not if I could help it.

"What do you intend to do with this – theory of yours?" I asked. It was the only thing I could think to say that wasn't an outright confession.

Professor Randall looked at his letter. "As a historian, I ought to expose this fraud. We have an obligation to the truth, you know."

My heart skipped a beat, but he continued. "But I don't see the need to do that just yet. After all, this deception could work to my benefit for a short time."

"To *your* benefit?" I laughed bitterly, thinking, again, of our nearly-empty bank account.

Again, he looked wounded. "No one needs to be ruined by this, Miss Warwick. I told you that before. What I have in mind is more of a collaboration."

As I stared, he explained, "As I said, I'm doing research on local activities during the Civil War. Finding the Chase treasure would be a fitting end to my inquiries. My classes get out at the end of June. What I propose is that I spend the summer here, maybe with a graduate student or two to help me with a book I'm on collaborating on, while looking for the treasure. If we find nothing, no harm, no foul. If we do find it, I get first rights to publication and Hadley University gets first option on purchasing."

I was regaining the power of speech. I couldn't believe that he expected me to fall for this. He'd gladly cover my deception for what? A chance to live on the farm and look for the treasure with no more hope of its discovery than anyone else?

"You must take me for a fool," I said carefully, and he jumped right in to contradict.

"No. Despite evidence to the contrary, I think you are probably an intelligent young woman who knows when she sees a bargain."

"By which you mean, free room and board for a summer is a cheap price compared to what you could ask for."

Randall sighed. "Miss Warwick..."

This time, though, I didn't allow him to finish. Instead, I went to the door and stood by it.

"Goodnight, Professor," I said.

He looked at me curiously.

"I don't like blackmail," I added. "No matter what the bargain. You will get out of my house and you will not return. And you will do it now."

He hesitated. Then he nodded, collected his things, and shut his briefcase. He held up the copy of Uncle Michael's book.

"Might I borrow this?" he asked. "I'll be in town for a few more days. I'll return it before I leave."

"Don't bother," I said. "Just keep it."

"Thank you. That's very kind of you."

He slipped it into his wide jacket pocket, looked around the room, and then came to the doorway.

I looked up at him. He had put his glasses back on and the lens seemed to shield my eyes from his penetrating gaze. He was close enough that I, again, caught the scent of his cologne, and I glared at him. He smiled indulgently down at me, completely unaffected.

He had been right on too many marks. The letter, its affects, our struggle on the farm. This deception of mine had been my most bold, desperate risk, and its results only just managed to justify it. I had to remind myself, as I stood in the doorway, trying to hold on to my courage, that for all the troubles we were experiencing, the letter *had* made a difference. We weren't as bothered, and I hadn't seen a hole for a week and a half.

He's wrong, I thought. *It has worked. It just took longer for the full effect to take place. It was worth the risk. It was worth the deceit.*

If only my stomach, the physical symptom of conscience, wouldn't churn so much. If only I didn't feel so exposed, so raw, so *helpless.*

He will not ruin me.

As if he could read my mind, his smile broadened.

"It was nice meeting you," Randall said, and extended his hand. "No doubt we'll meet again soon."

I ignored the hand, and pinned him with a resentful gaze. "You think you're so clever, don't you?"

"I do," he said, and reached into his pocket. "And so do you. When you change your mind about my offer, let me know. I'll be in town for a few days, conducting... Research."

He handed me his business card. Had I been able, I would have made him eat it. Professor Gregory Randall might know what he was talking about with the letter, but he'd never had to contend with the likes of Madeleine Warwick before. I could give as good as I got. I wasn't sure what, if anything, I could do, but I wasn't about to allow him to trample over everything I was working for.

I drew a deep breath. "Professor Randall, you'd better..."

But I never had a chance to finish.

"Maddie!"

The sound was more like a shriek and both the professor and I jumped. A door slammed and someone hurtled down the hall, gasping for breath, boots slamming against the hardwood floor. Ellen Gurney, one of my senior students, threw herself into the room, her tiny figure animated with panic. Her white face and wide eyes took in the professor and myself, standing in the doorway. She stopped, gesturing madly, her mouth working without making any sound.

"Ellen, what is it?" I demanded. Students weren't supposed to come into the house with their boots on, let alone without an invitation.

And what was Ellen doing here so late? No one was supposed to be here but myself and…

"It's Lindsay," Ellen rasped out. She looked ready to cry. "Oh God, you'd better come. There's been an accident – she's on the back trail. It's bad, Maddie. Really bad."

8

Despite all my training, it took forever to run to the scene of the accident. In the panic of the moment, none of us thought to take Ellen's horse, which remained saddled and tied near the house. We ran three abreast into the silent night. Randall stayed beside me, although he could have outpaced me handily, had he known which way to go.

Ellen ran next to me, wheezing. She was in her fifties, strong and hearty, but not a runner, and the exertion really told on her.

"Missy," she gasped out, referring to Lindsay's favorite mount. "She's… hurt… too."

We turned a corner and Randall shot out in front of us. Missy was on the side of the road, whinnying and wild-eyed and pawing at the ground. Lindsay was a pile on the path, her left arm flung out and bent at a sickening angle. A few feet away from her, a freshly dug, carelessly refilled hole sat tucked in the darkened bend of the pathway. Missy's stumbling marks were clearly evident in the soft dirt.

My knees weakened and I nearly fell. Missy whinnied and I called out, "Ellen, Missy."

She went immediately to take Missy's dangling reins and tried to soothe the mare in a voice that trembled almost as much as my hands when I reached out to touch Lindsay's prone form. Her face was white, luminescent in the darkness, and blood marred her paleness.

It was like being in a nightmare. For a moment, my vision blurred, and I saw Uncle Michael in her stead.

I don't know how long I would have stared, motionless, had I not noticed the slight movement of her twisted torso. Reality tore through my cloud of memories. Unlike Uncle Michael, Lindsay was breathing.

I tore off my jacket and threw it over her, the sudden movement drawing Randall's attention. He had one hand on her pulse, the other patting his pockets.

He looked at me sharply. "You have a phone?"

I already had it in my hand and was dialing with shaky fingers. Ellen came to hover over us, her face white.

"Is she…?" she asked and I nodded.

"She's still here." I looked up at her and saw Missy tossing her head and dancing in the middle of the trail, clearly terrified and unsteady. Even in the dim light I could tell that she was favoring her front left leg. Another small miracle – Uncle Michael's mount had suffered a clean break that very nearly sealed his fate.

"Get Missy back to the paddock and call the vet," I ordered. "Walk her slow and watch that leg."

My voice was gruff, abrupt, but Ellen was too grateful to have something to do to notice. She disappeared while I talked to the operator and relayed their instructions to Randall, who did them without question. When the paramedics appeared, backing the ambulance down the narrow trail, I called Lindsay's parents and left a message, promising to meet them at the hospital.

Lindsay was stirring as they examined her, but the paramedics wouldn't let me hover and told me to stand several feet away. I answered their questions as best I could, indicating the hole that I thought was the culprit. Randall was crouched over it, examining the gouge with the aid of his cell-phone light.

The paramedic was appalled. "That's a hazard," he said, and he looked at me in horror. "This should have been *clearly* marked off."

"I know," was all I could say.

I must have looked properly penitent, because his "I'll have to report this," was almost apologetic.

I nodded and when he was finished with me, I wandered off to stand by Randall. I thought I ought to thank him for coming, for helping, but the gratitude was lost in a tangle of guilt, anger, and fear. I stood there, numbly watching his light play over the freshly disturbed dirt.

When he looked up at me, I thought, *He's going to say it. He's going to remind me that this is my fault. And it is.*

But when he spoke, Randall said, "There's something wrong about all of this, Warwick. There's something very wrong about this."

The paramedics called me away – they were leaving. Did I want to ride along? I did, and sat in the back of the cab, watching as a paramedic - a competent looking woman with a professional's detachment - examined my assistant. I thought she was too calm, too dispassionate, and I remember thinking how fragile and *young* Lindsay looked, swathed in temporary bandages, her tee-shirt torn to reveal extensive bruising.

When we arrived at the hospital, doctors whisked Lindsay down the hall and I was left to address her parents in the waiting room. They arrived twenty minutes after I did, frantic and full of accusations.

I'm ashamed to say that I wasn't entirely up front at first. I explained that Lindsay's horse had tripped on the path and thrown Lindsay, and I thought that her arm was broken. I didn't mention the hole – there are plenty of reasons why a horse would stumble.

But Lindsay's father wasn't a horseman, and he had the layman's idea that a horse was like a machine and should work at a certain speed with a certain amount of reliability. Accidents were caused by mechanical failures, something that was both measurable and remedial.

When he asked, "What caused the trip?" I had no choice but to confess.

"Someone has been digging on the trail," I said. "They left an unmarked soft spot. The horse stumbled on that."

They stared at me.

"One of *your* people?" he asked.

I shook my head. "No. I don't know who did it."

He looked at his wife, whose welling eyes were spilling over.

"How could this happen again?" she asked, as though pleading with me. "I thought that was all over, I thought that ended with Michael."

The lump in my throat made it difficult to answer the question. "I thought so too."

"And what is Chase Farms going to do about this?" Lindsay's father demanded.

Lindsay's doctor entered in time to save me from answering the question. Lindsay was unconscious, and had suffered a concussion and a broken arm. They reset the arm bone and expected her to recover full use of it. The medical staff wanted her to stay overnight for observation, and afterwards, she would be on bed rest for at least a week.

"What about her competitions?"

I'm pleased to say I wasn't the one who asked the question. Lindsay's father was her biggest fan and had helped Lindsay to keep in the riding circuit, even when the family's financial situation looked shaky. Lindsay had been hoping to qualify for a riding scholarship at the regionals, which were only a few months away.

"She won't be riding for a while," the doctor said. "I know you're supposed to get right back up on the horse, but her head injury puts her at serious risk. If she were my daughter, I wouldn't put her on a horse until at least the fall." He winced and amended, "The autumn."

Lindsay's father sank back into the plastic-padded waiting room chair while his wife, who had said little in the exchange, turned to me with enormous eyes.

"How could this happen?" she asked in a haunted whisper. "How could this happen again?"

She might as well have been reading my mind.

9

Aunt Susanna asked the same question when I came home a few hours later. She had a sandwich and a cup of hot cocoa waiting when I walked in. I was too upset to eat, too nervous to do anything more than toy with my drink as we talked. My hands shook as I explained about the accident, so much that I had to let go of the mug until the story was over. My feeling of guilt was nearly overwhelming, but there was nothing accusatory in Aunt Susanna's tone when she spoke.

"How could this happen again? What would they be looking for?" she asked. "There isn't anything out there."

"I know, I know," I said, rubbing my forehead. I couldn't get the picture of the crumbled Lindsay and her broken arm only yards from the abandoned treasure dig out of my mind. And playing round and a round, like a broken record for a soundtrack, was Professor Randall's soft voice demanding, *Tell me, has that letter stopped* ***anyone*** *from trespassing on your land?*

Self-recriminations joined in the chorus. I should have known, I should have checked. Didn't I run that part of the paths this morning? Or was it yesterday? How did I miss it?

Aunt Susanna's voice broke through the clamor in my head. "….And I thought this was done when we found that letter. I thought it proved that there was no treasure, that Michael had been wrong..."

I looked at her sharply, but she was staring into her half-empty mug, her knuckles white on her elegantly lacquered hands. I noticed the deeply imprinted lines on her face. She suddenly looked old and hard. Something about her expression alerted me.

"It did," I said, pushing myself out of my slouch and into a sitting position. "It proved it beyond a shadow of a doubt."

"No, it didn't. We've got to close off the riding trails."

I gasped in surprise. "We can't do that, Aunt Susanna. We need them to exercise the horses – half of our boarders are here because of the trails."

"Do you really think they're going to use them after tonight?" she asked. "Once word of this gets around, they won't go near the trails, and I don't blame them. No matter what we do, word is going to get out. People are going to notice when Lindsay isn't there."

She was right. Lindsay was an integral part of the day-to-day operations. The damage from this accident was going to be considerable.

"It's going to be bad for business," I said.

Aunt Susanna snapped, "What are you, made of stone? Lindsay was nearly *killed* today. This isn't about business. It's about people."

"Don't you think I know that? *I'm* the one who had to bring her to the hospital and explain it to her parents. She's my friend too, you know."

"I know." She was silent for a moment, then she went on. "I won't have anyone else hurt, Maddie. We're lucky, and only lucky, that Lindsay is all right."

"I know. Lord, don't I know it."

"We're closing off the riding trails," she said firmly, but her voice was softer. "I don't blame you for what happened, of course, but until we can be sure these awful people stay off our property, I won't take the risk. If that means we lose the farm, so be it. I don't care anymore."

Her voice caught, exposing the lie. She did care. If we lost the farm, it would not only be the end of a business, but of a historic tradition. Chases had been on the property since the founding of the colony, and now we were the only ones left who cared enough to run it. If we lost the property, the banks would subdivide it and build. Uncle Michael's heart would have broken at the idea.

I can't let this happen, I thought. *But what can I do about it?*

We sat in silence for a moment. I wondered how I could convince Aunt Susanna that the trails were safe enough to keep open when I couldn't even convince myself.

Then she lowered the boom.

"What are you going to do about Professor Randall?"

After a long, weary day of unexpected surprises, you'd think I'd have grown immune to shock, but I hadn't. When I finally recovered my voice, I managed to squeak, *"What?"*

She was calm and steady. "What are you going to do about his proposal? He told me he talked to you tonight."

I remembered: she'd let him into the house. Of course, she must have had some conversation with him. I relaxed and was able to answer evenly. "Oh, right, yes, that crank. He wanted to look for the treasure. I told him to take a hike."

"You did?" Aunt Susanna cocked her head. "But - didn't he tell you about the letter?"

My heart sunk. "The letter?"

She regarded me soberly. "It's a fake, Maddie."

"A fake?" I squeaked. "When did he tell you that?"

He told her, he told her I forged it, he told her and she'll...

She was saying, "Darlene and I pulled up just as you left in the ambulance. I was frightened, as you can imagine. Randall was there, watching you go. He told us what had happened and then Darlene asked him what he was doing here. She recognized him right off, actually."

"Recognized him?"

I was horrified. So *Darlene* knew, too? Did Randall tell *everyone* what I had done?

"From his books – Darlene's read them and she recognized his picture. Well, he told me that he had watched the Dulles show and was interested in the McInnis robbery. Did you know that he's an expert in treasure hunting? He found those papers in New York and it made him the go-to guy for finding lost historical items. Even Mark Dulles consults with him."

"I'm not surprised Randall told you that," I said bitterly. "He struck me as a braggart."

Aunt Susanna's eyes flashed, but she continued. "Anyway, he showed us his copy of the letter and told us his theory." She leaned forward and I instinctively retreated. "We've been lied to, Maddie. Someone clever enough to fool Professor Maddox forged that letter from Beaumont and planted it where we'd be sure to find it. They wanted us to stop looking for that treasure, to stop looking for the truth about Alexander Chase. They wanted me to think that Michael was mistaken, but he *wasn't,* Maddie! Michael was right – all along, he was right! There's more to Alexander's story and Michael was right!"

Her eyes began to fill with tears and I stared at her, my mind whirling.

Someone clever enough to fool Professor Maddox...

Then Randall hadn't told Aunt Susanna about my involvement in the letter's creation. Surely she would guess soon enough... But why hadn't he clued her in? He knew I was behind the whole thing and he knew I would block his attempts to search for the treasure. So why hadn't he used his suspicions to try to drive a wedge between Aunt Susanna and me and convince her to go along with it?

"You don't know..." Aunt Susanna was wiping her eyes on a napkin, sniffing, and I braced myself. "You don't know what it meant to me to hear that, Maddie. All this time, thinking that your uncle died for nothing – that he'd been mistaken. I don't mean about the treasure, I mean about the theft. He was so convinced, that Alexander wasn't a thief. When the letter came out and we thought – well, it just killed me thinking that he'd been wrong all this time. That he'd been made a fool, and everyone knew it." She looked at me then, her eyes gleaming. "Now we have a chance to prove your uncle *knew* what he was talking about. That he wasn't just some old fool bent on keeping the family name. He was right, Maddie. He was *right.*"

I stared at her, aghast. With a rush, the blinders fell off and I could see the full extent of what I'd done. By fabricating the story, I'd ruined the one reputation that mattered. I had been trying to protect my uncle's legacy, but I had thought it was the land. I was wrong. My uncle's legacy was his family name – the same name I'd thrown away in a futile attempt at security. Thanks to me, Alexander Chase looked like a thief and a wastrel and I'd made a fool out of the man I respected above all else. I'd not only failed: I'd ruined that which I'd been trying to save. And what was worse, I also saw that it wasn't just my uncle's death which had my aunt prostrate with grief for so long – it was the death of a dream as well.

Aunt Susanna was wiping her eyes and I watched her, dully. *I have to tell her,* I thought. *I have to tell her who wrote the letter.*

But I was a coward and the words wouldn't come.

Aunt Susanna pulled herself together, sniffing and smiling at me as she straightened up. I cringed, expecting accusations that didn't come. Aunt Susanna wasn't angry. Behind her tears was a glow – a glow I almost didn't recognize.

It was hope and purpose.

"Randall is convinced," she continued, "that there is a lot to the McInnis story that we don't know and he's volunteered to look into it for us. He said that he already spoke to you about the book...?"

It was a question. I answered it dully. "Yes, he mentioned it."

She nodded briskly. "He's taken the summer off to write it, so we were thinking that that he could spend it here, with us, in the spare room. He could write his book and investigate the treasure at the same time. He wants to be on location because he thinks there's a lot of unexplored material, both at the farm and in the library. It'll be easier on site and living here, on Alexander's property, he'll get a better idea of the character of the people involved."

I bit back a bitter laugh. "Who came up with that idea?"

"Why... I think I did, why?"

Sure she did. After Randall put it in her head. Again, his voice rang loud and clear in my head: *I ought to expose this fraud. We have an obligation to the truth you know.*

Fine words coming from a blackmailer. I couldn't stomach the idea of letting him stay in my house over the summer, yet what would he do if I didn't?

I shook my head and pushed my chair away from the table. "Just curious, is all. He hinted at something like that when he was here." I grabbed my mug and brought it to the sink.

Aunt Susanna's eyes followed me where her weak body could not. "Randall even offered to lend a hand with the chores, to help offset the expense."

"Has he ever worked a horse farm before?"

"He said something about his spring breaks as a college student. Even if he doesn't have much experience, I still think it's a good idea – with Lindsay unable to work, you'll be needing even more help than before and it'll be for free."

I grunted, and ran the water over my mug, avoiding looking at her. Professor Randall, mucking out stalls and exercising horses? I couldn't imagine him wanting to get his hands dirty. "I suppose that was your idea, too?"

"No, it was Darlene's. But he jumped right on it. He said he'd welcome the exercise."

"Huh! Really."

"Maddie, don't you think it's a good idea?"

Aunt Susanna sounded worried. Well, so was I. I still didn't believe there was anything more than grass and seeds in those fields and I could live with that. My reputation and livelihood did not depend on finding something more, but Randall's did. When he came up empty-handed, what would prevent him from exposing my fraud anyway? Aunt Susanna might have been hurt by the idea that Michael had been mistaken, but what would learning of her niece's deceit do to her?

She repeated, "Maddie? Don't you think it's a good idea?"

"No, I think it's a terrible idea."

"You do? Why?"

"Because he's not going to find anything," I said, yanking open the dishwasher. "There's nothing out there to find, Aunt Susanna, we've been over this a million times! There's no bloody treasure!" I threw the cup in and slammed the door shut.

Aunt Susanna was frowning.

"I know," she said. "We discussed that. It doesn't matter whether there's treasure or not. The truth is all that's important."

"Is *that* what he told you, this – this *fortune hunter*?" I almost said "blackmailer".

"Yes, it is. The professor thinks there's a strong possibility that there may be something buried out in the fields. Both Darlene and I warned him that it wasn't likely, but he just said that wasn't what was important. Finding the truth was." When I laughed, she added, "Randall said that you agreed with him."

That rat!

"All right," I said, trying a different tactic. "That's all well and good, but what do we do when the press gets a hold of this? The only good that Beaumont letter has done is convince treasure hunters that there's nothing here. What will happen when they find out that we've practically hired a professional to look for us? We were inundated before – imagine the chaos then!"

To my surprise, Aunt Susanna seemed unaffected.

"We talked about that, too, and we decided that the best thing to do was to keep it a secret. Most people won't recognize him as a historian – Darlene will spread the idea that he's a novelist, working his summer here as background for his next book." She grinned. "Its subterfuge, but not that far from the truth, when you think of it."

"It's a bad idea," I said, shaking my head. "A bad, bad idea. We can't do this, Aunt Susanna. We don't even know the man. How can you trust him? How do we know he's what he says he is?"

"Darlene knew him," she countered.

I snapped, "From a photo in a back of a book. That's hardly a thorough background check."

Aunt Susanna looked at her hands, then at me, and her gaze was steady. "I want him to investigate, Maddie. I want him to find the answers and put this thing to rest. He thinks he can."

"He, also, thinks he's God's gift to American history," I growled. "He is a jerk, a blowhard, and a fortune hunter."

"He's *not* a fortune hunter," she said. "He's a scientist and a historian, and he's very interested in finding the truth, whether or not there's a treasure, just like Michael. Your uncle never wanted the money, you know. He only ever wanted the truth, and that's what I want. I thought that's what you wanted, too."

The disappointment in her voice was clear. I turned away and leaned on the counter. I heard her rise up behind me and take her walker.

When she spoke, her voice was clear and firm. "It's been a long, terrible night and you're tired and upset. We can talk more about this tomorrow. But Madeleine, I want this matter settled. I think this man has the wherewithal to figure things out, but if you are so dead-set against his involvement, then I insist that we shut the trails down. I won't have anyone else hurt because of this treasure. I *won't* have it, Maddie. You can decide. Goodnight."

With that, she left the room, her walker clumping awkwardly.

I stood for a long time alone in that kitchen, until Trusty started whining. I let her out the front door to do her business and stood on the porch as I waited.

The silence of the night rose. Spring was aging, summer was coming, and the symphony of night sounds sang their anticipation. I leaned on the post, sullenly refusing to allow them to lift my spirits, facing my second round of blackmail that night.

Professor Randall had been worse than annoying, but I couldn't afford to shut down the trails for even one day. My business couldn't handle it, any more than my conscience could deal with the idea of another accident.

I thought of Lindsay, how she'd teased me earlier in the day about the Fontaines and how she'd looked when we found her, a crumpled, shapeless form on the darkened trail. I thought of Missy's limp and wondered what the veterinarian had found. I saw Ellen's frantic face as she watched us checking Lindsay over, and I recalled Randall's puzzled expression as he looked up from the exploratory hole.

Something is really wrong here, Warwick... he'd said.

Well, he was right about that at least.

Aunt Susanna was right, too. We couldn't continue as we had. Something had to give. And if I didn't, we were likely to break. If I didn't, Randall would have no reason not to tell the whole world the truth. I was surprised he hadn't already told Aunt Susanna. Was he hoping to use it later?

It didn't matter. I really had no choice.

"All right," I said aloud. "I give up. Let him come. Let him look. It'll be August before he realizes that there's nothing to find and by then, I'll know what to do about it."

Resignation felt slightly better than floundering.

No one heard me but Trusty, who came running back, her ears streaming behind her. When I opened the door to let her back in, I caught the faintest whiff of cologne as I stepped into the foyer. Fragrant as it was, it set my hair on end.

ALEXANDER CHASE'S LAST KNOWN LETTER TO MARY CHASE

Discovered by Michael Chase tucked inside an old hymnal in the attic.

Written on a long half-sheet of paper, and reproduced here exactly with original spelling and emphasis.

June 1, 1862

Dearest Mother,
Your letter of the 12th arrived yesterday
And I was glad to receive it.
Any word from home is always welcome. I
Pray that you and Avery are well. I al-
So wish to thank you for your kind words of
Blessing – they are dew-drops to my soul. Marched
Long today and I am exhausted by hours
Of training and miserable Poe-like terrain. We shall meet
Johnny Rebel any day and I am itching for the introduction.
To glory we go, hungry and tired, but with
New vigor and eagerness. It may seem strange but I have no
Fear, just regret that I leave so little behind for my dearest
Mother – just the earthy good contained in my home soil.
Do pray for me, as I always do for you, knowing our God is
Just and loving and all is in His hands.
Yours, always,
Alexander.

PS: When I fear, I think on the August words in my beloved psalmery, especially no. 29. Read on this and think of me. – AC

10

June

Professor Randall moved into the spare bedroom in the back of the house in late June.

Despite my telling him to park around back, he rang the front doorbell. I was in the office and came out to find Aunt Susanna chatting animatedly with him while he wrestled two large suitcases through the door. My aunt was leaning heavily on her cane – she'd ditched the walker in a fit of pique a week before – and she watched him eagerly, as Maid Marion might have when Robin Hood came swinging in to rescue her.

Some hero, I thought sourly. I honestly did not understand her enthusiasm, but showing my displeasure would be tantamount to telling Aunt Susanna about the blackmail. So I put on my most congenial face and went over to help.

Professor Randall's car certainly looked the part of the poor academic. It was a four door sedan, several years old, and filled to capacity with his belongings. He'd brought a couple of suitcases, a laptop, a desk-top computer, and a box of books that was nearly the size of the twin bed in his room. Getting it up the stairs was some trick, and we were both winded when we finally made it.

"Are you moving in permanently?" I asked, as I helped him cram it into the far corner of his room. It wasn't a large space to begin with and the box dwarfed it.

"God forbid," he said cheerfully. "No, these are just a few references texts for my book and some manuscripts I've agreed to look over."

Aunt Susanna was in the room, having made the long, slow climb up the back stairs while we worked. She was fussing with a vase filled with the flowers that she'd insisted on putting in his room. It was a kind gesture, but it was, also, an excuse for her to hang around. I didn't want her getting attached to my blackmailer, but there was little I could say about it.

As we recovered from our labors, Randall spotted her moving an old book to better position her vase, and he pounced.

"Ah, now *that*," he said. He pulled a handkerchief out of his pocket and moved swiftly to pluck the book out her hands with the cloth. "That is a *very* valuable and irreplaceable old book. It's on loan from a friend – it's not even supposed to be out of its display. I'll have to ask both of you not to touch this in future. It requires delicate handling."

Aunt Susanna glanced at me. "Sorry, Professor."

I just rolled my eyes.

"I'll just put it over here," he continued, wrapping it in the handkerchief and placing it on a high shelf. "Now, then..."

He straightened, rubbing his back as he looked around the room. Aunt Susanna and I had decided to give him the rarely used room only after considerable discussion. She'd wanted to give him her old upstairs room, claiming that she never used it now that her knees had gone bad.

"It's just empty space now," she'd said, but I balked.

"You are moving back up there as soon as your knee heals," I insisted, and flatly refused to listen to her protests. "You're not a cripple, you know, just an impatient patient."

In the end, I got my own way and Randall got the back bedroom, which suited me for a number of reasons: One, it was one of the nicest rooms in the house - which meant he couldn't complain about his accommodations - and two, it was already wired for internet, which meant he wouldn't need the office.

The third reason was the most important: It was the furthest room from my own.

I'd decided that the best way to deal with living with the man was to avoid him as much as possible. I was even willing to let him off the hook with helping out around the farm, if it meant that he would just leave me alone. I wanted no part in his investigation, no part in his writing, and no part in his life - and his having the back bedroom suited the plan perfectly: his room was close to the back stairs, while mine practically opened on the front ones. I wouldn't even have to run into him on the stairwell.

Just get through the summer, I kept telling myself, even though I knew that the end of the season would bring another set of problems, specifically a disappointed Hadley history professor who still knew that the Beaumont letter was a forgery.

But that was weeks away. Surely I'd come up with some solution by then.

Now as Randall assessed the room, I realized how small it was. It had adequate space for the original bed, bureau, side table, but now, with the boxes, the computer equipment, and the small desk I'd moved in at his earlier request, the space was definitely cramped.

As he looked around in consternation, Aunt Susanna said, "I hope you'll be comfortable here. It's one of our nicest rooms."

She looked uncertain as she said it.

"Oh, is it?" he asked, and his gaze fell on me. I must have looked as I felt, for he returned to Aunt Susanna. "Well, I'm sure I'll be just fine in here."

I breathed a sigh of relief, turning to leave the room when he continued, "Now, where should I set up my research center?"

Before I could stop her, Aunt Susanna volunteered the office downstairs. *My* office. Where I did my paperwork at the end of the day.

"There's enough room in there for both of you, and all of Michael's research is still in there," she said. "There are two desks, so you can take one and just make yourself at home on the bookshelves. Maddie's only there in the evening, so you'll have the place to yourself most of the time. You won't mind sharing a space, would you, Professor?"

"Oh, not at all," he said. "As long as Maddie won't feel inconvenienced?"

They both turned to me, and although I burned with a desire to throw him out right there, I managed to mumble, "Fine, that's fine."

Then I ran downstairs to lock the filing cabinets and desk before he could start moving in. There was nothing of value or with particular privacy demands in either, but denying Randall something made me feel better. I spent the rest of the day outside, working with the animals and children, and avoided going into my own house as much as possible.

11

I worked until late that night, and not entirely because I was avoiding the people I lived with. With Lindsay out of work until at least August and being unsuccessful at finding a replacement, my lessons were scheduled further into the night, sometimes ending as late as ten o'clock. Late-night lessons meant bedding the horses down even later. It wasn't a healthy situation, but I kept hoping it was a temporary one.

Hiring extra labor help had become a tricky situation. Whenever I mentioned the possibility to Aunt Susanna, she always reacted with surprise.

"Why do that?" she would ask. "We've already got Randall coming to work as part of his room and board. Why spend money we haven't got on help that's going to be redundant?"

"He's an intellectual," I would protest. "How much help do you think he's really going to be?"

But she stubbornly insisted that we wait for Randall to show what he could do before we hired. I think she was unwilling to let go of the idea that she had brought about this "relief" solely through her own efforts, and her triumph undermined by my doubts. I briefly considered hiring a local boy anyway, but didn't for a number of reasons, not the least of which was that I hated to go against Aunt Susanna's wishes.

To make do, I employed the volunteer efforts of the young riders in the stables, organizing them to tend to their own horses' bedding and exercise, and to help out with others from time to time. But, like many volunteer situations, this was good only so far as it went. They were eager, but unreliable, calling in sick, getting summer jobs, going away on vacations, or just plain forgetting to come in. At the end of the day, the bulk of the work was still on my shoulders.

That night, I waited to go back into the house until I was quite sure that Aunt Susanna and Randall had already eaten and left the kitchen. It was late when I crept in. I popped a plate into the microwave, put the stack of mail by my cup, and went to wash up. Yet despite my precautions, they were both in the kitchen when I returned.

Aunt Susanna was by the stove, preparing mugs of coffee. Gregory Randall sat at the counter, setting up his tablet, notebook, and stack of files. The pile of mail I'd put by my glass had been pushed aside to make room for his propped-up cell phone, which was almost the size of the sleek, silver tablet he was working on.

He looked up when I came in and indicated the stool I'd set up earlier for my dinner.

"Ah, Warwick," he said. "Excellent, we can get started."

Warily, I went to the stool, but didn't sit. He fussed with the keyboard while Aunt Susanna pulled my plate out of the microwave and set it down in front of me.

"Eat it while it's hot," she said.

The scent of roasted chicken and vegetables reminded my stomach of how long it had been since lunch, yet I still hesitated to sit.

Aunt Susanna hobbled back towards the stove to tend to the coffee. I considered taking my plate and eating my meal in my room. But Aunt Susanna had three mugs ready by the stove for coffee and Randall was absorbed in his computer screen, one finger resting lightly against his lips as he scanned the screen.

After a moment, I gave in and sat down. I could afford to give them one night of my time.

Despite working outside in the muggy weather all day, the warm food felt soothing as I shoveled it into my mouth. I was starving, and I ate without noticing much else for a few moments. When I raised my head to take a drink, I realized that Randall was watching me, his finger still on his lips, a studious expression on his face that seemed oddly critical. I had eaten through half a plateful already, and under his scrutiny, I suddenly felt gluttonous.

"*What*?" I asked defiantly.

His eyes glittered behind the glasses, but he only shrugged slightly. "You shouldn't wait so long between meals," he said quietly.

My glass thudded loudly on the counter as I brought it down.

Aunt Susanna's bright tone cut through the silence.

"Maddie likes a little milk, and I like cream and sugar, but what do you like in your coffee, Professor?"

She was limping back over, two steaming mugs in her hands, and I reached over to take them from her. My cup was a fragrant hazelnut, but she'd selected a mild roast for the professor and I slid it over to him without looking.

"Black is fine," he said and took a sip. When he grimaced, I wondered if he'd said it just to be accommodating. "Have a seat, Susanna, and we can get started."

"Started?" I asked. Despite the discomfort of eating under his watchful eye, I worked through the rest of my plate. It had been a long day, and I knew going hungry would only add to my stress. "What's going on?"

"We're giving evidence," Aunt Susanna said. With some difficulty, she got up onto the stool next to mine and carefully leaned her cane against the counter between us. Watching her struggle, remembering all the times she used to hop up on the counter to hang decorations over it, I felt a sudden, intense urge to take the cane and break it over my knee. It seemed to be the awful symbol of change, of crippling injury, of restriction by violence - an object that held my aunt back, and I wanted it destroyed.

As if reading my thoughts, my aunt moved the cane to her other side, nonchalant, as though there was nothing wrong.

Randall was typing again. "Just a second," he said.

We sat in silence and waited.

The intervening weeks since Lindsay's accident had been busy, but productive. Darlene Winters' endorsement of Randall's abilities had aroused my curiosity, and I'd done a little research. I could still hear the surprise in his voice when he saw that I didn't recognize him by reputation. Now I knew how considerable that reputation had been.

Gregory Randall was something of a wunderkind. His discovery of the Dunstable cache was a fortunate event that launched the career of a wet-behind-the-ears history major working towards his doctorate. He'd gotten recognition and a book out of the deal, as well as nationwide coverage and offers of positions from several well-known universities. His articles were published in magazines and blogs across the country. Fifteen years ago, he'd been considered the rising star in the academic ranks and, luck aside, he seemed to have earned the recognition. One article even referred to him as "a modern age Indiana Jones". No wonder the man had an inflated opinion of his abilities.

"Have we decided on a name yet?" Aunt Susanna broke the silence. When Randall and I looked at her, she explained, "Your pen name. While you're here, so that people don't realize."

One of my few conditions on his conducting research in my house was that the investigation be kept quiet. The last thing I wanted was to encourage whoever was leaving the holes on my property and both Randall and I reluctantly agreed to Darlene's suggestion that he pose as a novelist.

"Lots of authors do that," Aunt Susanna had explained to me about a week before, when she, Darlene, and I were having dinner.

"It's common, but I don't," Darlene replied, her mouth curving into a grin. Her dangling earrings swung as she shook her head. She should know a thing or two about writer's habits. Darlene had been the author of an immensely popular travel column, globetrotting almost constantly until she took up novels instead.

Ten years of self-imposed exile in New Hampshire had not yet tempered her exotic appearance. Her vibrant Indian-print tunic and chunky jewelry was a shock of color against the pale early American color palette of the kitchen. When she held up her mug, her sleeve slid back to show a hint of her tattoo - a souvenir that she'd picked up while in Saigon.

Darlene continued, "But it's a good idea if you want to keep the neighbors in the dark. Mention the name 'Randall' in connection with the Chase farm and you might as well hang a 'Treasure Hunters Welcome' sign up."

"I don't know," I said. "It seems a bit – well, daytime-drama to me. A false name?"

She dismissed my concern with a wave of her arm, bracelets clacking with the movement. "Gregory Randall is still touted as one of the foremost historical detectives. People will assume the treasure is as good as found, and you'll have worse than what happened before."

Aunt Susanna nodded vigorously.

"We don't want anyone encouraged by Randall being here," she said firmly. "He could just go by his middle name. I think he said it was 'Vincent'."

I looked from one to the other. They were an almost comical contrast: Aunt Susanna thin where Darlene was generous, pale where she was dark, minimalist in dress while Darlene was bold. Aunt Susanna's walker sat close at hand while Darlene's beaten sneakers reflected her athletic spirit. Aunt Susanna was the quiet version of Darlene's strident strength. Salt and pepper, they were best friends and confidants. I owed both more than I could repay - had it not been for Darlene's presence and persistence, Aunt Susanna wouldn't have made it through the past couple of years.

Still, I had to object to this plan.

"It's dumb," I protested. "Besides, won't these people know him by sight?"

"He's a writer and an academic, not a TV celebrity," Darlene said. "I don't think anyone will recognize him from his second book photo – that picture was taken when it was written, about ten years ago."

"*You* did," I said, and she gave me a dour look.

"I didn't," she replied, with a sniff that spoke volumes. "I recognized him from a speech he gave at an event I attended. He has a very distinctive speech pattern. But most people here will not have seen him personally. He's been keeping a very low profile."

That was the oddity in Randall's profile. His career seemed to have stalled as suddenly as it launched. One day his was a best-selling book, another was promised, and he was waving away invitations to Harvard, Oxford, UCLA, and Princeton. There was even talk of his heading an investigation into the legendary La Noche Triste treasure, loot that was lost after Hernan Cortes and his Conquistadores fought their way out of Tenochtitlan.

Randall denied being a fortune hunter then, too. In an interview, he said, "Of course, treasure is not the object of the investigation. We hope to find a better understanding of the tragic events surrounding the Night of Sorrows, the causes, and the political and societal impact on the Aztec people. That's what we're setting out to find."

He had refused to comment on how much the missing gold artwork, looted from Moctezuma's Palace, would be worth in the current market.

Then, without warning, Randall disappeared. The prestigious positions dried up, his book published with little fanfare, his website was dismantled, and the La Noche Triste expedition was never spoken of again. The wunderkind, who once had Yale and Princeton beating on his door, accepted a position at a tiny, obscure Midwestern college, then transferred to Hadley. There was no scandal, no big story, no whisper of hardship, no explanation at all. Randall just simply faded away.

It was a fact that I found hard to reconcile with his attitude, but it worked for our immediate purposes and that was all I cared about.

"I thought we decided on 'Gregory Vincent'," Aunt Susanna continued, breaking the sudden silence that had filled the kitchen.

Randall paused before answering, shooting me a look I couldn't decipher. "Is that really necessary?" he asked. "It seems awfully dramatic."

I couldn't resist the opportunity to say, "Aunt Susanna, no one is going to recognize Randall now. It's been a long time since he's been in the public spotlight."

He stiffened, but hardly a moment passed before he looked me in the eye and grinned, inclining his head.

Aunt Susanna was too busy arguing her point to notice the exchange. "Even so, I think we ought to be careful," she said. "It's not like we have to lie completely. He *is* writing a book, and he *is* here to research one. We just don't want treasure hunting brought into it."

"Mmm, true," Randall said, tapping his mouth with his finger again. He posed as though he was thinking, but there was a wicked glint in his eye as he said, "I understand Maddie's point of view. We want to be as completely open and honest as possible. No secrets, only the truth."

He spread his hands on the counter and leaned on it, smiling in a manner that might have been reassuring, had I not known him better. "So why don't we just omit details as you suggest? When people ask, I'm researching a book. We don't say what it's about. We can imply that it's tied to a horse farm. And I'm not a proud man – just introduce me as Gregory. I think that will do, as I don't think you have many society soirees that will require a full introduction, do you?"

Aunt Susanna nodded her agreement, I glowered, and Randall, grinning, turned back to his computer.

"It'll only be for a few weeks," he said, his eyes on his screen. "I'll just do my research and investigation and be out of here before you know it."

Despite the reassurances and my own dig at his fall from fame, I wasn't sure that he wouldn't be known. Chester had a historical society and his research was likely to bring him in contact with people who might actually know what the Dunstable papers meant.

Do historians have groupies? I wondered. If they did, I felt quite sure that Randall would be the type who wouldn't mind the adoration. I would have to ask Joe.

If anyone would know about Randall's fall from grace, Joe would - or he would know how to find out. But between his summer classes, the articles he was writing, and the soul-searching that naturally came out of a divorce, he had enough on his plate without burdening himself with my problems. I wouldn't ask him anyway, because I was afraid the story of the blackmail would come out. I didn't know what he would do then – my imagination had him punching Randall's lights out, which stoked my womanly ego; but in practical terms, physical assault would make our position even more tenuous. I decided it was best to keep him in the dark about the whole affair for now.

My plate was empty and my coffee was growing cold. I sighed audibly and Randall's head snapped up, as though he were waking from a trance. Pulling off his glasses, he leaned back, sucking on the temple tip for a moment before he spoke.

"The first thing any good detective does," he muttered absently, and I found myself exchanging glances with Aunt Susanna, "is discover what the basic facts of the case are, from the source, or as close to it as he can get. That's what I want to do tonight. I want you to tell me, in your own words… Oh!" He leaned forward and tapped his propped-up cell phone. "We'll be recording this, by the way. So much more thorough than taking notes. Now, I want you to tell me everything you know about Alexander Chase."

He stared at us expectantly.

"Oh, really," I said, getting up and gathering my things. "What's there to know that hasn't been written down already?"

"I want to hear it from you two," he insisted, as I dumped my plate in the sink and rummaged in the cabinets for dessert. "You are the last living relatives on location. You by marriage, I know, Susanna, but both of you have lived and absorbed these stories for decades. There will be things that you know that are not what the scientific world would consider facts, but will be invaluable to me. Insight, family lore, legends – stories that are unproven but stubbornly refuse to die. I need you to talk to me. Tell me anything."

"Oh..." Aunt Susanna began to rub her hands together, under the counter where he couldn't see. I saw when I sat down next to her with a box of cookies. She only ever rubbed her hands when she was nervous, but there was no reason for her to be nervous now. I thought she probably didn't want to be recorded.

I patted her hand and shook my head at Randall. "I repeat, what's there to say that hasn't already been written down? I assume you've already read Uncle Michael's book, and the article about *Lost American Treasures*? There's nothing..."

I was cut off by Aunt Susanna. "Where do we start?" she asked, leaning forward and putting her hands on the counter.

Randall grinned again, an irritating air of victory clinging about him.

"Why not try the beginning?" he suggested.

12

Once she started, it didn't seem like Aunt Susanna would stop talking. I grew stiff in my chair, one of my legs went numb, and my whole body ached for sleep, but I didn't want to leave her alone. Several times I thought to interrupt, but whenever I opened my mouth, Aunt Susanna would start down a new track and I would find myself listening, fascinated in spite of myself.

She started at the beginning, all right: she began with Alexander's birth, his ancestry, and his mother's remarriage to Obadiah Chase, an upright citizen who adopted the boy, gave him his name, yet never really liked him much. She told him about the boy's strict upbringing, about his mischievous nature and the stories people would tell of his childish escapades with his friend, Reuben Hill. She told the story about their pranking the minister, how they'd run away and took a boat down the Exeter until Obadiah caught up with them. She spoke about how much both he and Mary Chase, his mother, loved to read, riding miles out of their way to pick up newspapers or to borrow books.

She talked as though Alexander was someone she'd known personally, a boy who was like the son she'd never had but probably longed for, and she spoke with a quiet, desperate eloquence that took my breath away. Alexander Chase was not a dusty historical figure with a checkered past: he was a man who lived, breathed, and was loved. I listened, my wonder growing. I'd always assumed that it was Uncle Michael's pet project – now I saw that she had been equally involved.

Randall didn't interrupt or ask questions. He nodded, jotted down notes, and listened. If he was impressed by her knowledge, he didn't show it; if anything, he looked almost satisfied, as though he was getting exactly what he'd expected.

Then, when Aunt Susanna looked about ready to wind down and I was thinking about my comfortable bed, he blinked through his large glasses.

"Excellent," he said. "Now, tell me about his family."

So she started in again.

She knew them very well. Mary Welles Chase lost her first husband from undisclosed causes when Alexander was only a few weeks old, and married Obadiah about six months later. She was an educated woman, well regarded and lovely, but Aunt Susanna thought that Mary may have been talked into marrying Obadiah, a wealthy farmer with a leadership position in his local church. By all accounts, their marriage was perfectly respectable, but there was no indication of love on either side.

"I think she made the best of a bad deal," my aunt said pensively, while I found myself imagining bright, dark-haired Mary Chase, living alone in the middle of a rough New Hampshire farm, trying to adjust to the verbose and vigorous Obadiah and his little boy. "Both of them were widowed, both needed help. I don't think Obadiah was unkind – well, I don't think he hit her, but he never really took to Alexander, and how can a woman love a man who won't love her son?"

Aunt Susanna didn't seem to like Obadiah much, so she went on to Avery, his son. Six months older than Alexander. Avery was more interesting: a reputed loner and skinflint who had never married, he died alone in the fields, still looking for a long-forgotten treasure. Despite pressure from others in the town, he'd not only refused to join the New Hampshire regiment, but actually paid for a replacement when he was drafted. That Avery would part with coin for anything was enough to excite talk in a town already overly familiar with Chase family affairs.

"No one knew about the robbery until long after Alexander died," Aunt Susanna said, eying the cell phone as though it would judge her accuracy. "It was only after the war ended that anyone knew about it."

"When was it reported?" Randall asked.

"Um... April 1865?"

Aunt Susanna looked to me for confirmation and I shrugged. Memorizing dates had never been my strong suit.

"I mean," Randall clarified, "when did the McInnis family report the robbery to the authorities? In Charleston."

"Oh, I don't know! We'd have to go look at the court records for that."

"You've got those?"

"Copies, yes. Michael and I..." Her voice faltered for a moment, but she continued. "We went down there for a long weekend. He got the copies then, read them all on the way home. I'm sure they're in the office somewhere. Maddie will find them for you."

"So you got the court records from the lawsuit – did you get anything else?"

She considered it briefly, then shook her head. "No, I think that was it. Well, that and the death certificates for Mr. McInnis and a few others. I don't think there was anything else."

"All right. Hold on a second."

He shuffled through his things, then bent down and rummaged around in the bag at his feet.

I checked my watch and saw that it was after eleven. I had an early morning, as usual, and I was about to suggest we stop until tomorrow when Randall popped up with Uncle Michael's coffee table book in his hands. It was more battered since I'd seen it last, and sticky notes had sprouted from the top of its pages.

He dropped it on the counter and pulled it open at one of the sticky notes, commenting, "Now, I need you two to fill in some blank spaces in this, if you can. A very helpful book, but it lacks references and sources. Your husband had a passion for family history, Mrs. Chase, but he was no scientist." He paused for effect. "Now, according to this, Alexander Chase went to work for McInnis in June of 1859. Where did he get that date from?"

"Where did he get it?" she faltered and I stepped in with, "What difference does that make? That he worked for McInnis was never in question. What made him leave is. What he did with the *loot* is."

"My dear Madeleine," he said condescendingly, "when one sets out to solve a mystery, it's important to make sure that you have all the dates and movements correct. I'll admit, it's unlikely that this particular fact will mean much in the overall investigation, but its source might prove to have other, more valuable information."

"Investigation? Mystery?" I asked. "I thought this was a treasure hunt, not an Agatha Christie. Aren't you supposed to be scanning the ground with metal detectors, or analyzing soil content for South Carolinian traces?"

"Later, perhaps," Randall said. "But I have a rule – never get your hands dirty until you know exactly what you're looking for. Now, Mrs. Chase," he turned back to Aunt Susanna, who was listening to this exchange wide-eyed. "Do you know where your husband got this information? It's too specific for me to imagine that it was just a guess."

She stared at the page with the look of a student who discovered too late that they studied for the wrong test. "That particular date?" she asked. "Gosh, I don't know... Mary's diary maybe?"

Randall choked.

"Mary's *diary*?" he gasped. "Alexander's mother left a *diary*?"

"Yes, didn't you know?"

"Know? How could I know? It's not listed in any of the source material." He shuffled through his things for a manic moment, then gave us an accusing look. "Why is it not listed in any of the source material? It wasn't on that show, or on any of the websites. Maddox never even mentioned it!"

I winced at the name as I said, "It doesn't have any bearing on the treasure hunt. Her last entry is in 1860, when she fell ill. That's over a year before the theft."

"It wouldn't help find it," Aunt Susanna said, and gain us both another disgusted look.

"Oh, totally useless," he agreed, his tone dripping with sarcasm. "Except as background information. Except as a witness to the character of our proponent. Except as a window into a past we can only guess from our distance. This diary could contain the very clue that the hymns failed to provide! I can't believe that no one thought of this! I credited you all with a sort of native intelligence in your field, but perhaps..."

"Mark Dulles said the same thing," Aunt Susanna said. Her eyes were flashing: apparently, Randall wasn't getting under only my skin. "He read it cover to cover, hoping to find a clue, too. He even quoted it during the show, but I think they cut it."

She looked to me and I nodded in confirmation. "They did. They wanted another shot of the magnificent Mrs. Bryant."

"Who is she?" Randall asked.

"She was the best looking rider in the stables, present company excepted," I said. "But she left when – after the accident."

"Good riddance," my aunt grumbled.

"So Dulles read the diary," Randall said. "Did he find anything?"

"No," I said flatly. "He gave it back and said that it was 'delightful'. He was a rather irritating man, too."

He ignored me. "Is it here? Mary's diary?"

Aunt Susanna nodded. "Yes, it is. All of Michael's materials are in the safe in the office, along with his notes to the book. He wouldn't throw away anything and neither did I. You're welcome, of course, to look at everything." She stifled a yawn and looked at the clock.

Randall nodded, looking pleased. "Does that include the letter Michael found? The Secessionville letter?"

This had direct bearing on the treasure. The last known letter of Alexander Chase, the 'Clue Letter', was dated just days before the battle of Secessionville, where he was killed in 1862. It had been lost until about six years ago, when Uncle Michael discovered it tucked into an old book in the attic.

Joe Tremonti's dig had given Uncle Michael a taste for historical research, and his discovery of the letter was the first domino in the succession of events that resulted in where we were today, for it was there that we first had what seemed to be evidence that Alexander knew of the treasure. It was Uncle Michael who first read into the letter and saw a clue. Unfortunately, like most of the clues in this "case", as Randall liked to refer to it, it had led nowhere.

"That," I said stiffly, "is in the safety deposit box along with the Beaumont letter."

As soon as I said the name, I wished I hadn't. Aunt Susanna, obviously fatigued, suddenly straightened up and looked at Randall.

"Speaking of which," she said. "I've been thinking about that. Someone went through a great deal of trouble to create that letter and make us stop looking for the treasure. Who's to say that they haven't already found it and made off with it?"

"Aunt Susanna," I managed through my suddenly dry mouth. "They can't have found it. They're still looking for it."

"Someone is still digging," she corrected. "It doesn't follow that our trespasser is the forger as well. What do you think, Professor?"

My heart began pounding in my chest. Randall leaned over the counter, chin on hand, and studied my aunt through narrowed lids. He didn't look at me as he spoke slowly: "I think it unlikely that anyone has found the treasure. If the McInnis report is to be believed, there are some very distinctive pieces among the collection and none have been found on the market yet."

"Would you know?" I couldn't resist asking.

"I've put out the word that I'm interested. I'll be told if something turns up."

Randall spoke with a finality that was impressive. I thought, *No way he has contacts that thorough,* but I didn't push it. The answer seemed to satisfy Aunt Susanna - but before I could relax, she asked another question.

"But shouldn't we expose the Beaumont letter as a fraud? Someone caused us to mislead people, including poor Professor Maddox. I'd hate to think that they're going to get away with it."

Her eyes narrowed as she spoke and I fought a sudden, intense urge to run away.

Randall spoke again.

"I understand how you feel," he said. "But exposing the fraud right now will only bring unwanted attention, and hamper the investigation. Besides, it would be embarrassing to admit that you were taken in by such an obvious fake. It'd be much better to release the information once we've discovered the treasure or at least solved the mystery of the McInnis robbery. Then we'll have a triumph to take the edge off."

I stared at him in disbelief. He avoided my gaze, and Aunt Susanna - oblivious to my shock - pressed with the question: "Solved the McInnis case? What do you mean?"

Now his eyes lit up and he leaned forward. "I mean that for all this research your husband did, we're still not absolutely certain what happened in Charleston in 1861. The story goes that Alexander Chase went to work for McInnis and met Beaumont, a drifter with a gambling habit. It's not much of a surprise that he and Chase would become friends. But Alexander was an abolitionist with the wanderlust and McInnis was a rabid secessionist with a habit of financially dabbling in politics. Would McInnis, the well-to-do up-and-comer, have ever invited Chase, his Yankee employee, into his house?"

"I doubt it," I said. "Why even ask the question?"

"Because if he didn't, how would Chase and Beaumont have known where and what to steal?" Randall asked. He dove for his papers, shuffled through them, then shoved the stack in front of me.

"That," he said, as Aunt Susanna leaned in to look, "is the list of items the McInnis family claimed were stolen: family spoons, heritage jewelry, a couple of silver candlesticks, and a few valuable nick-knacks. No cash, no coin. Not only that, but these weren't even the 'good' silverware and candlesticks that McInnis family owned at the time."

He pulled out a scanned reprint of handwritten ledger pages, stapled together at the top corner, and flipped through them quickly before throwing it on top of the robbery report. He jabbed a finger at a highlighted line.

"See that?" he demanded.

We looked. In elegant scrawl, the words, *Parlor: candlesticks, French, wrought gold, small,* were highlighted in green.

"What is this?" I asked, fingering the paper.

"This is an inventory of household goods made by Mary Anna McInnis, the spinster daughter and housekeeper of Mr. McInnis in the early months of 1861," Randall explained. "A friend of mine in Charleston found it for me. Mary Anna McInnis logged everything, including the missing items, and listed their estimated value. Why she did this, I don't know, except perhaps she'd heard the war rumors and wanted to know exactly what she had to protect. Whatever the cause, if she didn't exaggerate - and there's no reason to think she did - this list proves that they had *gold* candlesticks."

He said this triumphantly. A glance from my aunt told me I wasn't the only one who was baffled.

"So they had gold candlesticks," I said. "What does that prove?"

"It doesn't prove anything, Warwick, but it does raise the question. Chase and Beaumont break into a house to steal from their hated employer, take the silver candles sticks, and leave the gold behind. Why?"

There was a moment of quiet.

Then Aunt Susanna guessed, "They were locked up?"

Randall shook his head. "According to this inventory – Ms. McInnis was very thorough - the gold candlesticks were kept in the parlor with the knick-knacks, showing off the owner's wealth and station. If the thieves were already in the room taking the bric-a-brac, why not snag the candlesticks at the same time?"

He put his hand up to stop my objection. "I know what you are going to say: maybe there was some rearranging after this list was made. Maybe Mr. McInnis decided to put the candlesticks in his safe or in his room. That could be. But look at the jewelry. There is twice as much listed on Mary Anna's inventory than there was reported missing from the robbery. What was stolen was valuable, but old – Mary Anna's grandmother's, presumably –but there was newer, more fashionable pieces, worth much more. They were listed as…."

He pulled the inventory out of my hands, turned a few pages, and showed us more highlighted lines. In the same elegant handwriting, someone had listed broaches, necklaces, bracelets, rings, and pins, with varying descriptions, sizes, and prices. Next to all of them, where the cataloger listed the location, was the word: *Mistress' Bedroom, Chinese Bureau, locked.*

I looked at Randall. He was grinning as though he'd just let me in on a secret.

"They were all in the same place," he said, his voice dropping to a husky whisper. "A locked Chinese box in Mary Anna's bedroom. The new jewelry mixed with the old, yet only the old was taken. Now, if you were two men, breaking into a house to rob it, would you take the time to pick through the jewelry? Take the locket and leave the garnet necklace? Ignore the gold candlesticks in favor the silver ones? Pocket half the knick-knacks, but leave the rest, all of which are in plain sight?"

"There's a million reasons why they would," I pointed out. "Maybe they didn't see the gold candlesticks. Maybe Mary Anna was wearing the garnet necklace that night."

It was a weak argument and we both knew it. For whatever reason, he didn't choose to push that particular point.

"There is another question," he said, taking the papers back. "I've read some of the court papers from the lawsuit. Jarrod Carroll was the attorney for the McInnis family, and he was a most thorough man. Both Mary Anna and Mr. McInnis were dead when the law suit was brought to court, so he had to bring in a lot of outside testimony from friends, workers, business contacts, etc. One of those was the warehouse overseer, Greer, who directed both Beaumont and Chase in their day-to-day work. He didn't like either man very much. According to him, Beaumont and Chase argued with McInnis violently, and Chase threatened to 'smash his head'. McInnis was going to fire him, but never got the chance. The very next day, according to Greer, Chase left without notice. Just packed his things and disappeared."

He paused, I supposed for dramatic emphasis again. I sighed and checked my watch.

"It's generally agreed that McInnis and Chase hated each other, that Chase and Beaumont stole the stuff in order to get back at him," I said. "What you just said tends to prove it, don't you think?"

"No, I don't," he said. "Let's say the stories are true, that Beaumont and Chase get fed up. They know war is coming, so they sneak into the house, steal the second-best candlesticks, and leave McInnis, gloating that they'd one-upped their employer. That would work splendidly – perhaps they were just simply ignorant and thought the old jewelry was prettier than the newer stuff. It could be. But if it was, why does the overseer report that only Chase took off that day? Why doesn't he say Chase *and* Beaumont?"

"Maybe Beaumont stuck around?" I offered weakly, and he chuckled.

"Right. Not only is he stupid enough to not take the gold, but he sticks around to be discovered."

"Are you saying that Beaumont wasn't an accomplice?" Aunt Susanna asked.

"I'm suggesting that Beaumont may have had nothing to do with the robbery. I'm suggesting that this wasn't a simple case of snatch and grab. Maybe there wasn't even a robbery. Maybe this whole incident was a setup by a family, impoverished by war, who hoped to salvage something from this experience."

You could have heard a cricket sneeze in the dead silence that followed that statement.

Professor Randall sat back looking very pleased with himself. I opened my mouth, shut it, and looked at Aunt Susanna. Her expression was rigid, her face white.

"Are you saying," she said slowly, "that there was nothing stolen to begin with? That this whole – this whole treasure story… was *made up*?"

My aunt hasn't a cold bone in her body, but you could have gotten freezer burn from her tone. In the space of that second before Randall replied, I could almost hear her thoughts: that it had all been a sham, Alexander Chase was a victim of slander, and Uncle Michael died in pursuit of a shadow. It was worse than when she thought the Beaumont letter was true. This undermined everything. Not only had we'd been made fools, but so had the entire Chase family.

Just when it seemed that my aunt was about to explode in frustration, Randall answered.

"No," he said. "No, actually, despite all of this, I don't think that at all. If I did, I would be completing this project in Charleston, not here. I think that Alexander Chase did bring something back from Charleston, something that he hid on this farm, and I believe he put a clue to its location in the final letter to his mother. I'm almost positive that it is still here. I think there is more to the McInnis scandal than previously thought. Things were accepted as fact before they were tested. Questions need to be asked." He locked his gaze with mine. "And that's why I'm here. To ask the questions no one wanted answered."

His eyes bore into mine. I tore away to meet Aunt Susanna's quizzical look. Her mouth was twisted, like it always did when something worried her. Her hands weren't trembling, but they looked so fragile, laying on top of each other on her lap that I placed my hand over them before I turned back to Randall.

The man had me in a tailspin. I didn't know why he persisted in covering for me in regards to the Beaumont letter when it was likely that Aunt Susanna would be more easily brought to heel if she was trying to protect me. It would only be a matter of time before she figured out what had happened on her own anyway. But his motivations didn't matter tonight. I still didn't think there was a treasure, but it seemed to me that he might be able to answer some of those questions, ones that I'd never thought to ask.

"So how is this going to work?" I asked. "This summer, I mean. You've contracted to stay here for a few weeks, but it seems to me that most of the information you need is down south."

He shook his head. "I have a reliable contact down there who's much more familiar with the local the archives and already working on a few leads. What I need from you is complete access to Michael Chase's files, any evidence you have from the time period, and I need to see Alexander Chase's last letter to his mother. That is the most important thing: the original letter."

I could have made a crack about his not being able to tell everything he needed from the copy, but I restrained myself. No need to bring that up again.

"That won't be a problem," I said. "I'll show you Uncle Michael's files tomorrow, and when I have a moment go to the bank for the letter. But honestly, what new evidence do you expect to find?"

"I don't know yet." Randall grinned at me. I wondered if he thought himself charming.

I squashed the brief, horrifying idea that he might be, under different circumstances.

"But if there are the makings here for another book, I won't object." He looked at his watch. "It's getting quite late, so as much as I hate to do so, I'm going to say goodnight, ladies. Work begins in earnest tomorrow. I have a deadline to meet and a treasure to find."

He began to pack up his things, looking very satisfied.

I rolled my eyes and Aunt Susanna, seeming very concerned, broke in with another question.

"Professor, it sounds like you're going to be really busy, both with researching this project and writing your other book. Are you still going to have time to help Maddie with her chores?"

In the crush of information tonight, even I had almost forgotten that aspect of our deal. Professor Randall looked downright surprised.

"Chores?" he asked, with a touch of repugnance mixed in the question.

"You promised to lend a hand around the farm," Aunt Susanna said. Her expression would have been enough to melt an ogre's resolve, but Randall just looked at her with deeper confusion. "It was part of the deal, remember?"

"I hope you like horses," I said, suddenly jovial. "We've got a lot of stalls to clean out."

"Oh, that!" He chuckled. "That, yes, I'd almost forgotten. I did tell you about my hay fever, didn't I?"

"Hay fever?" Aunt Susanna repeated in disbelief.

I looked at the ceiling. *Naturally,* I thought.

"It's not deadly, but it is debilitating," he said. "However, rest assured, I'm a man of my word. I promised to aid in the day to day chores and I meant it. You'll see."

With that, he took his things, bid us good night, and left the room, leaving the pair of us sitting alone in the kitchen.

The antique clock chimed midnight, stirring Aunt Susanna out of her reverie.

"Well," she said, and her voice sounded very small. "That was – Interesting."

"Mmm..." I stared into my mug of cold coffee. I was tired, so exhausted that I'd gotten that false second wind that you get when you've gone too long without sleep. I was thinking, *Maybe he'll stay out of the barnyard then. If so, it'll almost make up for Aunt Susanna giving him the office to work in.*

As I had before, I wished for a laptop to do my office work on. This time, however, the wish was a little more fervent.

"I hope we haven't made a mistake, letting him stay here." She sighed. "When I first met him, he seemed... Well, less pushy."

I was unwilling to suggest that he'd only seemed that way because she had been blindsided by Lindsay's accident.

"I don't think we had much choice," I said and got up. "Come on – I'm going to bed. Morning will be here too soon for me."

I took her cup and my own and put them in the sink while she coordinated herself with her cane. Then I walked with her slowly back to her room, more for the company than because she needed help.

She opened the door, hesitated, then turned to me.

"What do you think he meant?" she asked, looking at me with large, soulful eyes. "That he was going to honor his promise to help but that he couldn't do it because of his hay fever? What do you think he has in mind?"

I read further into the question. She'd done a good thing by arranging for me to have help. Now it looked like she'd been sold a bill of goods. She was asking me if I thought so too. I did, but I answered, "I'm sure the good professor has something up his sleeve. I wouldn't worry about it, Auntie."

We both knew that she was going to anyway, but she went inside her room. I went back to the kitchen to tidy things, then took the back stairs to the second floor without thinking. When I went past Randall's door, I couldn't help but take a look.

His light was still on. It seemed the professor was working into the night.

I went into my room, and tossed and turned for a half an hour before dropping into a dream-filled sleep.

13

We didn't have long to wait before the meaning behind Randall's enigmatic explanation became apparent. The next morning, after I did my normal early morning chores and run, I came back to a quiet house. I assumed the professor's late-night research had him sleeping in late, which suited me just fine. If I could get out of the house before running into him, I would count that as a good morning's work.

I was nursing my second cup of coffee in the kitchen when there was a knock at the back door. It startled me. As a rule, only students and friends came to the back door, while strangers and new comers used the front door. It was too early for students, and our friends weren't in the habit of showing up without calling first.

After a hasty check to make sure my outfit was decent enough for company, I opened the door.

A young man I didn't know stood there, dressed in a band t-shirt and worn jeans. His thick, curly blond hair was well groomed. The phone he was concentrating on was large and expensive, as were his designer sneakers. If I was to make a stab at his age, I'd put him a year or two in college. That meant he wasn't my usual sort of customer, which was almost exclusively female, and fell either into the teenaged or fifty-plus age bracket. The sneakers meant he wasn't here delivering hay or other supplies - men in that business are savvy enough to wear boots at all times - so I was at a complete loss to explain his presence.

When he looked up from his phone to give me an uncertain once-over, I caught a glimpse of his face and was immediately glad that Lindsay wasn't around. Blue eyes like his were a menace to the teenaged female.

"Hey," he said hesitantly. I got the impression that he hadn't expected to see me, either.

"Hey yourself," I replied and crossed my arms. "Can I help you?"

"Um, yeah… I'm looking for Professor Randall? Is he here yet?"

It struck me like a slap across the face. Randall's presence here was supposed to be a secret, yet on his very first full day, this kid was asking to see him.

Professor Randall, you have a lot of explaining to do.

"I'm sorry, kid," I apologized. "I think you have the wrong house."

His forehead puckered in confusion. "Like, really? Because he texted me this address yesterday. He said to get here early."

"He… *What?*"

With a sigh that clearly showed his waning patience, College Boy scrolled through his messages, then held up the phone to show me. Sure enough, under the heading "Prof. Glasses" was a picture of Randall with the message, *Early start tomorrow* followed by our street address. It was dated the previous afternoon, when the man was supposed to be arranging his new room. Underneath that message was a later one: *Owner is a pill. Handle with care.*

No doubt about it – this was the professor's message, all right. It had been sent right after our late night conversation, and it was fairly polite under the circumstances. I mean, I would have described him in slightly stronger language.

I looked College Boy up and down. "What is this?" I demanded.

He shrugged and shoved the phone into his pocket. "If he's still asleep, I can wait." He looked over his shoulder. "I'll be out here. It's really nice out today."

I couldn't argue with that. Behind him, the farm was slowly wakening to the day. The sun just reached the tree line, bathing the paddocks in its soft, young glow, making the dew-drenched grass glitter like strands of emeralds. Greybeard and Missy nickered companionably from the nearest paddock, and the barn gleamed despite its peeling paint. Beyond that, the fields gave way to the warm, dark woods, threaded with the trails, at least some of which I knew didn't have holes marking them today.

It was a gorgeous day and this was a lovely spot in which to spend it, but while College Boy had time to waste, I did not. I plucked at his shoulder, tugging him into the kitchen.

"Come on in here," I ordered. "I'll wake him."

He followed, protesting, "I can wait."

"You can. I can't. Sit."

He sat at the counter, shrugged, and pulled out his phone as I slipped up the backstairs and went to pound on the professor's door. He appeared after a minute, sleepy-eyed, hair mussed, and tying his bathrobe. He fumbled with his glasses, then blinked at me.

"Did I miss the second coming?" he asked.

"I had thought that we agreed to keep your presence here a secret." I glowered at him.

He took a deep breath, looked to one side, then back at me.

"I've only just woken up," he pointed out. "There is no way I could have done something to tick you off already this morning - unless, of course, I was walking in my sleep. If so, in all fairness, you really can't expect a man to be responsible for what he does when he's..."

"I'm *talking* about Joe College downstairs," I hissed. "You promised to keep your mission here a secret, and yet one of your students showed up this morning for a meeting with you. What did you do, tell your whole class?"

"Joe – oh, good grief, you must mean Jacob. Is he here already? What time is it? Never mind, come downstairs and I'll explain. I hope you were polite to the poor boy. He's going to be your assistant for the summer."

He led the way downstairs as he spoke and my, "He's *what?*" echoed in the kitchen. College Boy was talking to Aunt Susanna, who was brewing him a cup of coffee. They both turned as we entered.

"Good man, Jacob," Randall said, and Jacob hopped out of his seat to shake his hand, an old fashioned gesture that seemed out of place for both of them. "Did you have any trouble finding the place?"

"Uh, no," Jacob said, shoving his hands back into his pockets. "It was easy. I used to skate on Wason Pond, you know. Like, back when I was kid, so I kinda know the area."

His phone was on the counter, blinking. Aunt Susanna was making gestures and mouthing messages to me, but I wasn't in the mood to interpret.

"Excellent, excellent." Randall ran a hand through his hair, making it stand up even further and I saw Jacob bite back a grin. Okay, so he wasn't so intolerable. "You've already met Miss Warwick, I see."

"Oh, yeah." He ducked his head, grinned, and bobbed it at Aunt Susanna.

"Actually," I stepped forward, "*I'm* Maddie Warwick and this is Susanna Chase. And you are?"

"This is Jacob Adamski," Randall announced, clapping a hand on the boy's shoulder. "He was my student last semester, and what he lacks in the science of history, he more than makes up for in eagerness to learn."

"A pleasure," I said dryly, and Aunt Susanna gave Jacob a warm smile as she limped over with his mug of coffee.

"Are you helping the professor with his research?" she asked.

"Oh, like, no," he said, accepting the coffee eagerly. "That is, partially. I'm here for the stable hand job."

When Aunt Susanna looked at Randall, he beamed proudly. "I promised to give assistance and here he is, ready and raring to go, right Jacob?"

"Oh, yeah. Like, I totally love working with animals, you know?"

"Now wait a minute," I protested. "The deal was that *you* were supposed to help, Professor, and that you weren't to let anyone else know that you were here working on the Chase-McInnis treasure."

Jacob choked on his coffee. Aunt Susanna snatched a napkin and handed it to him, while Professor Randall sighed heavily and leaned against the counter.

When he could breathe again, Jacob demanded, "Treasure? What treasure?"

I groaned. The professor gave me a sidelong look.

"Yeah," he said. "He didn't know about that. Until just now."

"All I knew was that he was researching some book!" Jacob's somewhat sluggish look was gone – in its place was a lean, hard expression that I knew all too well. "What kind of treasure? Gold?"

"Oh, boy," I said.

The full story came out. Randall, knowing that his time would be too pressed to be of much use around the farm, had offered Jacob a trade: he would assist on the farm for a few days a week and help the professor with the research in return for a passing grade in Randall's American History course. Both swore that Jacob neither accepted money from Randall nor needed any from me, but I didn't believe them. I would have thrown the boy out, but for that he claimed to have worked summers in a horse farm in Epping for a number of years and knew all there was to know about the business.

"I'm not, like, a great horseman," he said. "But I know how to clean stalls and stuff. It's weird, but I like the work. It's all real labor, you know? Good way to get a work-out and almost no stress. It'll be great. And there's, like, the treasure thing."

Aunt Susanna, having fallen sway to his large blue eyes, thought it was a great idea, but I had my doubts and expressed them to Randall when he followed me into the office to get the work-release forms.

"I can't afford to hire a boy I don't know," I groused. "I can barely afford one I do know."

"I know him," he said. "And it's volunteer work."

"Sure it is. Come on, Randall, I wasn't born yesterday. How much are you paying him?"

He mentioned a number that made me balk.

"I can't match that!" I gasped.

"Why would you?"

"I won't accept charity," I snapped. "We don't need your help or anyone else's."

"That's a debatable statement," he said dryly. "And it's not charity. I agreed to provide assistance in return for room, board, and access to your archives. My schedule makes it impossible for me to fulfill that part of my bargain personally, so I hired Jacob. He isn't the most talented conversationalist, but he's familiar with horses and he's surprisingly strong for his size. More important, he needs academic help in the worst way. He will benefit from my expertise, while you will benefit from his youthful eagerness to pitch hay and clean out stalls." He shuddered at the thought. "Most important of all, he'll keep me from having to shovel manure and for that, madam, I would gladly part with half my salary."

I tapped the pages against my chin, thinking. Jacob had the slouching attitude of a boy who hadn't worked in a while; but his face and arms were tanned from being outdoors and he did look strong. I had to admit, having a boy around for even just a few days would ease my work burden considerably. Randall was right. This was as much for his benefit as it was for mine, perhaps more so. Letting him pay the boy wasn't such a bad idea. It would ease my finances and save me the bother of having to look for extra help.

Besides, I had no faith in Randall's abilities to wield a pitchfork or drive a tractor.

Randall had been looking around the office as he spoke. In the silence that followed, he turned back to me expectantly.

"What do you say?" he asked, finally. "Let the boy work here? Give us all a break?"

I hated, *hated* giving way to him on one more thing. But once again, he presented a wholly logical plan, and it would be foolish to dismiss it simply because I didn't like the presenter.

"I'll give him a week tryout," I said, and a smile spread across his face.

"Excellent." He nodded. "I knew you could be reasonable. Now, if you don't mind, I'll get dressed."

He turned and had his hand on the doorknob when I, smarting from that last remark, called out to him.

"I've done a little research of my own, you know," I said. "On your background."

It may have been my imagination, but his spine seemed to stiffen. Nevertheless, his smile was still determinedly intact when he turned to face me.

"Oh?" he said. "Impressive, isn't it?"

"Very. But it did confuse me. I mean, if you are as good as you say you are and as good as *they* say you are, why are you working for a little nothing university like Hadley? Fifteen years ago, you were getting offers from Harvard, Oxford, and the Smithsonian. Then, suddenly, you just disappeared off the academic radar." I cocked my head, feigning the same innocent expression he used from time to time. "Jealousy in the ranks, Professor? Anything you care to tell me?"

There was a moment of silence. When he chuckled and the smile didn't reach his eyes, I knew that I had rattled the man, if only for a moment.

"I'll tell you someday, when I know you better. It has little bearing on our current business dealings. Now, may I go? Or was there something else?"

"There was, actually," I said.

The past two weeks before he'd come had been an experiment in living on a minefield. Aunt Susanna knew about the forged letter, and she no idea who could have done it: she was far too concerned with proving her husband right to worry about it. I was convinced that it wouldn't take too much detective work on her part to finger me. After all, Randall, who had known neither me nor the exact circumstances of the discovery, had done so rather handily. Randall hadn't told her yet, but why wouldn't he?

I didn't know what to make of the situation and the suspense was getting more and more difficult to live with. So throwing caution to the wind, I made myself ask him. We could hear Aunt Susanna chatting away with Jacob in the kitchen, her laugh and his echoing off the gray cabinets. There was no way they could hear our conversation, but I still lowered my voice.

"When you came here the other night, you practically accused me of forging the Beaumont letter. Have you told Aunt Susanna?"

Even in the process of creating the Beaumont letter, I'd never been able to bring myself to call my act "forgery" before. I'd thought of the process as one would think of installing a security system, and the fact that I was breaking into a house that was not my own to install it had simply been shunted to the side.

"My dear Madeleine," Randall said. "There was no 'practically' about it. I know you did it. And, no, I did not tell your aunt or her friend."

My heart was pounding in my ears and my hands were cold. The accusation was so stark and raw.

"Why didn't you?" I asked hoarsely. "You, with your so-called devotion to the truth. Why haven't you told everyone?"

"I could, but it wouldn't help my search very much. Having amateurs underfoot won't help me anymore than it would you, you know. Besides, I thought there was more to gain by keeping you in my corner. Was I wrong?"

Again, he wore that innocent look.

No, he wasn't wrong. In that instant, I knew I'd do almost anything to keep Aunt Susanna from finding out that I'd tricked her. How Randall had figured that I'd react that way was anyone's guess, but the second condition was clear: as long as I cooperated, Aunt Susanna wouldn't learn the truth from him. As long as I cooperated.

"I understand you perfectly," I said. If I could have spat venom, I would have, but he would have had to be deaf to misinterpret my tone.

"Excellent," he said. "Well, I have to get dressed. I'll see you later tonight?"

I didn't answer, but brushed past him to the kitchen with my heart thudding in my ears.

14

Orientation went very quickly. Jacob seemed comfortable around the barn and animals and even correctly identified several pieces of tack.

"I had to clean them all the time when I worked in Epping," he told me, as we toured the tack room. "My boss was kind of a snob and didn't like to ask the clients to do it."

"Our students all clean their own tack," I said, pushing aside the memory of Mrs. Fontaine. "But we help the younger ones."

"Like, that's a good idea, you know? It's good for them to do it. Keeps you grounded, like my grandmother says."

He was brighter and more talkative than I had expected, and in the short space of time proved that he was at least superficially competent with the animals, polite to the riders, uncomplaining about the mucking, and strong enough to heft bales of hay without breaking a sweat. More than once I found myself thinking, *Thank God Lindsay isn't here to see this.*

Despite his enthusiasm, I didn't like the idea of leaving Jacob alone on his first day. Leaving him to clean out the empty stalls, I went inside and voiced my concerns to Aunt Susanna. She immediately promised to hobble out to the stables and oversee his work while I was at the vet's office, and insisted when I hesitated.

"Professor Randall is going to be reading all day and I'll just be in the way here," she said.

"Did Randall actually say that?"

She brushed off the remark. "Oh, Maddie! Just go. I'll watch the boy. It's a nice day to be outside, anyway."

I bit my lip, but there was really no choice. I was already running late. Exacting a promise from my aunt that she would call at the least provocation, I raced upstairs to change and back down to grab my keys from the office desk. I pulled up short when I saw Randall, in dress pants and a button down shirt, sifting through the book shelves. I'd forgotten that I was supposed to pull out Uncle Michael's things for him.

Randall had already moved into my office. He'd cleared the big office desk, putting my piles of folders in a stack on the floor, and littering the surface with his own stacks: accordion files with yellowing labels, archival photo albums, a laptop, a netbook, a tablet, and a small sound system. Books were pulled out of the shelves and restacked in messy piles, and his mug of coffee sat on top of the floor safe.

"I got started without you," Randall said.

Since when have you done anything else? Somehow, I managed to keep the thought from verbalizing.

He was bent over a large green, water-stained hymnal that I recognized. Uncle Michael had bought it at auction, thinking it might have an alternate lyric version of *Come, Grateful People, Come.* It hadn't, but it remained in the pile of other books he'd collected from the period. They made an eclectic collection, ranging from the clothbound, worn church hymnals to battered prayer and political meeting tracts to personal prayer books like a miniature New Testament or the itsy-bitsy *Dew-Drops* daily reader.

I decided not to comment on the state of the desk or the room. I went behind the desk, pulled open a drawer, found the filing cabinet key, and went over to lock it.

"I don't have time to get the research out for you," I said. I found that it was already locked, then remembered that I had done so last night, when Aunt Susanna first offered him the room. "Will you be all right on your own?"

"I think I can be trusted," he said, and when I looked at him, he nodded at the filing cabinet.

Locking it had been instinct - even I wasn't rude enough to do it so pointedly - but considering my past behavior, it must have looked that way. I flushed, but decided against explaining. It would only sound like an excuse.

"All right," I said. I went over to the desk and was about to replace the key when I thought how silly that would look. So I pocketed the key, found my car keys, shut the drawer, and headed for the door, slinging my purse over my shoulder. "Aunt Susanna knows where everything is. She'll be out in the barn with Jacob most of the day, if you need her."

I stopped in the doorway, realizing that I had just volunteered her services without qualification. I turned. "But I must warn you – Aunt Susanna is still recovering from surgery, so she can't be running errands all day. She needs lots of time during the day to rest and relax. And it's best if she avoids the stairs altogether."

"Slavery," Randall said dryly, "has been outlawed since before the end of the Civil War."

"Right..." I said, hesitating. I had to leave, but I felt guilty about doing so. Aunt Susanna was used to a quiet house with little activity and plenty of time to rest and recuperate. How would she handle this first day with guests, especially a potentially demanding one like Randall?

"Since you are still here," he said, taking off his glasses and scanning the bookshelves through squinted eyes, "can you point out that diary for me? I wanted to start on that right away."

I glanced at my watch, stopped myself from sighing, and went over to the safe. I put my hand on the knob and gave him a pointed look until he turned back to his book. I knew the combination by heart, but some disquiet threw me off and it took me two tries before it opened.

There isn't much inside to interest the average burglar. On the top shelf are photos, memory sticks, and paperwork for the few horses we own. But the bottom shelf is stuffed tight with genealogical records that Uncle Michael found too valuable to risk losing in a fire and too useful to tuck away in the bank.

Among these was Mary's diary, a small, slim notebook of crumbling black leather and with the vestiges of gold embossing along the spine. How Mary had come to own such a handsome volume was beyond our explanation – but the real gold, as my uncle liked to say, was on the inside. She had filled the book with pages of elegant script in a variety of inks, some as vibrant as the day she touched paper, others so faded it was barely legible.

Without thinking, I slipped the book out of the bag and tenderly ran my finger down the rough edges of the paper. In my mind's eyes, I could almost see Mary Chase, bent over the book by candlelight, writing while her son played before the fireplace and her husband smoked his pipe. Or did she write during the day, when she and the serving girl worked long hours in the kitchen, while the men were out in the fields or fighting back the ever encroaching forests? Was it a secret hobby, her solace during the long monotonous days, or did her family know and contribute to the journal? Somehow, I always thought the former. Whenever I tried to picture Mary, I saw her as a woman with dark hair and large soulful eyes, ever looking towards a horizon she could never pursue.

I wasn't the only one who waxed poetic about the diary. Next to Alexander's letter, it had been Uncle Michael's most prized possession, and he treated it with as much respect as one would the Declaration of Independence. Holding it in my hand, tasting the scent of wood fires and old paper, I could almost hear his low, booming voice:

Think of it, Maddie! We have access to the thoughts of a woman who died almost a hundred years before I was born. Through her writings, we can touch the past, and learn about people who would have been long forgotten if not for her. That's the power of the written word – it bridges time and brings back those who are gone.

I wish it could, I thought, my eyes suddenly moist. *Oh, how I wish it could.*

"Have you read it?"

Randall's voice sliced through my reverie, pulling me back into reality with a wrench. He was crouched beside me, so close that the cover of the book in my lap was reflected in his large glasses. I felt as though I'd revealed something, and embarrassment washed through me.

"My uncle did, several times," I said, getting to my feet quickly. "He knew parts so well he could quote them to me. He thought there might be something in it that would clear Alexander. I don't know why he thought that. It ends before the incident. At best, it's a character study."

"How about you?" He tapped the book gently. "What did you think when you read it?"

"I haven't. Not the whole thing, anyway."

"No?" Randall sounded surprise.

"No. Some of us live in the here and now. The past is interesting, but it's dead." Slipping the book back into the bag, I held it out to him. "And there's little practical value in the dead."

He took the bag, his eyes strangely concerned. "There are many who would argue that point."

"Probably," I said. "People who have little else to do but dig up the bones of the buried. Those of us with responsibilities cannot afford the time to play in the past, Professor. The living must take priority. I have to go. If you need me, you have my cell phone."

"Oh, I shall be quite comfortable here," he said, as I headed for the door. "When will you bring me that letter of Alexander's?"

I paused in the doorway. "When I have time," I said. "You have enough to keep you busy here for a while, don't you?"

"Oh, indeed, but the letter – the letter is key. The sooner I have that, the sooner we'll have the solution." He smiled knowingly at me. "The sooner I'll be out of your hair."

I drummed my fingers on the doorframe, reluctant to make promises, but having to admit that the latter was an enticing idea.

"If not today, then tomorrow." When he turned away, satisfied, I added, "You take care of the diary. *That* is a very valuable and irreplaceable old book. It requires delicate handling."

He looked at the book in his hands, startled, then a slow smile spread across his face as he recognized his own phrase.

"I will," he said. "It'll be returned unharmed."

"I'll hold you to that," I warned. Then I hurried out into the hall. Once again, I was late for work.

EXCERPT FROM MARY CHASE'S DIARY

June 1st, 1858

Another letter from Alexander. He reports that he is well, yet his writing isn't as lively as it is when he is happy. I think this is because he knows that it is not only I who reads his letters and he is naturally cautious. Doubtless he knows, without my telling him, that I write with the same restriction. How hard it is to shape one's mind and words to the rule of another! It is only in this book that I feel the freedom to express myself as I truly desire.

I cannot say this to anyone, but I often long for Alexander's return. I love Avery as a son, and O., of course, but they have their work and I have mine, and the two spheres are worlds apart. I long for my son, who understands me as no one else seems to. Our minds, hearts, and tastes are so alike that we can speak volumes without saying a word and yet words are as comfortable and easy as walking. But I should not complain, for that is being ungrateful. Life is a hard thing and not many have the advantages that I do.

He is working for a merchant and reports that the work is good, the pay fair, and he is comfortably situated, except that he has not time to read as he used to. He misses his books, though he will not say so. I am arranging to send him a parcel with a few volumes in it, including a new copy of the little prayer book that has brought me so much comfort – God willing, it will reach him without damage. I'm ashamed to say that it is a wrench to part with the books. With hard times falling on the farm, O. will not replace them and without good books, I feel as though my soul will starve. But perhaps I can borrow some from my kind neighbors and, in any case, God will provide, if only I am wise enough to wait for His providence…

15

Despite my misgivings, the rest of the week passed quietly. Randall burst in on my dinner that first night to inform me that he'd just received a series of extensive revisions from his editor and he would be forced to attend to those first before pursuing the Chase matter any further. My lack of enthusiasm seemed to goad him until he finally cut himself off in mid-sentence with a frustrated, "Am I boring you?"

"I'm just wondering when I asked you to keep me informed about your schedule," I said. I was sitting at the table with my shoes off, a half-eaten sandwich on my dish, and a magazine open in front of me. I wasn't in the mood to talk, but then, I rarely was anymore, unless it was to Joe Tremonti. "Honestly, I don't really care what you do or when you do it, so long as you keep out from under my feet and out of the way of my clients."

"Oh," he said, then again, "Oh! Well, I can promise that."

"Excellent," I said and turned a page in my magazine.

A moment went by before he went back into the office, shutting the door behind him.

According to Aunt Susanna, he spent the majority of the week in there, locking himself in with his research materials and coming out only to help himself to coffee and to pace the front yard. He didn't eat much, talked less, and seemed, to her mind, to be wrestling with some terrible inner demon. She became so concerned that she called me at work and left a message with my co-worker, Che Che.

"Your aunt wants you to call," Che Che told me when I came back from my lunch break. "She's says she's worried about Vincent, that he's off his feed. Did you get a new horse? Do you need to schedule an appointment?"

I surprised her by sighing and rolling my eyes. "Vincent isn't a horse, he's a man," I said and her eyes lit up with interest.

"Oh?"

Che Che Randazzo is a petite woman with a quick mind, bright lipstick, and a motherly interest in my personal affairs. Her daughter, Melanie, was part of Joe's class that conducted the dig on the farm all those years ago, but I didn't really become acquainted with either woman until I started working at the vet's office. Che Che is a fixture in the place, having worked as a receptionist there for thirty years, and she had an intimate knowledge of every family, puppy, horse, and goldfish in a twenty-mile radius.

We've worked together for four years now, and despite my attempts to maintain a professional distance, she knows me almost as well as Aunt Susanna. I found myself confiding things to her that I couldn't say to my aunt. She knew, for instance, that I had been having lunch with Joe Tremonti today, so her next assumption was a natural one.

"Is this fellow your aunt's beau?"

"No!" I objected with such force that she was startled. I took a breath, shook my head, and sat down in my chair. "No, he's a houseguest."

When she arched her eyebrow at me, I said, "A paying houseguest. Of sorts. He's writing a book about, um, farms, and he wanted to get some real life experience."

The explanation sounded lame to me – so flimsy as to be unable to withstand the typical first round of Che Che's questions. I braced myself, but to my surprise, my coworker sat up straight and gasped in excitement.

"Really? Your place is going to be in a book? That is so exciting! What good advertising for your place! I read all the time – I wonder if I've read any of his books. What's his name? What kind of books does he write? Are you going to be in it? Leah, did you hear?" she asked, as one of the technicians came in with an armload of files and a tablet. "Maddie's farm is going to be in a book!"

"Cool." Leah was too busy to be very impressed. She thumped the stack of files on my desk, and frowned at the tablet as she made a note on it. "What kind of book?"

"A novel!" Che Che said. "The writer is living there right now, getting the feel for it. Isn't that exciting? It's like one of those TV movies."

"Who's the writer?" Leah asked. "She local?"

"It's a man," Che Che said, and that made Leah look up and grin at me.

"Does Joe know?" she asked, and I blushed up to my roots.

As a matter of fact, Joe did know. He'd found out that day over lunch, and his reaction had been a little less enthusiastic than my co-workers.

Lunch with Joe was a last minute thing. He'd sent me a text that morning, telling me he was working in Portsmouth and was dying for a decent lobster roll and intelligent conversation. Couldn't I take a little extra time for lunch and come meet him? Naturally, I was as incapable of saying no as the romantic-minded Che Che was of refusing me the extra time.

We had lunch at a ramshackle-looking restaurant on Hampton Beach that served what was possibly the best haddock I'd ever tasted. But although he'd said that he was starving, Joe didn't eat much. He'd been worrying about our situation ever since he learned of Lindsay's accident. Convinced that I was next to have an accident, he spent a good deal of the meal arguing with me, again, about closing down the trails. I was more flattered than annoyed by his interference.

Because of the circumstances, I didn't want to tell him about Randall and would have avoided the subject altogether if I could. But in trying to convince Joe that there was nothing to worry about,

I lied and told him that the hole-digging had ceased. Then he started hinting that he'd like to come up and ride the trails, something he couldn't do and keep ignorant of Randall's presence. Not inviting Joe seemed impossible – the very idea of riding along with him on one of the trails was too deliciously romantic to refuse.

Even so, I wouldn't have told him about our guest if Joe hadn't asked what my plans were now that Lindsay was no longer able to work.

"Will you be able to afford to hire someone?" he asked.

Had anyone else asked me that question, I would have been offended by the suggestion that I couldn't handle my own affairs; but the concern etched on his handsome face looked so heartfelt, so genuine, that I softened and wished that I could tell him everything. Something in the way he spoke, the way he looked at me, made me feel as though we were alone in that restaurant, despite the noon-day crowds.

Nevertheless, I was convinced that it was better he didn't know all yet.

"I'm not worried," I said, as lightly as I was able. "Someone, uh, recommended a boy to us. He seems to be working out well."

It wasn't a lie, but it felt like one and I flushed and looked at my plate rather than at him. After a moment, Joe reached out and covered my hand, squeezing it a little. My heart sped up and I found myself locking eyes with him, losing myself in their shifting depths.

How easy it would be just to stay here, I thought.

Falling in love with Joe would be too easy. As it was, our relationship was growing so slowly as to be almost imperceptible. His divorce had gone through quietly and easily and was finalized in March, and even though we'd been seeing each other on a fairly regular basis, there was no move on his part to take things beyond the friend zone, something that I was happy to report to Aunt Susanna even while I was privately growing impatient with the delay. Lunches were nice – but I wanted more. It was moments like this, when I was falling into his deep, dark hazel eyes, that I lived for.

"Maddie," he said softly. "You don't have to hide anything from me. Is it getting too much for you? The lessons and the job and the stable work – how can you possibly do it all?"

I would have regretted telling him about having to double up on the lessons since Lindsay's accident, only he looked so worried, so concerned, so involved, that I felt cared for. But warm as this feeling made me, I knew he was about to offer to help, something I couldn't accept. So I told him a novelist Darlene knew was looking to gain some experience on a horse farm and offered to help out for free at the stables in return for room, board, and research.

Joe was surprised.

"That's generous," he said. "What does he write?"

I shrugged and very nearly spoiled my story with the grin I found hard to suppress. "Romance novels," I said.

Joe immediately began asking me all kinds of questions about Randall's character, capabilities, and motives before finally letting it go.

"If he looks at you funny, you let me know," he said, and I had to stop myself from throwing my arms around him. "I don't want you or Susanna uncomfortable. He does anything and I'll be over like a shot."

Thinking about that made me grin again as I told Che Che and Leah that Randall was on the farm to write a romance novel. This stunned them for a moment, then Leah started to laugh and Che Che frowned. She'd read romances by the dozen and in all varieties, from the staple bodice rippers to the more modern paranormal romances. I could tell that, in the wake of this new knowledge, her suggestion that I was a character in the book was making her uncomfortable.

"What's his name?" she asked. "I've probably read something of his."

"Oh, probably," I said. "His name is Gregory Vincent."

"Oh?" She looked doubtful.

"He writes under a few pennames, I think."

"Oh!" She nodded.

"What kind of romances does he write?" Leah asked.

I shrugged. "He's written dozens in all genres, but I think he does the American dream-type romances now. You know, single mom meets broken, brooding Navy Seal-type and her ex doesn't like it."

"Ohhh!" breathed Che Che, looking dreamy. "Those are my favorites."

Leah was still grinning. "Are you going to be a character in the book?"

"God forbid!" I said. "Um, but I'd appreciate it if you didn't spread this news around. Vincent's on a tight schedule, and we can't afford to have too much attention drawn to him."

Leah, a practical woman who hardly ever let herself get carried away on the waves of fad or fashions, shrugged and promised easily. Che Che, however, had a wide circle of friends, including five sisters that she regularly played cards with, and I could tell that she relished the idea of having this juicy piece of information to tell them. In the end, her affection for me won out and she nodded acquiescence, but not without a request.

"Do you think you could get me an autographed copy of his book? Maybe a couple, for my sisters and me? We just *love* Vincent's books."

She looked so enthused that my guilt flared up. I promised anyway. There was nothing else to do at that point and, as it happened, I could actually get autographed copies of Randall's books, only it would be *The Dunstable Connection*, rather than *Dunstable's Dark Desires* or whatever they title those books now.

Thankfully the phone started ringing, forcing us all to get back to work.

I finally had time to call Aunt Susanna an hour later. She was out with Darlene and couldn't talk more than to whisper: "I'm so worried, Maddie. He just paces and frowns and he won't eat much. I keep bringing him things and offering to help, but he seems so – so intense."

"Just leave him alone," I advised. "He's probably just upset with his editor."

"But he's so thin – he should eat something. And I've got nothing better to do, I was thinking I could help, but he just won't..."

"I don't think Ran-Vincent is the type to neglect himself for very long," I said, earning a raised eye brow from Che Che at the desk next to mine. "Don't worry about him, Aunt Susanna."

"Well..." She seemed reluctant. "All right. I guess. If you think so."

"I do," I said, then after a moment's hesitation, continued. "I told the girls at the office about Vincent."

I emphasized the name, and she sounded surprised when she said, "You did? What did you say?"

"I told them about his research for his new romance book. I like that he's going in a new direction with this series – not as trashy as the others, more story, less torn shirt."

It was all I could do not to start giggling, especially when Che Che threw me a startled look. But on the other end of the line was dead silence.

Then, finally, "You told them he was a romance novelist?"

"Yeah. I figured it was better to come clean. They will keep it to themselves, though. I told them we didn't want too much publicity. Uh, until the book comes out, of course." I nodded at my co-worker.

There was more silence, then an unmistakable giggle.

"Oh my," Aunt Susanna said. "Oh my goodness. Oh, Maddie! Randall is not going to like that! Not at all!"

And then she was laughing, a hearty and full sound that rolled through the phone's speaker, filling my ear and making me laugh as well. It was so genuine, so unaffected that my eyes stung with sudden tears. She laughed so infrequently now – even with Darlene she only ever seemed to chuckle. To hear it now warmed me, and I quickly dashed the gathering moisture from my eyes. This was no time to indulge in emotional outbursts.

When the laughter slowed – too quickly in my opinion – Aunt Susanna said, "No, he is not going to like that one bit."

"I know! I can't wait to tell him."

"I'll let you do it – He's going to be livid."

"I don't see why he should be," I protested. "It'd give his reputation a much needed boost, don't you think?"

"Sounds more like false advertising to me," she retorted. "Poor Leah and Che Che are going to be expecting some broad-chested, rugged man with a torn shirt, instead of a fussy sort of - Ooops, he's coming. Talk to you later."

She rung off and I hung up, chuckling. When Che Che looked at me oddly, I had to come up with something to explain to her, so I said, stumbling with the name a bit, "Vincent just asked my Aunt to be a character in his book."

Her wide-eyed response set me off again.

16

I managed to avoid Randall most of that first week. He was busy with his revisions and my lessons ran late into the evening - and even when they didn't, I found reasons to hang out in the barn or in the stables. Aunt Susanna either didn't realize what I was doing or didn't notice, for she never commented on my absence, except to send me texts about dinner. She was growing restless, but there was little I or anyone else could do about that.

Jacob worked a few mornings and a couple of afternoons during this week and for all appearances was a model employee. He did his chores to Aunt Susanna's satisfaction and my own, filled in his time sheets properly, and only tracked manure into the kitchen once that I noticed. As he was careless with small details, I suspected that Aunt Susanna was cleaning up after him, but it didn't matter. The stalls were getting cleaned out, the supplies stacked properly, and he even volunteered to clean up the indoor ring on Saturday.

"I told him I had to talk to you first," Aunt Susanna told me on Thursday night. She was at the kitchen counter, hunched over some sheets of paper and beaten text books. We were talking and moving softly, but I wasn't sure if that was because of the late hour or if it was out of respect for Professor Randall, who was in the next room, working on his book.

It was half-past nine and I had only just come in from the stables. My eyes were heavy and I tripped over my own feet twice while putting together my dinner; but despite my exhaustion, I was feeling jubilant. Joe had called and asked me out to dinner on Saturday. Saying yes was easy – rescheduling the three afternoon lessons required a deft bit of tact, but I managed it and I was already planning my outfit.

"Jacob is coming on Saturday?" I asked. I was surprised, then remembered that asking him for his availability was among the many things I had forgotten to do. I would have to rectify that the next time I saw him, which would probably be Saturday, if my workload stayed the same.

Aunt Susanna rifled through her volumes, nodding distractedly. "Yes, he can work for a half-day then, but he can't work tomorrow. I asked him to give me his available schedule so that we could work out some consistency." She looked up at me and blinked through her glasses. "I thought that would make things easier for you."

"Yeah, that does, thanks," I said. "But Jacob's never allowed to use that tractor unless I'm here."

"Yes, I know. I told him as much."

I should have known she would. The microwave pinged, letting me know my dinner was ready, and I was happy to attend to it. "Thanks," I said. "How's he getting along with the riders?"

"He hasn't met many, but they seem to like him. I know Lindsay will."

"Lindsay?"

She turned then, her eyes shining. "She called today, Maddie, sounding so much better. She was hoping to talk to you, but you were out in the barn, so she said she'd text. She's coming out here for a visit soon."

"She must be doing much better then," I smiled. The idea that Lindsay was up and well enough to come around made my throat tighten with unexpressed emotion.

Aunt Susanna said, "She's not allowed to ride for a while yet, but she said she's getting bored. She's missing the horses and her girls and you, of course. Her parents are worried about her driving, so maybe Darlene and I will go and pick her up." She clasped her hands and beamed at me. "It'll be so good seeing her up and about again."

I had to agree. Even if she wasn't completely healed yet, seeing Lindsay without her bandages was sure to do my aunt – and me - some good. I felt as guilty about the accident as if I had dug the hole myself; but I was angry as well. I wanted find the people responsible for the digging, though what I would do when I met them, I didn't know.

"If she needs a ride, I might be able to pick her up, too," I said.

"When would you have time for that?" Aunt Susanna asked. She was over her papers again, her pencil scratching furiously. She had always had a talent for drawing and art, but I hadn't seen her working at a picture in a long time. I wondered what she was working on.

"You barely have time to eat your dinner at night," she continued, oblivious to my curiosity. "I doubt you'll have time to pick her up and bring her back. Besides, Darlene will enjoy the drive."

Of course, it would have to be Darlene who did the driving, she of the many speeding violations. Aunt Susanna's surgery wouldn't have affected her driving if she drove an automatic, but her car was a stick shift and she claimed it was too difficult to operate with a cane. Neither Darlene nor I bought the excuse, but we didn't see the point in disputing with her.

"I wonder what she'll think about Jacob," Aunt Susanna said.

I recognized the matchmaking glint in her eyes – she had that same look before, like that time a young man stopped by the farm to ask about lessons and pricing. He'd been tall, good looking, friendly, and my age. It took all of ten minutes to scrap Aunt Susanna's daydream. He was a struggling actor looking to improve his profile, which meant our rates were too steep for his budget, and he was engaged to a nice young fellow from Portsmouth.

I chuckled and got up to take care of my dishes. "Jacob. Nice, muscular, and available? I don't think there's much doubt about what she'll think. I'm more curious as to what she'll think of the great professor when she meets him – he's much more of a character."

I nodded in the direction of the office and was surprised to see the brief expression of concern etch across my aunt's face.

"Oh, I don't think they'll have much to do with each other," she said. "He's been so busy, he's hardly had time to do anything more than pace and eat sandwiches when he comes out."

"Think he'll ever get around to the treasure?"

She arched an eyebrow at me. "I thought you didn't believe in the treasure."

"I don't, but I'm going to hold him to it. Where did you put the mail?"

"On your desk."

I stopped and rubbed my neck. I really, *really* didn't want to go into the office. I didn't want to see how he'd rearranged things, I didn't want to be interrogated, and I didn't want to talk to Randall unless it was absolutely necessary. But the bills needed to be paid.

Maybe I could put it off another day. It was late after all…

"I think the mortgage bill was in the pile today," Aunt Susanna said. "And some checks. I sorted them for you."

So much for putting it off. If there was one thing our account needed, it was an influx of cash and we didn't need another late-payment penalty. I sighed, poured myself another cup of coffee. "I'll take care of it. See you later."

"I'm going to bed," she announced. "So I'll see you tomorrow."

I waved distractedly and went into the hallway.

The office door was shut and I paused for a moment, debating whether I should knock or not. Then I remembered that this was my house and that he was the intruder, and I opened the door with an air of authority.

Professor Randall was sitting in the soft glow of the floor lamp in my uncle's old soft chair, a cup of cooling tea and a plate with the neglected remains of a sandwich on the table at his elbow. He was frowning in concentration at the book that lay in his lap and didn't look up.

My dog Trusty was laying on his feet. Her ears twitched at my arrival and she lifted her head to acknowledge me before settling back down on her paws, looking like the devoted best friend sitting at her master's feet. It felt like a betrayal, and one that I hadn't been expecting.

The professor didn't look up until I shut the door behind me. The sound startled him, and he blinked at me through his oversized glasses.

"Oh, you're back," he sighed, and arched his back stiffly as he consulted his silver-plated watch. "Is it that late already?"

"Don't let me interrupt your reading," I said. "I'm just doing some deskwork." I took a step or two inside, then stopped. "If I can find the desk, that is."

I hadn't been in the room since the morning of Jacob's arrival, nearly a week ago. The place seemed awash in papers, files, and books. The professor's desk was buried under and behind piles of books, files, and boxes. Uncle Michael's shelves had been ransacked and rearranged, the genealogical books piled on their sides rather than in neat lines. Sticky notes in scrawling pen were scattered around, and charts were draped over filing cabinets or tacked to cork boards leaning against the shelves. His computer sat next to a small, sleek printer, loaded down with printed pages.

My desk, as promised, had been left untouched. I had to step around piles to get to it, but the surface was free from Randall's research, and the two small piles of mail sat in the tray. As much as I didn't like paperwork in principle, I was glad to do something that was organized, quiet, and routine. Some of that comfort was taken away by the knowledge that I'd be working under the professor's scrutiny.

It wasn't until he sighed again and rubbed his eyes that I realized that I'd actually awakened him. The glasses had disguised the fact that he'd been sleeping, which explained Trusty's calm demeanor.

"Sorry I woke you," I lied, smirking as I started up the computer. Then I thought, *What are you trying to do, start a conversation?*

"Not to worry," he said, getting up slowly. "I should be packing up anyway. Time for bed."

I grunted and focused on my computer screen and the small, but intimidating, stack of bills piled up by my keyboard. I studiously avoided watching him move about quietly, but I kept my dog in the corner of my eye.

Trusty jumped up at his movement, stretched, and watched him with a cocked head. She glanced at me, glanced at him, and took a moment to consider before trotting over to lay down on her bed next to my chair. When she'd settled in, she looked up at me with an adoring expression.

"Traitor," I whispered, and bent down to scratch her behind the ears. She leaned into my hand and licked my arm as I withdrew it, and the little kindness was like a balm.

My computer up and running, I started going through the bills and checks, working as fast as I could without looking like I was rushing. The repetitive nature of the work soothed me, even if the bills were still terrifyingly large. I printed and emailed invoices, applied payments, and worked through about half of the load before I realized that the professor hadn't left yet.

I looked up and saw that he was sitting behind his desk, frowning as he turned the aged pages of a little book. It took me a second to recognize it as the diary I'd given him earlier.

He caught my stare, then gestured to the book. "Hard to tear myself away."

I nodded and suddenly Trusty jumped up and yapped. I gasped, my heart pounding, and turned to find the dog was standing at the window, with her tail low and her ears up and twitching. Gone was her sleepy, comfortable nightly nature: she was rigid, her expression alert. It was so unlike her that it took me a second before I went and looked out the window myself.

The office is in the back of the house, looking over the "new" stables – new being a relative term, as they were built in 1968 – and the trail that runs along the perimeter of our land. The house sits at the farthest western edge of the property, next to the wooded lands that belongs to our neighbor. It's a pretty spot, with frequent late night and early morning visits by raccoons, moose, or deer, but Trusty knew these scents and rarely reacted like this. In any case, there was nothing to see there now.

"What's your problem?" I asked her softly.

The dog looked at me, then out the window again. Her tail started moving slowly, so I turned, shaking my head, to see Professor Randall leaning back in his chair. His arms were folded as he studied the two of us.

"She's done that a few times before," he said.

"She did?" I lowered myself into the chair, biting my lip. "That's not like her. Must be a coyote or something."

Then Trusty relaxed and turned away from the window with a yawn. She settled herself into the pile of blankets with a contented expression, and I couldn't help but stroke her head affectionately again.

"Dumb dog," I mumbled, and she looked up at me with an innocent expression. "Was there a cat out back?"

"There was a flashlight last night," Randall said, and when I looked up at him, he continued. "I guess it wasn't you, then?"

"No," I said, as steadily as I could with a heart that threatened to pound through my chest. "No, it wasn't me. You saw a flashlight in the back? Where? When?"

"Along the trail, last night around ten. I thought it had to be you or one of the riders."

"It wasn't," I stated firmly. "We have a strict curfew – no horses out after nine-thirty. I wish you had told me, professor. I need to know when we have prowlers."

He sighed in exasperation. "I'm new here. I don't know who goes about or when. Where are you going?" he demanded.

I had gotten to my feet, reaching for my barn coat with hands that shook despite my telling myself that I wasn't afraid. Blood was pounding in my head, and I honestly couldn't tell you whether I was more angry or scared. It didn't matter – the effects were about the same.

"I'm going to check it out," I snapped.

My voice sliced through the air, and Randall flinched, his mouth setting in unusual firmness.

"If Trusty is any guide, they're gone," he said.

"I'm going to check it out," I repeated firmly. "No need to trouble yourself."

Not that you offered.

I rushed out of the office and out the back porch, grabbing the baseball bat we kept by the back door. It's not a terribly effective weapon, but it gave me more confidence stepping out into the night by myself. I hadn't realized that Trusty was following me until the porch door bumped off her body before shutting. She yapped, and I hushed her, and we stood silently, scanning the night-shrouded backyard.

Silence settled over us like a heavy blanket, and the lights from the porch and the stables made the inky blackness of the surrounding woods seem even more ominous. As my heart calmed and slowed, I picked up other sounds: crickets chirping, tree frogs croaking, horses whickering. I could hear Trusty's heavy breathing, and the almost silent slap of her tail hitting my leg. In a distance, a car rushed by on the road running in front of the house. But there was nothing else - no light, no sound, no movement, nothing. I might have been alone on the edge of the world, for all my senses could tell me. And that terrified me.

I went down the porch steps and stood on the shadowed back lawn, listening, but too frightened to venture further. When Trusty began to sniff around the neglected weed patch, looking for a place to do her nightly business, I realized that we were indeed alone out here and began to relax.

Until the backdoor slammed again, making me jump six inches.

"Find anyone?" Randall asked.

"*No,*" I snapped.

If there had been someone out there, they were gone, further down the path than I cared to go at night with just a baseball bat and a dog. Making a mental note to check out that path during my morning run, I went back up onto the porch with Trusty, brushing past Randall to go into the kitchen.

As was her normal practice, Aunt Susanna had left on the lights over the counter. What wasn't her normal practice was the plastic-wrapped plate of cookies and the note she'd left under the lights. I picked up the note and read it:

> *Professor – I know you're working late tonight and didn't have time to eat much, so I made these for you. They're hearty and filling. I'll make corn chowder tomorrow night. I hope you can make it to dinner. – Susanna.*

My stomach growled suddenly – my quickly consumed dinner hadn't been enough, apparently, and the cookies were tempting. But they weren't for me. I tapped the note to my lips, wondering what we had in the cabinets.

I was avoiding thinking about the incident outside. There wasn't anything I could do about it, now that the trespassers were gone. Dwelling on the fact that there were people merely yards from the house would only make it that much harder to go to sleep tonight. I wished, as I had many times, that we had an alarm system.

"One more thing to add to the wish list, I guess," I said to Trusty, who was looking at me expectantly.

I knelt and got a biscuit out of the cabinet for her. The door clicked shut behind me and I held the note up over my shoulder. "It's for you."

Randall plucked it out of my fingers and walked around the bar so that he was facing me when I got back up. I rummaged through the cabinet until I found a box of crackers. When I faced him again, he was staring at the plate of cookies, frowning.

"Something wrong?" I asked.

He cocked his head at me and placed both hands on the counter before asking, "What were you planning to do out there? With that baseball bat, I mean."

He nodded to the corner where it was propped. I shrugged.

"I guess I was hoping to catch me a treasure hunter," I said, and popped a cracker in my mouth. "They're in season, you know."

I gagged. The cracker was so stale it was inedible, and I stumbled toward the trash can. The box followed the remains of the cracker and, when I stood up straight again, the professor was watching me with an expression of distaste.

"I haven't seen those crackers in that box design since the nineties," he said.

"Now you tell me," I growled, and went to the sink for water. When I came back, he slid the plate over to me.

"Help yourself," he said.

"Those are for you," I pointed out, hoping I was able to keep the hurt out of my voice. Being infirmed, Aunt Susanna didn't cook or bake much anymore. That she would start now for Randall rather than for me seemed unfair. But that wasn't Randall's fault, I reminded myself. Aunt Susanna had told me herself that he spent all his time in the office and only came out to make himself sandwiches. She would have mentioned if he demanded cookies.

Randall pushed the plate closer to me and took a stool. "Go ahead," he said.

I did this time, pulling off the cover and grabbing the biggest cookie to jam into my mouth. I was hungry, yes; but more than that, I was frightened and the chocolate chips melting in my mouth were almost as soothing as Uncle Michael's arm around my shoulder.

"Does this happen often?" Randall asked, and I shook my head.

"She doesn't bake often – her hips and knees don't allow her to stand for long periods of time," I said, as soon as my mouth was clear.

"I didn't mean those," he said, with a dismissive gesture. "I meant the trespassers. How often are you actually bothered by them?"

I shrugged and took the stool opposite of his. "Depends on the time of year. Obviously, they can't dig during the winter. Last summer they were tapering off – I had four, maybe five holes altogether. This year, though..." I shook my head and took another cookie. "This year, there's been a lot."

"Are you going to call the police?"

"What can they do? By the time I spot them, call the police, and wait for them to arrive, the night visitors are gone. Besides," I swallowed hard, "we kind of have a reputation with the police in this town. They don't welcome our calls."

"Cried wolf one too many times?" he suggested.

I scowled. "You could hardly call it that, not when there were actually people in our backyard. It wasn't my fault that they were quicker than the police."

"Yes," he said, thoughtfully. He was looking into the distance, absently crumbling my aunt's note in his hand. "Yes, I can see that. Well, I guess it just makes it all the more imperative to put this thing to rest. Can you give me a tour of the property tomorrow?"

"Tomorrow?" I asked surprised.

"It is Saturday. I presume you don't have to work at the office on Saturdays."

"No, but..."

"A tour is important," he said firmly. "I've been reading Mary's diary and she makes occasional references to specific areas of the farm. You were raised here and have the best the working knowledge of the land, aside from Susanna, who isn't physically able to walk me around the place. If I'm to make any progress in this matter, I need to know the lay of the land myself."

"Yes…" I said slowly, reviewing the morning's appointments in my head. Of all the things I had to cram into my day, a walking tour of the grounds with Professor Randall seemed the least important. But he was right – even Lindsay didn't know the land as well as I, and I might as well use the opportunity to check for recent digging. "All right, I'll take you around. But I don't have much time tomorrow. I have lessons all day and a… An appointment in the evening."

I couldn't bring myself to say "date" and if Randall noticed the slip, he gave no indication of it. Instead, he moved on to the next piece of business.

"And when can you bring me the original Chase letter?" he asked.

Going to the safety deposit box had slipped my mind completely, and I sighed as I remembered. "Good grief – I forgot. Well, it'll have to wait until Monday now. The bank closes tomorrow at noon."

Randall sighed too, sounding as put out as I felt. "That will hold things up, but I'll make do."

"You think the letter is really essential, then?" I asked. The cookie crumbled in my hand and showered pieces onto the clean counter. "What can you learn from the original that can't be seen in the copy?"

"I won't know that until I see it," he said, with a light hint of condescension. Then he slapped the counter with his hand and leaned forward, his eyes flashing with an intensity that gave me a start.

"There's a message in that letter, Warwick. I know it and I can't find it. Maybe it's encoded in the lettering, or it's hidden in the text, or it could be as simple as a stain in the background. I just don't know, but it's there, just out of my sight. Usually Civil War codes are so simple as to be *insulting*. This one – this one is trickier than you'd expect from a man of Alexander's upbringing, that's for sure."

He leaned back into his chair and I frowned at him.

"If it's so bloody difficult, then how can you be so sure that there is another message?" I asked.

The look he gave me was one of dismayed disbelief. "That's as plain as the nose on your face." When I didn't respond, he straightened up again. "You mean, you didn't see it?"

"You were just telling me that even *you* can't see it," I reminded him, annoyed. "Now you're telling me that it's as plain as the nose on your face?"

"The *clue* is, not the message. It's right there, for all to see. My dear Madeleine, have you studied the Civil War at all? You still don't know what I'm talking about?"

"No, I don't," I snapped. "I never claimed to be an expert in the Civil War, either, so quit acting like a pompous ass and tell me what on earth you're talking about. A clue that's not a message? What do you even mean?"

Randall reached into his pocket and pulled out a crumbled page, which he spread out on the counter. He slid it over to me and pointed to a line about half way down.

"Look there," he said. "And tell me you don't see it."

I looked and saw Alexander's letter, the text of which was practically burned into my mind: *Marched Long today and I am exhausted by hours Of training and miserable Poe-like terrain. We shall meet Johnny Rebel any day and I am itching for the introduction...*

"Practically poetry," I said sardonically. "What of it?"

Randall looked at me in disbelief, again then sank back into his chair.

"Sometimes," he said, "I wonder how you managed at all before I came."

I glared at him. "Don't make me throw the plate at you, Professor."

"The *Poe* reference!" he cried out and I hushed him, indicating that Aunt Susanna's room was within hearing distance. He dropped the volume, but not the arrogance in his tone. "Don't you see? It's Edgar Allen Poe he's talking about - the *writer*."

"Yeah, so I've heard. What of it? So the south reminded Alexander of *The Raven* – it's not flattering, but it doesn't mean anything."

"It does when you remember the other thing Edgar Allen Poe was known for."

"Dying of alcoholism?" I guessed, and grinned when he threw his hands up in frustration. "Oh come on. Give, professor. It's too late for guessing games."

"We'd be here all night if I didn't," he growled, which only made my smile broader. I liked getting to him, even if he was as good as I was at tossing the insults.

He leaned forward again and jammed his finger over the name. "I'll tell you what makes me sure that Alexander hid a message in this letter. He was writing to his mother - by all accounts, his best friend in town -and though he's not a man of many words, he describes the landscapes using the name of the best-known *cryptologist* of the eighteen-forties."

Now I stared. "Cryptologist? Edgar Allen Poe was a cryptologist?"

"One of the finest. He used to hold contests whereby people would send in their best efforts and try to stump the master."

"And could they?"

"Only very rarely," he admitted. "But the point was, he was a code cracker and known to be very good at it, and here is his name, nestled in the middle of your little mystery." He jabbed the paper with more force. "Now, doesn't that make you think that there might be a little bit more to this letter than meets the eye?"

I wrapped my arms around my waist, suddenly very tired. "Yeah, maybe. But you have to remember, others have tried to crack this letter and failed. I've got fields and trails pockmarked with abandoned attempts to prove it. Now, doesn't *that* make *you* think that if there ever was a treasure, maybe someone already found it? Someone like Avery Chase who was living in the same house as Alexander, and no doubt would have known about his hobbies?"

It was a good point, better than my average on a late night like this.

Randall frowned and drew back, taking the letter with him.

"You know what I like best about you, Warwick?" he asked, deftly folding the letter.

"No." I leaned forward. "Enlighten me."

"Your boundless sense of optimism," he said, annoyed. "Good night."

17

Saturday came soon enough. After my early morning run, I had two lessons simultaneously – both little girls around the same age. It went smoothly enough, until one of the mothers asked me about getting a refund for the summer camp.

"Elizabeth can't make it?" I stammered.

Elizabeth's mother looked surprised.

"I just assumed that with Lindsay gone, it was cancelled," she said, running a hand through her red hair. It glowed like polished copper in the early morning sunlight, and I found myself wishing that I had time to go to the hairdresser before tonight's date.

"Oh no, we're going ahead with the camps," I assured her. "We've got a new stable hand, Jacob, a new lesson plan, and I'm really excited about having a more active role in the camps." I paused to help her daughter cinch the saddle, then turned back to the mother with an expression of helpful innocence. "Of course, I'd be happy to refund your fees anyway, but the other girls would really miss Elizabeth. So would I."

She seemed doubtful, but said that, of course, Elizabeth would come. She was sorry that Lindsay wouldn't be there, but she wouldn't want to disappoint her friends. I agreed, sending up a prayer of gratitude for the narrow escape.

I entered the house hot, hungry, and wondering where my new stable hand actually was. Aunt Susanna had arranged his schedule for me, a schedule that had him starting at 8:30 on Saturdays. It was nine a.m. and he was still absent.

"*Kids*," I muttered, as I kicked off my boots at the door.

Randall stuck his head around the doorway. "Did you say something?" he asked.

"Just talking to myself. Have you seen Jacob?"

"He's in the study," he replied. He was making himself a cup of tea, with the hot water in one hand and a pint of milk in the other, looking for all the world like a proper English butler. "Something hot to drink?"

"Not unless it's coffee," I said. "What's Jacob doing in the study? He's supposed to be helping me in the stables today."

"He came in looking for you, but I, also, had a list and I knew you were with a client, so I grabbed him and put him to work." He put down the milk and began to rhythmically dunk his tea bag. "You don't mind, do you?"

"I do, as it happens. We've got a truckload of work today and I want to get it done early as possible," I snapped, grabbing a mug and a granola bar from the cabinet. "Besides, I thought he was hired as a farmhand, not a research assistant."

"Bit of both, actually. The boy needs help with his history, and I promised him that if he would condescend to helping out with farm chores, he would, also, have access to one of the finest minds in American History." He said this with a self-satisfied grin, his attention remaining on his mug.

I grunted. "Well, when David McCullough shows up, be sure to get his autograph for me. I loved the miniseries."

It took a second, but when the jibe sunk in, Randall lifted his head and exclaimed, "Hey!"

I waved it off, and decided that Jacob's time wasn't worth fighting a war over. "Seriously, when can I have him?"

"If it means I'll get my tour sooner, anytime you want," he said.

I'd almost forgotten about the promised property tour. I checked my watch while quickly considering my schedule, and nodded rapidly. "All right, all right. Give me a half hour with Jacob and I'll take you around the place."

His face lit up. "Excellent!" he said. "I'll gather my maps!"

"Professor!" I called after him, as he hurried with his mug to the office. "How do you want to go? Afoot or horseback?"

He made a face. "Very funny," he said.

I took Jacob out into the barn, where we sorted and put away the supplies that were dropped off Friday night. Several riders were around the stables, taking advantage of the bright morning, and they were very pleased to be introduced to Jacob. He grew more effusively polite as he realized that most of our clients were pretty young girls. It would be difficult to keep his mind on shoveling manure and cleaning stalls, but perhaps his presence would inspire my volunteers to keep a more rigorous schedule.

Aunt Susanna was in the kitchen when I came back to collect Randall. Despite the warmth of the day, she was wearing a long sleeve shirt and long pants, and she looked white and tired.

"Feeling all right?" I asked. When she nodded, I continued: "I'm taking Randall on a walking tour. Want to come? It's a nice day."

"I think I'll stay inside," she said quietly.

Randall came out of the office then, carrying a notebook, some folded pages, and his tablet.

"Where do we start?" I asked.

"Let's walk around the perimeter," he said. "I understand that it hasn't changed much since the eighteen-sixties."

"Oh, it hasn't," Aunt Susanna said. "Of course, there were more fields in those days. When the family gave up farming, the trees grew back like weeds."

"Not all of it is very walkable," I said. "You might want to change into boots or something."

"I don't own boots," he said.

I sighed and shook my head. "Of course you don't. After you, Professor."

"Oh, Professor!" Aunt Susanna stopped, blushing. When we turned to her, she continued, "I mean, *Gregory*, will you be having lunch with us today?"

To my surprise, the professor stiffened and looked as though he'd gone on his guard. "If it isn't too inconvenient," he said, glancing towards me.

I shrugged. "Might as well," I said. "Are you cooking, Aunt Susanna?"

"I was in the mood for grilled cheese," she said evasively. "And while you're out, shall I just tidy up the office? Or maybe you need some filing or..."

"No," Randall said firmly, and we both did a double take. "I mean to say, thank you for your offer," he said, in a gentler tone. "But I'd appreciate it if you left everything as it was for now. It's untidy, but it suits me - and if you should put anything away, it would set me back hours. So no, thank you."

Aunt Susanna looked more disappointed than upset, and she pushed him until he agreed - over my protests of her physical limitations - that she could dust the room, if she really wanted to. My warnings went unnoticed in her eagerness. She grabbed her cane and began limping for the office while the professor opened the door and ushered me out.

"What was *that* about?" I demanded, as soon as the door swung shut behind us.

Trusty, who had been following Jacob all day, spotted us and raced over, her tail a flurry of happy motion. She ran up to me, then jumped up at Randall, who seemed to have difficulty holding on to his maps while attending to her. Finally, he managed to calm Trusty down enough to pet her and still hold on to his work.

"I've been meaning to talk to you about your aunt," he said, straightening up, and I immediately went on the defensive. If he had *one word* of complaint...

"What?" I asked warily.

He took his glasses off and hung them from his collar, then rubbed his nose. "She's a lovely woman," he said, and held up his hand when I opened my mouth. "A genuinely lovely woman. She washes my socks. She makes me breakfast, lunch, the occasional dinner. She puts flowers in my room. She arranged that the bathroom should have my preferred brand of toilet paper..."

"Toilet paper!" I couldn't help exclaiming.

Again, the hand.

"She won't play loud music, and she won't allow her friend to exercise in the living room unless she's cleared the noise level with me. She's even given up her TV time to let me have control of the TV at night, when I'm finished work," he said, his impatience mounting with each word while I stood completely confused. "In short, she's done everything in her power to be the perfect hostess."

"And?" I interrupted.

He rubbed his nose again. "And, my dear Madeleine, she is driving me completely mental. She won't leave me alone! She asks me how I feel, if I'm hungry, if I'm too cold, too hot, too tired, too bored. She wants to clean my room, help with my research, maybe even clean my car if I'd let her. She's around all the time, driving me to distraction and keeping me from my work."

"She's friendly," I said.

"A bit too friendly," he growled. "I was looking for Yankee hospitality. Here's your bed, here's your meal, leave me in peace. Instead, I'm under constant scrutiny and investigation. Doesn't she have anything to do during the day? Any friends, any hobbies, a volunteer project, or *something*? I just can't get my work done with her constantly underfoot!"

I bristled. "Now, look here…"

But we were interrupted.

"Hello, Ms. Warwick!"

Shannon Granger, a bright sixteen-year-old with crazy curls and a blindingly pink polo, waved from the hitching post in front of the stables. Her mount, the placid Sarah Anne, barely twitched an ear at the sound, but the same could not be said for her human companion. Shannon's sister, the more bookish Erin, was holding Sarah Anne's bridle and burying her face in the horse's flank.

As we looked, Shannon waved even more eagerly. I was confused about her enthusiasm. Shannon is an excitable girl by nature; but being Lindsay's student, she had only a passing acquaintance with me. I knew that I was viewed as distant and difficult by most of the students, so I couldn't explain her friendly overtures until Shannon turned and poked her sister in the ribs. When Erin looked up, the older girl pointed to us and giggled. Erin turned pink, but couldn't help grinning in return, and that's when it hit me: they hadn't seen Randall before and they'd never seen me with a boyfriend. Being excitable, hormonal teenagers…

"Oh, for heaven's sake!"

I turned, exasperated, and found Randall waving back.

"*What* are you doing?" I hissed.

He looked at me with exaggerated innocence. "Being friendly," he said and waved again. A chorus of giggles tripped through the summer air.

"Don't encourage them!" I said, pulling his hand down.

"That's your job, equestrian," he said jovially. "Shall we mosey on over and say hi?"

I knew that would do no good. Say what I might about Randall being here for research, the Granger girls would think what they wanted and only the presence of a true boyfriend would convince them otherwise. Quelling the rumors was yet another reason I needed to invite Joe over for a ride when Randall was out. And, well, any excuse to have him close by…

"Maddie?"

Randall waved his hand in front of my eyes, frowning in confusion, and no wonder. One minute I was ready to kill him for waving to a pair of students, the next I was standing stock still, grinning like I was a teenager confronting my first serious crush.

I wiped the idiotic grin off my face and shook my head.

"Forget it," I said, and stamped off the porch. My boots sounded like they meant business and Trusty - who'd danced off to yap at the girls - came running back over to follow me. "Come on, Pro-Vincent, let's finish our walk."

My voice echoed off the stable wall and judging from the chorus of giggles, the girls heard every word. They were sure to tell everyone they met riding today that the stern Ms. Warwick was walking with her *boyfriend* in the woods; and if they didn't jokingly stress the word, "walking", someone else would do it for them. As if I didn't have enough on my mind.

"It's a lovely day for a stroll," Randall observed, a bit too cheerfully.

"What did you want to see?" I asked.

"Everything."

"Right."

We cut across the clearing, heading towards the trail. In the clearing, you can hear the rush of roadway traffic, chattering voices, and whinnies from the busy paddock, but behind the curtain of trees and struggling brush, everyday noises are hushed. Grandfatherly old maples spread their thick roots, disturbing the tumble-down rock walls that irregularly lined the trail. Tall pines, their tips so sharp as to seem to slice the sky, reached toward the sun and sheltered the old road under their gently green boughs, yet light gets through, enough to feed clumps of weeds and flowers that struggle to live in the ancient wheel ruts and hard packed dirt. Squirrels chittered, chasing each other around the tree trunks, while birds took up the chorus that the tree frogs left off at morning light. The Chase Farm was a busy place; but here, under the shadows, life fairly pulsed within every square inch.

Despite recent history on these trails, I always breathed easier here than anywhere else. I used to hide here as a child, wandering up and down the rutted path, out of sight - but never too far out of reach: hidden, yet close to the doings of the farm. The woods had sheltered and comforted me as a child and there was a short space of time where I might have believed in wood nymphs, had I known about them then.

Even now, when I was too old, too tired to believe in such thing, I could still sense magic in the atmosphere, even if somewhat dissipated with time and experience.

Once in the shelter of the tree-cast shadows, I expelled a sigh of relief. Randall, who was consulting his tablet, looked up and grinned at me.

"Out of earshot at last," he said.

He stopped to take a picture and I found myself wishing that I'd come here alone to think. Then again, I was always thinking that when I was with Randall.

"It'll only make things worse," I groused, running a hand through my hair before remembering that I hadn't washed it since putting Graybeard out to pasture. I withdrew it with a grimace. "They'll be imagining all kinds of things. If this was eighteen-sixty, I'd be worried about a scandal."

"Mmm hmm," he said, concentrating on his lens. "Although from what I've observed, your life could use a bit of scandal."

Not with you, it couldn't.

I considered continuing our conversation about Aunt Susanna, but he seemed to have forgotten about it and I didn't really relish another argument. Much better for me to advise Aunt Susanna on the sly that her help wasn't needed. Randall was right about one thing: she didn't have enough to do. Maybe I should talk to Darlene about that...

But that was a problem for another time.

While he focused on the tablet, squinting at the screen, I said, "We're facing south. This is the western edge of our property. The property line follows the road almost exactly and has done so since eighteen-thirty-two. At least, that's what my uncle said. But as you pointed out, he wasn't very good at citing sources."

He either missed the sarcasm or chose to ignore it. "It doesn't matter – I've already scheduled a trip to the town land records office for this week." He took another picture, then stopped, frowning again. "Road? Was this a road once?"

"Still is, technically." I swatted at a black fly. "I used to play here all the time. I got to know each side of the road pretty well. I used to like to tell my school friends that I played in the middle of a road all the time, no big deal."

"It's a wonder you weren't the cause of any accidents," he remarked and I grinned.

"That's what Uncle Michael used to say." I began to walk, Trusty trotting beside me. "Our neighbor took lessons with Uncle Michael, and she would take a shortcut through these woods. There's an old foundation somewhere. Whenever I saw her coming, I used to hide in it."

Randall snapped another picture before following me, pulling his glasses back on as he walked. "Was this part of the farm property back in Alexander's day?"

"No," I said. "This was Hill property then. According to Uncle Michael, they lost interest in it when they discovered gold in the Black Mountains. It's been forested ever since the eighteen-fifties, I think. This road leads – led – down to the back property, which was ours for a while, but that was lost in the twenties. Don't bother searching there, though," I said quickly, when his face lit up. "It was left wooded for the sap and the hunting. And because both Obadiah and Avery were too cheap to hire help."

"When was this road closed? Or was it?"

"Forties, I think? I don't know. It is closed, though, and we'd appreciate it if you didn't draw too much attention to the fact that it's not private property."

"Afraid they'll open it again?" he asked.

"It's a possibility," I said. "The back property is untouched, hemmed in by the surrounding properties. Right now, the owner doesn't want to sell - but if some bright developer discovers that he has access just by opening the road, he may make an offer the owner can't refuse."

"Do you think Darlene would sell?" he asked.

"Darlene?"

He gestured to the land on our right. "I thought your aunt said that Darlene Winters was your neighbor."

"She is. She owns all that land on the west side of the trail. Her husband bought it decades ago."

"They aren't into development, I guess?"

"He had a plane and built an airstrip on the property. He liked to keep the trees up to keep the plane and the strip hidden. I don't know if he was afraid of theft or nosy neighbors or what, but it works for us. Being surrounded by woods on three sides gives the farm a nicer feel and keeps things quiet."

"I wonder," he said thoughtfully, "if Winters would be willing to give me an aerial tour."

"She doesn't fly," I said. "And before you ask, Rich took the plane with him in the divorce. Darlene kept the land and Allison and turned the strip into a tennis court."

I smirked at the memory. Darlene, true to form, inaugurated the court with a "Freedom Party", celebrating her finally-official divorce. Uncle Michael and Aunt Susanna were invited, and since I was staying with them at the time, they'd brought me along. I was young and overwhelmed by the crush of people. I remember Aunt Susanna telling Uncle Michael that she didn't want me around people who'd been drinking so much.

"No one's fallen in the pool yet," he'd said, which confused me very much.

But what remained sharpest in my memory was Allison's face when she came over to talk to us. She was older than me and much taller, and I looked at her in awe.

She resembled her father, but had her mother's dark hair, and she was nervously fingering the necklace she always wore, a rustic looking accessory with a blue stone. The contrast between her black hair and her pale complexion was striking. I couldn't hear much in the din of the party, but I remember her saying, "It doesn't seem right, you know? We're celebrating the death of a relationship. It's weird..."

"Who's Allison?" Randall was oblivious to my ruminations.

Now I was the one who stopped, looking at him in disbelief. "Allison Winters? Daughter of Darlene Winters?" When he shrugged, I shook my head. "You haven't heard of the *Allison* Winters case?"

"Should I?" he asked.

"It was only the biggest story around here until the great and ongoing traffic light debate," I said. "Allison Winters, the girl who disappeared just after she had gotten accepted to Oxford for graduate studies. I can't believe you don't know – there was a nationwide search. The FBI got involved and everything."

He tapped his tablet meditatively, nodding slowly. "It's starting to sound familiar... That was about ten years ago, wasn't it?"

"Yes," I said, very slowly. "Ten years."

In some ways, it still felt like it had happened yesterday. Cloaked in the security of our landlocked existence, we didn't realize anything was wrong until the news came over the radio. Allison disappeared while on a road trip to visit a friend in California. No one even knew that she was missing until a friend called Darlene, who was overseas, and asking where she was. Knowing Allison's wanderlust, Darlene didn't immediately call the police, hoping she'd show up. By the time the authorities got involved, Allison hadn't been seen in eight days. The trail was cold.

Naturally, the press made much of the "absentee mother" angle. Darlene was a celebrity travel columnist then - a shining star in the dying art of reporting, as she liked to put it - and a regular on the talk show circuit. Allison was the bright, neglected daughter, with all-American good looks and a friendly, down-to-earth manner that made everyone like her. She'd just finished her degree and was working towards her Doctorate, eying a future in Forensic Pathology. Naturally, some friends reported that she was unhappy with her mother's frequent absences, and from this came the suggestion that Allison may have harmed herself.

Darlene staunchly denied the allegations, stating that her daughter was far too intelligent to be upset by her mother's career. She never stopped insisting that her daughter had come to harm, and pushed the authorities hard. But there was nothing to find - and eventually, other, newer cases took priority.

Like my uncle's death, Allison's disappearance left deep scars. The fight for her daughter and her own reputation sapped the strength out of Darlene. When the authorities informed her that the search was suspended, she responded by quitting her column, cancelling her appearances, and moving home, beginning a decade-long self-imposed exile from the world. She'd become convinced, she told my aunt, that if Allison were to turn up, it would be at home. She hasn't spent a night away from the house since.

"*Darlene* Winters!" Randall exclaimed now, again ripping me out of my memories. "I remember. She was that globe-trotting columnist-turned-hermit, right? I met her a few times when I was starting out, but I never would have recognized her."

"Time does that to people," I said shortly, and began walking again.

Randall caught up with me and matched my stride. "I wouldn't have known, to look at her," he said. "The hermit life seems to agree with her."

In a way, he was correct. Darlene refused to act the martyr - or the saint - and took great pains to dress and maintain a normal level of activity.

Nevertheless, I shot him a disapproving look. "She has never forgiven herself for Allison's going missing," I said. "For all her bold displays, she's still a grieving mother."

He nodded.

"It shows, however, in her writing," he said softly.

I was startled by his observation, and yet he was correct. The time alone, the soul searching, and the crush of grief produced a remarkable vintage, if you will. Darlene's books were dedicated to and based partially on Allison, and the prose was poetic and achingly beautiful. Even readers who did not know Darlene's story would review the book with words like "haunting", "soulful", and "tragically gorgeous". The carefree divorcee might have been a good columnist; but the grieving mother was a novelist of the highest order.

Randall met my gaze with a sad smile. "Oh, yes," he said. "I occasionally read fiction too, you know. All work and no play, and all that." After a pause, he observed, "Tragedy has seemed to hit this neighborhood rather hard."

He walked forward a few paces, kicking at the weeds. The stalks swayed and bent under his strikes, but they always stood again, bright green, without a kink in their straight lines. I envied that.

A pall seemed to have fallen over the warm day. We'd kept a brisk pace, and the sounds of the farm had given way to that of the woods, and gloom weighed on the otherwise pleasant atmosphere. Randall seemed to feel it too, for he walked with his head down and a pensive expression on his face. Only Trusty seemed unaffected. She loped up and down the trail ahead of us, like a puppy who's just discovered the great big world for the first time.

Watching Trusty play, the gloom dissipated. We came to a bend, where the trail separated from the road. Randall lifted his head, then his tablet, and snapped a picture.

"All right, Warwick," he said. "Before we get into another fight, tell me something about your family history."

After the heaviness of the earlier conversation, both of us made a concentrated effort to keep our discussion strictly on the historical puzzle he was trying to solve. I pointed out the areas that Mark Dulles' film crew visited, and showed him the paddock that we thought used to be the wheat field. I showed him where the orchard had been, where Alexander and Reuben Hill used to climb the trees and steal the apples, more to upset Obadiah than to enjoy the fruit. I showed him where the fields were, pointing out the one that Avery's body had been discovered in.

"He dropped dead of a heart attack, apparently," I said.

"Dulles covered that," Randall nodded. "Some said that he was digging a hole, looking for his brother's treasure."

I snorted. "More likely he was digging up yet another stone. They don't call this 'The Granite State' for nothing."

Like most old New Hampshire farms, finding the outline of old fields is often as simple as following the rock walls that the farmers built around them. They were built as much to get the stones out of the way as to divide the properties. New Hampshire is rocky, hilly country that prefers trees to wheat, bushes to potato plants, and the early colonists led a hard, meager life. Once land opened out west or down south, and trains began to freight food into Boston, the farms in the area closed up and were left to go to seed.

The trees were quick to move in. Walk through any woods in Southern New Hampshire and you find pines, maples, and birch trees, most about the same age, growing amidst broken threads of rock walls and abandoned foundations. For all the lush greenery of the summer, this part of New England does not like the farmer.

When we were finished and heading back to the house, Randall said, "This has been very helpful, but I may call on you again for more information or another tour."

"Fine," I shrugged.

"You don't object to taking long walks in the woods with me?" he teased, but I shut him up with a look that was impossible to misinterpret.

18

Aunt Susanna had lunch ready, but I had time only to grab a sandwich before running back to the barn to relieve Jacob and take on my next lesson. I spent the rest of the day teaching and readying the release forms for the upcoming camps. I completely forgot to warn Aunt Susanna about crowding Randall.

Despite the busyness of the afternoon, time dragged. I was impatiently looking forward to the evening, even while dreading the spectacle of dressing for a night on the town and leaving under the watchful eye of Randall and my aunt. But when I came in, Aunt Susanna was in the living room, moodily watching TV, and Randall's car wasn't in the driveway.

"Where's the professor?" I asked.

"He had a meeting or something," she said. "He won't be back until late."

I was relieved and so eager to get out of the house that I barely noticed her subdued state. I showered, pulled on one of my little-used and almost out-of-style dresses, pulled my unruly hair back into a bun, and applied a little lip gloss. When I came back downstairs to say goodbye, Aunt Susanna was in the kitchen, frowning at the contents of the fridge.

"Going out?" she asked.

"Yes. I'll be back late."

"Joe Tremonti again?"

"Yes," I said, trying not to let her make me feel defensive. "Will you be all right tonight? You seem kind of down."

She sighed and shut the fridge door. "Oh, I'm fine. Darlene is coming over to keep me company."

She really didn't seem to want to talk to me, something that both worked in my favor and made me feel guilty at the same time. Both feelings melted away when I walked into Ranalli's Italian Restaurant in Salem and caught sight of Joe, studying the menu with a look of concentration on his handsome face. He rose when he caught sight of me and pulled out my chair.

"I'm sorry I'm late," I said, consciously trying to keep my hands from pressing against my stomach, which seemed to house a dozen fluttering butterflies.

"I get it – you're a working girl," he said. His breath was on my neck as he pushed in the chair and I couldn't repress the shiver of electric excitement that went down my spine. Then, with his mouth close to my ear, he murmured, "Besides, you're worth the wait."

That held me tongue-tied for the next few minutes.

The waiter came to take our wine order, and I let Joe pick the wine and the appetizers, claiming - a little incoherently - that I didn't have the expertise that he did for such things. He chose a hearty red with a dry finish, and it paired perfectly with the dinner that accompanied it.

I didn't need alcohol to induce a heady feeling. Just being in Joe's presence was enough to make a girl need a designated driver.

Our talk, at first, was platonic. I asked about his work and he talked about his summer courses, the students he had, and the twists and turns of his book project - which reminded me uncomfortably of the writer back home. He was looking for a new house, as the one he was renting now was starting to feel cramped, and he'd rented a little Catalina in Boston harbor and was looking forward to taking it out.

"Of course," he said, focusing on the ruby liquid in his glass, "I'll need a first mate. You can't run a proper ship without one. It just isn't as much fun."

His eyes, hazel green in the soft light of the restaurant, shifted to mine. Time had chiseled his face, sharpening the strong jaw line, weaving delicate patterns around his eyes, and dusting his hair with just the right amount of white. He could easily have graced the cover of any magazine - and I, with my wild hair only just contained in its bun, my hands hardened through outdoor work, and my figure maintained only by stress and physical labor, could not understand what on earth he was doing here with me.

But good fortune came rarely enough that I wasn't about to question it now.

His smile deepened, and my heart rate rose in response. It was only with great difficulty that I managed to say, "Are you still accepting applicants?"

"Yes, from a very narrow pool," he murmured.

We ordered dessert, even though I could barely eat, and a sweet wine to go with it. Then over coffee, he mentioned that he was considering moving out here permanently. That piqued my interest, naturally.

"You're ready to leave Braeburn?" I asked. "But I've heard that you were being considered as head of your department."

He laughed, stirring sugar into his mug. "Where did you hear that?"

For a moment, I panicked. Was it something that Randall had said? I couldn't remember, so I said, "I don't know. Just picked it up somewhere. It isn't true?"

"I think I did make the short list, but since Amber left..." He shrugged again and took a sip. After a moment, he said, "I guess, I just feel like it's time for something new. Leave my old life behind. Find something else to do with it."

I took a deep breath and leaned back against my chair, staring at my china cup. Around us, the din of the restaurant had died down as pair by pair, patrons finished their meals and left. Joe and I had lingered longer than most. The fire flickered low in the reproduction brick oven, the hostess by the entrance yawned and checked her watch, but I wasn't ready to leave yet.

Joe was leaning back, too, regarding me with those intense eyes of his.

"That sounded," he said, "like the sigh of Atlas, groaning with the weight of the world on his shoulders."

I laughed self-consciously. "Sorry. I was just thinking… I know this isn't what you wanted for your life, but I wouldn't mind a chance to leave everything behind."

"Oh? Has there been more trouble?"

I shook my head, then decided to come clean. "We – I thought I spotted someone digging out on the trails the other night."

"Near the *house?*" He sat up straight.

"Down the trail behind the house. You know, the old road. Anyway, when I went out to check, they'd gone. They heard us and ran off before they could do any damage." I paused and looked at my hands. Without suppressing the bitterness, I added, "I keep thinking that they're going to stop, you know? But they don't. They just keep coming back. They just keep digging."

"Did you call the police?" he asked sharply.

"No. I didn't see the point."

He hesitated, then said, "Yes, I suppose you're right."

We sat in silence for a moment. I broke it with another sigh and an apologetic smile.

"Sorry, Joe. Just thinking about leaving it all behind, to start again with a clean slate, shaking off old responsibilities sounds like – well, like heaven sometimes." I reached past my mug and took my wine flute instead. There was still a few ounces of the sweet wine left – I'd been pacing myself for the drive back home. "But it is what it is," I said, and drained the glass.

Joe leaned forward. "Why don't you?"

I shook off the effects of the wine, and wished I'd eaten more and stared less. I blinked at him. "What was that?"

"Why don't you start over? Sell the farm, move… Somewhere else. Start again. Or just start. You never got a chance to go out on your own, to do what you wanted to do with your life. Why not start now?"

I stared. "Start over?"

"Why not?" He covered my hand with his warm one and my heart nearly stopped. "Maddie, let it go. That place is consuming you and giving nothing back. Sell the farm, let your aunt find someplace to live, and *go* and *live.* Do it now. Do it before you get too old, before it's too late."

The ice in my fingertips was giving way to the warmth of his grasp. He didn't just hold my hand: his fingers roamed over it, stroking and caressing.

I was confused, even without his touch complicating matters. Joe understood, if anyone truly did, why the farm was so important. Although I didn't like to talk about business matters with him, I'd thought I made it clear that the farm stood for more than just a family business that needed rescuing. Here he was, pressing me to give it up, with touching urgency. He was concerned, truly concerned about me - and I'd rarely felt so conflicted.

"Give up?" I breathed. "Just give up?"

He studied my face for a moment, then shook his head with a sad smile. "I guess that isn't in the cards yet, is it?"

I withdrew my hand reflexively, regretting it in almost the same instant. "Not yet," I said, and was surprised when tears stung at the back of my eyes. "No, not yet."

He nodded, then sighed heavily. "All right," he said. "But promise me you won't dismiss the idea entirely. Consider it. Some things aren't meant to be saved."

"I promise," I said, but the lump in my throat was so large it hurt to speak.

"Promise that you also won't go out chasing trespassers in the night anymore. You see something, you call the police. Or me."

"And you'll be there, zipping all the way up from Cambridge?" I teased, and he turned sober.

"Yes," he murmured, and the look in his eyes had me floating in a cloud the whole way home.

Despite missing him, I was glad to have the drive home to myself. I mulled over his words and found myself wondering – why did I continue? Weren't two years proof enough that the farm wasn't profitable?

Yet the idea of giving up was so repugnant that I felt guilty for even thinking it.

Perhaps, I thought, as I pulled into the driveway, *the idea will grow on me.*

It was late when I got back. I let myself in the front door and Trusty ran over to greet me. We went out the back again - her to do her business and me to check the stables, as was my custom. There were a few whickers of protest when I snapped on the aisle light, but the horses were comfortably bedded down and all seemed well. My favorite, Greybeard, stuck his head out to greet me and seemed almost as impressed by my unusual outfit as Joe had been.

I stayed a few moments with Greybeard, hugging his neck, stroking his nose, and breathing in the familiar scent of sweet hay. A thousand happy memories competed with the few negative ones connected with the smell, and I remembered the first time I'd led Greybeard into the stall. He had been ten years old then, a gelding who used to run the racing circuit, yet he was a gentleman of a horse: well mannered, calm, and hardly ever out of temper. I'd loved him at first sight, the deciding factor for Uncle Michael.

When someone smiles like you did, he'd told me, *you know there's something special about the horse. A man would be a fool to let him get away.*

Trusty came running up to me, her ears streaming behind her, and I bid Greybeard goodnight. I felt refreshed as we walked up the porch steps. Time in the stables with my horses, on my land, had that effect on me.

"Joe may be right," I said to Trusty, and she cocked her head at me. "That's a decision that I'm going to have to make someday. But not tonight, at least. Not right now. Right now, we remain."

By the wagging of her tail, I knew Trusty agreed with me.

EXCERPT FROM MARY CHASE'S DIARY

July 5th, 1855

There were fire-works in the town center today and Obadiah drove us all into town to view them. Naturally, Alexander would not ride in the wagon, but went on ahead, where he and Reuben H. met and played a few sly pranks on the good townsmen. I watched him dancing with the girls in the square and wished, not for the first time, that he would marry one and settle down somewhere near me, so we could visit and I could have conversation with my best friend.

But I know Alexander, better than most, though that might be mother's pride. He is a restless spirit, this son of mine, a man roaming a world that he persists in keeping at a distance. He has always been the stranger in the midst of the crowd, the sailor adrift in a crowded sea. He will not settle down, but only because he feels that there is no safe ground. It is not true – there are many that would see his good qualities, who would welcome them into their hearts and families, if only he would allow them to.

I cannot help but feel that if he had not lost his father, my beloved Justice, he would not feel so alone. Obadiah is a good man, but has not the qualities that would draw a boy like my son. I feel great guilt about this sometimes...

19

The next morning, I tripped into a hole on my morning run. It was my fault that I hadn't seen it. I'd been running on a cloud of giddy thoughts, memories of last night's date running through my head like a musical montage scene from a romantic comedy.

I dwelt longest on when we said goodbye. Joe had just told me that he was heading back to California in the morning, for a few weeks, for business. My face must have fallen, because he stepped closer and lifted his hand to trace it along the outside of my face.

"Going to miss me, Maddie?" he asked, smiling, his eyes moving over my face and hair.

He was so close that I couldn't breathe. When I didn't answer, he cupped my face and leaned in until his lips were close to my ear.

"I'll miss you, kid," he said, and my heart stopped when he kissed my cheek.

I savored that exciting, roiling feeling, when my foot touched air where earth should have been. I went flying, but I was sharp enough to catch myself with my hands and roll almost before I knew I'd been tripped.

I landed on my back, bewildered, watching the flashing emerald of leaves dancing in the morning sun. I laid there for a long moment, allowing my surprise to cloud my mind and forbidding it from considering and processing reality.

I didn't want to acknowledge it. I wanted to lay on the ground, staring at the clean, clear sky, and believe - if only for a moment - that my life was every bit as fresh and comforting.

But reality made no allowances for my mood. The ground was uncomfortable under my back and the growing, throbbing pain in my ankle competed with the stinging of my palms. When my breathing returned to normal, I rolled up onto my feet, brushed my knees off, and went over to sit by the hole.

A hole is such a silent thing. It's a danger unlike most others, where the absence of matter is its greatest weapon. I pondered that it wasn't dirt that killed my uncle, but the lack of it.

Lindsay had been broken by a tree, but it was because the path had been removed that her horse had fallen.

We'd fallen on hard times, not because of a treasure, but because of the absence of one.

Sitting there beside the trap that had so neatly caught me, staring into its shallow depths as calm as any Bhuddhist in his mountain top retreat, I thought: *You could almost say that Uncle Michael was killed over nothing.*

It was a thought clear and detached, as remote from me as my emotions seemed to be at that moment.

But the longer I stared at that shallow crevice - the nothing that was ruining everything - the volcano of fury that I'd been holding at bay for years erupted.

I screamed.

It was long and painful, ripped from the depths of my soul. The sound echoed off of the shimmering trees, silencing the chorus of forest sounds, and making Trusty jump and bark anxiously.

When the first sound died away, I screamed again, longer and even louder than the first time, and Trusty was frightened into stunned stillness.

After that, I was beyond noticing what else was happening. Ignoring my throbbing ankle, I jumped up and ran back and forth on the path, furiously kicking at stones, pounding on the trees, throwing branches, and finally - in a fit of pure fury - I grabbed my music player and smashed it against the trunk of a sturdy old oak. The screen cracked under the impact, and I counted it as victory. I threw it into the bushes and then returned to the hole.

My rage didn't abate until I had filled it by hand. I threw rocks into the hole, so forcefully that many bounced out again. I piled on branches and then used my hands to shovel dirt into it.

By the time it was filled, my hands were bleeding, my face throbbed with heat, and my spirit was spent. It wasn't until I was halfway to the house that I realized I was still sobbing.

Randall was in the kitchen when I returned. He was yawning, rubbing his bleary eyes, and frowned when he saw my dirt-stained outfit. When his eyes took in my bleeding hands and the mess that was my face, he jumped out of his chair and raced around the counter.

"What happened?" he asked, alarmed.

I waved him off with an impatient hand and wrenched the refrigerator door open. My throat was raw from rage, but I grabbed the orange juice from the fridge and reached for a glass.

How Randall knew where the emergency kit was, I don't know, but he had it out and open when I turned with my glass and jug. He presumptuously took them from me, insisting over my protests that I wash my hands. I did so, moaning when the soap stung my open flesh; but he paid no attention then, nor when I objected to his slathering on the antibiotic. The cuts were minor, but he put bandages on the bigger ones anyway, his mouth set in a line that was almost as hard as the look in his eyes.

"Care to tell me how this happened?" he asked, when he was finally finished. "Or am I supposed to guess?"

I was pouring orange juice into the glass, silently cursing as my shaking hands dotted the counter with spots of orange juice. I told myself that I shouldn't have come through the kitchen. I didn't want anyone to see me like this, let alone Randall. I had this half-formed idea that if I ignored him, he'd drop the matter, but he didn't take his eyes off of me, not even as he moved to close up the emergency kit.

Finally, I gave. As much as I *didn't* want to talk, I couldn't leave him standing there without some explanation.

"I tripped," I grunted, and he snorted.

"On what? A landmine?"

"On another hole. On the west trail."

He gaped at me. "On the *trail*? What is it doing on the *trail*?"

"You're the expert," I snapped. "You tell me – that's where they always are. Anyway, it isn't there anymore. I filled it up, hence..." I held up my bandaged left hand. "Guess I won't be playing the piano for a while. Damn hunters." I drained the glass in one long swallow, and nearly choked on the lump in my throat.

Randall rubbed his mouth, his face pinched with thought. When I finished my drink, he asked, "Are you sure it's the treasure hunters that left the hole?"

I heaved a deep sigh. "Of *course* it's the treasure hunters. Who else goes about leaving open holes for people to fall into?"

Despite my best efforts, my voice cracked on the last two words. I buried my head in my hands, trying to calm the whirling pattern of torturous thought.

Let it go, let it go, let it go, Maddie...

I thought I might as well try to stop Niagara from going over the falls.

"They keep coming back," I fumed. As I continued, my pitch grew, even if my volume stayed the same. "They keep coming back and they just. Keep. *Digging*. It's like a game, where they dig the holes and I have to find them before someone else falls in them. And I can't run fast enough. I can't find them all. I planted a phony letter, pound my feet off in the morning, and ruin my hands filling the holes, and I still can't keep up. There's always more piles, more digging – if this is a game, I'm losing it. And if I lose this, I lose *everything*. *Damn* them!"

I brought my fist down hard on the counter, taking perverse delight in the pain that radiated up in a spider webbing of nerves from the impact point.

Randall gazed at me with a new understanding.

"That's why you run in the mornings?" he asked softly. "Because you're looking for the holes?"

I stared at him, disappointment almost supplanting my fury. *Of all the people in my life, why is it that you are the first person to put that together?*

Aunt Susanna, for all her fretting, only ever questioned why I would run in extreme weather. Lindsay assumed I was doing it for my health and figure. And Joe didn't know about my morning activities.

I answered more abruptly than I meant to.

"Yeah," I said, and shoved the juice container back into the refrigerator. "Not that it helps much. I can only run about a third of the trails in the morning. This hole could have been there as long as two days, I don't know. These amateurs treasure hunters don't exactly keep regular business hours. I'm just lucky one of the girls didn't ride into their latest excavation like Lindsay did..."

The idea was like a physical blow and with it came anger. I slammed the fridge door, then I sank into the stool and buried my face in my hands to ward off the sudden images - memories that came hard and fast, falling figures and crushing accidents, and helplessness joined the anger in twisting my gut.

I wanted to call Joe. I wanted to ask him to not get on that plane, but to come back to help me fight this. But as much as I wanted to call him, I wouldn't. This wasn't Joe's fight. It was mine and mine alone. And I'd never felt more alone in my life.

"*Damn* them!" I whispered into my hands. "*Damn* them all!"

The silence stretched out. It was so quiet that I could almost hear the beating of Randall's heart. I kept my hands pressed tight against my eyes, as though by doing so I'd keep the craziness at bay.

I heard Randall shift, and I wished that he'd leave the room. But he didn't leave. Instead, he moved closer, taking the seat beside me.

I did *not* want to deal with him at that moment. I sat up abruptly, preparing to get up and leave; but as though he knew, he stopped me.

"Madeleine," was all he said.

Live with a man for four weeks and you can't help learning something about him. In Randall's case, I'd learned to tell a lot from what name he called me. "Warwick" meant that he was thinking of me as a colleague and was probably going to tell me something in an impartial and informative matter and, perhaps, be open to my commentary. "Maddie" meant he was feeling friendly, or that Aunt Susanna was present and he thought he ought to be on his best behavior. "My dear Madeleine" preceded an admonishment of some sort, usually delivered in the tone of a father exhausted from the intellectual struggle with his two-year-old.

But he'd never called me just plain "Madeleine". For that matter, hardly anyone did, and none with a tone infused with such...

I didn't dare decide what his tone was infused with, but I looked at him. My eyes were bleary, but not too much to see the concern lines etched on his face.

"Don't give up now, Madeleine," he said. He took my hand, which had fallen to the counter, and squeezed it gently, his thumb rubbing circles on the back of it. "You're stronger than that. We just need a little more time. Don't let them beat you. Not these people. Not yet. Not when it's just starting to look like we're on the right track."

"Right track?" I asked. My voice was thick and clumsy, affected by my emotional outburst. I was too worn to even remove my hand from his grasp. "How do you figure that?"

There was no denying the glitter in his dark eyes. "Because their pattern has changed. They're doubling their efforts, as though they knew I was here. I don't think these are just amateurs, Madeleine - although they aren't professional archeologists, if their holes are anything to go by. But they are serious and they are persistent, which means this is more than just a nightly recreation. They're *working* at this. Think about it: they aren't digging in the fields anymore. They're digging in the trails. Why?"

I groaned and shrank away, taking my hand back to cover my face.

The trails...

The whirling slowed and faded as the words came into sharp focus. Why the trails when all of the clues pointed to the fields? They ought to be churning up the paddocks and the hay field, places that were not only mentioned in the so-called clue, but also a good enough distance from the house that, with a little care, trespassers could avoid detection. Back when all of this started, that's where most of the vandalism happened. Uncle Michael's hole had been a singularity. Now the reverse was true. It was the path where they were digging, not the fields.

Why?

I asked it out loud before lifting my head to look at him again.

"I think that, like me, they've realized that there's more to that letter than meets the eye," he said. "If a century of empty-handed searches of that field isn't enough to convince someone that there's nothing there to find, I don't know what would. But there is something on this farm, Maddie. *That's* what we both know, these intruders and I – Alexander did leave something behind and someone is going to find it. If we don't move fast enough, it's going to be them."

It wasn't until that moment that I ever, even briefly, thought that there was anything to find. Randall spoke with such authority, such conviction, that I found myself sitting up straight with one loud thought flashing through my head: *Over my dead body.*

He opened his mouth, but I waved him into silence, sorting through my racing thoughts. It was one thing if Randall and a few amateurs thought that there was something to find. I could dismiss the latter as amateurs, and the former as an academic desperate to re-establish his credibility with a big find. But if Randall was right and this was an organized effort by a group of intruders willing to risk jail time to find it... For some reason, that made the impossible possible.

If there was an actual treasure, that changed everything. I wasn't in a race simply against exposure of fraud. If Alexander Chase did rob the McInnis family, we had a chance to put it right, albeit a century and a half late, but only if we could prevent the cache from disappearing into the underworld. If it did, I would have lost the one chance we had to restore the Chase family honor.

Even as I thought it, the word *honor* seemed so old fashioned as to be laughable. But this wasn't just about some philosophical idea about family pride: this was about finishing what Uncle Michael had started, about making his death something more than just a tragic accident. This was about vindicating him as much as it was about completing Alexander's condemnation.

Randall waited, rubbing his hands together slowly as I thought this through.

"You think they aren't professional," I said.

He nodded.

"But you still think that they're on to something. That they're more than just ordinary thrill seekers?"

"I'd stake my reputation on it." He grinned. "And for the record, it's still a good one, just not as well-known as it once was."

I dismissed the caveat with another wave of my hand. "I just don't know what I can do..."

He interrupted me again. Leaning closer, he covered my bandaged hand with his own.

"Madeleine," Randall said. "Bring me that letter and I promise you, one way or another, we'll put a stop to this for good."

His eyes, dark as mahogany and deep as the fathomless sea, caught mine and held them. I hesitated.

"Work with me, not against me," he said again, "and I *promise* you, we will find it. Together, we will end this."

He said it as though I'd believe him and the funny part was, I did. For the first time since we'd met, I believed that what he was telling me was the simple unadorned truth. We could work together and we would find it.

Yet I hesitated. I faltered, not because I thought at last that he might be right. I faltered because here was offered help.

But again, it was the wrong person offering it.

Joe offered – in his own way, he offered and you didn't accept.

If I worked with Randall, there was still that chance that there was nothing to find – that we'd both end up empty-handed, looking like fools. The truth about the Beaumont letter would come out, because I knew that if I worked with Randall, I would have to cleanse my conscience of that stain. If there was nothing to be found - or worse, there was, but these hunters beat us to it - I would be ruined. Financially, personally, and irreparably.

Joe had offered me a way out, permission to leave this mess behind and start fresh. I could give up, sell out, and move on. I might be able to use Joe's influence to mitigate the Beaumont affair and come out, if not ahead, at the very least even.

So yes, Joe had offered a form of help, but it wasn't one I could accept. For one thing, I wouldn't feel right relying on him until our relationship was cemented, and I knew I wouldn't allow that to happen until this digging stopped. But beyond that, today's accident made me realize that I was living in fear, cringing through life, waiting for the next hammer to fall. I'd allowed these hunters, these *intruders* as Randall called them, to dictate the kind of life I lived. No amount of financial freedom could make up for the loss of self-respect.

All of this ran through my head in a matter of seconds; but in that short span of time, my entire life pivoted, and the new direction took my breath away.

Randall was still waiting, the lines deepening on his face. I was surprised to see resignation wash over his expression. Then I remembered that we'd had this conversation before, and he'd made practically the same promise. I scoffed at him then and did my best to make his life miserable - not that his ego couldn't use the humbling. He must have thought my hesitation was due to doubts about his abilities, a wounding thought. He had no way of knowing that hurting him was no longer at the top on my list.

I found my voice.

"All right, professor." My voice was shaky, but resolute. "Consider us partners until the treasure is found."

His surprise was so great it was nearly audible.

I withdrew my hand and avoided looking at his face as I rose. "Today is Sunday. I'll get you that letter tomorrow," I said, and left him sitting in the kitchen.

I took a shower, got dressed, and got on with my day. When Aunt Susanna asked about my injured hands, I told her I'd tripped. And when Joe texted me from California, I asked him about the weather.

20

Monday dawned and I rose early, conscious of the fact that for all the changes that had taken place yesterday, much had remained the same. I had an ally, but we were still under siege.

I ran for longer and only barely managed to cover a little more of the trails than usual before having to come in for chores, breakfast, and then rush to open the office. There was another hole, this one on the far end of the property, too great a distance for me to run back and forth for the shovel. I filled it with nearby rocks and branches, making an obvious lump for the riders to avoid.

This new hole unnerved me and for the first time, I found myself seriously considering closing the trails down. It was impossible to cover more ground than I was already doing, and I worried that there were other holes that I was missing. I was concerned enough that I left a note on Aunt Susanna's coffee mug, warning her that I'd found another and leaving the decision to close the trails for the day up to her.

Also on my plate were the riding camps that were due to start next week, which I'd be doing without Lindsay's aid for the first time. This meant I'd have to take four weeks off from work. I'd asked for the time off a few weeks earlier, and reminded my boss of the fact when she came into the office this morning. She remembered, though reluctantly.

"It's the usual summer rush," she said, pursing her lips and tapping them with her steepled hands. "Everyone's dog has ticks, everyone has time to come for the annual checkups. Do you think Che Che can handle the load?"

"I'm sure she'll be fine," I said, although I wasn't sure at all. Even during the slow times, the office work could be daunting - and here I was taking not one week off, but two this month and two the next.

My boss looked concerned.

"Maybe I should get someone in to cover," she mused. "Someone who can be more reliable during the summer months..."

I left the meeting in vague discomfort. I was already taking three of these weeks off without pay, a financial loss that was covered by the camps, which I was convinced was the way of the future for the farm. Now I wondered if I'd have a job to come back to.

I worried about it so much throughout the day that Che Che, noticing my taciturn mood, asked me if everything was all right with Joe. I let her assume that my preoccupation was with him. Being lovelorn was easy. Being besieged by treasure hunters, little girl riders, and job worries was a little more difficult to explain.

As promised, I went to the bank during my lunch break and withdrew Alexander Chase's letter from the safety deposit box. I returned home to find Jacob by the back door, working on Uncle Michael's bicycle.

It was a fine, expensive bicycle, a sturdy off-roader that Aunt Susanna had bought him several years ago, when he was considering joining a men's trek team up Mount Washington. But the team never formed and the bicycle was rarely used, for he much preferred riding horseback to biking. When he died, Aunt Susanna couldn't bear the sight of it, so we'd put it in the barn and forgot about it.

Seeing it in Jacob's hands was disconcerting, but I rallied, thinking, *Better someone should make good use of it.* I even managed to smile when Jacob raised his head to greet me.

"It's a fine bicycle," I said quietly. "Do you ride often?"

"Yeah, it's all right," he said. "It'll be ready for tomorrow, no problem."

I thought it an odd thing to say, but chalked it up to "things teenagers said" and went inside.

The kitchen was empty. According to his usual schedule, Randall would be in his office, either finishing a new chapter or editing an old one, but not to be disturbed in any case. The letter, the precious, troublesome Alexander Chase letter was in a protective sheet in the briefcase that I'd brought just for the purpose. It was safe enough, but I burned to have it out of my hands and in someone else's care. I could do without yet another responsibility.

I was tempted to interrupt the professor, but the happy babble of female voices coming from the living room drew my attention. Two of those voices were easily identified as Aunt Susanna and Darlene, sounding brighter and happier than I could recall hearing in a long time. The third voice was so quiet that I couldn't make it out.

I was standing in the hallway by the office door and listening in on the conversation in the living room, when Aunt Susanna hobbled out into the hallway, laughing. She broke off when she saw me.

"Oh, Maddie, you're home, good! Come and join us. I have someone here I want you to see." When I gestured to the office door, she said, "He's out walking around the grounds and won't be back for a while. Come on! We have a visitor."

She looked mysterious and I couldn't imagine who it was that could elicit that reaction. Thus I was completely unprepared when I walked into the room and saw Lindsay sitting in the armchair beside Darlene.

It is one thing knowing, intellectually, that someone is healing from an accident. It is another to see them sitting in a chair, holding a glass of lemonade, smiling up at you from under their familiar bangs, looking as though nothing had changed in the four weeks since you'd seen them last - as though that awful night in the ambulance had never occurred.

"Hey, Boss!" Lindsay said, her voice low and musical. "Miss me?"

I don't remember dropping the briefcase, but it wasn't in my hands when I wrapped my arms around her. She was laughing, protesting, her voice welcome in my ear.

"Not too tight, Boss," she said, her laughter taking the sting out of the admonition. "The doctors say I'm stubborn, but still pretty fragile."

I could feel the brace under her printed t-shirt, and I loosened my grip. When I pulled away to look at her, I could see its faint outline under the thin material. There was an arm brace, too, black and unobtrusive, another reminder that she might be back, but she was no more whole than any of the rest of us in the living room that afternoon.

I was assailed by another wave of anger against the thugs that were digging up my beautiful farm, but I bit it back. I reminded myself that they weren't important. What mattered was that we were here, together. Battered and bruised, but not shattered.

Aunt Susanna poured me a glass of lemonade. Darlene made room on the couch and for a little while, chores were forgotten. The lemonade was tart and sweet, the laughs quick and frequent. Lindsay, though a little slower than before, was as bubbly as ever. She had already visited the stables and said hello to all of her buddies, both four-footed and bipedal, and she was enthusiastic about Jacob.

"He's awesome," she said, and didn't even flinch when the two older women nudged each other. "I wonder where Professor Randall found him."

When the three of us exchanged looks, she laughed.

"Don't worry," she said. "I know that he's here to find the Chase Treasure, which is *so* cool, and that it's a secret, which is even cooler, *and* that he's undercover as a novelist for the summer - which is just, like, so awesome I can't *stand* it."

"But how did you know?" Aunt Susanna asked.

Darlene folded her arms and fixed my assistant with a mock-stern look. "I suppose," she said, "that you wheedled it out of Jacob. Most boys can't resist a pretty face."

Lindsay smiled wryly.

"It wasn't entirely his fault," she said. "I guessed most of it from what my girls were telling me and what you three *weren't* telling me. Did you really expect me to believe that Maddie would let a romance writer bum a free summer's stay off of her? She's smarter than that." She leaned forward, suddenly sober, her large eyes connecting with mine. "Anyway, when I realized that you hadn't called the police about the diggers after my accident, I figured you must have a better plan in mind. After all, relying on them didn't really work any better than the Beaumont letter, even when we thought it was real."

I physically flinched; but, of course, none of them knew the whole truth about the Beaumont letter. What worried me was the thought that the knowledge was spreading fast, too fast. The professor needed time to conduct his investigation properly.

If I can't stop the truth about the Beaumont letter from spreading, I'd better help Randall get to the truth faster.

The thought came fully formed and unprompted, surprising me with its clarity. It was true: helping him was the only option left to me. And Randall needed help. I was by no means an expert, but I could provide knowledge that might take an outsider hours to uncover. After all, I'd picked up a lot over the years. It was time I stopped balking and put it to good use.

The idea of working with such an irritating snob still grated on me. I wasn't sure I could do it without wanting to wring his neck, but now it was clear that doing so was a necessary evil. His expertise would go a long way towards clearing up the issues surrounding the treasure myth. And if nothing else, his testimony might help, should the Maddox family decide to sue.

In the briefcase at my feet was the letter from Alexander, the supposedly coded letter that he sent to his mother on the eve of his imminent death. The professor wasn't the first person to think that it was the key to everything, but he was probably the only person who could prove that it actually was. It would be my first gesture of real cooperation.

All of this whirled through my mind in a mere moment. I had only just resolved everything when Lindsay reached for the backpack at her feet, still chattering.

"...So that's when I came up with up with this new lesson plan," she said, and I was surprised to realize that I had missed some conversation.

"What?" I asked, blinking. "What did you say?"

Lindsay's brace creaked ever so softly as she pulled her tablet out of her bag, stray wisps of hair falling into her eyes as she bent. "Daydreaming, Boss?"

"She's had so much on her mind lately," Aunt Susanna said.

"Working overtime, too," Darlene added, her keen eyes fixing on me until I flushed. "It's a wonder that she's able to stay awake at all."

"I'm fine," I objected. "I was just distracted. What were you saying, Lindsay?"

She brushed the hair out of her eyes as she waited for her tablet to load. "I said that you owe me for a few day's work from home."

The pleased grin on Aunt Susanna's face only deepened my confusion. "Working from home? How does that work?"

Lindsay practically bounced in her seat. "It works. You see, I figured you and the professor had enough on your plates without having to worry about the day camps, too. After all, you weren't expecting to have to run those. They're my babies, and I really didn't want to give them up, even after the accident. By the way, it isn't fair that I have to stay off of horses for so long. I'm perfectly fine."

I pointed a finger at her. "If you think for one instant that you are going to lead those lessons while you're still under doctor's orders, you're crazy. I won't let you."

She only grinned. "You will when you see what I have in mind. Anyway, you're already outvoted. Darlene and Aunt Susanna think it is brilliant, which it is. Look at this and prepare to be amazed."

She flipped the tablet around and showed me a spreadsheet, five days of lessons, planned by the hour. She'd reorganized the whole thing, devoting the mornings to non-horseback activities like tack care, exercises for the girls, equestrian history, and detailed care studies. The afternoons, she told me as I read it, would be when they actually got on the horses. For three of the afternoons they would stay in the ring, where Jacob - who'd already been recruited - would guide the horses while Lindsay and Aunt Susanna coached from the sidelines.

"Aunt *Susanna* will coach?" I asked in disbelief.

Both of them nodded.

"It's time I got back into the saddle," Aunt Susanna said. "Figuratively, of course. With my knees, it'll still be a few weeks before I can actually get onto a horse."

While I stared dumbly, Lindsay said, "It'll work perfectly. This way, you only have to take two afternoons off a week, if you still want to do trail riding. Between Jake, Aunt Susanna, and me, we've got everything else handled. Darlene volunteered to help with the lunches, so that's all set..."

"I've got nothing else to do anyway," Darlene shrugged.

"...And I can still take care of all the paperwork and everything," Lindsay chirped. "I get to keep my job, and the girls can still do their camp while you and the professor are out chasing bad guys and finding buried treasure." She clapped her hands together and grinned like a child who has just discovered the cookie jar. "It's perfect."

I looked at the plan mutely. It was a very good plan. Better, in fact, than the camps we'd had in the past. Lindsay had obviously put a lot of thought into it. I hesitated to have her work, even superficially with the animals. But if Jacob was there, maybe it was possible to do it safely.

It would solve so many problems, not the least of which was allowing me to work mornings at the vet's in the summer, something that would greatly ease the financial burden. But still, I couldn't just say yes.

"What's the catch?" I asked. "What are you all up to?"

They looked so innocent that for a moment, I thought I was mistaken.

Darlene said, "Is it so impossible to think that we just want to help?"

I knew, from her tone, that I was not mistaken.

"It's entirely possible," I admitted. "And this would be a great help, an enormous help. I can't even tell you… But I don't think helping me is the entire reason you're volunteering in this way. I get the feeling that there is something more going on here and I want to know."

They glanced at one another and hesitated. Not surprisingly, it was Aunt Susanna who finally responded.

"Well, it isn't every day that you have a real, old fashioned treasure hunt right in your backyard, Madeleine," she said defensively. "Can you blame us if we want to get involved?"

"All we want," Lindsay added, "is a piece of the action. We want in."

"Is that too much to ask?" Darlene asked.

Under the circumstances, I had to admit that it wasn't.

"Anyway," Lindsay said, as though in summation, "the sooner we solve this treasure mystery, the sooner you can get these diggers off of your land and make it safe to ride again."

Her shiver was so slight that Darlene and Aunt Susanna didn't notice. But I did. If I needed anything more to solidify my resolution to work with Randall, this would have been the last straw. It was one thing to terrify and annoy me – but scaring Lindsay was something else altogether.

"I guess that's it, then," I said.

Suddenly, there was nothing I wanted more than to see Randall and get started. I was on my feet so quickly that the other women were startled, and I was half way to the door when Aunt Susanna stuttered, "But what about the plan, Maddie? Is it a go?"

I stopped and looked back at them.

"You're all hired," I said, then grinned. "Looks like we're about to have a very busy couple of weeks, ladies."

As I left, I heard Lindsay say, "It is *soo* good to be back to work."

I had to agree.

21

Randall still hadn't returned to his study. I put the letter into the safe, taking care to shut it before I left. In the brutal light of day, the treasure seemed as unlikely as ever, but that letter was probably the only way we'd find out.

I went out into the backyard and found Randall striding out of the woods, carrying his walking stick with Trusty trotting at his side. The professor's face was pinched up in an expression that I now recognized as puzzlement. Judging by the sharp way he swung the stick, I figured he was working through a particularly tough problem. He brightened a little when he saw me and picked up his stride, no doubt eager to find out about the letter. But Mrs. Fontaine reached him before I did.

I didn't know she was even on the property before she appeared, zipping out of the barn with one arm waving frantically and the other clutching something to her chest. I'd never seen the woman move so fast, nor look so eager. She was so intense that the professor, on seeing her, took an instinctive step backwards before righting himself. Not that he had any chance of an escape. Mrs. Fontaine was on him and plucking at his sleeve long before I could get there.

Mystified, I hurried and came into range in time to hear her say, "…So if you could just autograph these for my mother, she will be *so* thrilled. You are, without a doubt, her favorite author. When my daughter told me you were staying here, I collected all the books I could find and here, I've brought a pen..."

She pulled one of out her pocket, so delighted to hand it to her bewildered prey that she even condescended to give me a smile as I jogged up to them.

"Hello, Maddie," she said, and I was taken aback by her friendliness. "This is so exciting, isn't it? The farm *my* daughter takes lessons at is going to be in a book! Alice was so excited – not that she'll be able to read these for quite some time yet, but I did promise her that I would save a copy for her when she's old enough."

She noticed that Randall was standing, making no motion to use the pen, so she indicated the title page encouragingly. "Sign it to Alberta," she said.

The jig is up! I thought, panicking. *She's figured out who he is!*

Professor Randall looked at her, then plaintively at me, the "help me" so visible in his face that it was almost an audible cry. It seemed to confirm my suspicion, and I dropped my head into my hands. Just when we were getting started, this had to happen. Now the secret would get out and we'd be inundated.

Mrs. Fontaine continued to gush at Randall, all admiration and awe, and I thought, *Never would have pegged her as a history buff.* Then Randall said, in a tone as confused as my jumbled thoughts, "But why would you want me to sign *these*?"

He said it with such obvious distaste that I looked up. He was holding one of the books high so I could see it. I nearly choked. It was a large print hardcover with a gaudy cover, featuring a man and a woman grappling against a Moorish background, under the title, *My Lord Chieftain.* And in elaborate script under the tumbling, passionate pair was the name of the author: Gregorianne Vincent.

I clapped a hand over my mouth to keep from laughing.

"I was curious about you, so I looked your name up in the local library," Mrs. Fontaine explained. "When I couldn't find anything, I asked the librarian for help and she told me that it's common for romance writers to use an assumed name and even an assumed gender.

She guessed right away that you and Gregorianne Vincent were one and the same because she's a fan, too, only her favorite was *One Night in Bangladesh*."

She paused when she realized that Randall was still staring at her, then said defensively, "Well, I know this looks like a library book, but my mother is on Social Security and she bought it in a sale, so it's perfectly all right for you to sign it."

I heard someone, probably Alice, calling my name, but I ignored her to watch the interplay of emotion and thought on Randall's face as he sorted through the information. He took another quick look at the cover. He must have spotted the author's name for the first time, because he practically reeled.

Mrs. Fontaine went on anxiously, "You aren't upset, are you? I hope it's not an imposition. I know you're here to write, but when I learned that my mother's favorite author, Gregorianne Vincent, was here, I just couldn't resist…"

He cut her off, pointing to the cover, "You think I wrote *this?*" he sputtered, then looked around her at me. "*This?*" he asked again.

I shrugged, and Mrs. Fontaine turned defensive.

"You needn't be touchy, Mr. Vincent," she said, then surprised me when she added, "Maddie didn't tell us anything more than you were a writer. She told us you were to be left alone to study. She didn't give us your penname or anything, but when she said that you wrote romances, it was easy to put two and two…"

The look on his face was absolutely priceless. It was all I could do to keep from laughing aloud.

For a moment, Randall couldn't do anything more than stare. When he did regain his voice, it was a roar.

"Romances! My dear Madeleine…"

"I've got to go," I interjected, jabbing behind me. "Duty calls."

I sped off, leaving them to work things out. I heard Mrs. Fontaine say, just before I went out of earshot, "Honestly, I've heard of temperamental artists, but you are carrying this just a little too far, don't you think, Mr. Vincent?"

Alice was at the barn, trying to find her gear for a ride she had planned over the weekend with her friend. I helped her find it, chatting about the camp; then, Mrs. Fontaine came striding back in. It only occurred to me then that my joke on the professor might very well cost me a customer, if Mrs. Fontaine was sufficiently insulted. Anxiety swept over me, but to my surprise, she seemed calm, even happy.

"Everything all right?" I asked warily.

She was typing in her cell phone as she nodded. "Oh, yes. We got everything straightened out. I don't envy you, though, sharing a house with a touchy fellow like that. Still, it must be fascinating to live with an artist. He's so intelligent, isn't he? For a romance writer, I mean."

"Oh," I said, trying to make sense of this. "Absolutely. He signed your book?"

She beamed then, her face transforming. "Every one. Mom will be so pleased! But don't worry. I won't give them to her until August, as requested. We have to go. Have you got everything, Alice?"

They left, happy enough, and I went into the house. Jacob had gone home, but left the bike behind, leaning against the house and gleaming in the dying sunlight. I thought it must need more work, but as I ran a hand over its sturdy frame, I couldn't see anything wrong with it.

Teenagers, I thought, and went inside.

Randall was in the kitchen, pouring himself and Trusty a drink of water. There was no one else in the room, so I felt comfortable giving him a hard time.

"So, Gregorianne," I said, leaning against the counter with my arms folded. "You signed your book for Mrs. Fontaine?"

He was lowering a bowl of water to the floor for Trusty and shook his head in irritation. "Gregorianne! What a ridiculous name! Yes, I signed the bloody books. What else could I do without giving the game away?"

"But I thought you told me that the truth was worth getting into trouble for," I said. He gave me a sidelong glance that spoke volumes, but I was enjoying myself too much to stop there. "In fact, I seem to recall that you abhor forgeries of any kind."

I was a little surprised at myself, to tell the truth. It seemed only an hour ago that I couldn't bear even the mention of the name Beaumont, let alone verbalizing the word "forgery". Now here I was joking about it.

But even as I marveled at this, Gregory addressed me with another one of those looks of his, freezing my smug smile in place.

"I do, and I did, and I still think so," he said. "But I gave my word that I wouldn't tell anyone my true purpose here. I promised *you* that I wouldn't do so, and then you went and created an unbelievable story that I am a *romance* writer!" He ran his hand through his hair and exclaimed, "Romance! My dear Madeleine, of all the genres, why did you have to pick that one?"

I shrugged, but I won't deny that I was feeling a little ashamed of myself. Not that I was about to let him know that.

"I don't know," I said. "I guess I thought Gregory Vincent needed a more solid background story, and romances seemed the most likely genre to have pennames. No one would be surprised that there wasn't a Gregory Vincent. How was I to know that there was a Gregorianne?"

He grunted. "I guess you couldn't, unless you read the things yourself. But honestly, it was awful! I had to *pretend* that I wrote them, and that I'm writing another. She asked if you were going to be in it."

"Really? What did you say?"

"I said, of course you are. She got a giggle out of that."

I grimaced. "Thanks a lot."

"Turnabout's fair play. Anyway, she insisted that I sign the stupid things, so what else could I do? I signed them, and told her that she couldn't give them to her mother until the end of the summer. I made up a story about being mobbed by my fans and she bought it, and promised not to say anything, so I minimized the damage somewhat." He sighed, martyr-like. "Now I've got to get her mother some books signed by the real Gregorianne Vincent, if she even exists. I signed them G. Vincent, so it wasn't a complete lie, only I forgot and started writing 'Randall' in one. I had to finish it with 'Regards'. Imagine: *G. Vincent, Regards,* like I was a bloody robot or something!"

He sounded so put out, so suddenly *human,* that I burst into laughter.

Randall looked at me in sharp rebuke. Unfortunately, that only made me laugh more, and I dropped my head into my hands, letting my shoulders shake with the force of it.

"Gregorianne!" I laughed. "If you could have seen your face – oh my gosh, it was priceless!"

"Gregorianne," he repeated wearily. When I looked up, he was leaning on the counter beside me. While he still looked like he'd swallowed something disgusting, there was a distinct softening in his eyes, and I knew that the humor of the situation was beginning to get to him. "That's an awful name. A truly awful name."

I shook my head, wiping my eyes. "Oh, it's not so bad. It's just a girly version of yours. If you ever have a daughter, you can use it."

"A daughter!" His eyebrows rose in surprise.

"Well, you seem like the type of man who'd name his first born after himself."

To my surprise, he smirked at that and looked at his feet. "Yeah, probably. But…" he lifted a finger in defense. "It is a family name, so…"

"Gregorianne?"

He snorted. "No. '*Gregory*'. I come from a long line of Gregory Randalls."

"I didn't know that."

"Now you do," he said. "For your information, my family has a long and distinguished history in this country *and* in the one before it." He stopped, shook his head, and grinned at his feet. "So I'm undercover as Gregorianne Vincent, the bodice-ripping romance writer."

"Looks that way."

"I suppose it could be worse. You could have told everyone I was writing a cookbook, or one of those supernatural teenage dramas."

He shuddered and tightened his arms. "That would have been truly intolerable."

"I'll remember that for next time," I said, and he grinned wryly as our eyes met.

I was thinking, *He's not too bad, once he's put on the spot.*

What he was thinking, I don't know, but his expression changed subtly, and I realized I was being studied. It was as though he was seeing me for the first time. But where I was finding common ground, he seemed to be digging deeper, looking into what might be called my soul.

"Watch yourself, Warwick," Randall said softly, his smile still mischievous, but with an edge. "Leave the backstory to me, or I'm liable to start spreading some rumors about you and a certain shirt-tearing novelist."

I did a double-take as a sudden image caused my cheeks to burn. I tore my eyes away, snorting in feeble derision, saying the first cutting thing that came to mind: "They'd never buy it. The first rule of deceit is have a believable story."

Randall winced, but before he could come up with a comeback, I said, "I've brought the letter, by the way. It's in the safe in the office."

"It's *here*?" he asked, leaping from the counter like his hands were scorched by the contact. "Alexander's letter?"

"As promised," I answered and he bolted for the doorway, shouting, "Why didn't you say so before?"

Trusty barked and raced after him, and I was a step or two behind her. We were quick, but Randall was already at the safe, spinning the dial frantically and undoing the combination in his haste.

"Let me," I said, as I crouched beside him to work the door.

I pulled open the door at last and gestured to the safe and he dove into it, pulling out the precious plastic-wrapped item with as much reverence as though he were handling the Shroud of Turin.

"Excellent!"

He jumped out and rushed out of the room. Trusty and I followed.

He went back to the counter, pushed aside the various cups, pieces of mail, and kitchen instruments left on its surface, and laid the letter on it. Then he deftly pulled a pair of plastic gloves out from his back pocket and pulled them on, his eyes never leaving the page, his lips moving in silent recitation of the well-known words.

Trusty and I stopped on the other side of the counter, and I watched him as he carefully extracted the letter from its covering. Behind me, I heard the laughing chatter from the living room.

"Don't you think that we ought to do this in the office?" I asked.

He shook his head, completely absorbed in his work. "Better light in here," he said. "Oh, you have the envelope, too – fantastic! I had no idea this still existed!"

There was a gleam in his eye that was unfamiliar to me. He pulled the letter out and laid it carefully on top of its covering, then bent down to read it, adjusting his oversized glasses as he did so.

I leaned over and read what I had, over time, nearly memorized:

June 1, 1862

Dearest Mother,
Your letter of the 12th arrived yesterday
And I was glad to receive it.
Any word from home is always welcome. I
Pray that you and Avery are well. I al-
So wish to thank you for your kind words of
Blessing – they are dew-drops to my soul. Marched
Long today and I am exhausted by hours
Of training and miserable Poe-like terrain. We shall meet
Johnny Rebel any day and I am itching for the introduction.
To glory we go, hungry and tired, but with
New vigor and eagerness. It may seem strange but I have no
Fear, just regret that I leave so little behind for my dearest
Mother – just the earthy good contained in my home soil.

> *Do pray for me, as I always do for you, knowing our God is Just and loving and all is in His hands.*
> *Yours, always,*
> *Alexander.*
> *PS: When I fear, I think on the August words in my beloved psalmery, especially no. 29. Read on this and think of me. – AC*

It was written on what we were told was cheap, common paper at the time, and there were stains on the page from both dirt and moisture, maybe sweat or rain, or possibly - as the more poetic observers suggested - tears. There was a ragged tear in one section, where his pen dug a little too deeply, and several deep wrinkles that marred the beauty of the unexpectedly clear and well-formed cursive.

Seeing it gave me a feeling similar to what Mary's journal provoked: that this was a bridge to a time before, to people that were connected to me but never seen, whose lives - though ended - were as present now as they were then. Looking at the letter, I got the sensation that the dead hadn't gone as far away as one might think.

My morbid thoughts made me shiver.

Randall stirred, nodding vigorously.

"*Yes*!" he shouted.

"See something?" I asked.

He looked at me, his expression one of triumph. It took me aback – I'd never seen him look so happy, nor so young. He looked like a different man entirely: a man so alive, so full of life that his vibrancy was barely contained. I found myself remembering his crack about the shirt-tearing novelist and blushed like a schoolgirl.

Not that Randall appeared to notice.

"It is here, Madeleine," he said, his tone hushed with reverence. "It's here, I know it."

"What's here?" I asked.

"Give me another minute."

He pulled out a small, square magnifying glass and went back to his examinations, pouring over the envelope with almost as much care as he did the letter. This puzzled me, as there was nothing more on the envelope than the address and the usual markings of travel. With nothing else to do, I studied it, too, though I couldn't see anything more on it than had been on the copied version.

I was about ready to chalk up his statement to mere excitement when he interrupted my thoughts by pointing to the letter with his gloved hand.

"Look at that," he demanded, then pointed to another spot, then another. "Look at those wrinkles. Here's where the paper was folded and put into the envelope. You can tell that these are the primary folds because of the dirt that gathered on their outer spines. But if you look here... And here, you can see that this letter has been folded before, in a smaller square. See?"

He pushed the magnifying glass towards me, but I didn't need it to see what he was talking about.

"I see it," I mumbled and he went on before I could ask what it meant.

"And *here,* on this line. The ink is just a shade different color than the one before it. Also, the writing is a little different. Here, where he writes 'Long today and I am exhausted by hours', his hand is firm, his lettering is clear and solid. He isn't tired, not like he is here, where he writes 'We shall meet Johnny Rebel any day'. There his hand shakes, wavering a little on the 'H' and 'N', and here, where the pen went through the paper. And it changes *again* down below, but that's at the PS, were one would expect a change, so that's not out of the ordinary. Except for the obvious question that it should and has raised: why did he feel it necessary to add that line? Usually postscripts were written on the envelope and they were direct messages, like, 'Tell Uncle Ben that I am sending the books', or something like that, not this - which can only be described as a poetic afterthought." He tapped the page. "This was one of the reasons why I thought there was a message in this letter. Putting aside the clumsy wording, which seems to announce 'Here is a clue!' The fact that it was put in after the main body of the letter suggests that Alexander *wanted* special emphasis on this line."

"Which would confirm the treasure hunter's theory," I said. "That he wanted his mother to look at the hymnal and find the lines that point to the fields. But those fields have been gone over with a fine tooth comb, and not even a coin has been found. So where does that leave you?"

Pinching the letter delicately in his fingers, he lifted it up and dangled the envelope next to it.

"It leads me to the source," he said, and the gleam in his eyes grew stronger. "Look at these both, Warwick, and tell me what it is that you see."

I studied them for a moment before shrugging impatiently. I was annoyed by these guessing games, perhaps embarrassed by my lack of observation. My tone was sharp when I said, "I see an envelope and a matching letter. Nothing more. What else is there to see?"

Randall dropped them back on the counter and pointed to the deep lines on the envelope. "You have to know where to look. See these creases?"

"Yes."

"They correspond to the secondary creases in the letter, meaning that this envelope was folded with the letter in it. Perfectly normal - and that in itself means nothing, before you ask. So, the primary folds in the letter were to fit it in the envelope, the secondary ones were made after the letter was in the envelope, presumably sealed. But how do we explain the third set of folds?"

I frowned and looked closer. Yes, the third set of folds, weaker and much less noticeable than the others, were there. Now I was really confused.

"I don't know," I confessed. "But does it really matter?"

"Of course it *matters*, Warwick. I wouldn't have brought it up if I didn't think so, just as I have chosen to ignore the coffee stain in the corner, here. They matter because if you add this to the changes in the writing, you draw one unmistakable conclusion: that this brief, rather unimaginative letter was carefully written over a period of time. And *that* indicates that I was right, that there is more to this than meets the eye. I wonder if this is what our rivals knew when they decided to start poking around here..."

"But..." I protested, but he wasn't listening any more. The chattering laughter from the living room had grown louder, and the women were heading for the kitchen.

He swiftly placed the letter back into its packaging, along with the envelope, then put his finger to his lips with a significant look towards the hallway, and darted out before I could comment. I heard him hastily greet the ladies before the office door slammed shut.

Darlene came into the kitchen first, looking bemused.

"He looks very happy," she said. "What did you do, give him the keys to the Smithsonian?"

"You've got me," I said, shrugging. "The man is weird."

I kept his revelation - which didn't seem like much to me - to myself, puzzling over his excitement. What difference did it make if Alexander took a few days to write the letter? Maybe he was busy. Maybe he was a slow writer. Perhaps he was uncomfortable writing, and it took him a while to write what would be for most men of the age a momentary chore.

That might be the answer – but the easy dismissal didn't sit with me as well as it used to.

Lindsay, Darlene, and Jacob stayed for a hastily put together supper. I joined them after chores and even had time to enjoy coffee with them, thanks to a last minute lesson cancellation.

Jacob offered to drive Lindsay home, something that delighted not only her, but the matchmaking Darlene and Aunt Susanna as well. As she waited for him to bring the car around, Lindsay saw me bringing a stack of paperwork out of the office to sort on the kitchen counter.

"You can start leaving that for me now," she reminded me, and when I started protesting, she put her hands on her hips. "You want me to earn my paycheck, right? Besides, you've got detective work to do."

I laughed as Jacob came back in, insisting that he carry Lindsay's backpack for her.

"Don't forget your bicycle," I said as they turned to go.

He blinked at me, confused. "Bicycle?"

I began to despair about the future of our country. "The one Aunt Susanna gave you?" I hinted, and when his confusion seemed to deepen, I added, "The one you were working on outside?"

"Oh! That one!" He looked relieved. "That isn't mine. The professor asked me to clean it up for him."

"The professor?"

"Yeah. He said he wanted to start riding in the mornings. Well, see you tomorrow."

"Later, Boss!" Lindsay chirped, and they left me balancing a pile of pages on the stairwell, wondering what on earth would inspire Aunt Susanna to surrender Uncle Michael's bike to the professor.

I didn't have a chance to ask Gregory himself. He stayed in his office way past the wee hours of the morning, long after I'd given up on the paperwork and gone to bed.

The bicycle was gone when I returned from my run the next morning, drenched in sweat but grimly triumphant. I'd found no hole, but as I showered, I began to worry again. Just because I didn't find it didn't mean the diggers hadn't been there last night; and until I was sure, how could I allow the riders to use the trails?

On the other hand, how could I close them without arousing suspicions?

For the second time in two days, I found myself desperate to talk to Randall. But when I went back into the kitchen, there was only Aunt Susanna, pouring herself a cup of coffee while Trusty attacked her breakfast in the corner.

"Good morning!" Aunt Susanna greeted me as I entered. "Isn't it a beautiful day today?"

It was, but I hadn't noticed until that moment.

"Have you seen the professor?" I asked, tossing my purse on the counter and checking my watch. I barely had enough time to make a cup of coffee to go before I left. My haste, added to my anxiety, put enough stress in my voice for Aunt Susanna to take notice, her head tilting with curiosity.

"I haven't seen him," she said. "Something wrong?"

I'd already decided not to tell her about the new onslaught of holes and she seemed satisfied with my explanation: "I gave him the letter last night and I was just curious if he found anything, that's all."

"Ooh!" she said, perking up. "Now things will *really* start happening."

As I made my coffee, the back door opened and to my surprise, Randall came in, flushed, sweaty, dust-stained, and glowing with the after-effects of a good workout. He nodded to us.

"Fine morning for a ride," he said, wiping his forehead breathlessly.

"Did the bike work well for you?" Aunt Susanna asked. "It's been such a long time since anyone rode it."

"Oh, it worked like a dream," he said, and looked at me as he continued. "I covered more than half of the trails this morning alone."

Aunt Susanna was every bit as pleased as I was flabbergasted, and when he left to clean up, I asked her about the bicycle.

"He asked if we had one," she explained with a shrug. "He said he needed to get some exercise in the mornings if he was going to maintain his health while writing this book. I remembered Michael's and thought it might as well not go to waste. I must say, though, I didn't take him for a bicyclist."

"I don't think he is," I said.

I kissed her goodbye as I left. As I turned on my car, my cell phone vibrated with a text. It was from Randall.

Covered the other end of the trails. No holes today. Together, we can cover them all each day and keep track of our rival's progress.

Together. My partner and me. An enormous, crushing weight rolled off my shoulders.

Together.

My reply was pathetically brief: *Thank you.*

It was all I could think to say.

LETTER FROM ALEXANDER TO HIS MOTHER, CIRCA 1862,

Dearest Mother,

We wait for our marching orders and the dreary weather continues. I can hardly write for fear that the rain will dampen the paper and render it too soft for my pen. It seems the only soft thing in this harsh world. I do not mean to be morbid, but I look around at this sea of men and realize that I am the oldest among them, and this saddens me. I have had experiences, I have made my mistakes, and lived a life that was less than what it could have been. For me to offer my life in the service of this nation seems only a fitting end to my story.

Do not take this to mean that I am ready to die, for I am not. I have plans, some of which you know, others which must remain with me for the present, that render life too sweet to consider its termination. But if it is my lot to fall on the fields of battle, they can at least say that I have had my time and used it. You cannot say the same of James or Timothy – they have hardly started to shave.

The promise of the nation is marching off to battle, not in some foreign country, not against a hostile alien, but against our own kind, men whose ancestors threw off the shackles of white slavery and joined us in the common cause.

Now we are fighting each other. We are a divided nation, with half determined to permanently sever the bonds that tether us, and the other half trying to maintain them. But, how much more divided will we be once the blood of our sons stains the grassy knolls? When we leave behind a generation of widows and orphans? When we have churned up the ground, burnt the towns, and ravaged each other's fields? We say that we are fighting to free the slaves and to save the union. The one we may, indeed, achieve - indeed, I hope and pray that we might, that some good may come out of this war. But union, true brotherhood, is not to be bought, even at so dear a price.

I fear for my fellow soldiers, these boys with whom I work and train. I fear for myself and for those I hold dearest. I fear for those who live in the towns we have yet to invade, Americans in all but proclamation.

But when by myself, I fear most of all for our union. Others fought dearly for its creation – we fight equally against its destruction, but in fighting, are we not just digging a deeper crevasse to separate ourselves….?

22

We worked out a schedule. I would run one end of the trails, Gregory would take the other; if either of us found a hole, we would text the other to see the location before we filled it.

The second part was his idea, because he was convinced that he could learn something about the diggers from the placement of their digs. That sounded plausible to me, and I was put out when he seemed surprised that I wanted to be called to view the holes he found.

"What's wrong?" I demanded.

He shrugged. "It just doesn't seem necessary. I mean, you're not really an expert…"

"I've been tripping over these stupid things for three years straight. If that doesn't make me an expert, I don't know what does."

Randall conceded the point and for the next few days, I ran and he biked the trails in the morning, often meeting in the middle and walking back together before working our several jobs during the day. He was still redrafting the project that he referred to as "that blasted book" and it was impacting what time he could spend researching, something that he lamented to me more than once as we filled holes together.

"Never collaborate, Warwick," he told me once after a particularly grueling conference with his editor and co-writer. "It'll be the death of you."

"Aren't *we* collaborating?" I asked innocently.

"No. We're partners. That's different."

I didn't ask how, and he offered no explanation.

Joe texted from the west coast and I continued to ask him about the weather, driving the conversation as far away from the holes as I could. I managed this with varying degrees of success when we were just texting; but it was harder when he called, because I hated lying to him. Fortunately, these calls were infrequent and short: he was extremely busy and recognized that I had things to do.

"I do miss you, Maddie," he said one afternoon. "You just can't get good lobster out here."

"You are *such* a poser," I laughed, "pretending that you like me just to have an excuse to go out for lobster."

"Maddie," he said, his voice husky. "I don't have to pretend."

I felt at times as though I was having an illicit relationship. I couldn't talk about it with Aunt Susanna, Lindsay was more like my little sister than a close friend - and obviously I couldn't speak to Gregory about it. In fact, if Joe called when Randall was within earshot, I let the call go to voicemail rather than risk him overhearing. It was a reaction I had with him alone.

Gregory would have had no reason to link us together, except for the photo of us at the Dig's End party ten years ago in the office. He was studying it once when I came in to the office to get some papers. I was in such a hurry that I didn't notice his interest until he asked, "You know Joseph Tremonti?"

Startled, I looked up and met his gaze, but the sun glinting on his glasses veiled his expression.

"He taught a summer class on the farm when I was in high school," I said, then turned to my papers as though there was some urgent business with them. "Why, do you know him?"

"Oh, yes," he said quietly. "I know Tremonti."

I wouldn't take the bait. I left him in contemplation, scooting out of the room and counting myself lucky to escape a more intense interrogation.

Still, I wondered. The academic world was small enough that the two men knowing each other wasn't that much of a surprise. But the way Greg spoke made me wonder if they didn't have a history together.

If they do, it's probably best Gregory doesn't know about my relationship with Joe. Nor Joe my relationship with Gregory.

Every morning, Gregory started on one end of the trails, and I on the other, but we always ended up walking back together. And since people can't just walk each morning without making some conversation, we began to learn something about each other. I talked about the farm, my office job, my aunt, my uncle, and even a little bit about my personal family history. Gregory talked to me about his students, his job, his 'pet' research projects, and what drew him to history in the first place.

"Just knowing the names and the dates never seemed to be enough," he told me. "These were *people,* not statistics. They deserve to have their whole story told."

I couldn't help but agree.

He told me he was contacting other people to research aspects of the Chase/McInnis case, including that friend in the Charleston area who was employed in parks and recreation. One morning, as we walked back to the house after successfully filling another hole, he told me his friend was now looking into the official investigation of the McInnis robbery and lawsuit in the local records.

"The robbery report was filed *three* weeks after the event," he said. "*Three* weeks, Madeleine! Simply ridiculous. There is something wrong there, so I'm having Charlie look into it."

"What do you think he'll find?" I asked.

"Not 'he'," he corrected. "'She'. Charlene Schaeffer."

"Old girlfriend?"

He grinned at me. "Jealous, Warwick?"

I punched his shoulder. "Shut up. What do you expect her to find?"

"I don't know. But if there's anything, Charlie will find it. She's like a bloodhound once she's caught the scent. For instance, she's already found out why McInnis' list-making spinster daughter wasn't present at the lawsuit after the war."

It had never occurred to me to ask that question. Of course, if Mary Anna McInnis was concerned enough about the household goods to write a painstaking inventory, it would follow that she would be the first to report the crime, then follow up with the lawsuit.

I felt rather foolish as I asked, "What happened to her?"

"She died," he said matter-of-factly. "She went to live out the war with relatives in the country and caught a fever. She never saw the end of the war, nor the beginning of the lawsuit."

"How sad," I murmured. "And she was the one who filed the robbery report?"

"No. That was done by her father. According to what Charlie's been able to find out, Mary Anna left to live in the country about a week before, but that date is suspect."

I barely heard Greg's reply. I was thinking about Mary Anna and her careful inventory, and wondering if she'd left a diary. What did she think of the war? Was she a segregationist, like her father? Or did she harbor feelings of a different nature, nurtured and hidden from the bombastic man she lived with, like Alexander's mother? Would we ever know?

Given the length of time and the scattering of the McInnis fortune, it seemed unlikely to me that we'd ever know more about Mary Anna McInnis than we did now, and that was a pity. I would have liked to have known what she thought of the robbery, and the dangerous man from New Hampshire who had spirited it away. Probably the prevailing image of her, a snobby, cold woman obsessed with her wealth, was close to the truth. But what if it wasn't?

It was an idle thought, but one that stayed with me until we reached the house – where another idea occurred to me.

As Gregory leaned the bicycle against the porch and turned to brushing the mud from his shoes, I asked, "Gregory, could she have taken the goods with her?"

He looked up at me, startled, a lock of thick, dark hair falling across his face. "Pardon?"

"Mary Anna. Could she have taken the goods with her? To the farm? I mean, as you said, there was a significant delay in the report of the theft and she was awfully careful with everything. Couldn't she have taken them with her to protect until the end of the war?"

Shaking his head, he knocked the last of the mud from his shoes. "It's possible, I guess, but extremely unlikely. She would have known her father filed the report. Surely she would have told him what she did and cleared everything up."

"Unless she was stealing it from him," I said.

He stopped and stared at me for a long moment, blinking. "Why would she do that?"

"I don't know," I said, unable to shake the thought of Mary Chase, living in constant longing for books in the dark New England forests. "Perhaps... she was trying to escape."

He opened his mouth to protest, closed it, then said, "All right. I'll suggest it to Charlie. If she did steal the stuff, she would probably have brought it with her to her relatives. I doubt there's any trace left, but I'll ask her to poke around. Some of the family still lives on the farm. They might know something."

"The McInnis family still exists down there?"

"This would be Mary Anna's mother's family, the Carvers." He held the screen door open for me, and commented as Trusty and I passed through, "It's not a bad thought, Madeleine, but I don't like the idea. I still think the letter, the last letter, holds the key."

He hadn't made much progress in decoding the letter. He spent hours pouring over it, studying various Civil War era codes. He even went so far as to check out every Edgar Allen Poe book in the local library, using Aunt Susanna's card. But he found nothing. If there was a code, he couldn't see it. And while this frustrated him, it did not deter him: the more he looked at the letter, the more he was convinced that there was a clue within it.

"What makes you so certain?" Darlene asked him one night when we were all sitting around the dinner table.

Aunt Susanna and Lindsay had worked together to cook dinner – a spicy gazpacho and hot tamales - in celebration of the upcoming riding camp. They insisted that not only Jacob stay for dinner, but that Gregory come out of his office and join us as well.

"Celebrations aren't any fun unless they are shared," Aunt Susanna said when he protested. "Anyway, you'll work better on a full stomach."

He surprised me by acquiescing gracefully, and it was a bright, interesting conversation. Darlene was her usual, witty self, and Aunt Susanna was livelier than I'd seen her in months. She and Lindsay had been working on the new lessons plans and she grew more and more enthusiastic about the work.

"I can't believe it starts next week," she kept saying. "I just can't wait."

It was then that Lindsay asked about the investigation, questioning until Gregory and I explained about the investigation in Charleston - and Greg's insistence that the treasure was here, and the clue was in the letter.

"Why do you think that?" Darlene asked, leaning forward gracefully. Her eyes were shining, almost the same sapphire blue as the pendant she wore around her neck. The necklace caught the light and I was startled, a sharp memory piercing my mind.

For a moment, I thought she was wearing her daughter, Allison's necklace, a distinctive Native American piece that she'd never been seen without. This one was similar, with the same leather cording; but as it quivered against Darlene's neck, I saw at once that it couldn't be the same necklace. For one thing, that necklace was reported missing - along with Allison - and was used in the descriptions issued to find her. And for another, Darlene's stone was cut in a smooth oval. Allison's had been square.

No one noticed my reverie, because they were too interested in Greg's discourse about the letter. It was the usual one about his gut feeling and the careful lettering, and so on; but even as he explained, I could see the enthusiasm waning from his audience. Finally, when Lindsay and Jacob exchanged significant looks, Gregory jumped up from his chair.

"It's easier to understand if I show you something." He waved a hand over the table. "Clear this and make sure it's clean. I'll be right back."

We had finished eating anyway, so no one protested. Aunt Susanna started the coffeemaker and took Trusty outside, Lindsay and Jacob cleared the table, and Darlene and I took care of the dishes. The increasingly giggly teenagers made their way back and forth, jostling each other until I finally had to issue a warning in order to save the dishes they carried. As they made their way back to the table, quieter but undaunted, Darlene turned to me with a dish towel in hand. Her smile was wide across her expressive face, but the ever-present sadness kept her eyes hollow with loneliness.

"I think that's what I miss most of all," she said. "The noise."

She didn't need to explain that she was talking about Allison. I didn't know what to say, so I just nodded, murmured something about being sorry, and handed her another dish to dry. I wondered how long it took before the sting of a loss like hers faded.

As though she heard my thoughts, Darlene leaned against the counter next to me and responded.

"It's moments like these that you miss the most," she said, watching the two kids wipe down the table. They were talking in hushed, shy undertones, and it didn't take much imagination to see what was happening there. "The little, everyday things. Like eating together, driving her to school, sitting in the living room and picking on the show we're watching. I miss making her dinner, squabbling with her about the calories, and I even miss the mess she used to leave in the bathroom. I still find myself grabbing her favorite kind of ice cream when I'm in the grocery store. It's been ten years and I still can't adjust to the idea that she isn't coming home."

Her eyes welled, but not quite to overflowing. She stared at Lindsay and Jacob as though grimly determined to face life without giving way to her feelings.

I had long since ceased doing the dishes – how could you continue with something so mundane after an admission like that? I'd never heard Darlene say these things before, at least not to me, and I didn't know what to do with the information. Should I try to commiserate? Offer her a hug? Touching her would likely induce the very tears she was fighting against, and how could I empathize when I'd never had and then lost a daughter?

As I battled myself, she continued.

"I was robbed," she said.

"What?" I gasped. Instantly, my mind turned to the treasure hunters – had they gone from trespassing to housebreaking?

"I was robbed," she repeated. "And I was a fool. I was a fool because I put my career above her at times. I loved her, and I loved my career and I thought… Well, I thought, 'She's young and healthy, she'll outlast me, but how long will I have these opportunities?' I wasn't to know that she would…"

She caught herself and took a deep, shuddering breath. I couldn't move. The world seemed to have slowed to a halt, with the giggling teens in an outer orbit around this silent planet that Darlene and I inhabited. The coffee machine made hissing noises, signaling that it was nearly finished, and I found myself wondering when Greg would be coming back in. I wished he wouldn't. Not until Darlene was composed again.

"I didn't know that it would end so soon," she whispered. "I was robbed of a chance to say goodbye, to finish what I had started when she was conceived all those years ago. Intellectually I know she's…. I know she won't be coming back. But my heart doesn't know it. And as long as we *don't* know what happened to her, how can I leave the house? What if she comes home and I'm not there?"

Darlene's whisper had intensified until it was almost loud enough for the teens to hear. She stopped abruptly as the coffeemaker beeped, indicating that it was done. She glanced at me with embarrassment and put the plate she was drying carefully on the counter.

"I hope she brewed it strong," Darlene said.

I was struck by the idea that, for a few minutes, she had switched roles with Aunt Susanna. I wondered how often her usual attitude was a mask for her friend's sake.

For the first time, I was grateful that we'd been able to bury Uncle Michael. I couldn't imagine anything worse than his simple disappearance.

To move past the awkward moment, I said - a little too enthusiastically - that Aunt Susanna always brewed it too strong. I pulled out some mugs, and when I turned from the cabinet, Darlene was standing in front of me.

"I'm sorry," she said, and held up a hand when I started to protest. "No, you didn't need this tonight. But I am going to give you a piece of advice, as an old, old family friend."

"Not that old," I protested, and was rewarded with a worn smile.

"Older than you might think," she said. "But do yourself a favor, Maddie. No matter how busy you are, never forget to stop and enjoy the people you have now. The people in your life are a gift and, if you aren't careful, they'll slip away before you have the time to enjoy them."

I stared into those intense blue eyes, wondering what she saw that would make her feel that she had to warn me.

It was then that Gregory came back in, waving two freshly made copies and carrying a stack of worn books under one arm.

"Come on, class," he said, as he dropped the books on the table. "We have a mystery to solve."

23

Aunt Susanna and Darlene poured the coffee as we gathered around the table. With our steaming mugs in hand, we examined the pages in silence for a few minutes while Gregory arranged his materials.

When he was finished, he leaned on his fists on the table and looked around at each of us.

"All right," he said. "Since you asked, you've been drafted. What we have here," he indicated the copy of the Alexander Chase letter, which had been blown up to twice its size, "is a puzzle with two questions: One, did Alexander Chase steal from his employer? And if he did, is it hidden on this property?

"According to the facts that we can verify, Alexander Chase went to work for McInnis in Charleston in 1860. In 1861, weeks before Sumter, Chase abruptly went home to New Hampshire. Three weeks after he left, McInnis filed a report, accusing Chase of stealing from him. Then war broke out, and Alexander joined the New Hampshire regiment, later dying after Successionville. After the close of the war, the McInnis family filed suit against the Chases, who denied all knowledge of the affair.

"The existence of the Chase treasure is supported by three pieces of evidence: the report of the robbery in Charleston, the testimony of the Chase farm hands during the lawsuit, and the contested interpretations of this letter. We can't, from our position here, challenge the Charleston report. The farmhands testified five years after the fact and were so vague as to be next to useless – they claim only that they saw Alexander go out one night with a medium sized trunk and that he returned without it. When pressed for details, they unable to give anything more.

"We can't bring the witnesses back to cross examine them anymore than we can talk to the McInnis family about the robbery. What we do have to work with is this letter, a strangely constructed piece that many believe is Alexander's veiled confession to his mother and directions to the burial spot. But if he did include directions, they are very well hidden, leading some to believe that there is nothing to find."

He didn't look at me, but Aunt Susanna and Lindsay did, and I flushed.

Greg said, "Despite the confusion, I believe there is something buried on this property and that this letter is key to its location. With your help, I intend to crack the code."

In a few words, he laid out his reasons for thinking that the last letter was deliberately written, including what he'd already told me about the folds and the careful lettering. Then he pulled out another letter and laid it beside the first.

"This is a letter written by Alexander shortly after he joined the regiment in Concord," he said. "According to Michael Chase's notes, it was discovered tucked in Mary Chase's diary and it was used to verify the authenticity of the last letter. I've sent samples to experts who agree that the same man wrote both letters. Now, I want you to examine this letter closely."

We bent over it. He had copied it in full color, so we could see the water stains on the blue-tinged paper. Like the other letter, it was one page long - but this page was crammed with text, so full that Alexander had to sign his name along the side rather than on the bottom.

It was far more poetic – Alexander was ruminating on the efficacy of the war they were about to fight, and bemoaning the youth of the men he was fighting alongside of. In fact, the tenor of the letter was so different than the last that, despite Gregory's reassurances, I found myself wondering if they were written by different people.

I wasn't the only one who thought so.

"This one looks different than the other," Jacob pointed out.

Randall nodded. "Yes, it does. Yet all three of the handwriting experts swore to me that these letters had the same authors. So let's examine why they look different."

He pulled the earlier letter up and held it out, pointing to various places to demonstrate his theories.

"Look at the construction here," he said. "Look at the handwriting. Sloppier than the clue letter, indicating that he was writing fast in cramped quarters. Understandable enough, but look at the prose. He writes like a poet, with full sentences and lofty ideas, and with the kind of rhetoric that you find among these early self-taught philosophers. You can tell that he's probably read some of Thoreau and Emerson or at least was aware of their world view, though you couldn't escape it if you lived in New England during that time."

He paused reflectively. "So here he is, writing thoughtful passages anticipating reconstruction in this letter, apparently composing it in normal haste. Then two weeks before he dies, he spends several days carefully composing his last letter, which is beautifully penned, oddly constructed, and simplistic – a complete change in tone and delivery."

"Indicating that he was in a different state of mind," Darlene said.

"Yeah, 'cause in the first letter, he's almost against the war and in this one, he's talking like he wants to go to battle," Lindsay mumbled, scowling.

"And in this second one, he's almost saying that death would be welcome," Aunt Susanna said, tapping the second letter with a concentrated frown. "In the first he says he has a reason to live. Something must have happened between these two letters to make him change his mind. But what was it?"

"Had they, like, seen any action yet?" Jacob asked.

Gregory shook his head. "No. Except for some minor skirmishes, this regiment didn't see any actions until the Battle of Successionville, which is where Alexander received his mortal injury. It was a torturous death, but that occurred after this letter had been mailed. I agree with Susanna. Something must have happened to change his mind about death, but I can find no indication of what it might have been. His stepfather died shortly after he departed for the army, but they weren't close, and it's unlikely that he would take so long to mourn a man that he barely got along with. Mary Chase died a year after Alexander did, and there's no indication that there was anyone else in his life besides Avery." He sighed. "But his change of mind doesn't entirely explain this letter. There has simply *got* to be something else in it. There *is* a message within this letter."

He spoke with great impatience, but it was directed at himself. He'd been working on this for days - weeks even - and was no closer than when he began. I felt sympathetic, but I knew no good would come out of stewing over lost time. So I asked a dumb question.

"Everyone thinks that the code was in the postscript of the letter, right? The part where he says that she should look in his hymnal at number twenty nine?"

"Right," Gregory answered.

Jacob interjected, saying, "But it says 'psalmery' here, not 'hymnal'."

"Most hymns at the time are based on the Psalms," he explained. "We think that it was shorthand for hymnal."

"So then it doesn't indicate Psalm 29?" Lindsay asked.

There was a moment of dumbfounded silence. Then Darlene said, "Surely someone checked that?"

We all looked at Gregory.

He muttered, "If they did, I've no evidence of it."

We were silent for a moment.

Aunt Susanna said, "I'll get my Bible," as she left the room.

Jacob asked, "What I don't get is, why did he leave it in code? Why not just tell his mom, like, it's under the apple tree or something?"

"We think that he was trying to keep it from his stepbrother," I said. "Avery was a miser and Alexander would have wanted his mother to be provided for."

"So he encoded it to keep his brother from finding it." Jacob nodded. "Makes sense."

"Except that it's pretty obvious," Lindsay said, scrolling through her phone. "I mean, anyone in those days would have known where to look. It's tricky for us, because we might have the wrong hymnal, but Avery would have known exactly where to look. Oh, here's the psalm!"

"Get the King James Version," Gregory ordered, just as Aunt Susanna returned, lugging her big Catholic Study Bible.

Psalm 29:

Give unto the Lord, O ye mighty, give unto the Lord glory and strength.

Give unto the Lord the glory due unto his name; worship the Lord in the beauty of holiness.

The voice of the Lord is upon the waters: the God of glory thundereth: theLord is upon many waters.

The voice of the Lord is powerful; the voice of the Lord is full of majesty.

The voice of the Lord breaketh the cedars; yea, the Lord breaketh the cedars of Lebanon.

He maketh them also to skip like a calf; Lebanon and Sirion like a young unicorn.

The voice of the Lord divideth the flames of fire.

The voice of the Lord shaketh the wilderness; the Lord shaketh the wilderness of Kadesh.

The voice of the Lord maketh the hinds to calve, and discovereth the forests: and in his temple doth every one speak of his glory.

The Lord sitteth upon the flood; yea, the Lord sitteth King forever.

The Lord will give strength unto his people; the Lord will bless his people with peace.

"That's not exactly specific," Darlene sighed. "So the treasure might be buried in the Exeter, or in the woods, or in the fireplace, or was fed to a unicorn."

"You said that part of the fields flood regularly," Jacob said, turning to me.

"Yes, but that part has been searched a dozen times with a metal detector," I answered. "If the treasure was there, we would have found it by now."

"Maybe it's in the woods," Lindsay said.

Darlene rolled her eyes. "He might as well have said, 'I buried it somewhere in Chester.' If he wanted to tell his mother were it was, he would have been more specific. And before you say it, no, we don't have any cedar trees in the area."

"Bummer," Lindsay mumbled.

"I have to go along with Lindsay," I said to Greg, who was studying the Psalm with a scowl. "If he was worried about Avery finding the treasure first, surely he would have made the clue a little harder to find. Avery's dad was a deacon. Avery would have been as familiar with the hymns and the Bible as Alexander himself."

"Yeah," Jacob said. "But, like, did they even have codes then?"

That brought Gregory out of his reverie. He fixed the poor boy with a withering look that had even the usual oblivious Jacob looking embarrassed.

"Did they have *codes*?" he repeated. "Jacob, don't you remember that class we had on George Washington's spy network? If they had codes and counter signs back then, don't you think they would have had them in the Civil War?"

Jacob shrugged. "Like, I guess," he said.

Randall was about to launch into a lecture when he saw my expression. He sighed, rubbed his eyes, and resumed in a milder tone.

"There were many codes used during the Civil War, mostly word substitution, symbolism, or encrypting using a common book. And the use of code wasn't restricted to just the military – there are cases of gossipy soldiers encrypting their personal diaries to protect their careers.

"I think there is an additional code in this letter: If the intention was to keep the treasure from Avery, the hymnal clue would be too easy for him to break. But I can't see where the other code is hidden. If it were like a Stager code, there would be an odd pattern of words. If it were Vigenère or Caesar code, there would be a string of letters somewhere and a clue word to decode it. But I don't see either."

"I don't either," Jacob said. "It is written weird, though. Like a sonnet or something, but it, like, doesn't rhyme or anything."

"What's the Caesar code?" Lindsay asked.

Gregory pulled out a book and flipped it open to a page that showed a circular decoder. "It's a letter substitution. Let's say the letter A stood for F: in that case, Maddie would be spelt Rfiinj and Chase would be..."

He stopped, thought for a moment, then wrote "HMFXJ" on his pad of paper. He straightened, looked at the word, then at us.

I was gaping at him. Lindsay said softly, "Whoa. Dude, that was fast."

Greg shrugged and grinned. "A simple frequency analysis will break the Caesar cipher in minutes. During the war, both sides used it, but it was so simple, it was useless. So the Union started using the Stager code while the Confederates preferred to use the Vigenère cipher, which is a little trickier."

"How does the Vigenère code work?" Aunt Susanna asked.

He turned the page and showed us all a square filled with columns of the alphabet.

"It uses twenty-six Caesar ciphers in a sequence with different shift values and a keyword or phrase to decode it. It's trickier to decode because simple frequency analysis can only be useful if the code keyword is really short."

We stared at the letters in defeat.

Frowning, Darlene turned the book and leaned forward on the table to study the square. Her long nails playing over the columns, accompanied by the jingle of her bracelets, and I wondered if she was on the brink of a breakthrough. I saw Gregory watching her carefully, probably wondering the same thing.

I sat back in my chair and took a sip of my now-cold coffee. Trusty jumped up from under Aunt Susanna's chair and wandered off to the back door. It was dark outside and I thought, *I should take her out.* But I didn't want to leave yet.

I pulled the copy of the Alexander Chase letter closer and studied it. This time, instead of focusing on the words, as I normally did, I looked at the letter as a whole, as though it were simply a picture.

That's when I saw the pattern.

My hand began to shake. It was easy to see, once you knew where to look and everything pointed to it: the odd length of the lines, the awkward phrasing, the obvious care that went into forming the lettering... The cipher had been in plain view all the time.

No one was paying attention to me. Gregory and the teens were bent over an explanation of the Stager code while Darlene whispered to Aunt Susanna. My heart pounded so that I could barely speak and, when I did, it came out in a squeak that only Aunt Susanna heard.

"I found it," I said.

She stopped and leaned toward me.

"Found what?" she asked.

Gregory heard and turned around sharply. Shoving his glasses back up with his thumb, he whipped around the table and was looking over my shoulder before I could even begin to form the words.

"What is it?" he demanded.

"It's the layout," I said. "Jacob had it. It's written weird – like a sonnet, only it isn't a sonnet. It's a cipher. And it's written carefully, oddly, so that..." I took my hand and covered the paper so that only the first letter of every line was showing. "So that the cipher would fit along the side of the paper, where no one would notice it. He even emphasized the first letters ever so slightly, just in case Mary missed it."

Lindsay gasped. Aunt Susanna put a hand over her mouth while Jacob whistled low.

I turned in my chair to grin at the wide-eyed Professor Randall.

"You were right, Professor," I said. "Alexander *did* leave a message. And it's been here the whole time."

He nodded at me, his dark eyes shining.

It was then that Trusty, who had been pacing impatiently in front of the porch door suddenly threw herself at it in a frenzy of fury. Her barks, sharp and angry, cut through the celebration like shards of shattered glass and Aunt Susanna jumped, grabbing at her heart. Darlene, the closest to the door, leaned to peer outside. She pulled back quickly.

"Someone's out there!" she gasped.

24

Instantly, Gregory was tearing open the door, calling to Jacob. Jacob dashed for one of the cabinets, yanked open the door, and pulled out the heavy flashlight we kept there. They were out the door before I knew what was happening.

"What are they *doing*?"

My question came out as a panicked squeal. I was on my feet, my head and heart pounding, trying to see out into the dark.

"They're going after the diggers," Darlene said. By the time she finished speaking, I was out of the kitchen, heading in the opposite direction.

I raced down the hall to the office, my anxiety making me stumble when I entered the room. The gun safe was concealed behind the door, where Gregory had left a rolling chair full of books. I threw them aside, whipping through the combination with a hand so steady that it surprised me. I was all too aware that I was running out of time.

I yanked open the door and was greeted with the metallic scent of polished metal.

Uncle Michael wasn't much of a hunter; but having served a brief stint in the military, he liked his rifles and handguns and kept a small, carefully maintained collection. I had learned to shoot while I was a girl, and as Aunt Susanna didn't much care for the sport, she left me to take care of the collection. I hadn't shot much since Michael's death, but I'd kept the guns clean and always made sure that there was ammo close at hand.

I grabbed the shotgun, loaded the shells, dumped a handful into my pocket - and then nearly ran into Lindsay in the doorway. I brushed past her, leaving her staring open-mouthed as I raced through the kitchen, where Aunt Susanna was already on the phone.

It wasn't until I was outside that I realized just how dark it was. The moon was in its last quarter and its light was barely able to penetrate the inky shadows cast by the trees.

I knew where to go. I raced for the path, taking care to keep my fingers away from the trigger as I ran.

My heart was thumping, the blood pounding audibly in my head. I was barefoot, but I barely felt the roughened earth under my feet. Up ahead, I could hear Trusty barking hysterically, then she abruptly cut off.

Gregory was shouting something. I couldn't make out what it was. I was running faster than I'd ever done before, but it wasn't fast enough.

I came upon the scene suddenly. Randall was pulling himself unsteadily off the ground, calling, "Jacob, *stop*!" in a terrible tone.

The flashlight was on the ground as though someone had just flung it away, and in the near distance, my terror-heightened senses picked up the sounds of someone running away - and then the sound of someone in pain.

Randall whipped around at my approach.

"Gregory!" I cried. "Where's Jacob?"

I tried to push past him, but he caught my arm.

"Maddie, don't."

My eyes were adjusting to the dark and I could just barely make out the fresh pile of dirt. My stomach lurched so violently that I was nearly ill. Someone had been here, and I'd only just missed them.

When I tried to continue, he held on tighter.

"He's gone, Maddie. He's gone. Let him go."

Gregory staggered and let go of my arm as I called out for Jacob, relieved when he answered. I bent to pick up the flashlight and played it slowly over the hole before bringing it up to Randall. It was then that I noticed the blood.

"Gregory!" I gasped, and grabbed his arm in a panic. But he shook his head.

"I'm all right," he said, his voice thick. "Find Trusty."

"Trusty?"

I found her, faintly moaning, just as Jacob came stumbling back through the unfamiliar terrain. Trusty was curled inches away from a large stone that anchored the ancient rock wall. I handed my gun to Greg, the flashlight to Jacob, and then gathered my faithful friend in my arms.

Darlene and Lindsay took Trusty to the emergency vet clinic while we waited in the kitchen for the police to arrive. We treated Gregory's bloody nose, a souvenir of his brief encounter with the intruder. It took a while for the bleeding to stop and he seemed embarrassed by the attention.

"All I need is a long shower and short glass of brandy," he said, his annoyance muffled somewhat by the cotton Aunt Susanna insisted on shoving up his nose. "Where's the police?"

For all of Aunt Susanna's hysteria on the phone, fifteen minutes passed before they arrived. The officer, who was familiar with our trespassing problems, told us in no uncertain terms what he thought of our trying to confront the burglar on our own.

"You were lucky to get off so easy," he scolded, taking notes as he spoke, holding the pad out so that he could read his own writing. "Next time, call the professionals."

"And you would have been here in time to catch them, would you?" Gregory asked, and earned a scathing glare for his trouble.

Jacob volunteered to show the officer the scene of the crime, and he reluctantly followed the teenager out into the dark. Aunt Susanna, too nervous to stand still, went out on the porch to watch.

Gregory and I sat in silence in the kitchen. He pressed a wad of paper towels against his nose and looked at the ceiling. He seemed as angry as I normally would have been.

But I wasn't angry this time. I didn't feel anything. It was as though I was completely numb. I shredded a stray paper towel and watched my phone, even though I knew it was too early to expect a call from Lindsay. I knew if I thought too much about what happened tonight, I would either become angry enough to do something stupid or I would break down and sob, neither of which would help.

Gregory leaned over and grabbed another wad of paper towels, muttering in an impatient undertone. His muffled voice broke through my thoughts, and I turned and pinned him with a stare.

"You should go to the hospital," I said.

We'd had this conversation earlier, and his response was the same: a vehement shake of his head, a scowl, and, "It's nothing, I'm alright. Anyway, there's too much to do here."

He threw the used paper towels into the trash with a sharp movement.

I looked away and my gaze fell on the table, where only an hour before we'd been on the verge of a breakthrough.

As though he knew my thoughts, he said, "The intruders don't know either. They're stabbing in the dark. They've figured out that there is something here, but they don't know where. We've still got time."

"Do you think they've figured out where the cipher is?"

"If they had, they would have cracked it by now," he said. "These kind of ciphers are pathetically easy. We've got time."

I nodded slowly. I believed him, but I knew something that he didn't. Charlie White, the reporter, monitored all the police calls in the area and had a mole in town politics. It would be only a matter of days before word of this intrusion got out locally and from there, who knew how far this would spread.

I thought about Joe Tremonti, out in California, then shook the thought out of my mind.

One problem at a time, I told myself firmly.

I turned back to Gregory.

"We haven't got much," I said. "We'd better crack this quickly."

He nodded, gingerly pulling the paper towels away from his face.

The bleeding had stopped, but his face was a mess. I grabbed a wad of paper, wet it, and then surprised him by taking hold of his chin. He tried to pull away, but I stopped him.

"Hold still," I said firmly, and began dabbing the blood away.

Funny how this little act did so much to relax me. I suppose it was because of all the injuries on the trail, this was the most minor and the one I could do something about.

But even as I worked, a new feeling began to softly take hold of me, making me uncomfortable. It must have been the same for Gregory, because instead of teasing me or making some kind of joke, he stayed silent and looked everywhere but at me.

Then, when the blood was nearly gone and the feeling had grown too uncomfortable to ignore in silence, I said, "That was pretty stupid, you know. Running out there unprotected like that, letting yourself get beaten up. What were you thinking?"

He shrugged, glanced around the room, before focusing his dark eyes on mine.

My breath caught.

A lock of hair had drifted across my face. Gently, Gregory reached up and tucked it behind my ear, leaving a trail of fire where his hand brushed my face.

"I was thinking," he said softly, his eyes never leaving mine, "that I'd better get out there before you did."

For the second time that night, my heart started pounding.

THE CIPHER

Dearest Mother,
Your letter of the 12th arrived yesterday
And I was glad to receive it.
Any word from home is always welcome. I
Pray that you and Avery are well. I al-
So wish to thank you for your kind words of
Blessing – they are dew-drops to my soul. Marched
Long today and I am exhausted by hours
Of training and miserable Poe-like terrain. We shall meet
Johnny Rebel any day and I am itching for the introduction.
To glory we go, hungry and tired, but with
New vigor and eagerness. It may seem strange but I have no
Fear, just regret that I leave so little behind for my dearest
Mother – just the earthy good contained in my home soil.
Do pray for me, as I always do for you, knowing our God is
Just and loving and all is in His hands.
Yours, always,
Alexander.

PS: When I fear, I think on the August words in my beloved psalmery, especially no. 29. Read on this and think of me. – AC

25

Civil War ciphers might be easy, but Alexander's just did not give.

Despite his injuries and the excitement, Gregory was up half the night of the accident working on it - and went right back into his office after our morning trail inspection. He was still there when I left for work.

Before leaving, I poked my head in and asked how things were going. I received a dismissive grunt, from which I took that things weren't going well at all. I left for work and to check on Trusty.

Leah showed me the kennel where Trusty was recuperating. She was weak and obviously in pain, yet she wiggled when she saw me, struggling against her restraints to get up before finally giving up and licking my hand in fervent greeting. I cooed and stroked her and reassured myself that she was still my loveable mutt before I turned to Leah for the prognosis.

"She's broken a rib," she said, her lips tight with concern. "I want to keep her in here for a few days, keep an eye on her. I don't know what kind of prowlers you've got wandering around on your farm, but, if they're willing to do this to a dog, I don't know what they'd do to you or to the horses."

"We've called the police," I said, as we walked back into the receptionist area. Che Che was tapping away on her keyboard, carefully keeping her eyes on the screen. "They're looking into it. Anyway, they're too cowardly to even go into the barns, let alone get close to one of us."

"That's not what Darlene Winters told me," Leah said, and Che Che couldn't help but perk up at the name of our local celebrity. "She said that someone was hurt last night."

"The police are *on* it," I insisted. "What else do you want me to do? Call the FBI?"

Leah's lips grew tighter, but a client happened to come in with a whimpering Cocker Spaniel, and Leah had to tend to her.

I sat at my desk and resisted the urge to call home and see if Greg had cracked the code yet. It was annoying to be so far away from the scene of the action, yet I knew that it was probably best to let Gregory have his time alone to study it.

Over the next few days, we devoted every spare minute to cracking the code. Lindsay, Aunt Susanna, and Jacob spent their days teaching the camps, and their nights around the dinner table with Gregory, Darlene, and me. We poured over the cipher and the letter, looking for clues, and trying every conceivable combination of words from the two hymns and the Psalm mentioned in the letter.

Once Jacob grasped the cipher, he became fascinated and started encoding his own messages. He was proud of his new talent and sticky notes covered in his heavy scrawled began to appear on the fridge or in the barn, for Lindsay's eyes only. We all found this amusing, even Gregory, but I knew he was growing frustrated. Nearly a week had gone by and we weren't any closer to an answer.

However, we had learned one thing. Using deductive reasoning, Gregory had decided that the 'D' in Dear, wasn't part of the code. It wasn't stressed – it was just ordinary. That left us with Y-A-A-P-S-B-L-O-J-T-N-F-M-D-J-Y.

This deduction put us back at the beginning, double-checking each of the word combinations that we'd tried before, back when we thought 'Dear' was part of the cipher. But it was no good. The cipher held just as strong.

One night, Gregory and I were sitting morosely in the kitchen, a copy of the letter at hand and notebooks full of rejected key phrases tossed on top of it. It was late and we were tired, but our awkward silence wasn't simply from exhaustion and defeat.

Ever since the night of the attack, a sort of uneasy peace had settled over our relationship. Something had changed, making our old conversation style inappropriate and the new one impossible, at least for me. I'd been growing more aware of him as time went by and this new sight was as unnerving as it was unconscious. I felt as though we were going someplace that I wasn't ready for.

What he felt was impossible to determine. His whole focus seemed to be on cracking the cipher and, to everyone else, it seemed as though nothing had changed between us, at least on his end. Even I wondered if I had imagined it - it was only when we were alone that I knew he, too, was struggling with this change.

Of course, talking about it was out of the question, so we sat side by side, drank coffee, and stared at the opposite wall.

Gregory grunted and shifted in his chair. "It's just as well that I have to run to Charleston tomorrow," he said suddenly. "This thing is liable to drive me crazy."

"You're going to Charleston?" I asked. I tried not to sound too interested, but I don't know how well I succeeded. I felt massive relief that there would be at least a day where I didn't have to deal with my houseguest and his distractingly dark eyes.

This was tempered by the thought that time would be lost in the treasure hunt, time that would be used by our rivals. Not that they'd been particularly active lately. Actually, since the attack, neither I nor Gregory found a single hole or sign of their presence. Gregory took full credit for this, of course.

"Only took one encounter with me to make them stay away," he quipped earlier that morning as he was putting his bicycle away. "The so-called unstoppable force meeting the immovable object."

"By which you mean your face?" I'd asked, grinning.

The more logical reason was, of course, that they reckoned on our calling the police and decided that it was prudent to keep their distance.

But they would be back. If I knew anything, I knew that, and it kept me returning to the code and to long hours working with the professor, when every other warning sign told me I ought to keep my distance.

He was nodding in response to my question.

"We're finished with the book," he said. "Well, not finished. The first draft is finished, and now we're on to editing. My editor and my agent called me in to have a conversation about it and a new project next year. I figured, since I'd be down there anyway, I'd check in on Charlie's progress. You know how the academics are. Unless you sit hard on them, they'll never finish a project."

He smiled, but I wasn't able to enjoy the joke. I made a half-hearted attempt at a laugh, looked at my toes, and tried to clear my head. If I was so glad he was going, why did my heart feel like it had sunk to the floor?

Not now, Maddie.

"How far are we from a solution to that code?" I asked.

He sighed heavily and rubbed his eyes.

"Bloody thing," he muttered. "We could be days away, or weeks, or hours. I don't know. Today, Jacob and I ransacked the first hymn again, using every combination of words we could think of, but nothing even comes close to working. So we're going to start on the next one when I get back. I may send this out to a friend of mine, who cracks ciphers for fun and profit." He looked at me. "That would mean bringing someone else in on the project. I wasn't sure if you'd be comfortable with that."

"Not very," I admitted. "But we have to crack this quickly. Charlie White just published his story about the intruders, and we're bound to have curiosity seekers start trooping in."

Charlie White's story had, indeed, hit the online stands that afternoon. I'd been watching for it, checking his site every day, praying that he would overlook this one little story.

Of course, he didn't. The story came with the prerequisite sensational headline. His writing hadn't improved in the year or so since the farm had been featured; further, his information was superficial and weak, forcing him to pad it - adding more sensationalism than it needed.

Thankfully, Greg was reported simply as a "farm hand" and the story was creating only minor ripples. But I assumed it was the calm before the storm, and I was bracing myself.

Gregory was looking at me in that curious way of his, his dark eyes taking me in and studying me. I felt enveloped, as though I was being held without being touched.

"Easy, Warwick," he said gently. "Rome wasn't built in a day. We'll get there, don't worry about that. Anyway," he broke off eye contact and straightened, as though readying himself for something. "Anyway, if I can't crack it, it's a cinch that our rivals can't. I'm the best in the business. They are mere amateurs. You can hardly even call it a contest."

Relieved that he'd broken the moment, I couldn't help but laugh at this return to his egotistical self, which I think was his intention. He went back to business then, telling me that he was sending Jacob to look at the town land records the next day, after his chores were finished.

"Why do that?" I asked.

"He's getting underfoot. The classes are running smoothly, and Susanna couldn't come up with any farm work for him to do," he said. "But it's not a total loss. I'm sending him to determine that no land changed Chase hands during the war. It occurred to me that perhaps we haven't found it because the boundary lines have changed. It's a long shot, but I want to eliminate it."

I sighed. “Fine by me.”

I checked my watch and found myself reluctantly taking note that it was late, and I had to go check on the stables. I think he might have volunteered to go out with me, except Aunt Susanna wandered into the kitchen, wrapped in her bathroom and moving carefully without her cane.

She invited Gregory to share a cup of coffee with her. He agreed, and I was allowed to escape into the safety of the lonely night.

26

Gregory left early the next morning, before I got up. There was a note from him on the counter, telling me that he'd asked Jacob to check the trails in the mornings and warning me against any more "nighttime theatrics".

"*Wait for me before you go dashing out into the woods again,*" he said. "*No need for both of us to have bloody noses.*"

I was a little annoyed by this: I was certainly old enough to run things myself, and I was smart enough to know not to go into the woods at night without a fully-healed Trusty at my side. But I was relieved that I wouldn't have to mind the store entirely by myself and I realized that he was worried I would try to chase the nighttime raiders off on my own – judging from my earlier actions, it was not a far-out assumption.

As I was ready to leave for work, Jacob showed up and cheerfully took off on the bicycle, whistling in the clean morning air - the picture of health and good spirits.

The days passed slowly. I thought I should have been relieved by Randall's absence, but I wasn't. I was restless and irritable. With Randall down south tending to other business, Aunt Susanna and the others busy with the classes, and me at the vet's office visiting Trusty and filing forms, the code work ceased just when it was at its most interesting. The nightly meetings ceased, too, as Lindsay and

Jacob claimed that they were too tired to work and went off to hang out together.

Trusty was kept in the hospital - for observation, the vet said, but we both knew that she wasn't comfortable letting the wounded dog go home to a house under siege. That left me roaming alone around the house and the office, moodily sifting through the old books, trying to occupy myself so that I wouldn't have to admit how empty the house seemed.

I even brought a copy of the letter to work on during slow hours at work. Che Che found this amusing, and tried to help, but neither of us got very far.

Randall texted every once in a while, but I didn't want to encourage communication, so I was slow to answer. But he called me at work on the second day, I grabbed my cell phone, told Che Che I'd be right back, and dashed outside to take the call.

It was a gorgeous but sweltering summer day, almost too hot for pacing in front of the office while we talked. Randall was rushed, prefacing the conversation by telling me he had only a few minutes before he and his Charleston connection went to some library.

"Library?" I asked.

"More like a historical house with lots of unstudied journals, letters, and the like. Charlie has turned up something interesting down here, Warwick," he said, excitement infusing his tone. "It seems the McInnis family was remotely tied to the Lee family, and one of them wrote about Mary Anna's funeral in her diary."

"Oh, really?" I said, swatting at a hornet. "Anything important about it?"

Randall hesitated.

"I don't know," he said. "Probably not. It's just a brief mention in a gossipy journal, and the only reason Charlie found out is because she is friends with the curator of the collection that owns the diary, which has never been published. Charlie doesn't think there's much in it – just some speculation about a necklace Mary Anna McInnis was wearing when she died."

"A necklace?" I asked. "Was it one of the ones reported stolen?"

"No. According to the journalist, Mary Anna died wearing a simple ring on a leather cord around her neck."

"A ring? Like, an engagement ring?"

"We don't know. We're going to take a look at the journal now. I'm going to scan and forward the passage to you later. Like I said, it's not much, but it is interesting - a spinster dying with a leather cord around her neck."

"There was more to Mary Anna than we first supposed."

"Yes… And the date of her death struck me. It's almost dead center between the time Alexander wrote the letter from his training camp and the last one he wrote with the clue. Curious, isn't it?"

I frowned. "You think he found out about her death and *that's* what made him depressed? That Mary Anna and Alexander Chase were a *couple*?"

"I don't know," Randall said again. "It seems unlikely, but look at the evidence. Chase leaves, and stuff disappears from the carefully curated McInnis household. But Mary Anna, the sharp-eyed mistress, says nothing. It's not discovered until *after* she goes visiting. That makes me ask a few questions: Why didn't she notice the loss? If she did, why didn't she say anything? And why did she choose then to go visiting her relatives? Was it really to get out of a besieged city? Or is it that she had, let's say, personal reasons to stay out of the way?"

"That's a lot of leaps in logic, isn't it?" I asked.

"I'm only asking the questions. Let's say they were a couple. Maybe Alexander is in love with her, maybe he's just interested in her wealth. He convinces her to marry him. It probably wasn't hard to do – she's a spinster after all, and past her prime."

"Watch it," I laughed. "It's not polite for a gentleman to point out a lady is not as young as she used to be."

He laughed, then plunged back in. "But let's say McInnis found out about it and that's what lead to the argument in the warehouse. McInnis wasn't about to let a Yankee wanderer come in, marry his daughter, and walk off with the wealth. And by his actions, it's pretty obvious that Chase wasn't interested in marrying her without the money. So he steals the goods, and hightails it for New England, leaving poor Mary Anna with nothing but wounded pride."

"If that was the case," I countered, "then she would have called the police right away."

"Not if she was too embarrassed to," he said. "The man who claimed he loved her went ahead and proved that her father was right. Some women would rather part with their money than admit they'd been played for a fool."

I sighed and rubbed my eyes. I didn't like it. It meant that Alexander was worse than a mere thief: he was a philanderer, too. I could almost see Uncle Michael's disappointed face. He'd worked so hard to prove that Alexander had been misunderstood, to clear the family name. Were we about to prove that he was even worse than was previously thought?

"If he did betray her," I said, "she'd never keep the ring. The man broke her heart and stole from her father. She'd have gotten rid of it."

"Hell hath no fury, and all of that. Yes, you're probably right. We have another clue, but we're not really any further, are we?"

Deflated, I went back into the office. Che Che beamed at me from over her computer screen.

"Was that your young man?" she asked as I sat down.

I was confused for a moment, before I realized that she meant Joe. As I assured her that it was not him, it occurred to me that he hadn't called in several days and that his text messages weren't as frequent as they had been. He was busy, of course, but he'd been so attentive that first week he'd been away.

Just as well, I thought. *It isn't as though I haven't enough on my plate.*

Che Che's daughter, Melanie, came in the next day with her cat. Seeing her was a welcome break. We'd gone to the same high school and college, though at different grade levels, and she'd been among the group of students who worked the dig at my farm. Melanie was practically the spitting image of her mom, down to the same style clothing and French features, only she was two inches taller than her mother, just tall enough to lean on the counter while she chatted with the two of us.

We were still talking when Darlene and Aunt Susanna unexpectedly showed up at the office.

I was glad to see them and they were happy and noisy - bringing iced coffee for Che Che and me, and biscuits for the recuperating Trusty. Aunt Susanna was so lively that her cane hardly touched the floor as she moved about.

"What happened to the camp?" I asked, gratefully accepting my coffee.

"They're having lunch with Lindsay and Jacob," Aunt Susanna said.

Darlene chimed in. "We decided to sneak out and bring poor Trusty a snack."

She shook the bag of biscuits and the two dachshunds that were waiting in their crates for their owners began to whine pitifully.

Che Che hopped up. "She's in the back. I'll show you."

"Don't let the boss catch you feeding her," I warned as they followed Che Che, chattering happily.

I turned back to Melanie and found her shaking her head.

"Darlene Winters," she said softly, so the others in the waiting room wouldn't hear. "Now seeing her brings back a lot of memories. Allison and I went to school together. We weren't really close, but we hung out every once and a while. I couldn't believe it when she disappeared."

"Tragic," I said. The unfinished nature of Allison's disappearance always made me uncomfortable, and I looked for something else to talk about. Fortunately, the vet was ready for Melanie's cat so the conversation concluded naturally.

But as I was turning back to the computer screen, Melanie stopped and leaned over it.

"Do you know, the last time I saw Allison Winters alive was that night at your place?" she whispered, her eyes aglow. When I looked up, she nodded eagerly, shifting her hold on the cat's carrier. "I'll never forget the look on her face. She was coming up to ride that big bay horse, the one that was terrifying, and she looked as though she was going to her execution."

Her tone dropped even lower, making me lean closer to hear it.

"Why, what was wrong?" I asked.

"She didn't say," Melanie said. "She just looked as though she were dreading the next step. I was convinced for a while that she'd killed herself. She looked so… determined. I invited her to join us, but she waved me off and never looked back." She shook her head. "It was at that epic party your folks threw for our last dig day with that delicious Professor Tremonti."

I stared at her, shocked. Allison had been at our stables that night? I hadn't seen her and it was never mentioned in any of the reports. But then, why would it be? It was a week before her disappearance was even reported, and it was not unusual for her to go riding at dusk.

Still, it was chilling to think that she'd been there on that night of mixed highs and lows. While I was growing to hate Amber, Joe Tremonti's would-be-bride, the ill-fated Allison was taking her last ride on our grounds.

Melanie obviously felt the same way.

"It's odd, isn't it?" she said. "You just never know, from one moment to the next, when fate will change everything."

I went home at noon to help Lindsay and Aunt Susanna with the riders at the camp, but my mind wasn't on them or their proper riding techniques.

Melanie's words haunted me. I couldn't believe that Allison had been there, on the grounds, and I hadn't known. There was no reason why I should have: she'd contacted either Aunt Susanna or Uncle Michael for permission to ride, and I would have been far too distracted by the party and my crush to pay attention. What Melanie said about Allison's fateful attitude I dismissed as hindsight colored by later events, but what I couldn't dismiss was the idea that, if we had been paying more attention, the situation might not have ended as it did.

The girls were too busy riding to notice my distraction, but Aunt Susanna and Lindsay both commented on it.

"Something worrying you?" Lindsay asked when the girls were busy cleaning their tack.

I lied and said no, but Aunt Susanna asked, "Missing Greg? I know I am – the house doesn't seem the same without his noise."

"*No*," I said sharply, and left the stables before they could respond.

I went into my room to change, then down into the kitchen to grab a snack. It was only about 3:30 and a long, unusually empty afternoon stretched out before me. I was nervous and irritable, and I suppose it was inevitable that I should wind up in the office.

Alexander's letter was in the safe, of course, but copies of it lay scattered about Gregory's workplace along with notes and books and hymnals. My desk alone was free of the clutter, an island of the present amid the sea of the worn past. It seemed out of place.

I tried to pay a few bills, but my heart wasn't in it. I wondered what Gregory was learning in Charleston, annoyed that he wasn't calling me with updates, and annoyed with myself for wanting him to call. My attention wandered from my accounting software to my cell phone, but it lay by my hand silently, receiving messages from neither Gregory nor Joe.

When the silence and stillness grew too much for me, I gave up on the bills. I turned on some music to cover the silence, and began to tidy the room. I straightened the shelves and the papers on the desk, and began to clear the floor of the overflowing stacks. As I worked, the music and the activity began to work on my mood, soothing my troubled thoughts and relaxing my tension.

The corner of the room with Uncle Michael's old chair seemed to have been devoted to code-breaking, for it was piled high with old hymnals, devotionals, copies from Mary's old diary and Alexander's letters, well-covered with Gregory's penciled notes.

There were more books than I remembered Uncle Michael having, and I wondered how many Gregory had brought into the house. I loaded them onto the nearby shelves, double-stacking them in some places.

With the books out of the way, I went to work on the paper. I couldn't help but start reading snatches from the letters as I cleaned, reading until eventually I was sitting on the floor, paging through their correspondence. I noticed how similarly Mary Chase and Alexander wrote – they worried the same way, thought the same way, and expressed their concerns with rich detail. The pages that Randall had copied out of her diary were filled with concern about her only son and her loneliness, while Alexander wrote about the war and the country and his growing discontent. It was touching to see how they cared for each other.

Know that my thoughts are with you, my best friend on this earth, Alexander wrote to his mother.

(Alexander) misses his books, though he will not say so. I am arranging to send him a parcel with a few volumes in it, including a new copy of the little prayer book that has brought me so much comfort – God willing, it will reach him without damage, Mary had written in her diary about a month before. She then went on to lament how hard it was to get good books in her area, a further indication of her willingness to go without for her son's sake.

Sitting on the office floor, surrounded by the remnants of their relationship, I felt their bond almost as strongly as if they had been in the room with me. I couldn't help but wonder about Mary Anna McInnis, and the conclusions that Gregory was coming to. But how could a man who worried so about the youth in his regiment steal from a woman he was leading on? How could he, who seemed to understand his mother's isolation so well, take advantage of a spinster like Mary Anna? I was convinced that he couldn't. Gregory had to be wrong. But, if Alexander hadn't been romancing her, then how did Mary Anna McInnis fit into this story?

"This is impossible," I grumbled, looking down at the copies spread across my legs. With a frustrated sigh, I got up and began, again, to collect the scattered pages.

How can we solve a case that's been dead for a century and a half? How can we ever understand what was going on in the heads of people who wouldn't write it down? It's impossible. This whole thing is just too-

Suddenly, my mind wrenched itself from its spiraling pattern. I had just placed an enlarged copy of Alexander's last letter on top of the pile, when my eyes fell upon a sentence that I knew by heart, but had never actually noticed before:

> *...I al-*
> *So wish to thank you for your kind words of*
> *Blessing – they are dew-drops to my soul...*

Dew-drops...

I'd wondered before why the words were hyphenated, but today it jumped out at me, almost as violently as the emphasized lettering had jumped out on me the other night.

The papers fell from my hands. I nearly slipped on them in my haste to get to the bookcase, frantically scanning it for the book I placed there only moments ago. It was still there, the worn cover bearing the remains of a gilt pattern, a tiny volume that my uncle had bought on a whim at an antiquarian book fair years ago. Its faded orange binding was pulling away from the pages and there were only traces of the gold that once adorned the page edges. It was an elegant, but practical book with a Bible verse for every day, and it was obvious that my copy had been well used by one of its owners. Despite its wear, the print was crisp and clean and the title page was as bold as ever:

> *Dew-Drops.*
> *My speech shall distill as the dew. Deut. 32:2*
> *Published by the American Tract Society, 150 Nassau Street, NEW YORK.*

I held it in my shaking hand. This had to be it. This book had to contain the key word that Alexander was trying to convey to his mother.

Gregory.

I needed to call him. I had to let him know what I'd just found.

I dashed for my desk, looking for my phone. It wasn't on top, so I cast about, rummaging through his desk, the shelves, the piles of books, and even under the rocking chair. It wasn't until I sat down on the chair that I realized my phone was where I always left it – in my back pocket.

I pulled up his contact information and was about to call when the doorbell rang suddenly – almost causing me to drop the phone.

No, not now!

I was on the cusp of a great discovery, about to solve a mystery that had tormented my family for generations. The last thing I wanted was an interruption.

But curiosity is a powerful influence. No one I knew ever rang the front door, and ignoring it might mean losing a new client. Reluctant as I was to leave the office, I locked *Dew-Drops* in my desk drawer, and shut the office door behind me.

The bell rang again and I grit my teeth. No matter who it was or what they wanted, I was determined to rid myself of them quickly so I could call Gregory and get started on the cipher. I imagined the look on his face when I told him what I'd discovered.

"Darn it!"

I wrenched the door open, fully intending to send the visitor packing. But when I saw who it was, I froze.

"Hello, Maddie."

Joe Tremonti leaned against the door jam, his phone in his hand, and his BMW convertible just visible in the driveway over his shoulder. He was dressed in immaculate casual wear: jeans, rugged shoes, a polo shirt that strained to contain his shoulders, and cologne that wrapped around my senses and held them hostage. He was just inches from me, looming so large that there seemed to be nothing else in the world but him.

I gasped, gripping the door tightly, fighting the feeling of unreality. He couldn't be here. Not now.

"Joe! You're here. But – you're in California!"

Thank God Gregory is in Charleston.

Joe smiled at me, an assault that sent my brain reeling. The effect doubled when he stepped closer.

"So I was," he said. Then he bent down to whisper in my ear, "Let's just say I decided there was more fun to be had back here."

His lips were so close I could feel the warmth of his breath on my cheek, and it sent waves of fire through my system, burning away whatever vestige of interest in codes and ciphers that might have remained. I was completely taken.

When he kissed my cheek and murmured, "I couldn't stop thinking of you, Maddie, and your offer of a ride... Today a good day?" it was all I could do not to throw myself in his arms and give him whatever he wanted and more.

27

My memories of that afternoon have an ethereal quality to them.

I don't remember if it was Joe who suggested we start with a ride around the property or if it was me, but that's what we wound up doing. I had the dubious pleasure of re-introducing Joe to Aunt Susanna, whose frosty exterior was quite at odds with her normal demeanor.

"What brings you to Chase Farm?" she asked, after the normal pleasantries were exchanged. She was alone in the stables. Lindsay was out back, watching Jacob lead the girls in a run around the paddock. Aunt Susanna's eyes ran up and down Joe, but she showed nothing but a casual disinterest.

I didn't know how tense I was until Joe wrapped his arm around my shoulder and tugged me into a one-armed hug.

"Oh, several reasons," he said. "Some of them… Sentimental."

My heart did a little backflip, but Aunt Susanna was not impressed. She leveled a cold stare at me, which I had to brush off. This was not the time to discuss my choice in men.

I helped Joe select a horse and tack and met Aunt Susanna again when I went back into the barn for my helmet. She hobbled up behind me and tapped me with her cane.

"What is *he* doing here?" she asked, in a whisper that nearly echoed in the empty room.

I shrugged, trying to push away my own concerns. "He said he wanted to ride. I told him to stop by whenever. Is there something wrong with that?"

"We're in the middle of an investigation," she protested. "We're hardly in the position to entertain guests. I thought you said that he was in California."

"He was, but now he's back. And the investigation is stalled until Randall gets back," I said, faltering at the name. Somehow, it was difficult to mention Gregory in the same breathe as Joe. "Besides, don't you think I've earned an afternoon off?"

I brushed past her to join Joe outside. I found him surrounded by admiring little girls, while being watched by a confused Jacob and a bemused Lindsay. When I introduced Joe as my friend, one of the smaller girls asked if he was my boyfriend.

Joe answered the girl, looking at me with a twinkle in his eye.

"I'd say that was up to the lady," he grinned.

The girl was confused, but thankfully Colleen was on hand to stop her from asking what had happened to my *other* boyfriend. Lindsay and Jacob herded them back into the stables, allowing Joe and me to ride off without further explanation.

It was a glorious ride. Joe wanted to see everything, to refresh his memory of the old days, and his memory was sharp. He took the lead, and we went everywhere - down the old trails, across the old fields, and dismounted to walk alongside the narrow river that bordered part of the property.

I was tongue-tied, but Joe was witty and charming, maintaining a steady stream of conversation that had me laughing and blushing the whole time. We walked and rode and wandered and I remember thinking, *This must be a dream.*

But like any dream, reality tugged at the edges of it. When Joe asked about the hole-digging and the encounter in the woods, I left out Gregory's part in it. When Joe asked how I was holding up, I didn't tell him that I was doing much better, now that I had help. I just told him that I was managing.

He was obviously worried, but he let it go and spoke instead about his trip to California, about how uninteresting it now seemed to him, and how glad he was to be back on the East Coast. He talked about the kind of place he wanted to settle in and write, because he had decided that he wanted to devote less of his time to academic politics and more time to writing.

"I need a retreat to work in," he said. "You know, some place quiet and calm, peaceful but with a history. Kind of like what you have here."

I laughed. "With everything that's been going on around here, you could hardly consider Chase Farm a peaceful retreat."

He regarded me sympathetically. "It's been bad, has it?"

We were on our way back home at this point. It had been a long and full afternoon and our mounts were hungry, tired, and ready for the stables. I was buoyant, feeling both satisfied and eager to see what was going to happen next, but not so much so that I was unable to feel hungry. I was going to invite him to have dinner with Aunt Susanna and me, hoping to avoid answering his question, but Joe had drawn up and was waiting for my answer.

I drew up, too, patting my mount as she impatiently whickered at me.

"It's getting better," I said cautiously. "There hasn't been any activity since the incident in the woods."

He shook his head impatiently and looked around, as though looking for someone.

"I just can't believe their blatant disregard for you and the farm," he said. "It's unbelievable! I thought when that Beaumont letter came out that it would take care of everything. We talked about that and it should have worked. What did we get wrong?"

I could have told him, but I didn't, of course. He'd asked about Gregory, still thinking that he was a harmless romance writer, and

I'd told him that he was away on a research trip, which was the truth. But it had made me uncomfortable nonetheless. Gregory was a specter that lurked on the edges of the entire afternoon, despite my best efforts to banish him. I wasn't about to bring him up now.

"Some people," I said, "just don't want to let go of the dream of treasure. They insist that there's something out there, however unbelievable it is."

He nodded and sighed heavily. He believed me. But then, he had to. There was too much risk in believing the treasure story and we both knew it.

"People will believe the strangest things," he said. "I just hope that this is the last time we'll have to deal with them. I'm worried about you, Maddie. I'm worried about your safety. If anything ever happened to you... Or to your aunt..."

A cold chill made me shiver. The usually gentle woods once again assumed a sinister look and the gathering dusk turned ominous. I found myself wishing I was safe inside the stables or in the farmhouse.

But when he turned back to me, his grin had returned and the somber moment was broken.

"How about inviting me to dinner?" he asked.

There was nothing I'd like better; but in spite of all the potential, dinner wasn't the success I was hoping for. Lindsay and Jacob had gone home and Darlene had an engagement - so it was just Aunt Susanna, Joe, and myself around a plate of store-bought lasagna and a salad that Joe and I put together. I even found a bottle of wine in the pantry that Joe declared was just barely drinkable, and we buried it in a bucket of ice until Aunt Susanna emerged from her room.

At first, she seemed ill-disposed to talk. She sat with a preoccupied expression on her face, pushing her noodles around on her plate and refusing the offered glass of wine. I felt awkward - but if Joe did, he didn't show it. He effortlessly split his conversation between me and my aunt, until even she couldn't withstand his charm and began to soften.

We were nearly finished when Joe asked Aunt Susanna about how she was holding up against the trespassers.

"We're holding our own," she said cautiously. "Of course, we're going to beat them to it."

Joe looked blank. "Beat them to what?" he asked.

"To the treasure," Aunt Susanna said promptly, before I could stop her.

Joe asked, "So you believe there is one?"

Aunt Susanna opened her mouth, then looked at me in fright. In her effort to shield Gregory's work, she had forgotten that the forged Beaumont letter was not common knowledge yet. Now she fumbled to cover.

"My husband thought so," she said simply and to our relief, Joe accepted that explanation.

I suggested that we were ready for coffee and dessert. Joe helped clear the dishes while Aunt Susanna made coffee, and I daydreamed about making this a permanent arrangement.

It was after I set out cookies for dessert and was dreamily stirring milk into my coffee that Joe dropped the bomb on us.

"I was asking because I heard that someone else might come around here inquiring about it," he said, settling back into his chair and accepting the coffee Aunt Susanna offered him. "I don't suppose you've heard of a man named Gregory Randall, have you?"

Aunt Susanna nearly lost hold of her own mug and glanced at me in a panic, but Joe wasn't looking at her. His eyes were focused on me.

For some strange reason, I was calm. It was as though every emotion had abandoned me. I was being tested. I'd already resolved that Gregory Randall was not going to be exposed - not yet, not even to Joseph Tremonti. Not until I was ready.

"Randall?" I said, leaning forward to take a cookie that I had no interest in eating. "Sounds familiar. Should I know him?"

I feared that I sounded too disinterested, but Joe released my gaze and continued.

"He's known in some circles. He's a historian, used to have quite a good reputation. But that was a while ago, back when he showed some talent."

Aunt Susanna's lips tightened noticeably, but she didn't respond.

I wondered at Joe's tone. He sounded positively disdainful and a dreadful thought washed over me: that gap in Gregory's history. I hadn't yet found out what caused it.

Stay the course, Maddie…

"Oh?" I said, my curiosity pushing me beyond where I should go. "Sounds like there's a story there."

He shook his head, grinning, and Aunt Susanna said, "Why did you bring him up? Do you expect him to cause trouble or something?"

Joe looked up at her in surprise. "More trouble than you've already experienced?" he asked, and she did a double take. "I'm sorry, that was crass. No, it's just I heard that he'd been asking around about the Chase letter… And the Beaumont one."

This time it was I who was startled, but I recovered before Joe returned to me.

"I wondered if he'd contacted you at all?" he asked. His eyes, now a shade of metallic green, caught and held mine. His mouth curved into a slow smile.

In the corner of my eye, I saw Aunt Susanna gaping at me. She expected me to follow my usual practice, of course, and confess all. Joe's penetrating gaze and the Hollywood good looks usually had that effect on me.

I looked deep into his gold-flecked eyes, leaning forward until his cologne washed over me again.

I lied without blinking.

"No," I said. "I haven't heard from anyone like that."

After that, the conversation became warm, comfortable, and lively, with even Aunt Susanna joining in. Much, much later, I walked Joe out to his car.

It was a brilliant night, warm and just humid enough that the air felt as though it was a blanket embracing my shoulders. The sky was a velvet arc studded with diamonds, and the moon was the polished silver centerpiece. Tree frogs and crickets chorused loudly, reminding me that for all the darkness, there was life.

We walked out together in silence, and Joe reached out to take my hand as we strolled. I was thrilled at his touch, and I found myself wishing that I didn't have to let go. His hand was so strong and his presence so stable while my life was so shaky, filled with shadows and ambiguity. I wished to be part of his safe and strong world; yet it wasn't something that could be asked for. I needed to be invited.

When we reached the car, Joe turned to me and took my other hand, pulling me close. I lifted my face to his.

"Thanks for today," he said in his husky voice. "I needed this."

"Me, too," I smiled, then, "I missed you while you were away."

His grinned widened. "Why do you think I came back so early?"

My heart began to pound. I was so wrapped in a tormented dream-state that I didn't expect what he said next.

"Maddie," he said, his voice as softly caressing as his touch. "Randall's here, isn't he?"

It hit me like a siren, shocking me into reality.

"What?" I stammered.

His smile was warm, his eyes roaming about my face without a hint of disappointment in them.

"Gregory Randall has been here, hasn't he?"

When I stared at him, flabbergasted, he nodded knowingly and even laughed. "Oh, Maddie. You just aren't any good at lying, you know that?"

I very nearly pulled my hand out of his grasp, but I didn't. Alarmed as I was, there was no doubt that he knew and no point in denying it any more.

"How did you know?" I asked.

He shrugged. "It's a small world. I know people that he knows and word gets around about these projects, especially a figure with a reputation like Randall's." It was not a compliment. "He's been asking questions and some of them got back to me. It wasn't hard to put together the pieces. What did he want?"

"He wants what everyone wants." I did pull my hands out of his then, and turned away to lean on the side of his shiny convertible. The metal felt cool under my hands. "He wanted a crack at finding the treasure."

"And then what happened?"

It was an odd thing to ask. I frowned and shook my head. "I thought we agreed that there was nothing to find."

"That's not what I meant," he said, stepping closer. "Did you let him look for it?"

My heart was pounding and for a moment, I couldn't speak. That must have alarmed Joe, because he reached out and turned me back to him, firmly but gently. I looked up at him, but his face was in shadow.

"Maddie," he asked. "Did you allow him to look?"

"Yes."

It came out as a whisper, a frightened little noise that at any other time, I would have despised. I felt absolutely defeated, like a small child who has failed her parents. I almost wanted to run away; but like that small child, I didn't want to leave the man who faced me. His opinion still mattered.

His hands tightened on my shoulders. "Randall is the man you let me think was a writer, the one you said wrote trash. Right?"

I nodded.

"Maddie, why did you lie to me? Couldn't you trust me?"

His plaintive tone cut deep. “I didn’t want to worry you. I didn’t want to involve you. I thought, after a few weeks, he’d get discouraged and go away again. But he didn’t and he – I… And he…”

I trailed off. What was I trying to say? That he’d remained convinced that there was something to find? That he’d sucked me into the search as well? What would Joe say then?

Joe’s hands dropped from my shoulders suddenly, leaving me stranded in the middle of the dark while he took a step back.

“Why?” he asked. “Maddie, I thought we… Did he ask to see the Beaumont letter?”

I’d always known that Joe was sharp, but I’d never realized just how quick he was. It unnerved me.

“He didn’t have to, Joe,” I said simply. “He knows *I* forged it.”

His look was measured, cautious. “And the letter itself?” he asked. “Did you burn it, like you said you were going to?”

My throat tightened. I had promised him I would do just that and I hadn’t. Joe had warned me long ago that Maddox’s word was only good as long as no one looked too hard. As long as the letter remained in existence, the truth was only a few short tests from exposure. He’d warned me, and I’d promised.

And the letter was still in the bank.

“No,” I whispered hoarsely.

There was a sharp intake of breath. And then Joe Tremonti turned away from me. He was walking away, leaving me. My heart lunged after him, dragging me along with it.

“Joe!” I said and he stopped short. “Joe, please…”

He looked at me, and this time I could see his face clearly. Etched in it was the disappointment I’d heard in his voice.

“I told you to burn it. I told you that you were safe, all you had to do was burn it and no one would ever know.”

“But it didn’t make a difference, Joe. It *didn’t.* Gregory didn’t need to see the original. He knew it was fake before he came to see me – whether or not he has the letter in his hand, he can prove it. In the end it just didn’t matter.”

I was pleading now and his face, shadowed as it was, was impossible to read.

Then he said simply, "Maddie, why didn't you come to me? Why didn't you trust me? Why did you go to Randall, of all people?"

"I didn't, Joe. Once he knew about the letter, I had no *choice.* It was that or exposure." And then, as his fists began to clench, I went on, gaining confidence as I went. "But that doesn't matter now. He's on to something. I'm sure of it. I thought he was a fraud at first, but he knows what he's talking about. There's really something out there, Joe. I couldn't believe it at first, but it's true – there is something. We just found..."

"He's a thief, Maddie."

The statement cut me off mid-sentence, leaving me gulping for air. As I stared, he stepped close to me, looming above me until his head and shoulders blocked the moon and I was covered in his shadow.

"What are you talking about?" I asked, when I could finally speak.

His voice was like honey - smooth, sweet, smothering.

"Gregory Randall is a thief, Madeleine. An intellectual thief. Oh, he made that Revolutionary War find all right, but it was a lucky break, one that gave him a reputation far beyond his ability. It made him into a quasi-celebrity, and when he realized that he couldn't make lightning strike twice, he surrounded himself with talented underlings, and stole their research."

I was trembling, shaking as though I was standing in my short sleeves on a winter's day.

No.

"But Joe," I protested feebly.

He interrupted. "I'm not saying he's without talent. He's smart enough to negotiate his way out of that fiasco with only the slightest stain to his character. But he's without scruples, and he's been known to use little events like this one to build his legacy." He looked around, rubbing his face with his hand. "It doesn't matter to Randall whether or not there's actually a treasure here, Maddie. All that matters is that he gets a story, a book out of it. If he doesn't write about the treasure, he'll write one about the family that ruined itself chasing fool's gold. It's what Randall does." Then, through clenched teeth: "And now he's got *you* in his clutches."

My head was whirling. This didn't make sense, yet Joe was saying it and I had no reason to doubt him. Quite the opposite, in fact. He'd always dealt squarely with me, while Gregory had blackmailed his way into my house. I'd instinctively mistrusted him from the start. Perhaps I'd been right.

But he promised... He rides the trails with me...

But couldn't that just be another snow job? Didn't Gregory Randall have a vested interest in making sure I didn't give in to the trespassers? Didn't he have a reason to keep me indebted to him?

The letter – I didn't make up the clue in the letter. I found that clue, not Gregory. Whatever he might be playing at, he didn't fake that.

But that meant only that his gamble had paid off this time. It didn't mean anything more, and it certainly didn't mean...

I didn't finish that thought.

As I struggled through these conflicting emotions, Joe was sating, "You've got to get rid of him, Maddie. He's nothing but bad news. You can't let him use you."

I was shaking again, but my voice was steady when I answered him. My tone was flat, almost dead.

"I can't do that, Joe."

He was taken aback. "Why not? Has he threatened you?"

He had. There was no real guarantee that Gregory wouldn't expose the Beaumont letter if I threw him off the property now. In fact, it might goad him into keeping his promise, a promise I'd nearly forgotten about.

But Joe didn't need to know that. In fact, I decided that he'd better not know. I trusted Joe, but not to keep his temper where I was concerned. And Gregory must not be harmed.

"No," I snapped then calmed myself. "No. We made a deal. Whatever his motivations, I promised and I'm sticking with it. It's as simple as that."

"Maddie..."

I put my hands up and shook my head.

"I can handle this," I said, even though I didn't believe it. "I think Randall's on to something and, when he finds it, I'm going to be there to make sure it's claimed for the Chase family, if only for Uncle Michael's sake. I don't think Randall's playing me, but if he is, it doesn't matter. Two can play at that game, and I *am* going to be there when he finds it."

My determination gave an edge to my voice, cutting off any protest on Joe's part. We stood in silence for a few moments.

Joe ran a hand through his hair, looked around, then stared at me. His smile was enigmatic, somehow menacing.

"If he hurts you, I'll kill him," he said.

I stared, stunned. He stepped forward and I held my ground, letting him come close to me. Our eyes met and held and everything but his presence faded to the background.

"Will you let me run him out of here for you?" he asked gently.

I swallowed hard and looked at my feet. "No. Not yet. Please..."

He was turning from me again, turning to his car, nearly stomping his feet in frustration.

"Madeleine Warwick," he said and pulled open his car door. "You are the most stubborn woman I've ever met."

He couldn't leave, not now, not like this. Not angry. Yet I would not stop him any more than I could stop the little audible cry that involuntarily left my lips, nor the sudden tears that stung my eyes.

He heard the cry, then he saw my tears. And before I knew it was happening, I was in his arms.

"And Madeleine Warwick," he said, his face so close to mine that his breath caressed my face. "You drive me absolutely crazy."

Then he kissed me.

It was confusing and overwhelming. He was insistent, demanding, and my physical senses were so overwhelmed that all thought fell away. As his arms tightened around me, a dizzying, triumphant feeling rushed over me: here, after all this time, was the moment I'd been waiting so long for.

I responded, leaning into his kiss, my arms snaking around his neck. One thought emerged clearly:

So this is what it's like to be kissed by a strong man.

I don't know how long the kiss lasted. It seemed both an eternity and a moment later when he pulled away, stepping back from me. He was as breathless as I; but where I was weak-kneed and confused, he seemed to have gained in confidence. He smiled at me, then reached to trace my face with his hand.

"That's dangerous," he whispered. "A man could get addicted."

Taking my head in his hands, he kissed me again, lightly. Then, without another word, he got back into his car and drove off, leaving me alone in the driveway.

I stood watching him go, my thoughts a jumbled riot, wondering, *What happens now?*

"Well, well."

The familiar voice cut through the night air like a knife.

My first thought was: *He saw.* Guilt swept over me, chased just as quickly by the thought, *I've done nothing wrong, whatever he might think.*

I turned to face Gregory.

He was silhouetted on the porch steps, the light glinting off of his glasses. His arms were folded, and he leaned against the post in a pose that normally would denote ease and disinterest. But I knew him pretty well now, and I knew better.

"You're back," I said. My voice was surprisingly steady. I forced myself to walk up to the porch under his unblinking scrutiny.

"I am," he said, in a tone that was flat - so void of emotion it was almost frightening.

"I wasn't expecting you until tomorrow," I said.

I was on the porch at that point, leaning on the post opposite of his. I tried not to look at him; but his presence, for once, was more overwhelming than Joe's had been.

He was staring out into the night, and I studied the outline of his face. The light created deep shadows, and the man looked haggard, aged beyond what travel fatigue could explain.

"I caught an early plane," he said, then nodded towards the road. "So we had a visit from the great Joseph Tremonti. I wonder what he wanted."

"Do you know him?" I asked.

He laughed. It was a brittle sound. "Better than I'd like. What did he want?"

There was a harsh note in his tone, one that made me lift my chin in defiance.

"Dinner," I said, and when Randall looked at me, I explained, "He came for a visit. We're old friends."

"So I saw," he said dryly.

I was glad that my face was in shadow.

"Is that all he wanted? Dinner and... Dessert?"

Anger swept over me, righteous and dangerous. I clenched my fists, but my words made for a far more effective weapon.

"Not exactly," I said, matching his tone. "He came here to warn me against a Professor Gregory Randall."

Eyebrows raised, he turned to me.

I continued. "Joe said he's been poking around the archives, looking for the Beaumont letter. Apparently, *Randall* has a habit of making a nuisance of himself, poking his nose where it doesn't belong, uncovering things better left alone."

I saw the curve of his grin.

"Sounds about right," he said.

"Yes, it does," I snapped. "Joe didn't want me to be inconvenienced."

"Very considerate of him. Naturally, you thanked him for his trouble."

My nails were digging into my palms. "Naturally," I said coolly. "And I told him that you weren't a threat at all."

"Aren't I, Madeleine?"

His voice was infused with something that set off all my warning alarms.

Run.

"No," I said shortly and I turned to go into the house.

"Tremonti helped you with that letter, didn't he?"

I stopped short, then turned.

"What?"

He hadn't moved, except to shove his hands into his pockets.

"The Beaumont letter. He helped you forge it, didn't he?"

I opened my mouth, but when no sound came out, he turned and the light from the house lit his face clearly. He was grinning, but it was an awful, cynical expression that cut me like a dagger.

I managed to gasp, "What are you talking about?"

He looked at his feet. "You're smart, Madeleine. Quick, strong, beautiful - but all along, I knew you didn't have the technical knowledge to do that on your own, let alone convince a man like Professor Maddox to authenticate it. You needed help. You needed connections. Tremonti has both and he helped you. Then, when he learned that I was snooping around, he came here to see if I had put two and two together yet. Isn't that right?"

The pounding in my ears was so loud I could hardly hear my own whisper.

"How did you know that?"

"I saw the picture of the two of you in the office," he said. "It wasn't hard to realize what that could imply. Tremonti helped you with the Beaumont letter and now he's panicking. He came here to see if you'd destroyed it, right? That's the usual procedure in these affairs."

He almost spat the last words out, and my pride returned with a rush. I took an angry step toward the insufferable man.

"He did ask me about the letter." And when he started to grin again, I snapped, "But that wasn't the only reason why came here tonight. He wanted to warn me. To warn me about *you*."

"Me? I'm surprised he'd take the time."

"He told me that you have this cute habit of swiping material and stealing research that wasn't yours."

"That *I*..."

"Yes, *you*. Joe wanted me to throw you off the farm tonight. Had I asked, he would have stayed here to do it himself. Frankly, the only reason you're still standing here is because I've decided I'd rather put up with you than lose a chance at the treasure. Is that the *truth* you were looking for, Professor?"

Dead silence fell upon us. Gregory didn't say anything. He didn't move. He just stood there in the dark, an outline against a royal blue sky, absorbing the blow I so easily gave.

I stood watching him, waiting – hoping - but the only reaction I got was when his head dropped for a moment.

I found the silence worse than the argument.

Randall shifted and looked up at the road again.

"He said that?" he asked. There was no jest, just the same flat, dull, lifeless tone.

"He said Gregory Randall was a thief," I said simply.

He straightened, his stance becoming rigid. Softly, he said, "Well, now. Isn't that just like Joe?" There was a long, shuddering sigh, then, "I suppose you believed him. We do tend to believe the ones we're in love with."

I staggered, but recovered quickly.

"Can you give me any reason I shouldn't?" I demanded.

I waited for that denial, my stomach churning. Inwardly I was pleading with him, *Say something, Gregory. Tell me Joe is mistaken. Please, tell me he was wrong.*

But he didn't say anything. He stood there with his head down. Suddenly, I couldn't bear to stand out in the warm darkness, not with him so close.

I turned and went towards the house, feeling his somber gaze on my back as I left. But he let me go. He didn't say anything to make me stay.

It wasn't until I was in my room, with my door safely shut and laying on top of my old comforter that I was able to identify what exactly I was feeling: a keen sense of disappointment.

And loss.

28

My alarm clock jerked me out of a restless sleep and into a gray, rainy day that perfectly suited my mood. I took two pills for my headache and laced up my sneakers for my morning run. I went out the front door to avoid the kitchen and forced myself to start jogging.

Of all my bad runs, this was the worst. I slipped on slick earth, splashing in puddles, and ran into branches bent low with water-logged leaves. What was worse than all of these was the awful, sickly weight that seemed to pulled at my shoulders and upset my stomach. Try as I might, no conjured memories of Joe Tremonti's kiss could quite erase the picture of the expression on Randall's face last night nor the odd feeling of loss. When I came upon Randall, sitting on his bike in his slicker, waiting at our usual meeting place, the encounter was so startling as to nearly cause me to slip again. I reminded myself that I had done nothing wrong, and jogged passed him with as courteous a nod as I could manage.

I remember being glad that the glasses and hood obscured his face.

The noise of the rain aided in my determination to stay silent and not a word was said until we came to the back porch. While Randall parked his bike, I bolted up the stairs and was through the kitchen door when he called my name. I pretended not to hear it.

I raced up to my room to shower and change. I didn't want to eat, but habit took me down the back kitchen stairs anyway. I caught myself just before I entered the room, but not before I heard Aunt Susanna say, "…always had a crush on him. I just assumed that it was a teenage thing – not lasting. I'm sorry I was wrong."

A rush of heat flushed my face. As I crept silently back up the stairs, I heard Gregory say, "She deserves better," with a ferocity that seemed foreign to him.

It made me stop and listen.

Aunt Susanna spoke in a tone too soft for me to hear, then Randall said, "She's a fool. A silly little fool. She can do so much better than him."

"I know," Aunt Susanna said. "I know."

That made my fists clench tight and the blood pound angrily through my forehead. It was only with an effort that I tore myself away from the rest of the conversation. I couldn't listen to anymore of it.

In my mind, I argued with them the entire way to work. How dare they judge me! Aunt Susanna I could excuse somewhat – she didn't know the risk Joe ran for me in forging that letter. Its discovery could have cost him his career. But Randall? There was no excuse I could think of for his dismissive judgement except for jealousy, professional and otherwise.

How dare he? I fumed. *How* dare *he butt into my personal life!*

I decided I was glad that he saw the kiss. With difficulty, I dismissed the picture of his hollow face silhouetted in the porch light last night.

I was glad to get to work. Trusty was feeling better and Leah told me she would be ready to go home tomorrow. Despite distraction of the work, and Che Che's cheerful presence, the phrases, *We do tend to believe the ones we're in love with* and *She's a little fool,* chased each other around in my mind, like a manic dog chases its own tail.

We do tend to believe the ones we're in love with.

That one bothered me the most. It was said like a condemnation rather than a simple statement of fact. It was unjust and wrong, yet I could not or would not put my finger on just why this was so.

The morning stretched on forever, the lunch break was much too long, and it seemed the afternoon would never end. I was distracted and irritable, oblivious to the ringing phone, absent-minded when dealing with clients, and careless while typing emails and invoices. It was so noticeable that even Che Che commented on it.

"Good heavens, Maddie!" she asked in the mid-afternoon, when the waiting room was empty. "What happened to you? Did you have a fight with your boyfriend last night?"

I answered "Yes," then realized that she was talking about Joe Tremonti.

"No," I hastily amended. "Just some personal issues, that's all."

She nodded, unsatisfied, but was too good a friend to ask further questions. And it was a good thing, too, because it was about then that I realized that I never told Gregory about my discovery about the Dew-Drops clue.

I spent the rest of the afternoon agonizing over how to tell him. I didn't want to talk to him, wanted less to see him, unless it was to rip him apart for talking about me and Joe behind my back to my already overly protective aunt. At the same time, I wanted nothing more than to do just that, to get him so excited about the clue that he would forget about last night and we could go back to where we were: easy, teasing, free – and distant.

It never was about friendship, I reminded myself. *It was always about business.*

As long as I viewed him as a business associate, I could keep my temper in check. I could do that. I had, after all, had years of practice dealing with difficult people – one more shouldn't make a difference.

The sooner this is over, the sooner I'll have the farm to myself again.

For some reason, this was not nearly as reassuring as I had expected.

The long day finally ended and I set off for home, gritting my teeth and mentally preparing myself for the battle ahead.

The house was quiet when I got back. Aunt Susanna, Lindsay, and Jacob were in the barn with the students and I only remembered when I saw Aunt Susanna's note, that this was Friday, the last night of the riding camp. She and Lindsay had decided to throw a little party at the end of it for the students and the moms and nannies who came to pick them up. Naturally, as head of the stables, I would be required to attend, a duty that was a mixed bag: While I appreciated the excuse to stay away from Gregory tonight, it also meant that I wouldn't be able to work on the code with him.

I changed out of my work clothes into soft jeans and a short-sleeved flannel shirt over a tank top with my riding boots. The students expected me to dress the rustic part. Then I gathered my courage and went to knock on the office door. When I got no answer, I opened it.

Randall wasn't in. The room was in its usual chaotic state of work-in-progress, with my desk the island of almost sterile calm. It was quiet, too, the melancholy atmosphere disturbed only by the presence of a vase of bright flowers left on my desk, Aunt Susanna's touch no doubt. As I stood in the doorway, hesitating to enter and wondering what had become of the tiny book that I had in my hand only yesterday - I caught the scent of his cologne, hanging in the air as though marking his territory. I suddenly felt a breathless sense of loss.

Brushing the feeling aside, I went to my desk, unlocked it, and pulled out the little *Dew-Drops* book. Holding the tiny thing in my hands gingerly, I flipped through the pages, wondering how on earth we were going to find the key word in the midst of all of these pages.

Maybe there's another clue in the letter...

I went over to Gregory's desk and looked at the pile of pages, hesitating. Some of the piles had to do with his book, some of the others about the Chase farm, but it wasn't immediately apparent which of the many would contain a copy of the Chase letter. I began to gingerly poke through the piles, trying not to disturb them too much.

Greg's leather bound journal was under some discarded graphs. I was surprised to see it there – he normally kept it close at hand, jotting notes, careful to close it before anyone got a look at it. I tugged it out and placed it on top of the pile, then ran my hand along the edge, wondering what was inside. Dry notes about the McInnis affair? Snatches of his next book? Daily observations about life on the farm, maybe.

"Lose something?"

Gregory's voice came from behind me, making me gasp as I turned. He was standing in the doorway, watching me with a carefully blank expression on his face. The walking stick in his hand told me he'd gone for one of his rambling walks around the property. The exercise had brightened his face and the wind had played with his thick locks until some of them drifted across his forehead boyishly - and I suddenly found myself wondering why I'd never before noticed that he was so handsome.

I checked myself: *Silly little fool, Maddie, silly little fool.*

"You're back," I said at last.

"I am," he said.

His eyes were as veiled as I ever saw them, and he didn't hold my gaze for more than a moment. As he strode into the room to where I was standing, I took a step back, but he didn't approach me; rather, he went around the desk, and took the journal from me.

"Boring stuff," he said, and dropped in into the drawer while I stared.

He leaned his walking stick against the bookcase, where he normally left it, then stood studying it for a few seconds with his hands shoved into his pockets while I tried to find something to say. Then, I remembered the book and held it up just as he turned to me.

"Madeleine," he said quickly, "about last night..."

But I shook my head firmly, waving the book and fighting back a surge of resentment. I couldn't allow him to speak. If we started talking about last night, any hope we had of returning to the way things were would be hopelessly lost.

The mystery had to be solved. That was the primary concern. Not my feelings, not his. In the end, neither would really matter anyway. The only way forward was to pretend as though nothing had happened last night.

"I didn't come here because of that," I said abruptly. "I found the key."

"The key?"

His arrogant mask was back. He couldn't have sounded less interested.

I ignored it, pushing aside my discomfort as I nodded and held out the tiny volume.

"The key," I said, "to the letter."

As he stared, I bent back over his desk and rummaged until I found one of the copies of the Alexander Chase letter. I found the line and pointed to it triumphantly, holding up the copy of the little book as I read it out loud: "I also wish to thank you for your kind words of blessing – they are dew-drops to my soul..."

I'd scarcely finished when Gregory was at my side, his shoulder brushing mine as he bent down to examine the line through his glasses. Something like an electric jolt went through me at the touch, but I ignored it and handed him the book. His fingers brushed mine in the exchange.

He open it carefully to the title page and stared at it a long moment. He was so still that I began to doubt. When he shook his head, my heart sank.

"He *is* referring to that book, isn't he?" I asked weakly.

"It looks like it..." he said, frowning in concentration. "But where is it? Usually they would identify the page number and line or would have prearranged the number, but I don't see an indication in the letter..."

Gregory looked at the letter again, froze, then grabbed a pen and made some wild strokes on the page. Looking at his handiwork, he smiled - a genuine, disbelieving smile that encompassed both triumph and childish excitement.

"*There it is!*" he whispered hoarsely. "Right under our noses the whole time. Look, Madeleine, *look*."

He shoved the page at me. He'd underlined two words: *...I think on the August words in my beloved Psalmery, especially no. 29.*

He was whipped through the devotional, flipping pages until he found the devotional reading for August 29th. He read it out loud:

"The fear of the Lord is the beginning of Knowledge. Prov. 1:7."

His eyes met mine, shining brightly, furiously excited.

"We've got it, Madeleine," he whispered. "At last, we've got it."

For a brief moment, we were united and fearless. As I stared into the depths of his dark eyes, it occurred to me then - as it hadn't before - that once this mystery was solved, there was no reason for Greg to stay. He would return to his university and the next project, and I would go back to teaching lessons and balancing the budgets. The house and land would be free from trespassers, and mine alone once more.

Alone...

I swallowed hard and turned my face away.

"Then what are we wasting time for?" I asked. "Let's decode this thing."

29

Having the key phrase and decoding the message were two entirely different things.

I explained to Gregory that I had to attend the work party, but that I could work with him until it started - a resentful offer of assistance. I half expected him to throw me out, but he didn't; instead, he cleared a chair for me to sit on and we worked in close, somewhat uncomfortable proximity for the next forty-five minutes.

Conversation, oddly enough, was not a problem: we focused on the puzzle at hand and avoided personal comments as much as possible, and only once did I look up to find Gregory gazing at me in the haggard manner of the night before. As soon as he saw me looking, the expression disappeared and he threw himself into the puzzle with renewed vigor.

I tried not to wonder how the process took so long. For all our eagerness, the decoding process went in a slow, methodical manner that was only just efficient enough to exonerate both of us from any suspicion that we were deliberately slowing things down. At least, I told myself that wasn't what *I* was doing. I knew that the sooner Gregory left, the sooner my life would settle. In theory, I should have been working as fast as I could to find the treasure and speed his departure.

That was the theory, anyway.

We tried a combination of words first, using the first three words: *The fear of,* then *the fear of the Lord,* and then the whole phrase, and then single words: *fear, Lord,* and *beginning.* We were still working on *beginning* when Aunt Susanna and the class came in for the promised Farewell Party. The noise of their chatter and giggles gained in volume until Gregory dropped his pen, exasperated.

"So hard to concentrate with that racket," he complained.

My phone vibrated then and I absently pulled it out.

Dinner tonight?

Just a glance at Joe's name was enough to diminish the temporary comfort Gregory and I had discovered in the past forty-five minutes. I could feel my face flush and, when I glanced up, I saw Gregory was looking away with tightened lips.

I felt overwhelmed with the urge to run from the room.

I forced myself to answer the text and to answer it honestly: *Love to, but am working late tonight for last night of camp. Tomorrow night?*

He answered immediately: *It's a date. Don't work too hard.*

My stomach fluttered.

Then he texted again: *How's Trusty?*

I resisted the urge to show Gregory the thoughtful message. Instead, I replied that Trusty was fine and would be returning tomorrow. I slipped the phone back into my pocket, aware of Gregory's gaze.

Then, as the girls grew noisier in the kitchen, I rose and gestured to the kitchen.

"I'll go quiet them," I said.

The girls cheered when I came in. They were happy, flushed with the triumph of a successful week. Their four teachers - Lindsay, Jacob, Aunt Susanna, and Darlene - looked as happy and as exhausted as the rest.

It was a nice night, so I ushered everyone outside, and we served the treats on the back porch. The girls clustered around the food tables, chattering and laughing. Darlene worked the grill while

Lindsay and Jacob scooped ice cream, and Aunt Susanna and I filled in where-ever necessary.

For some reason, I was very popular that night. The students clustered around me to gush about their riding camp, brag about their achievements, or show me one of the simple trophies they'd won over the course of the week. I was glad for the distraction, something to keep me out of the office, even as I was consumed with curiosity – how was Gregory getting on?

One by one, mothers and nannies turned up to collect their charges for home and most of them were persuaded to stay a few minutes for ice cream. The night stretched on. Eventually the party dwindled and ended. Jacob took Lindsay home, and I shooed Aunt Susanna and Darlene into the living room to drink wine and chat so that I could be alone with my discomfort.

I cleaned the porch, filling a trash bag with plates, cake, and forgotten souvenirs, and wiping down the table, grateful to have something to work out my restless energy on.

Then I went inside and started the kettle. I stood, watching it warm, absolutely miserable. I thought about Joe and his kind inquiry about Trusty, seethed about the conversation in the kitchen this morning. That, and the phrase, *We do tend to believe the ones we're in love with,* was whirling through my head when I heard the office door burst open behind me.

I turned, but Greg was already in the room, waving a piece of paper, his face alight with excitement. He was in front of me in a second, grabbing my shoulders in delight, his eyes dancing.

"I've got it, Maddie, I've cracked it!"

"What!" I gasped. "*What?*"

He was so excited he was chuckling, practically dancing. He released my arms and waved the page. "Right here – read this! Read it, read it!"

I snatched the paper from him and tried to focus. His handwriting began carefully, then turned to scrawling, but I was still able to make out what he'd written:

Code: YAAPSBLOJTNFMDJ
Key: KNOWLEDGEKNOWLE
Message: INOLDFOUNDATION

I read it three times.

This was it.

This was really it. Here, in my hands, was irrefutable proof that Alexander Chase was a thief - that he'd stolen from the McInnis family, and left the loot here for his mother to find. Here was proof that I had been wrong, that Joe had been wrong, that the treasure hunters had been right all along: there was something buried here, and the old stories were true.

Here, too, was proof that Uncle Michael had been as wrong as he had been right. He knew that there was more to the story than historians would allow him to believe; but he had always insisted that Alexander Chase had been maligned - that he was a scamp, but not a thief. It was something that would have disappointed him, something I would have spared him if I could have; but I knew that he would have persisted until he found the answer anyway. I knew then, sure as I was standing there with Gregory Randall hovering over me, that Uncle Michael would have allowed the truth to be made public, no matter how disappointed he might have been. He never would have condoned the forged letter, no matter whose idea it was.

Unexpected tears stabbed at my eyes and I squeezed them shut, trying to shove away the sudden longing to see Uncle Michael just one more time. He'd died in pursuit of this information. How unfair was it that he never got to see the conclusion.

But I was glad that he never had to know about my lies, or seen how I'd betrayed his trust. Of everything that had happened to us over the past years, what I'd done to Uncle Michael had been the hardest to bear. It poisoned everything, altered my relationships, and made the one man I admired most a laughing stock. This clue, this direction, made my betrayal impossible to put aside any longer - and for the first time in years, I longed to see the inside of a confessional.

Forgive me, Father, for I have sinned – I have betrayed the man who'd offered me a home, a legacy, belonging. I made a mockery of the man who gave me everything I ever cared about.

Forgive me, Uncle Michael.

"Forgive me..." I breathed raggedly.

"Madeleine?"

Gregory's voice was distant, but tender. It was a tone that put me on guard. I opened my eyes and found him regarding me with concern, and I turned away abruptly.

He shouldn't look at me like that.

"We have to tell Aunt Susanna." As I said it, it occurred to me that we were actually going to see the treasure. My heart started pounding. "Oh my... It's really *real.* You were right. It's actually real!"

My voice rose into a squeak, and Gregory smiled at me.

"It is," he said gently. "And we found it."

There **is** *no* ***we.***

I shook my head. "Old foundation - what old foundation? What is he talking about? *Our* foundation? This foundation?"

"Think, Madeleine. This house – when was it built?"

I looked up at him, blinking. "The original building was built in, um, the 1830s? The new addition was put on in 1845."

His grip tightened. "They didn't move the house? Or renovate the basement?"

"The *basement*?"

The words caught in my chest. I gaped at him. But he'd never seen the basement. Even I hardly ever went down there.

"The *basement?* But if it's there... It can't be there – not here the whole time."

"There's only one way to find out. Show it to me."

It was an order and I remembered, *Silly little fool...*

I bristled.

And then something occurred to me and I said, "But..."

"Come on, Madeleine!" he said, striding over to the basement door. "There's no time to lose!"

It was no good trying to get him to stop. I shook my head and followed him as he charged down the wooden steps.

"You're in for a disappointment," I called after him.

I was correct. He stopped short at the bottom of the stairs, and his face fell as he gazed about in dismay.

The basement hadn't changed all that much since the house was built. It was low, dug out as a root cellar rather than the modern idea of a basement, and the succeeding generations hadn't seen fit to improve upon it. After all, there was plenty of room upstairs and our lifestyle kept us outside. But Uncle Michael's father had done one, significant thing to modernize it, way back before I was born.

"It's cemented!" he exclaimed as I approached. He turned from one wall to the next, then looked at the floor, running his hands through his hair. "It's cemented, Madeleine! We can't get at the old foundation!"

"I know," I said. "They covered the old walls and floor in the sixties. I tried to tell you..."

"But did they – did they change anything?" He looked around, then strode over to me impatiently. "Think, Madeleine. Did they dig out the walls or the floor? Did they find anything? Did they push anything out? Think, Madeleine."

He was standing inches away from me, and I stepped back, scowling.

"I don't have to think. I *know*," I snapped. "They did this in the sixties. As far as I know, all they did was put up cement over the existing walls. And if they found anything, don't you think one of us would have mentioned it by now?"

He didn't notice my sarcasm. He was back at the walls, checking the cracks, glaring at them, stalking around as though he'd be able to see the treasure just by pacing. He shook his head in annoyance, almost condemnation, and my irritation grew.

"It's behind here," he said, as he struck the wall with his fist. "It's behind one of these walls, and we can't get to it. Not without metal detectors and jack hammers. We're going to have to bore through them just to take a look! We're so *close*! So *close* and we run into bloody *cement!*"

He struck the wall again, then turned on his heel and returned to me, shaking his head. "What a mess! Whose bright idea was it to put up cement here in the first place?"

"I think," I said dryly, "that it was my grandfather's."

Something in my tone brought him up short, but not short enough. He sighed and looked around the basement.

"I was hoping to have something to show you tonight," he said, and his tone was almost wistful. "I thought it would be so easy. Now we're going to have to get in detectors and excavators. We could be looking at another few weeks of work in here."

"Oh, terrific," I said. "More confusion, more disruption, and we're going to start tearing apart the house while we're at it. And all of this is dependent on the idea that the cement pourers didn't actually discover the treasure first and steal it. Marvelous."

He looked at me in confusion, a confusion that I ignored as I continued, "And before you bring in the jackhammers, you *will* think to ask Aunt Susanna first, won't you? She might not be so keen to bore into the walls at random, especially since we are the ones that are going to have to pay for the repair and the cleanup."

He caught my arm as I turned to leave. "Madeleine, don't worry about the expense. We'll work something out, the two of us."

I threw his arm off, all the pent up frustrations of the day exploding at last.

"The two of us?" I spat back at him. "The *two* of us? There *is* no us, Professor Randall, there is me and there is you, and that's it. Do you understand me? That's it, and that's all, and that's all there ever *was*."

Randall stood totally still for a minute. I couldn't read his eyes, because the light was reflecting off of his ever-present glasses - but for once, I didn't need to. The red stain blossoming across his face told me that my message had gotten through.

With visible effort, he maintained his calm. "Madeleine," he said slowly, "about last night…"

I cut him off.

"I don't owe you a *word* about last night," I hissed. "Since when have I given you permission to pry into my personal life? You have no right to it and no right to judge. Who I date and who I fall in love with is *none of your concern.* Joe Tremonti was part of my life long before you *blackmailed* your way into it."

He looked shocked. I stepped in and pushed the point.

"That's right. You're here because you're a blackmailer, a manipulator. Joe is here because I *want* him here. I may be a 'silly little fool', but I'm smart enough to know what I want and how to get it. I'm just smart enough to know which man is on my side and which one is here to just make a name for himself." I jabbed my finger at his chest. "Whatever you and my aunt might think, I know where to put my trust, and it's not with the man who uses extortion to get ahead."

His hands were flexing and clenching as his jaw worked, and I thought, *He's going to punch a wall and break his hand.*

But he didn't. Instead, he reined himself in, and the tone he used when he spoke was so flat it was terrifying.

"So you've decided that Tremonti is the man you can trust?" he asked.

I refused to flinch. "I know he is. When I needed someone to lean on, Joe was always there for me. Like he is now. Like he'll be permanently, once this whole matter is finished and I've sent *you* packing back to Hadley College."

I turned on my heel, intending to stomp out, but his quiet voice stopped me in my tracks.

"Always there for you?" he asked.

I turned and found him glowering at me, his jaw so rigid the words could hardly get out.

"After all that we've gone through these past weeks, you still think of *Joe Tremonti* as your rock? Your knight in shining armor? Do you even know the man?"

"I know him enough to know that he's a real man," I said. "That's enough for me."

Although I didn't think it was possible, the color on his face went a shade darker.

"Before you go make this proclamation public," he said, "let me ask you this: what kind of 'real' man convinces the woman he loves to lie?"

The question hit me like a blow to the chest. Before I could recover, he was pushing on.

"What kind of a man has her put her integrity on the line? Convinces her that she is too weak to face the truth head on, and then helps her to risk her reputation and livelihood by forging documents?" He took another step forward. "What kind of a man helps the woman he loves to construct the lie, and then *leaves* her to bear it alone? What man leaves the woman he cares about alone in her hour of need? What is your definition of a *real* man, Madeleine? Who lies, then walks, and only comes back when it's convenient for him to do so? Is that what you want? A pretty boy who encourages you to avoid what you ought to face? The man who thinks that you are a…"

"A silly little fool?" I interrupted, cutting him off. "I heard you this morning. Discussing my personal life, as though you had a share in it. You don't. You never have. And before you get all high and mighty, do I have to remind you exactly *why* I allowed you to stay here? Do you want to talk about manipulation? Do you want to talk about leaving someone high and dry?"

"I *haven't* left!"

He practically roared at me, with a force that made me take a step back.

"I wouldn't leave you, Madeleine. I haven't and I won't, not until this is finished, not until you're safe. If I haven't proven that by now, then..."

The words strangled in his throat. His hands dropped to his sides helplessly as he slowly shook his head at me.

"Oh, God, Maddie," he finally said. "What else can I *do*?"

In the sudden silence, I stared at him, stunned. He must have seen something in my face, though what it was, I have no idea. Whatever he saw, it brought that mask down again and the cynical twist back into his lips.

"You don't love him, you know," he said. "But I guess that doesn't matter, does it?"

I wavered. For one brief moment, I wondered if I was as sure about my decision as I claimed. But the moment passed and I squashed the thought.

The burning dark eyes, no longer veiled by the reflection, caught mine and held them.

"After all of this," Gregory said simply. "It's still Joe Tremonti, isn't it?"

I raised my chin defiantly.

"It's always been Joe Tremonti," I said. "Always."

I couldn't stand it anymore. I turned on my heel and fled up the back steps.

30

I stormed up the stairs and slammed the door shut behind me. My breath was coming in shallow gasps, and the feeling that I had just stepped off a cliff into empty space had my knees shaking. I couldn't stay where I was – either Aunt Susanna would come in and demand an explanation or Greg would appear and the whole argument would start again. But where to go?

I heard Darlene in the hall, so I darted through the kitchen and outside into the misty, warm air. If anyone asked, I was checking on the horses. It was what I had to do anyway.

The stables did not hold their usual charm for me that night. I checked bedding, rubbed noses, and spoke soothing words to the boarders – while in my head, ragged shreds of the argument chased each other.

What kind of a 'real' man convinces the woman he loves to lie?

Greybeard whickered at me, nosing around the pocket of my flannel shirt for a carrot, but I barely noticed. I absently noted that all seemed in order, that Lindsay and Jacob had done their usual thorough job of cleaning up after the daily events.

I checked the supply cabinet. It was locked and there was a sticky note on it - in code - from Jacob to Lindsay, and I smiled in spite of myself.

Jacob had grown on me in the previous few weeks. He'd proven himself to be hard working, able, cheerful even when tired, and not too proud to do any of the jobs put before him. He had greatly eased the burden of my chores, and was a hit not only with the girls, but with the adult riders as well. He was a real find – and Gregory had been the one who'd found him.

What man leaves the woman he cares about alone in her hour of need?

Joe Tremonti was part of my existence long before you blackmailed your way into it.

Stop this, Maddie. Stop this.

It's easy to tell yourself to let something go. It's hard to actually do it when fury surges within, swaying your emotions from one extreme to another. It was only through great effort that I kept myself from breaking down, either in sobs or in another argument with my former partner. I had no idea which extreme would be worse.

I checked everything in the stables twice, bid goodnight to the boarders, and now had no reason to stay outside. Yet I did *not* want to go back inside the house. I did not want to face Greg or Aunt Susanna or anywhere near that office. With restless energy surging through me, I felt an intense longing to disappear. To run.

I grabbed the battery-operated lantern we kept in the barn for emergencies, and headed for the riding trails.

I never let my riders or guests do the trails at night. Even without the trespassers, the winding paths, low branches, and root-pocked terrain are not safe for nightly strolls.

But I wasn't in a reasonable mood. The moon was full, shining strongly through the overhead canopy of branches, and walking the lonely trails was a good deal better than facing the reality waiting for me back at the house.

It took only a few steps into the trail before I started feeling isolated. I took deep breaths and long steps with great care. The moonlight was strong enough that I didn't need my lantern - which suited me well, because I didn't care to signal my location to anyone at this point. I walked firmly, battling fears and memories, too busy being angry to turn back.

Around and around in my head, I read off the list of Gregory's crimes, starting from when he first appeared in my house and threatened to expose my secret about the letter. The way he insinuated himself into my home, got out of doing the chores by hiring Jacob, and complained about Aunt Susanna's fussing, how he constantly bothered me for information, keeping us up late at night to pump us for information, and - worst of all - ruining my moment with Joe. I remembered the arrogance, the intrusions, and the insinuations, until my blood began to boil.

The sooner Gregory Randall gets off my property, the better.

Then the path turned, the trees cleared a little, and a shaft of moonlight shone down on an expertly filled hole.

I stopped short.

It was here, not that long ago, that Gregory and Trusty were attacked by the trespasser. I remembered Trusty's whimpers and the blood running down Gregory's face as he stopped me from charging after Jacob. I remembered touching his face in the kitchen, and the look he gave me when he said, "I knew I had to get out there before you did."

Joe Tremonti was part of my existence long before you blackmailed your way into it.

Maddie, what else can I do?

I had the sensation of cold water running down my back as I stood there in the dark. The memories swarmed me again, same memories but changed somehow, as though I was seeing them in person now, when before they were reflections in a flawed mirror.

I remembered Gregory insisting that he would pay Jacob's salary, as it was part of the deal. I heard him cautioning me against running outside the first time Trusty heard the digger. I saw his smile when I cracked a snappy remark; but this time, I saw that he hardly ever returned it. I felt his hands on mine on that morning I fell into the hole, and his voice telling me that we would find the truth and end the siege. I had believed him then.

Just like I believed him now.

I remembered the look on Joe's face just after he kissed me, the look of satisfaction.

A man could get addicted.

I shook my head, my fingers going to my lips.

What man leaves the woman he cares about alone in her hour of need?

I buried my head in my hands, the lantern clunking down at my feet.

I wasn't wrong about Joe. I couldn't be. Joe was the mainstay. Joe was the standby, my fallback and first choice, the one who rode to my rescue the first time and promised, albeit tacitly, to be there forever. Joe was the man most women only dream about, but the one I got to know.

Joe was part of my future. That had been decided. It had been decided long ago, back on that day when he found me sobbing at Uncle Michael's funeral.

What kind of a "real" man convinces the woman he loves to lie?

Memories surged over me. I recalled Joe explaining that the only thing I needed was proof that the treasure didn't exist. "A statement," he'd said, "or a sale that proved that the treasure was lost before Alexander ever got to the farm."

I don't honestly remember whose idea it was to write the Beaumont letter. It may have been mine, it might have been his, but Greg was right about one thing: I didn't know a thing about forgery. It was Joe that found the ink and paper, and arranged to buy it so that there was no connection to me or the farm. His hand was the one that wrote the words, that aged the paper and arranged for Professor Maddox to authenticate it – because Joe knew, as few did, that the good professor was starting to show the first signs of dementia.

"It'll work, Maddie," he'd said. "No one will ever know. No one will ever care. Just trust me. It'll all work out."

Oh, it worked out, all right. Look at me now, Joe, and tell me if this is what you consider, "working out."

I felt a sudden revulsion for the man who'd allowed and encouraged me to do this, giving me this burden of guilt that was almost impossible to bear.

Not that any of this excused my part in it. It was I who agreed, and then did the research on Beaumont, and I planted the letter in the attic and made sure that Aunt Susanna found it. I planned and schemed to ruin the family name and the reputation of the man who'd taken me in, and treated me like a daughter.

But then Joe had taken an almost incredible risk for the sake of friendship. If we'd been found out, I would have been disgraced - but Joe would have been ruined. His professional reputation and standing, his marriage… All were all put on the line for me. Surely that said something about Joe, even though the debt I owed was enormous, almost overwhelming. Not only did I have the burden of the lie that was meant to protect my family while betraying them, I had been responsible for Joe's professional reputation as well.

I'd failed him in that. I hadn't burnt the letter as I'd promised, and now Greg knew. What was to prevent him from blowing the whistle on all of us?

Even as I thought that, I knew better. Gregory never once told me that he'd ruin me. He'd only ever said that the truth would come out – after we'd found the truth to temper the news of the fraud. Had he ever actually threatened me?

He hadn't.

I felt sick. I felt beaten. It was for my aunt's sake that I had lied, for Joe's sake that I'd taken full responsibility for the forgery, and for a legacy's sake that I'd betrayed Uncle Michael. Now I was about to lose them all: Aunt Susanna, Joe, Greg…

Oh, Gregory…

Everything you touch you ruin, Maddie Warwick. Everything you touch, you ruin.

I wished that I could find a place to bury myself, to hide from the reality that was exploding around me. It was a childish impulse, one I used to give in to when I was young. I was always running. Running into the woods, hiding among the trees, lowering myself into the ruins of the old foundation by the path. I'd wait until everyone had gone, until no one was looking for me - until I was quite sure that there was no one left. Hiding in that hollow in the ground, I learned to wait out the storms of my early life. When I was a child, I hid.

As an adult, I ran.

But there are some things you can't outrun, and some things you can't hide from. I could no longer hide from the fact that if I was in love, it wasn't with Joe Tremonti.

I am not a child. I'm too tired to run and I can't hide in the old foundation anymore.

The old foundation...

Realization poured over me, stripping my thoughts away, leaving only one clear, bare idea:

INOLDFOUNDATION

I turned back, sprinting to the house before the thought was complete. My head was pounding, my heart racing, my mind focused on one thought.

I knew where the treasure was.

Gregory was outside, pacing around the back yard with his hands in his pockets, kicking at pebbles and looking absolutely miserable. Under any other circumstances, I would have hesitated; but tonight, with the thrill of discovery pounding through my veins, I ran for him full-tilt.

He turned, surprised.

"Madeleine, what is it?" he demanded, and looked confused as I grabbed his arm.

"I've found it," I gasped. "I've *found* it!"

His eyes were impossible to see in the darkness.

"Found what? The treasure? Where?"

I gestured behind me.

"The old foundation. I know what he meant!"

"Wait here," he said, and dashed back into the house. He emerged a moment later with a flashlight and his walking stick.

"Show me," he said.

It wasn't far, and the way was so familiar to me I could have run there with my eyes closed. As Gregory easily kept pace with me, I flashed back to the first night I met him, how quick he'd been to run to the scene of the accident with me, and how then - as now – when he could outrun me with so little effort, he stayed at my side.

We reached the bend in the road. Greg hesitated. I plunged into the forest, following a tiny footpath that was so little used that it was nearly grown over, and only someone who knew what they were looking for would have found it. He was behind me, the beam from his flashlight bouncing off the trees, lighting my way.

We turned on the lantern as we slowed our pace, watching the ground carefully. The way was strewn with fallen branches and new growth. Leaves slapped my face, thorns clawed at my shins, and something skittered away from me in the undergrowth up ahead. But I was too driven to be frightened. The foundation was only a short distance from the path, so close that I nearly stumbled into it.

I stopped short and got my bearings, letting my beating heart calm. The light of my lamp seemed a paltry defense against the dark that pressed against us. Above my head, the trees whispered to each other and under them, fire flies winked in and out.

Greg came up behind me, playing his flashlight in the hole in front of us. It was all that remained of the Hill family home. No one really knew when it had been built: some said in the 1820s, but my uncle had maintained that it was earlier than that. One thing everyone agreed upon was that it was built as the eldest son's main living quarters. They had lived in it until a fire consumed both the structure and the fledgling family that lived in it. After, the remaining family let it fall to ruin, focusing on other parts of the property, which included the piece that Darlene Winters lived on now.

All that remained of the house was the stone-lined root cellar and the remains of the granite fireplace. The timber used to build the house had long since rotted away. Leaves, the trunk of a fallen tree, and other debris had collected in the place that once stored a family's winter food supply and, much later, hidden a little girl desperate to be alone. Looking at it that night, I marveled at how the younger me once had the courage to sit in such a deserted place.

Greg's voice broke the silence.

"You think it's in here?" he asked.

I nodded, uncertainly. "Yes."

"It's not on Chase property."

"I know, but..." I shrugged. "I just had a feeling."

He played the light about the remains.

Thinking the treasure was here was a long shot – and it was getting longer the more I thought about it. For Alexander to stash the money here meant that he assumed the Hills wouldn't touch this place while he was gone, a risky assumption. But Avery would surely never come across this by accident. The clue fit better, too: Alexander would have said, "in the basement" rather than "foundation," if he'd meant the family home. And if he'd meant the basement, why did the farm hands testify that he'd gone out of the house to bury the treasure?

They could have lied, of course, just as Alexander could have said "foundation" when he meant the family basement. But I didn't think so, and there was only one way to find out.

Greg was saying, "We ought to wait until morning..."

I jumped into the foundation.

My landing was unsteady, the floor made slippery by fallen leaves, but I didn't lose my balance. I recovered and lifted the lamp triumphantly.

"If you think I'm going to wait for a little thing like daylight, you're crazy," I said.

He stared. Then, through the night air, I heard him laugh, and the sound made my heart skip a beat.

"You know, Madeleine," he said, and then he jumped into the pit beside me. My lamp light caught the smile on his face as he landed. He steadied himself and continued. "I always knew you were a treasure hunter at heart. Just like me."

He was standing a little too close, his presence just a little too much. My angry words came back to taunt me: *It's always been Tremonti.* He'd looked so crushed then, so excited now. Could he have recovered so quickly? Or, like me, was he just trying to put it behind him?

It didn't matter.

"Let's start looking," I said.

"Let's," he nodded. "Flip you for the south wall."

"As if you knew which one it was."

"As if it *mattered,*" he returned cheerfully.

We separated and went to opposite walls. The hole was not as deep as memory or shadow indicated. My eyes were almost level with the ground, a fact which greatly lessened the trapped feeling I had. I lifted the lamp and moved closer to the rock-embedded wall.

The debris under my feet made an unsteady platform, forcing me to move slowly and carefully. I walked around the perimeter, checking the walls for scratch marks or loose rocks, or maybe an "X" to mark the spot. I didn't know what to look for and I felt rather foolish – an amateur doing what a professional could do better, but I didn't stop.

The walls had held up pretty well over time. There were a few loose stones, but I hesitated to pull them out to examine what was behind them, worried that I might find more insects than treasure. The walls had caved in a few places, loosened by rain and time, the rocks now partially buried under the debris. I felt the softened, root-threaded earth, but found nothing to indicate that there had been anything buried there.

Every once in a while, during my brief examination, the sounds of the woods seemed to change. There would be a snap, like someone stepping on a twig. Or the tree frogs would momentarily hush, as though silenced before a looming threat. I would freeze in response, my nerves taut, my mind roving through possible explanations - all of them life-threatening and most of them absurd. Once, I swore I heard slow-moving footsteps through the leaves, but it ceased almost before I identified it. I looked to see if Greg noticed the sound, but he seemed absorbed in his examinations.

Relax, Maddie.

I focused again on my search and found that I was back to where I started. I lowered the lantern and sighed in defeat.

"Maddie!"

The sound made me jump, and the note in Gregory's tone quickened my pulse. I ran to where he was bent over.

He pointed to a spot. "Put your lamp there."

I did as he said. He handed me the flashlight and knelt in front of a pile of fallen stones. He began to throw them to one side, almost recklessly.

"So loose," he muttered to himself. "Can't have been here long, but..."

That's when we saw the box.

It was tucked into a hole in the wall behind the stones: a plain tin box, with a handle so rusted that it had molded back into the side of the box.

"Gregory!" I gasped. "It's..."

He was already scraping away the imprisoning earth. "Help me, Maddie."

I kneeled beside him, and between the two of us, we dug enough out to start pulling at the box. It took a bit of effort to move it, because it was heavy and the ground had fallen in around it. Looking back, we probably should have waited, should have documented the site better. But we were both fueled with impatience, and nearly tore the box apart in our combined urgency.

"Is it really...?" I asked.

He said, "I don't know. I don't know."

The earth suddenly gave way, and we fell backward, taking the box with us. I, still holding the flashlight, rolled to one side as he rolled to the other.

As I did so, the light shifted, exposing another part of the ground, and something else caught my eye - something that was so out of place that it was enough to take my mind off of the long-lost treasure for a moment.

It was buried under branches, faded with time, and so coated in dirt that I could barely make it out. It was a plaid horse blanket. Only someone who had been at Chase Farm for more than seven years would have recognized it. Uncle Michael himself had decided to change out the old plaid horse blankets for the more modern weave in a stylish gray color, giving away all the plaid to a recycling plant.

I pushed aside some of the debris and assured myself that this was, indeed, the Chase Farm blanket, but what was it doing here? Had I brought it here one time and forgotten it? That would have been most unlike me. Had someone else? But who?

Greg interrupted then.

"Maddie, bring the light."

He was kneeling in front of the box, brushing off the dirt. I crawled around the front of it, telling myself that it could be anyone's box, that it needn't be Alexander's. It could just as well belong to the Hill family. Judging from the tense look on Greg's face, he was thinking the same thing.

"There's something stamped here," he said, gesturing to the top of the box and squinting in the dim light.

I lifted the flashlight and the light fell across the top, where it had been stamped with one word: *McInnis.*

We'd found it. Here, on the wrong piece of property, the McInnis treasure, after 150 years, was sitting right in front of us.

"Oh my God..."

My voice echoed in the empty darkness. I stared, my heart pounding. Here it was, the answer we'd all been waiting for, the treasure that Uncle Michael had been so sure existed. This box proved my uncle right, even while it disappointed his hopes that Alexander was a righteous, misunderstood man - if, that is, the box contained the McInnis family fortune.

Greg was shaking his head, brushing the dirt off of the top of the box.

"I can't believe it," I muttered, and he looked at me. "I just can't believe it. After all this time… It's here. It's really here."

"It is," he said. "And you found it, Maddie. You figured it out and you knew where to look for it. After only a few weeks with me, you're getting to be quite the detective, you know. If you ever give up horses, you might want to consider this as a new career."

His voice was an odd mixture of tones and implications, and I flushed with pleasure before I remembered the argument that had me charging out into the dark by myself.

How different everything seemed now.

The feeling of triumph was short-lived. Looking at him across that trunk, I realized that the end was coming. Now that the treasure was found, he'd be leaving for good. Our collaboration would be at an end.

I couldn't let him go after that terrible argument. But what could I say?

I looked at the box.

"Aunt Susanna," I said. "We have to tell her."

"Better than that," he said, springing to his feet. "We'll show her. Give me a hand."

We dragged the box back to the edge of the foundation; then he sprang up, climbing the walls easily, surprising me with his agility. I tossed the flashlight up to him. Then he laid flat on the ground as I tugged and grunted, and lifted the end of the box to him. He pulled it up easily.

"Need a hand?" he asked.

"I forgot the lantern," I said, and turned to retrieve it.

It was then that I heard a snap, echoing like a gun shot in the night air.

Startled, I jumped, and then I stepped back. My foot caught on something. I twisted and went falling forward on my face. I threw my hands in front of me and they plunged into the debris, my left hand tangling in the branches, the other protecting my face.

"Maddie! Are you all right?"

Something moved past my face, and I jerked back instinctively. As my left hand moved, it tangled in a mess of fibers that were whispy and rough, like grass - only much finer. It freaked me out and I pulled it back hard, scraping the back of my hand on some of the undergrowth and bringing a handful of dirt and grass that wove its way around my fingers.

"Madeleine?"

"I'm fine," I assured him.

I sat up, but as I brushed the dirt from my hand, I realized that there was something more than just grass dangling from it. Something cool and hard bumped against my arm, and it was too dark to identify it. I reached out and touched it, intending to pull it away, but the feel of the smooth stone brought me up short.

"Hurry up," he said. "I want to get this thing open."

"Sure..." I said absently.

The lantern was glowing just out of reach in the little hollow where it had fallen. I crawled over and pulled it up, casting a bright light across my left hand.

It wasn't grass that was entangled in my fingers: it was hair. Long, dark, wavy hair. Human hair. The dangling stone I'd felt was oval, in a Native American setting, hanging from the remains of a badly decaying leather cord. I recognized it at once.

I jumped up with a sound that was somewhere between a gasp and a squeal.

"*Gregory!*"

Gregory was standing with the flashlight playing over the trunk. He flashed it in my direction, blinding me as I stared at my arm.

"What is it?" he asked.

My breath was coming fast. I couldn't tear my eyes from my arm as I lifted it up to show him. I felt like I had a mouthful of sand as I spoke.

"I've found Allison Winters."

"*What...?*"

He barely finished the word.

Something flashed through the night air, close at hand - and Gregory folded, dropping to the ground like a dead man.

The flashlight fell as the sound of the impact hit my ears. I screamed, probably his name, and jumped forward to grasp at the wall.

Another beam of light hit my eyes. Someone was standing over Greg's prone body. The same someone who'd laid him out.

I froze, blinking, unable to see.

A familiar voice sliced through the night air.

"Hello, Maddie," Joe Tremonti said, shoving back the hood that obscured his face. "Fancy meeting you here."

31

I gaped up at him.

"Joe!" It was a sound somewhere between a gasp and a scream. "Joe, what are you doing here?"

Joe had lowered the light to bend over where Greg had fallen. For a moment, he was clearly silhouetted in the moonlight, and I saw the outline of the backpack he was wearing - and the spade that he bore like a spear in his free hand. It was new and shiny and it glinted, knife-like, in the moonlight.

I still couldn't grasp what had happened.

"Is he all right?" I asked. Begged, more like. "Joe, is he all right? What happened?"

He turned then, and stared down at me from the edge of the pit, his figure looming up in the night and casting a shadow over me.

And I *still* didn't get it. I didn't want to.

"Help me up," I commanded, lifting my arms. "Lift me up. Please. Quickly."

He didn't move. He just grinned at me.

"Isn't it a little late for a dig, Maddie?" he asked.

"Joe! Help him!"

"Oh..." he said softly, almost crooning. "Yes. Your houseguest and blackmailer, the man you thought you could handle. You don't have to worry about him, Maddie. He won't be bothering you anymore."

I stared up at him.

This is insane. This is ***Joe.***

"What did you do?" I whispered. "Joe, what did you *do*?"

He hefted up the shovel again. "I took care of a problem. Now I have only one."

With a sharp movement, he thrust the shovel into the ground beside him. The force cut through the hard-packed, root-lined ground so deep that it stood quivering on its own, and I realized then just how strong he was.

"You *are* alone now, aren't you, Maddie?"

Alone…

He's killed Gregory.

I thought I knew what pain was. After all, I'd had enough experience with it. But what I was feeling now was as powerful as a full-on collision with a freight train, a dizzying, heart-stopping sort of pain that nearly drove me to my knees.

Secondary realization spread like a wild-fire through me, sucking the air from my chest and shrinking the world to a pin-point of awareness. I stared at him, unable to speak, rage building up in me. But even then, I thought, *This is crazy. That's Joe. You know him. You know him.*

"Maddie," he said, watching me as one would watch a caged pet. "You just don't know when to quit, do you? Why did you come out here tonight? Why couldn't you stay at the party, like you told me you would?"

"Joe," I said, and my voice was surprisingly steady. "Is Gregory all right?"

He sighed and hunkered down to look at me.

"You're all alone now, Madeleine," he said. "Just you and me."

Rage flooded my system. Grief took over, and I lost control. I charged the wall, scrambling up it, wordlessly screaming, determined to hurt him. I came within inches of his smug face and he, without flinching, put his hand on my forehead and shoved me backwards into the darkness of the abandoned foundation.

I fell hard and unprepared. My head bounced off the ground and something jabbed at my rib cage. My arm hit a rock or a log, and Allison's stone broke free, disappearing into the night. I don't know what happened to the lamp, but it must have shattered against something, for I was plunged into sudden darkness.

Pain spread through my side and I laid there, panting, fighting sobs.

Joe's voice reached me through the night air.

"I've come for the same thing as you, Maddie," he said, lightly. "And I've come to get Allison. As you've just discovered, you're laying right on top of her. I know because… Well, I put her there."

Groaning, I rolled into a crouch, clutching my side. I was shaking, my teeth chattering, and his words filled me with a nameless dread.

"No," I whispered. "This isn't happening. You didn't kill her. This is a joke. Tell me it's a joke. You couldn't – and Greg…"

I had to stop as his laughter rolled over me, smothering me. When I looked up, he was crouched on the side of the pit, a predator sizing up his prey.

"Would you really believe me now, if I said I didn't?" he asked. "You may be a little on the weak-minded side, Maddie, but you aren't stupid. You don't really believe that I'd come out here in the middle of the night, under the cover of darkness, and kill a man just because I thought there might be a treasure around here somewhere."

The last time I saw her was at that epic party your folks threw for our last dig day with that delicious Professor Tremonti.

Drink to my health, friends, Joe had said, when he was making the wedding announcement. It was a memory seared into my conscious by keen disappointment; and I could see now, as clearly as then, Joe's white complexion and the way his hands trembled as he lifted his glass to toast.

It was then that I believed him. Funny how easy the admission was, as though it was the last piece in a puzzle that I'd long wanted to finish. Joe had killed Allison, and now Greg.

But this was no time for grief. I had to stay alert. I had to keep him talking. It was the only way I had a chance to stay alive – and see to it that he got caught.

If I could get out of this pit, that is.

Get him off guard, Maddie.

"You killed her the night of the dig party," I stated, my voice a monotone.

Joe cocked his head at me, surprised.

"You remember it," he said. "That was ten years ago. You were there, following me around with that adoring expression on your face. First crush, I think, but I didn't mind you hanging around. You were just a kid."

"So was *Allison*," I snapped. "What was she, twenty-one?"

"So she was," he said. "Allison Winters was attractive, and she knew it. She was helping me with a research project for my first book. That's when she found out that I…"

He broke off and looked at me sharply. While he was speaking, I had gotten to my feet, slowly, carefully, trying to look as though I was defeated. I was in the middle of the foundation, which was still only inches away from his reach, surrounded by softened earth that was chest height or higher, and there was no way I could get out and run before he caught me.

Joe saw my position, and guessed my intention; but he knew, like me, that I was fairly trapped. He got to his feet, and in a display of nonchalance more terrifying than any open threat, he sauntered around the perimeter. He seemed bigger then I remembered, and his shoulders moved in sync with his steps: easy, relaxed, completely at ease.

"I might as well tell you," he said conversationally, like we were discussing his new book over a cup of coffee. "We're already here, after all."

He paused and turned his back to me, his hand on his chin, as though he needed to recollect. But his purpose was to show me the handgun tucked into the waistband at the small of his back.

My knees went weak, but I was determined *not* to give in. When Joe turned back, he found me where I had been.

"You were about to tell me," I said, "that Allison was going to expose you as an intellectual thief."

He looked startled, but he quickly recovered and his grin widened.

"Why, Madeleine Warwick," he said, mocking me. "Who knew you'd turned detective? Now how, I wonder, did you discover that?"

"It what you accused Gregory Randall of," I said. "We usually accuse other people of the things we're guilty of ourselves. What you said about Gregory wasn't true at all, was it?"

Joe nodded slowly, then sighed.

"No," he said. "It wasn't. Quite the opposite, actually. You won't find a man less interested in glory than he is in truth." He paused and, with malicious delight, said, "I should have said, *than* he *was*."

I glared.

He began to pace again. "I was worried when I learned Randall was here. His reputation exceeds his actual ability, but he is still a decent historian and he's almost as persistent as you. I knew that if anyone could find the McInnis treasure, it would be him. And I couldn't allow that."

"You knew where it was?"

"Of course I did," he snapped. "I practically tripped over it the night I left Allison here. I didn't know what it was then. I had… Other things on my mind." He waved his hands impatiently, as though to stop me from getting ahead of him. "You see, like you, I didn't believe in the treasure. My only interest was finishing that course with my class and getting back to California to start my real career. The east coast was a dead-end, as far as I was concerned. My life was out west – that's where my career was, my wife…" He shook his head, as though driving off a bad memory. "Allison knew that. She was just a summer thing. We were adults. She *should* have known. But when she found out about Amber and me, she became emotional. She didn't want to listen to reason and she threatened to tell the truth about the research."

"And you couldn't allow that," I said.

"No. I couldn't. It didn't matter, really. The man who'd done the work was dead - suicide - and not really in position to publish or protest. But she kept insisting that he deserved the accolades, even though it was I who'd discovered the work and I who finished it."

"So you finished her."

"Yes," he said softly. "I did."

He started pacing again, and I looked again for an escape. Nothing seemed promising – I would not be able to out-run him and fighting him off would be difficult, if not impossible. He had at least seventy-five lean-muscle pounds on me and he had a gun. My only weapons, if you could call them that, were my lamp and whatever I could find on the ground. That he would kill me wasn't a question.

I needed more time, and the only way to buy it was to keep him talking.

So I said, "You buried her here, then what? How did her car end up in another state, when you were on a plane to California?"

He waved a hand dismissively. "That was easy enough," he boasted. "I knew that she was taking a road trip and I wasn't supposed to leave until the morning. I had to change planes anyway, so I left the night of the party in her car. I drove it all the way to somewhere outside of Chicago, ditched it, and caught a bus to the airport. I made my connecting flight with about fifteen minutes to spare and no one put two and two together. It was genius. As long as no one discovered where the body was, I was safe.

"I had stumbled across the treasure box when I was covering her up, but I didn't realize what it was. It's not on Chase property, and I didn't believe in the story anyway. It was only when Mark Dulles' special came on that I had second thoughts."

I remember thinking that if I ever met Mark Dulles again, I'd probably punch him in the eye for all the trouble his special had caused.

Joe had continued. "But even then, as long as the search stayed on your property, I was safe. No one would look on the Winters property,

I thought, and I was right, as long as it was the professionals looking. Then, when the amateurs started, I got nervous. They have no method or discipline. They wouldn't necessarily know where the property lines were."

He was pacing again, his hands behind his back, walking in circles around me. I still hadn't found a way out, and was cursing myself for having left my cell phone at the house. I wondered again if Greg was really dead or if he was just hurt, bleeding out into the ground as this insane stand-off continued.

Oh, please...

Joe stopped and turned to me.

"Then your uncle died," he said simply. "And I knew I had to do something to stop the searches before they found her. As you just have."

A chill washed over me. I forced myself to speak, to break the moment: "You must have known that someone would find her eventually, even if they weren't looking for the treasure."

"Oh, I knew that," he nodded. "But it isn't easy to dispose of a body, you know, especially when you don't live in the area. I needed to put it off for as long as possible. After all, evidence erodes. And I had – and have – no intention of letting anyone else find the treasure. It was my discovery, and I would reap the benefits of it. That's when I came up with the Beaumont Letter."

"A stall," I said, and he nodded.

"A stall. Even though I knew you didn't believe in the treasure, I wasn't sure you'd go for it. But you fell for the scheme, hook, line, and sinker. You bought me, what, four more years, Maddie? I'm grateful."

"Don't mention it," I said through gritted teeth. Bad enough that I'd made my uncle a laughing stock – I'd gone and aided a murderer as well.

Not now, Maddie.

"What then?" I demanded. "So you bought more time. So what? That would run out eventually."

"True. Eventually."

He stopped and pulled the pistol out of his back pocket. It glinted dully in the moonlight and I froze, terrified.

He studied it, frowning and stroking the barrel. His grip tightened and he stood, silhouetted in moonlight, one hand twisting at the barrel, the other keeping firm grip of the handle. It was as though he was wrestling with the weapon, one hand trying to wrench it out of the other's grip.

I had backed away as far as I could in the foundation, pressing against the rock wall, watching in fear-fueled fascination.

Then, as quietly and suddenly as the wrestling match had begun, it was over. He let go of the barrel and whipped around to face me - but it was not the end, as I assumed it was. Instead, he crouched down at the side of the hole and continued as though he'd never paused.

"I knew that time would run out," he said as I stared. "But for the moment I was safe, and things were working for me in California. I decided that the treasure would keep. Besides, extracting it after going through all that trouble with the Beaumont letter would be difficult, even though I'd built in safeguards. I'd made sure that none of the supplies were traceable to me and when I presented the letter to Maddox, I made sure that he and everyone knew that I was doing this for an old family friend."

He chuckled. "Maddox was starting to slow down, but most of the world didn't know just how far he had slipped into senility. Refuting his find later would be a breeze, provided I kept far enough distance. I just had to wait until Maddox either broke down completely or died. When he finally did, I was free to act.

"The next step was to drive you out."

His face was hooded in darkness; but the pistol, held loosely in his hand, was easy enough to make out.

My throat was constricted, so dry that I could hardly rasp out my question. "Drive me out?"

"Yes," he said. "It was a simple idea. California was becoming... Unfriendly, shall we say? So when the job opened up here, I moved back, established contact with you, and then hired a man to dig the holes for me. He got scared off when Randall and that kid chased him into the woods, but the plan was for him to do the digging while I stayed just close enough to ride to your 'rescue', so to speak."

Flames of humiliation competed with my icy fear. I gaped at this man, who'd understood me so completely – so well, that he knew just where my weak spot was.

Before you go and make this declaration public, Maddie…

Oh, God!

I found enough spine to glare at him.

"I hope I wasn't too predictable, Joe," I practically spat.

He chuckled. "Actually, you were a much tougher nut to crack than I expected. I had to keep upping the stakes."

My mind was whirling with the implications. The last sentence made me gasp.

"Lindsay!" I snapped. "You *arranged* that, didn't you?"

There was a long pause. Then he shook his head.

"That," he said, "was a… fortunate accident."

Flashes of memory swept over me. The panic in Ellen's voice as she ran to get me. The pale form that was Lindsay on the ground, the terror on her parents' faces when I told them what happened, the grim summation by the paramedics. Greg looking up at me, after examining the hole.

There's something wrong about all of this, Warwick. There's something very wrong about this.

Joe's voice cut through my reverie.

"That should have done the trick," he said, and his voice grew taut with annoyance. "If anything could break you that should have done it. But just when I thought you were going to crack, a writer moved in and messed everything up. So I had to up the charm."

"You *used* me," I hissed. It burst out of me, startling both of us; but once it was out, I pressed further. "You knew I was attracted to you, and you *used* me."

His laughter rolled out, deep and hearty, and it drove the point home with callous precision.

"Attracted to me?" he laughed. "You practically salivated every time I walked into the room. You were so *desperate* and so *easy* to play, it wasn't even fun. Yes, I used you, Maddie. But you played into my hands so easily, it was as though you were working with me the whole time."

And just when I was about to commit suicide by rushing him in pure anger, he went on.

"Although you did have me worried for a while. Once I realized that your writer was Randall, I panicked. He has his drawbacks, but he is – was - clever, and I thought you might get distracted. I didn't want him upsetting everything, so I arranged for our little play date." He shook his head. "I was surprised at how long it took before you would admit that he was here. You'd grown more attached to Randall than I'd thought, but it didn't take much to bring you back in line. All I had to do was threaten to walk, and you fell apart."

Joe paused, grinning at me. "The kiss was entirely for his benefit," he said. "A massive ego like his needs the occasional kick."

I saw that his hands were caressing the pistol again. He was shaking his head too, looking for all the world like a man mulling over the fickle nature of fate.

"If I'd known from the first that it was Gregory Randall who was staying here," he said softly, almost tenderly, "I would have arranged for this accident a little sooner."

If I was chilled before, that made me feel as though I'd just stepped under an ice-cold waterfall.

Keep him talking.

With a great effort, I kept my voice steady, my fear and anger under control. "So what happens now?" I asked.

He looked at me sharply. "I was going to move Allison before that dog of yours came back and scented me, and then I was going to oust Randall and discover the treasure. But you're here and that... Changes things."

I took a step back.

"It'll never work," I said desperately. "How are you going to explain away three bodies?"

It was as if he hadn't heard me.

"When they find you," he said, looking around as though for inspiration, "it'll break your aunt. She'll fold up. You're her last link to the property. With you and Randall gone, she'll be ripe for the picking. She won't think twice about selling to me after you're gone."

While I was still reeling from that stark declaration, I saw that he was looking behind me. I turned, but all I could see was the shovel, standing erect and ready.

I looked back at Joe. He was fixated on the shovel, moving towards it while shoving the pistol back into his waistband.

He was muttering, "A shot will be heard."

Joe was halfway to it when I realized what this meant. Panic and adrenaline surged through me. I ran to the opposite end of the pit, and threw myself at the wall, my hands scrambling for a hold. I couldn't find a grip. The rocks had fallen out of the wall there, leaving nothing but smooth dirt with thin roots jutting out. I was trapped.

I glanced over my shoulder. Joe had reached the shovel and pulled it out of the dirt with one fluid motion, his eyes fixed on me. And then he jumped.

He was in the hole with me.

He'd already killed Greg.

Rage wrestled with fear. There was a rock in my hand and I threw it. I'm no athlete, but this shot went straight to its mark and his head whipped around with the impact.

He hesitated. I launched myself at him.

Joe caught me by the shoulder and shoved me aside like a rag doll. I landed on my hands and knees, but I didn't have time to recover before his shovel caught me in the ribcage.

Some instinct kicked in, and I rolled with the blow. The shovel missed my head by inches, hitting the wall behind me with a heavy thud, and he brought it around for another go. I rolled again, and this one glanced off my shoulder.

Joe was over me almost before I stopped moving, swinging the shovel. I had just enough presence of mind to kick upwards.

My feet made contact, and he grunted, staggering backwards as the blade whooshed by my face. I rolled onto my feet and fled across the uneven ground towards the other wall. This one wasn't as tall - if I could just jump high enough to catch the top…

I heard Joe's breathing, practically felt him on my back, but I ran. I had to reach the wall, had to… Then my foot plunged through a gap in the bedding. I fell with another shout.

The impact knocked the breath out of me. I forced myself to roll onto my back.

Joe loomed over me, his shovel raised to strike.

When they find me tomorrow, they'll think I ran into one of those trespassers.

The shovel never landed. Something, someone, jumped down from the wall, landing just inches away from my attacker. There was a flash of movement, then a ringing thud.

Joe roared, staggered back, and I saw Gregory, holding the flashlight he'd just cracked Joe across the head with.

On the face of it, it was not an even match. Gregory was muscular but slim built, a scholar who, having already met that shovel, was supposed to be dead. Joe Tremonti was taller and wider, a man who liked to work out and spar. More than that, he had two weapons and he wasn't afraid to kill.

But Joe never stood a chance.

Even as he attempted to change direction, to bring the shovel down on Gregory instead of me, Greg ducked under his swing and drove his knee straight into Joe's gut. Joe grunted, then cried out when his arm was caught in a hold that seemed about to break his elbow. Greg pressed harder, and the shovel clattered to the ground. Gregory let go of the arm hold.

I saw Joe's hand move and I screamed, "Gregory, the *gun*!"

But he had only released Joe's arm in order to set up a haymaker. I heard the *crack* as fist met jaw.

Joe went up and back, and fell like a crumbling brick wall. He landed on his side, his head bouncing off the ground. The handle of his pistol glinted in the moonlight.

Greg reached down, wobbling a little as he picked the gun up. Joe made a feeble movement as though to grab Greg, and his punishment was swift: two rapid-fire kicks in his gut.

"Sit and *stay*, Tremonti, or I'll be the one using the shovel," Greg muttered through gritted teeth.

Stunned, Joe subsided.

Gregory stepped backwards, then aimed and fired three shots - but at a mound of soft earth and not Joe, as I'd immediately thought.

Gregory turned. "International distress signal," he muttered weakly.

He staggered over towards me.

The light shifted, and moonlight poured through the trees, flooding the pit in eerie silver light. I could see the pistol, held limply in his hand, and there was a dark stain growing on his shirt.

My heart clutched painfully.

"Are you all right, Madeleine?" he asked. His voice was hoarse. He swayed, but did not fall. "Did he hurt you?"

I was frozen, watching the surreal sight, still in disbelief. Gregory was here – but he was dead. Or I thought he was... But he'd come back for me, just as he'd promised he would. I gaped up at him.

"Are you hurt?" he asked again. His glasses were gone and he squinted, peering through the dark at me.

I found my voice.

"No," I whispered. "I'm all right."

There was a long pause. Then he sighed, and smiled at me.

"Excellent," he said.

Through the suddenly still air, I could hear the voices of people running towards us. Thanks to the gunfire, help was already on the way. Gregory heard it, too, lifting his head painfully towards the sound.

"Excellent," he repeated.

Then he collapsed again. Only this time, I was there to catch him.

Life can change in the blink of an eye.

I know this to be true, because it happened to me twice: once when I watched my uncle die on the trails, and once again, when I held the man I loved in my arms and willed him back to life.

LETTER, WRITTEN BY ALEXANDER CHASE, FOUND INSIDE THE MCINNIS TRUNK

To whomever may find this,

If you are reading this, then you've found it necessary to remove this trunk in my absence. If I am not here, then it is very likely that I have fallen in battle. If so, I hope I died honorably, but I regret that my passing may have caused my mother and another pain.

No doubt this secrecy has caused you to doubt my motives. After all, an honest man has no need to hide what he has earned. But the contents of this trunk are not mine – they are merely in my custody.

While working in Charleston, I became attached to a lady and I am engaged. It has been kept a secret because, in these troubled times, the lady worries that her father, a southern gentleman, would not take kindly to a northern son-in-law. She has considerable wealth and worries that the coming conflict will ruin her father, whom she loves above all else. She begged me, therefore, to leave her behind, to take a stock of her goods and preserve them for her family until after the war. They say it won't last long, but much damage can be done, and so I agreed, although it nearly killed me to leave her side. When I arrived here, I was disturbed by the vehement war fervor. Fearing that others would seize these goods in false patriotism, I have hidden them here, on the land I have contracted to buy from my neighbor.

I intend to join the army, to serve honorably until the war's end. Then, God willing, I shall return this to its rightful owner and claim her as my own. But I beg you, my reader, that should I not return, fulfill my charge and restore this in my stead. It belongs, in whole, to Miss McInnis, and her father, Jasper McInnis, of Charleston. Please assure Miss McInnis that to the last, I remained her faithful and devoted servant,

Alexander Chase

32

I spent that night in the waiting room. The hospital staff weren't too pleased about it and kept trying to convince me to go home and rest, but I flat out refused. My injuries had been mild and easily tended to. Gregory's were a different story: I'd heard the EMT's talking about head trauma and blood loss, and I told the staff, in no uncertain terms, that I was not leaving until Gregory woke up and that was that.

"Are you family?" they asked.

"No. I'm his partner."

They eventually accepted the situation, and left me to make myself as comfortable as I could on the teal and pink seats.

Aunt Susanna came around midnight, carrying a backpack and a thermos of milky tea. She gave me a hug, then the thermos, and sat in the chair next to mine.

"I brought you a change of clothes, and his laptop and notebook," she said, patting the backpack. "How is he?"

I shook my head. "I don't know. They won't tell me. I'm not family."

As she sighed and looked at her hands, I asked, "How's Darlene?"

Darlene Winters was in our house when everything went down. When she was told about the discovery of her daughter's body, she'd collapsed. Even ten years of speculation had not been enough to prepare her for the reality of Allison's murder.

Aunt Susanna had stayed behind to take care of her while I accompanied Gregory to the hospital. As glad as I was to have her with me, I was surprised that my aunt had left Darlene alone.

"She's asleep," Aunt Susanna said. "I should get back to her. I don't want her to wake alone."

I nodded solemnly. "Yeah. I know what you mean."

She looked at me sharply, but I refused to meet her eyes. My tears were starting, and sympathy from my aunt would be sure to cause a deluge. I didn't want to make another scene in front of the hospital staff that night.

I could feel that she was about to ask me another question, a question my composure might not survive answering. Before she could speak, I said, "Poor Darlene. After all this time, all that waiting, and she lost it all anyway." A lump rose in my throat, and I swallowed hard as Aunt Susanna stared at me.

I whispered, "Sometimes, it hardly seems worth it."

In the silence that followed, I struggled with myself. I thought it odd that Aunt Susanna had not yet asked me about Joe. She seemed to simply accept the situation, almost as much as I had.

The time alone in the waiting room made one thing clear to me: my affection for Joe Tremonti had been as much of a smoke screen as the Beaumont letter. I never really loved him. He was the unobtainable lover - safe to obsess about because there was no risk of a real relationship. As long as I told myself that I was infatuated with him, I could keep all others at bay and preserve my heart from further trampling.

Like a lot of my other theories, this one didn't quite play out.

When I did look at Aunt Susanna, she was studying her wedding ring, her face thoughtful. It was then that I realized she'd come without her cane.

"When your uncle died, I didn't think I would survive," Aunt Susanna said softly. "It was so... wrenching. I didn't know I could be so lonely. If it wasn't for you and your determination to see us through, I don't think I would have survived it."

I was shaking my head, but she stopped me with a look.

"*No*," she said. "I mean it. You and Darlene saved me. I would have given up. But once the initial storm had passed, when I finally let go of the anger – anger that he left me, anger at those who'd left the holes, angry at myself for letting him ride so recklessly - I felt like I'd been cheated. Robbed. But once I let that go, I was able to finally see clearly. I hadn't been cheated. I was the luckiest woman in the world. I had loved and been loved in return. I had a lifetime with the best man I'd ever known. And while I would have loved to have more time with him…" She paused and steadied herself, then smiled at me through tear-filled eyes. "I have what most other people would give anything for. I have memories. And I know that I'll see him again, eventually."

She reached out and squeezed my hand. "All things considered, I came out ahead. Way ahead. Darlene has, too. Once she gets through this, she'll be able to treasure what she had with Allison. Her death will leave a hole. Every death does. But it's such a small price to pay for a lifetime."

She smiled, a motherly smile I knew so well and had missed so much.

"It's a funny thing," she continued, "but that old saying is right: it's better to have loved and lost than never to love at all. When I was your age, I didn't believe it, but I know better now. It's worth the risk. If you believe nothing else that I have taught you, Maddie, always believe this: love is worth the risk."

After she left, I barely slept at all. The seats in the waiting room are comfortable enough for waiting a few hours with an outdated magazine, but they are not constructed for a stubborn woman to get a comfortable night's sleep in.

By the time morning rolled around, I was a sleep-deprived mess. I checked at the front desk and was told that Gregory was doing fine, and that the doctors were with him. Visiting hours didn't start until ten a.m., but the desk nurse, whose name tag proclaimed her as "Rosemary", told me that she thought it would be all right if I went up earlier.

"I'll take you up myself," she offered. "I want to meet him anyway. We're all fans of his work – it must have been exciting, having him at your place." She leaned forward. "I'm told that all of his work is based on true-to-life experiences," she whispered. "That he conducts extensive… research, if you catch my drift."

There was a sly expression on her face, as though we were girlfriends exchanging a juicy piece of gossip. It confused me, but I was too tired and too strung out to worry about it. I shrugged.

"Yes," I sighed. "That's entirely true."

Her face lit up, and she slapped the counter triumphantly.

"I *knew* it," she said. "You can't write like that unless you've been there, right? Now, it's none of my business, but someone told me that you were working with him on the new book. Is that true?"

"Yes," I answered, and was startled by the wide-eyed look of shocked delight that spread across her face. "Um, is there some place I can get a cup of coffee?"

She directed me to the cafeteria. I stopped at the bathroom to try to tidy up as best I could, then got a cup of coffee and a granola bar before returning to the waiting room.

I drained the coffee and nibbled at the bar distractedly. Behind the desk, the nurses were chatting. Rosemary gestured to me, causing the two women to giggle confidentially.

I was already feeling a little foolish, waiting in the hospital all night. I resolved, though, not to let their behavior get to me. I really didn't want to leave until I'd seen Gregory.

Finally, Rosemary told me to follow her. She led me down a maze of corridors, chatting the whole time about how she loved to read and was always at book fairs and, by the way, how frightening was it that I had been attacked on my own property?

"That is just *so* scary," she said, as we strode down the hallway. "I wouldn't go back home either, just so you know."

"I didn't stay here because I was scared," I growled.

She nodded understandingly.

"You were lucky to have a rescuer," she said. "The night nurse told me he was calling your name during the night, while he was unconscious. You must be..." and here she grinned slyly again, "...very close."

Before I could respond, she reached for a door, and threw it open with a cheerful, "And how are *we* feeling this morning?"

I pushed past her and found Gregory laying on top of the bedclothes, dressed in a robe and hospital gown, his head swathed in bandages. A pair of drug-store mini-glasses was perched on his nose, and he was reading a battered scientific journal. There was an I. V. stand near his bed, but he wasn't hooked up to it. The knuckles on his left hand were bruised and swollen and his eyes, when he looked up, were red and strained.

But he was awake, and he was alive, and that was enough for me.

He sat up quickly when he saw me, only to fall back, holding his head.

I stepped forward, but Rosemary was faster, scolding, "Now, now, you can't move that quickly, not for a few days yet, you know."

He brushed her hands aside, his gaze fixed on me.

"Warwick!" he said, happily. "You're a sight for sore eyes. Have you brought my glasses?"

I'd taken another step forward - torn between wanting to rush to him, and my need to maintain my restraint in front of Rosemary. The sound of his voice was enough to make me want to dance, while his use of "Warwick" and the impersonal request made me want to stomp my feet with impatience.

His spare glasses were in the front pocket of the backpack. Aunt Susanna had thought of everything. I handed them to him, and he tossed the cheap glasses aside, rubbing his eyes while Rosemary went about straightening the room.

"How do you feel?" I asked.

"Like I've been hit over the head with a shovel," he said wryly, pulling on his glasses. He blinked through them, then smiled broadly at me.

"Ah," he said softly, and his eyes caught and held mine. "Now, that's better. Warwick, you look like..."

"Like she spent the night in the waiting room?" Rosemary's voice bisected the moment. She stood by his nightstand, holding his chart, grinning at us like she had the inside scoop on a delicious secret.

When Gregory glanced at her, she nodded eagerly. "That's what she did, you know. Flat out refused to go home until she knew you were all right."

"*Really*?" He looked at me with amused interest mixed with feigned shock. "Why, my dear Madeleine, that's so *sweet*."

"I shouldn't have bothered," I muttered, and gestured at Rosemary. "It seems you were in good hands."

"Oh, the very best," Rosemary hastened to assure me. She turned to Gregory and gushed, "You have a lot of huge fans here, you know. I've read all your books."

"Have you? How very gratifying! Did you hear that, Warwick? She's read every single one of my books."

"Awesome," I said.

"You know," he said, leaning closer to Rosemary, "the nurse before you told me the same thing."

"Louise is a huge reader, like me. I can't wait until this next book comes out. I think you are brilliant."

I rolled my eyes.

"Why, thank you," Gregory said and grinned at me. "It helps when you enjoy what you do for a living. But I can't take all the credit for the next book. Maddie's been my right hand in all of the investigation and she's going to help me to write it. Surprisingly enough, she has quite a flair for this kind of work. Almost as good as myself."

I looked at him in surprise. Rosemary surprised us both by giggling like a school girl, and she blushed when we looked her.

"Oh," she said, and giggled again. "Oh, I wouldn't want to ask about that. Oh, no, I wouldn't – though I guess I'll be reading all about it soon enough, won't I?"

She slapped her side and then pulled something out of her scrubs pocket. "My goodness! I almost forgot! Can you autograph this for me? I just got it the other day and I can honestly say, it's your best yet."

He took the paperback. "Absolutely. Warwick, do you have a pen…"

The words faded from his lips. He stared at the book. He looked so surprised that I went around his bed to check it out.

On the cover, a man and a woman grappled with each other. Her dark hair flowed over her bare shoulders, her hands flat on his impressive chest, resisting his passionate embrace, though not enough to break away.

The title was *Her Lord and Master.* The author was Gregorianne Vincent.

Rosemary was saying, "My friend, Delia Fontaine, told us about you, Mr. Vincent. I hope you don't mind that she passed it on to me about you and your, um, research assistant."

She winked at me.

I pointed to the book. "You think he… That I… That I'm…"

Rosemary shrugged primly, but grinned again.

My face went hot.

"I'll say this for the artist," Greg said. He was studying the cover with exaggerated fascination, his mouth tight from restrained laughter. "The eyes are the wrong color, but he's captured the real you, Maddie. The essence of the character, the bow-like mouth, the firm…"

My face was flaming now. I snatched the book out of his hands and smacked him across the shoulder with it before tossing it back to the nurse. She caught it, her eyes wide.

"There'll be no autographs today," I snarled, and she took that as her cue to exit.

I turned to Greg, who raised his hands protectively.

"Now, now, easy does it, Warwick," he said. "I'm grievously injured, you know."

He was laughing, the insufferable man. I pointed to the door.

"Do you know what she thinks? She asked me downstairs if I was your *research assistant*! And I told her *yes!*"

"And fine assistant you were, too," he nodded. "In fact, in a dozen or so years, with the proper tutelage, you'll make a reasonably good treasure hunter. And that's not a compliment I give out to just anyone."

"Oh, thanks!" I fumed. "That's fine. That nurse is going to tell all her friends about this. The entire hospital is going to think that we're... That you... How am I supposed to live that down?"

"Why, Madeleine Warwick," he said. "There are worse things than to have your name linked to mine. Some people might think it's an honor. Besides, if you'll recall, this 'Gregory Randall as the new Barbara Cartland' wasn't *my* idea."

I stopped and sighed. I'd spent the entire night worrying about him and beating myself up over the cruel things I'd said, intending to go straight to his side to set things right. Now, not two minutes in his presence, here I was reaming him over a case of mistaken identity that was essentially my fault. I didn't know whether to be relieved that he was feeling well enough to tease about it or just annoyed.

"So you say," I said, and decided that it was time to change the subject. I reached into my pocket and pulled out a folded piece of paper in a plastic bag. "This is for you."

He took it suspiciously. "What is it?"

"A letter from an old friend," I said. Seeing his confusion, I explained. "It's Alexander Chase's. We found it in the old trunk."

"You *opened* it?"

Only once before had I heard him sound and look so upset. I shook my head.

"It *wasn't* me," I said. "The police opened it to see what the fuss was about. Aunt Susanna laid them out but good, then she had them repack it and put it in the kitchen."

When he opened his mouth, I interrupted. "I was with you in the ambulance. With your blood on my shirt. Under the circumstances, I couldn't really object too much."

That put things into perspective. He opened the letter.

I'd already read it, so I studied his face as he absorbed the contents, memorizing every line and crease. I noted the way his eyes jumped around the page - as though he was not just reading the letter, but taking in the page, the texture, and the various markings. I wondered how much he saw that I didn't.

He caught me staring and I looked away quickly, focusing on the floor.

"Well," he said, slowly folding the letter and returning it back to the plastic wrap. "This seems to explain everything. Your uncle was right. Alexander didn't do it for money or revenge."

"No," I said. "He did it for love."

When I looked up, he was smiling at me.

"Not bad for an amateur," he said softly.

I nodded, and the moment held.

Then he cleared his throat.

"Well, that's that, then," he said, and swung his legs around so that they were hanging off the bed. "You'd better go, Warwick. I'm going to get dressed now and we wouldn't want the nurses to have too much to talk about." He tried to stand, but he moved too quickly and had to sit down again.

"What are you doing?" I demanded, alarmed. "You can't leave!"

"I can't stay here," he said. "There's far too much to do. I have to get this letter back to my lab at Hadley, and the treasure, too, for proper study. Then there are the reports and the meetings and the press releases and..."

"You're going back?" I asked, my heart sinking. "Back to Hadley? Today?"

"The sooner the better," he said, holding his head. "My job here is finished - It's time your aunt had her house back. I was serious about the book," he said. "About writing it with you, I mean."

I stared, so he continued.

"This is a rare opportunity. You know how I feel about collaborations, but I think it would be interesting to have your perspective. The exposure would be good for your farm and, of course, there would be the revenue. I may not be the academic star I used to be, but my name still can sell a few hardcovers. You might even find it fun. And you'll get a chance to work with one of the best-regarded professionals in the business."

All I could do was gape as he resumed, "It's a good opportunity for both of us. I know this is coming on fast and not that I wish to exploit what happened last night, but putting that in the book – talk about a solid ending. It's a win-win situation. What do you think, Warwick?"

Warwick.

The name he only used when he was talking business. Not Madeleine, not Maddie – just Warwick.

I stared at him, aghast.

"How can you take this so lightly?" I whispered. "Leaving and... Gregory, you almost died last night. I was in that waiting room all night, worried sick and all you can talk about is writing and business relationships and asking me to..." I groped for words, my tone building as I continued, "to exploit Joe's attack to sell a few miserable books?"

My voice rung in the room.

He winced.

"When you put it that way, it doesn't sound as good," he said. "But you've got to admit that we've got a good story here. It would be criminal to throw it away."

"You are *crazy*," I yelled. "You're lying on your back, calmly talking about business ventures and book sales and I was downstairs, thinking, he's hurt, he's dying, it's my fault... I thought you'd *died* last night. Do you know what that did to me?"

He looked up at me, suddenly still. "No," he whispered. "What did it do to you?"

I stood there for a moment, debating.

Then I thought, *He called me Warwick.*

That was my answer. There was no need to stay.

"Not a thing," I lied. "Why don't you just go back to your precious Hadley U?"

My words caught in my throat, my eyes filled and I panicked, turning, running for the door before he could see.

"Madeleine."

His voice stopped me dead in my tracks. I didn't turn. I stood there with my back to him, biting my lip hard so that I wouldn't cry.

"Oh, my dear Madeleine," he said softly. But this wasn't the same dismissive "My dear Madeleine" that I was used to hearing. This was a soft, tender whisper, something new. "Don't leave. Not yet."

"I'm going home," I insisted, taking a steadying breath, thinking about life on the other side of that door. It would be as cold as before – and lonely. Loneliness stretching out like acres of neglected, weed-choked fields. No one there to run along beside me. No one there to tease me into eating properly, to push me out of my comfort zone, to need me to listen, to ask me to work with them, to look for me when I came in, to bandage battle wounds, or to wander about the trails, talking about nothing. I'd be alone, as lonely as when Uncle Michael died. Only worse. Much worse.

I squished the images before they overwhelmed me, but the truth came out in a savage rush: "I don't want a *business* agreement with you, Gregory. That isn't good enough."

There. It was out for both of us to hear.

He was silent. Absolutely still.

A desperate need to salvage my pride made me add hastily, "I really have to run…"

But as I reached for the doorknob, he said, in the same quiet tone: "Madeleine, aren't you tired of running? I know I am."

My hand dropped to my side. I didn't turn. I couldn't bear to see his face. I couldn't leave, either.

"I don't want just a business relationship with you, either," he continued. "It would never be enough for me."

I couldn't move, couldn't speak, so Greg went on.

"You know," and there was a wistfulness in his voice, "when you spend your life as I have, buried inside books and genealogies and maps – and the endless hunts for other people's fortunes, you can look up one day and realize that you neglected to look for the real prize."

I turned to face him then, tears flowing down my face. He was sitting up, leaning forward as though to stop me, his head wound forgotten.

"But that was the life I chose." He smiled, but it was tentative, unsure – something I'd never seen in him. "Until I met you, that is. I couldn't dismiss you like I could others. You're unforgettable, Maddie. Just being with you makes me want to be more than I am. Being away from you is a kind of loneliness I didn't know existed." He shook his head. "I know I drive you up the wall sometimes..."

I had to smile at that. "Goes both ways, I think."

He didn't return the smile or agree. "Last night you said that there is no 'us', but Madeleine, don't you think someday, there could be?"

I felt as though my heart were swelling painfully in my chest. There was a look on his face, in his dark eyes. A look that made me think I could, maybe, safely lose myself in their depths.

He continued softly, "I don't want to just work with you. I want you in my life permanently, but I'll accept whatever you can give, even if it means saying goodbye to you today or tomorrow or after the project's done. It's up to you. Working together on this book – it's a poor substitute for a life, Maddie. But when a man's in love with a woman who loves someone else – well... can you blame him for taking whatever time with her he can get?"

My throat was so constricted I couldn't speak. I remembered how I felt when I thought he'd died. I thought about Joe, and how duped I'd been. I thought about Uncle Michael's death, and how it had nearly ruined me - as Darlene had almost allowed her daughter's death to do to her.

And then I heard Aunt Susanna's voice, clear and strong and sure: *It's a small price to pay for a lifetime.*

I couldn't promise forever. Not yet. We were still too raw, still too new, with too many hurdles to jump over before either of us could promise that. But I couldn't dismiss him, either. To do so would be tantamount to ripping my heart in two.

He was watching me, his heart shining through his eyes, his hand stretched out for me to take.

"I was never in love with Joe," I whispered. "And I don't want to say goodbye."

I put my hand in his.

Gregory's face lit up like the dawn.

"Then don't," he said and pulled me to him. "Please don't."

As I melted into his arms, one clear thought bubbled above the heady waves of emotion that rolled over me:

So this is what it's like to be kissed by the right man…

TWO YEARS LATER

From an article by Charlie White in ***The Triple Town Sentry:***

Chase Book Published:

> *A book launch party for the newly published* ***Read On This: The Chase Treasure Hunt*** *was held at the Chase Farm last night. Written by Professor Gregory Randall and Madeleine Warwick Randall, this non-fiction book outlines their search for the legendary McInnis treasure, long thought to have been stolen by Alexander Chase.*
>
> *Back in 1861, Chase was accused of stealing from his wealthy employer. The scandal ruined the family reputation, a stain that lingered until the climatic affair two years ago, when the treasure, and the explanatory note was discovered on a neighbor's property. The note exonerates Chase, who had secured the goods at the behest of his fiancée, the daughter of his employer.*
>
> *"It's really exciting to finally have the truth about the whole affair," said Susanna Chase, who had just returned from an around the world trip with her friend and neighbor, novelist Darlene Winters. "My husband always believed in Alexander and in the treasure. It's nice to have his theories proven."*
>
> *Ms. Winters, also releasing a book this year, wrote the introduction to* ***Read On This.*** *"This is such a fantastic book – it reads more like a mystery thriller than a history. And the old saying is correct: truth is stranger than fiction."*
>
> *Charleston Historical Society President, Charlene Schaeffer, attended the party. Her museum is hoping to obtain joint ownership of the collection and she spoke at length*

about the ties between the North and the South. Also present at the party were such literary notables as local author A. Glen Bernard and romance writer, Gregorianne Vincent.

Randall, who teaches at Hadley University in Massachusetts, announced that his next line of inquiry would take place in Philadelphia, concerning some pre-Revolutionary War material, but he declined to give any details. He and Warwick married last year, and will be working on the new book together, leaving care of the farm to Susanna Chase.

Madeleine Randall said, "I'll miss the farm, of course, but I know I'm leaving it in good hands." The couple are expecting their first child in August, and she said that she's looking forward to having a family, something she never expected.

"Having the right person by your side just changes everything. Every day it seems there's something new. We're looking at a bright future – and I just can't wait!"

ABOUT THE AUTHOR

Killarney Traynor is a New England-born writer, actor, and history buff, living in New Hampshire. *Necessary Evil* is her second book. Her first, *Summer Shadows,* is also based in New Hampshire. Find Killarney on the web at www.killarneytraynor.com.

25318232R00221

Made in the USA
Middletown, DE
26 October 2015